Stoneseekers

By Catherine Milner

Copyright © 2014 C. M. Milner

All rights reserved.

ISBN: **1503180158**
ISBN-13:978-1503180154

CHAPTER 1

The monster blinked. A pair of huge orange eyes glowed from the darkness of the forest, the pupils just slits of black that bulged when the creature's stare settled upon me. I held my breath as I took a step forward, soft dead leaves under my feet and my heartbeat sounding steadily in my ears. This was the moment I had always known was coming. The moment I'd have to risk my life to find my birthstone. I squinted at the beast hiding in the darkness, imagining that I could see the glint of a Rubine stone clutched in its bloody claws. I released a breath and took another tentative step towards the monster.

"Go on Fearless Fen!" A sudden shout from behind me was accompanied by a hard shove that propelled me forward into the darkness. I lost my footing, tumbled over a snarl of roots and landed in a heap of grubby skirts, mucky clogs and red curls. From the shadows, the orange eyed monster hooted and took flight. A few disrupted feathers drifted across the clearing as the great white owl swooped low beneath the branches of the finkle trees, glided out of the gloom of the Blackwoods and disappeared across the meadow.

Before I could clamber to my feet, my friend Duckie piled roughly on top of me. "Where's your stone Fen?" He teased, pinning me to the ground and nipping me all over. "Where'd the monster go Fearless Fen?" He went on. "Got your birthstone hasn't he, that big bad owl!"

I cackled with laughter, pulling my legs up to avoid his painful pinches. "Duckie, get off!" I shrieked. "Get off me!" I managed to push him away and struggle to my knees, the pair of us giggling and breathless in the shady clearing.

"Duckie, I bet you'd never even…" I began, intending to start one of our frequent and heated arguments over which of us was the bravest; which of us would dare to go furthest into the woods. Before I could finish, something caused the playful words to fade abruptly on my tongue. Duckie was red faced and panting but he clapped a hand over his mouth and his eyes widened when he realised why I'd fallen silent. The pair of us cocked our heads to one side like nervous bunnies, listening carefully as a soft breeze rustled the branches above our heads.

As we crouched on the forest floor, a mournful sound echoed from the depths of the Blackwoods. A sound like a baby crying, a pitiful mewling sobbing noise that gradually intensified until a shrill scream filled the quiet afternoon air. The hairs on my arms stood straight up and I grabbed Duckie's hand, dragging him from the darkness of the finkle trees towards the safety of the meadow. We ran from the forest as the scream echoed in our ears, leaving the shadows behind us as we raced out into the warm afternoon sun. The village lay on the other side of the meadow and as the scream faded away, Duckie and I slowed to a trot, comforted by the sight of the thatched cottages and grey smoke curling from the crooked chimneys.

"A real monster then, Fearless Fen," puffed Duckie as he paused to catch his breath. He spoke nonchalantly but I could tell he was a little rattled.

"Probably just a Bobkitten," I said, not very convincingly. Duckie and I both knew that the Blackwoods were dangerous; home to codgers and sinflints and snipes. The noise we'd heard was most likely a cariad, a siren of the woods that would lure folk deeper into the forest by imitating the cries of an injured child or the sweet song of a beautiful maiden. "Anyway," I went on. "It's all good practice for stone seeking." I shot a side wards glance at Duckie and he nodded.

"Won't be long now." He said in agreement, his tone light but I saw a shadow of fear darken his face. We walked on in silence, trudging through the long grass. When we reached the high fence that surrounded the village, Duckie leant down and pulled back a loose plank so I could wriggle through. Duckie followed and tugged the plank back into place, smoothing down his hair self- consciously as we made our way between the cottages towards the village square. He always straightened his hair and brushed down his clothes when we came home from our adventures. His mother worried about him; she was always happier when Duckie looked like he'd been up to gentle sports like reading or playing pinecones. She'd have a fit if she knew we'd been in the woods with a cariad lurking about.

"Fancy a game of pinecones?" I asked as we emerged into the village square where an old tree stood, crooked and stooped with age. I knew Duckie would feel better if he only had to tell his mother a half-truth rather than a bald-faced lie. Duckie nodded and pulled a couple of pinecones from his pocket, tossing one to me. I caught it with one hand.

"Best of three?" Duckie asked and I nodded keenly, turning toward the circles scratched in the dust at the foot of the old tree. I had lost our last game and hated losing to Duckie; I was eager to be the queen of pinecones once more. Before either of us could aim a throw into the circles, I heard someone calling my name. "Fen! Come on in now, it'll be dark soon!" My father's familiar voice drifted over the thatched roofs of the cottages and Duckie looked at me, one eyebrow raised.

"We'll play tomorrow Duckie, I promise." I said, tossing his pinecone back to him.

"Alright Fen," he said with a sigh. "I can handle being the best pinecones player in Millings Beck for another day." I laughed and darted forward to tug hard on one of his ears.

"Enjoy it while it lasts," I said as he yelped in pain. "I'll beat you tomorrow, and the next day and the day after that!" My father was calling me again so I turned and trotted across the square. "See you later!" I shouted over my shoulder and Duckie raised one hand to wave as he rubbed his sore ear with the other.

Duckie and I had been friends since we were small but Duckie had grown tall in recent annums with his pink cheeks, dark eyes and black hair that fell around his face. His real name was Duqorlias Erland but of course everyone called him 'Duckie' for short whether he liked it or not.

I ran across the square and past the mill, its wheels turning relentlessly through the cool waters of the beck from which the village gets its name. The beck gushes down from the hills and meanders between the ramshackle cottages, merrily making its way towards the rivers further south.

I scurried past the tavern, The Twilight Stop, and glanced through the crooked window catching sight of a few villagers gathered inside playing cards and setting the world to rights.

I have lived in Millings Beck for all of the sixteen annums of my life in a simple cottage with my father Dryden and brother Leif. My mother died of the Sphyx when I was ten and Leif just a baby so it's just the three of us now. The village nestles in a lush green valley in the middle of this land we call Immentia, surrounded by dense leafy woods and fertile hills. A set of sturdy gates and a watchtower stand at the southern edge of Millings Beck, high fences around the village borders and a few narrow lanes within the safety of the boundary. Life is simple enough and the people work hard, farming the surrounding fields or grinding grain on the millstones turned by the tumbling waters of the beck.

It was the middle of the month of Greenleaf, unusually warm and humid for springtime in this part of Immentia. The sun was just going down behind the hills to the west as I hurried down the lane towards home. Low clouds lumbered across the sky, dark and heavy with rain, the dwindling sun casting a murky light across the rooftops. As I rounded the bend I saw that Mr Burle was already out lighting the lanterns that hung from the cottages on either side of the lane.

"Oi! Fen Hadwyn!" he called from the top of his little ladder. "You'd better be heading home, looks like a storm coming!" He looked up at the troubled sky with a frown and I did the same as I trundled past him.

Mr Burle was the safekeeper of Millings Beck, in charge of lighting the lanterns each night and keeping watch from his tower at the gates. He would stand there for most of the day, stroking his moustache and surveying the surrounding countryside for "beasts and travellers". There weren't many travellers visiting Millings Beck but no one got through the gates without Edmund Burle knowing exactly who they were and what they wanted. As he always says, "Dangerous folk out there, got to look out for our own".

"I'm off home Mr Burle, don't worry!" I called back, taking a sharp turn down the narrow alleyway running along the side of our cottage. He shrugged, grumbling to himself about his "old bones" as he folded his ladder and trudged on to light the next lantern.

The houses of Millings Beck were roughly built from wood and thatch with small leaded windows that glowed dimly at night from the light of firepits and candles. The cottage next to ours belonged to the Edsels, a friendly couple with a couple of young children and an eldest son Elvyn, a big lad who was an annum older than myself. As I slowed to a walk in the alleyway I passed the Edsels small kitchen window and glanced up to see Elvyn's mothers standing there, looking out into the dusky evening light. She was white faced, ashen, her face streaked with tears and when she saw me I smiled at her and raised my hand in a small wave. As I did so, her expression hardened and she stepped away from the glass, pulling the curtain back quickly. The smile faded from my face as I passed the window and a shiver ran through me. I knew that there was something badly wrong. I also feared that I knew exactly what was troubling Mother Edsel.

Elvyn had become a Seeker last spring and had left Millings Beck with his good friend Dagda Folkborn, setting out on a journey that we all have to take when we reach our seventeenth annum. At this age, we approach the end of the first circle of life so we leave our homes and venture into the sprawling cities and vast wilderness of Immentia to find something. Something very important to each of us. Something small and often difficult to find but a thing with the power to save our lives.

Our birthstone. One of the nine gems linked to the seasons of the annums and the day we were born. We never know where our birthstones might be found, these mysterious gems that glow with power, the stone of each season a different colour and unique shape. A stone will last for a short while and then it turns to dust, others appearing in hidden places and secret corners elsewhere in the mountains, swamps and forests of Immentia.

If we are lucky enough to find our stone and hold it between our fingers, its power seeps into us, providing the energy we need to live on. The Seekers have until the first second, of the first minute, of the first day of their eighteenth annum. If we seek it too early then the power is too great but if we find it too late then the hourglass of life runs out. This is a harsh fact of life in Immentia that we accept because it has always been this way. We know that not everyone is lucky enough to find their stone and many die trying, never to return home. There is an old saying that the elder folk of the village like to repeat in somber tones, heads nodding sagely over mugs of ale in the Twilight Stop; "The Seekers leave with sword and pack, six set out but none came back".

Elvyn had gone in search of his birthstone filled with a braggart's confidence, a shiny new sword hanging from his belt. His friend Dagda had gone with him; Seekers close in birthdate often set out together, thinking they would be safer and have more chance of finding the stones they needed. Elvyn was a few weeks older than Dagda, born in the month of Greenleaf and birthed under the stone of Veridian. Having spoken with a wise woman over in Lark-on-Farthing they had journeyed to the Vale of Sighs far in the south-east of Immentia in search of Elvyn's birthstone. That was the last we'd heard. I thought of Mother Edsel's face and shivered again.

I pressed on down the alley and opened the little gate into our yard; a tidy square with a neat boundary of stout sticks hammered into the earth and a fence knitted together with twigs and twine. There's a small vegetable patch in one corner and a coop for the chickens that we keep for eggs and meat. I kicked a chicken gently out of the way and it flapped in displeasure, scratching its way off into the corner of the yard with the others, clucking to itself. I made my way down the cobbled path and lifted the latch on the heavy wooden door into the cottage. In the stone floored kitchen, candles illuminated the room softly with a cozy glow against the foreboding gloom outside.

My Pa, Dryden, was stirring the contents of the cooking pot hanging over the firepit. "Now then," he said, glancing up at me. "There you are. Good job you hurried home otherwise you'd have been in for a soaking. Burle said a tinker arrived this afternoon from Feybridge telling of a storm coming in from the south." Pa glanced up at the window. "It surely feels like something's brewing out there." Just as he spoke, a fork of lightening flashed across the twilight sky and a rumble of thunder rolled over the village. The chickens skittered about the yard and headed into their coop to huddle together. "Told you," Pa said, smiling as he added a handful of herbs to the pot. "Go and fetch Leif. Suppers almost ready." I skipped over to my father and took the spoon from his hand, peering into the pot.

"What are we having?" I asked, the Edsel's quickly forgotten as my mouth watered and I stirred the meaty stew bubbling over the fire. Pa sat down heavily onto one of the three legged stools surrounding our small kitchen table. "I caught a rabbit today," He said. "Couple of carrots and some potatties in there too." He smiled tiredly at me and his face looked serious. Sad even. "Now go and get Leif. We will eat, and then after supper you and I need to have a talk."

I trotted into our front room to find Leif, my little brother; 8 annums old and cute as a button. I don't actually have any buttons. The few clothes I have are held together with wooden toggles or yarn but I have heard of the big cities where merchants and traders ply their wares in markets, selling beautiful buttons and brooches made of precious metals that are smooth to the touch and sparkle in the sun. I entered the front room of the cottage to find Leif crouching on the floor, his hands mucky with charcoal and a piece of paper spread in front of him.

"What are you drawing little one?" I asked kneeling beside him and resting my hand on his curly head.

"I'm drawing the mountains," he explained, his little tongue poking up over his top lip in concentration.

"What do you know about mountains Leif?" I exclaimed, smiling. "We've never left Millings Beck!"

Suddenly his face was serious. "No Fen," he said solemnly. "But we will do. We have to. We both have to. You will have to leave Millings Beck very soon, and I don't want you to go." His big brown eyes suddenly brimmed with tears.

"Oh, Leif I know," I said soothingly, knowing he was thinking of my looming seventeenth annum. "But I will come back," I reassured him, resting an arm around his shoulders and looking into his face as he rubbed at his eyes with a grubby fist. "Plenty of people go to find their birthstone and come back safe and sound. Just like Pa!" I added, wishing I felt as brave as I sounded about the task ahead of me. Leif seemed to cheer a little at my words.

"I think you will too Fen," he said. "Look; I have drawn you in the mountains. This is you slaying a snow giant and this is you climbing a huge crag with eagles circling overhead. And look here, at the top of the crag, almost in the clouds - here is your stone!"

I laughed and tousled his hair "I hope my stone is a bit easier to get to than that!" I said, rising to my feet and looking down at my little brother. "Wherever it is, I will find it and I'll be home safe with you and Pa soon enough. And you don't need to worry about finding your birthstone for a very long time. By then you will be big and strong and you'll be able to fight giants too."

Leif brightened at that and laughed. He carefully rolled up his drawing and followed me back into the kitchen where Pa was ladling up rabbit stew with wedges of bread. I wondered what Pa wanted to talk to me about. We didn't talk of serious matters very often and there were very few words uttered by my Pa that didn't come with a twinkle in his eye. His serious and somber mood made me uneasy but I pushed the feeling aside; my growling belly being a more pressing matter.

Pa tossed another log into the fire pit and we all settled at the table as the storm broke overhead. Rain pelted down on the thatch and thunder boomed as we tucked into the warming stew, rich juice dribbling down our chins.

CHAPTER 2

After dinner, I brought in a bucket of rainwater from outside to wash the pots. I would usually go and fill the bucket with fresh water from the beck but the downpour had provided more than enough. "Go and play in the other room Leif," Pa said, "I need to talk to your sister."

"Why can't I stay and listen?" asked Leif, inquisitive eyes darting between the two of us.

"Well my little soldier," Pa said seriously. "This conversation is for folk more grown up than you. And anyway, soldiers need to concentrate on practicing their sword fighting!"

Pa playfully flicked the back of Leifs legs with a damp cloth and he scuttled, giggling, out of the room as I carefully rinsed the dinner plates. I hung the cooking pot back over the firepit, filled with water and herbs ready for the endless cups of mintleaf tea my Pa liked to drink. Whenever I went looking for my Pa in the village, I knew I'd find him doing some odd job or other – working at the mill, picking vegetables, mending someone's thatch or laying still as a statue down by the beck, patiently tickling for fish. Wherever he was, he'd always have a tin of mintleaf tea nearby and the fresh scent would always remind me of him, as familiar as the smell of the new grass in the summer or wood smoke in the chilly air on a winter's night.

"Fen," my Pa began wearily, rubbing his eyes as he sat back down at the table. "I have some news." I wiped my damp hands on my grubby skirts and crossed the kitchen to sit down opposite him, my eyes wide as I bit my lip. "I saw Mother Edsel earlier," I blurted out before my Pa could continue. "She looked upset. Did something happen? Did something happen to Elvyn?"

My father sighed heavily and rested his head on his hands, suddenly looking very old. "Yes Fen. That's why I need to speak to you."

My heart sank. We'd had this conversation many times before. I had seen the Seekers come and go throughout my childhood in Millings Beck. They would head off into the wilderness beyond the boundary of our safe little village, sometimes giddy with excitement, sometimes with looks of terror on their pale faces. Their families would stand for days in Burles' gatekeep tower, looking out across the horizon hoping to see their beloved son or daughter returning exhausted and battered, perhaps hurt and limping, but victorious having found what they were looking for. All were received with joyous relief by everyone in the village and a huge celebration would be held in the square or at the inn. They were the lucky ones. Some returned in weeks, some came back after several months. Many were never seen again.

"I knew he hadn't come back," I said bitterly. "I could tell by her face." My Pa lifted his head and looked at me sadly. "It's not as simple as that my love," he said quietly. "Elvyn made it back. He came home. But he failed. He turns eighteen tonight and has not found his birthstone. He was out in Gobbs Pass, a long way off to the east, three weeks ago with Dagda. They found a stone of Glisston, Dagdas birthstone, but not the Veridian stone that Elvyn needed. Elvyn knew then that he could keep looking or he had just enough time to get home to his family. He chose to come back to Millings Beck."

I looked at my father aghast. "So, he gave up?" I asked, disbelieving. "He just came home to die?"

"Yes Fen. He did. He had searched high and low for nearly an annum and didn't have the strength to go on. He only just made it home. Dagda had to carry him the last five miles to Millings Beck. That is why Mother Edsel is grieving. Elvyn Edsel is home but he is at the brink of his eighteenth annum and nothing more can be done."

We sat in silence for a few long moments as the rain drummed down loudly on the cottage. "I don't understand," I said quietly. "Why does this happen?"

Pa looked away, gazing out of the window into the now dark and windswept night. "It's the first circle of life Fen. We come of age and we need the power of our birthstone to give us the energy to go on to the second circle. Those talented at fighting, with the wiles to survive and a good dose of luck may find what they seek and will come home with the gift of life. But there will always be those who don't."

My stomach was churning as my father spoke. I thought of poor Elvyn in the once happy and warm cottage next door, remembering the many times he had waved at me in the morning as he headed off to the fields with his Pa. "Morning Fennington!" he'd shout, gently teasing me.

"Good day to you Elvynton," I would respond with sarcastic formality, smiling and raising my hand in mock salute.

Now he was laid in the dark cottage next door, tired and beaten, waiting for his life to ebb away. His family would be around him weeping, holding his hand, speaking softly to him in the hope that he would leave them feeling warm and loved and at peace. Dagda would be standing in the dark doorway, chewing his knuckles and biting back tears wondering why he was chosen and Elvyn was not. The first circle of life.

My father was watching me intently, his wise eyes nestled beneath bushy eyebrows. "You know Fen," he went on. "We would do anything for our children but we can't do this for you. Once gifted we can't touch another's stone – even to go too near can be dangerous. I could search Immentia high and low for your birthstone but I already found mine. It gave me life but the power of finding another would kill me and the magic within it would be gone. I would be dead and the stone would turn to dust. It's something our children have to do for themselves when they come of age. You will soon turn seventeen and we need to make sure you're ready when it's time for you to go." He sighed heavily again, gazing at me as he waited for me to speak.

I thought for a few moments, my chin resting on my hands as I stared into the fire. I didn't want to think about poor Elvyn or the fact that I would soon have to take the same dangerous journey. I pushed the dark thoughts from my mind and turned back to my Pa. "How did you find your stone Pa? Tell me the story again." I had heard the tale a million times but never tired of it. He stood up and took his tin mug to the firepit, ladling in some hot sweet-smelling tea. I could hear Leif play-fighting with his wooden sword in the other room as Pa settled back down opposite me and looked off into the distance over my head, thinking of days long passed.

"Well, as you know," he began, as he always did. "I was a couple of annums older than your mother but I knew, as we all do, that I would have to find my birthstone when I turned seventeen. There was an old man who lived just outside Millings Beck out in the Blackwoods, beyond the meadows on the far side of the village. His name was Thumbleton. Dickings Thumbleton." Pa smiled at the memory and his eyes misted.

"I was out in the woods one day, hunting and climbing the finkle trees and I had wandered further from home than I was supposed to. The finkles were dense and the ground was soft and springy, covered in dead leaves and moss, tree roots knotting across the woodland floor. I was following a small stream, watching the damselflies hovering over the water when I came across a glade where the stream flowed into a small pond. The pond was still and stagnant, surrounded by tall grass with sludgy weeds floating on the surface of the water. One side of the pond rose steeply into a large mud bank, creamy and damp, ferns clinging to the moist soil and trees overhanging from above.

I crept through the moss and leaves of the forest floor, looking down into the water for brown trout, maybe a crab, and I noticed the sun glinting off something across the glade. I squinted to look a little closer and that's when I saw it. A real surprise it was. Right there in the mud bank were couple of dirty little windows and a door. It was a little house carved right into the soft earth! The strangest thing I had ever seen! A plume of smoke drifted out of the little crooked chimney in the grassy overhang above and a rickety wooden jetty hidden by reeds lead to the front door. A little brown boat was tethered up right outside, resting low in the pond water, covered in weeds. I once asked Thumbleton where he went in his boat. He said he would row off for the day, out of the pond and up the stream, further into the woods looking for mushrooms and dragonflies.

I stood beneath a finkle tree for a long time, watching the house. The boat bobbed lazily on the pond and a Queenfisher flitted across the water, blue feathers flashing. Apart from that the glade was completely still. I stood there wondering what kind of creature could possibly live in a house so strange, out in the woods and away from the safety of the village. As I stood there pondering this, there was a sudden yank at my ankles and whoosh! I was hoisted up into the air and found myself hanging in a finkle tree by my feet, completely helpless! I tell you, it knocked the wind out of me and gave me a real fright! Made me wish I'd listened to my mother and not ventured beyond the third lamppost out of the village! As I swung there catching my breath, I heard a voice.

'Ah ha! You'll see what happens to spies in Thumbleton's Glade!' the voice cackled as if it found my predicament very amusing. I twisted and turned, swinging there in the tree, trying to see who had strung me up. I could see nothing, only hear the cackling laughter as my captor playfully tugged on the rope, causing me to bob and sway like a fish on a line".

My Pa was smiling and laughing at the memory. It was infectious and I caught his excitement, even though I knew what came next. "Who was it? What did you do?" I asked, clasping my hands under my chin and leaning eagerly across the kitchen table.

"Well," Pa went on. "When he'd had his fun he eventually lowered me down. As I got to my feet – a bit shaken up I might add - this little man appeared from the trees. He wasn't *in* the tree or *behind* the tree, he was standing right in front of it but you couldn't have seen him even if you'd been looking. He was wearing a long cape stitched together from tree bark and reeds and there were streaks of dried mud encrusting his ankles, hands and face. His pointed hat seemed to be made from hanging moss and covered most of his face so the whole peculiar outfit rendered him virtually invisible! The hat was coated in glistening silvery trails made by a couple of snails creeping across it, their horns turning this way and that.

He blended so well into the woodland surroundings that he could have been there an age watching me and I wouldn't have known. I should've been frightened but he was so small and smiling so gleefully that I was more intrigued than alarmed. We stood there, staring at each other for a few moments and eventually he spoke.

'So, boy,' he said in his peculiar creaky voice. 'I'm guessing you don't get out of Millings Beck very often. You shouldn't make it so easy for folk to creep up on you. Not surprising I suppose," he muttered as he freed me from the vines around my ankles. 'Got to keep your young 'uns safe and, as I of all folk knows, it's not safe for anyone out here. How old are you boy?' he asked, straightening and peering up at me from beneath his moss hat.

'I'm sixteen and a harvest,' I said. My tone was a little defensive as I was a bit put out having been strung up in a tree.

The little man cackled again. 'Sixteen and a harvest?' he crowed. 'Nothing left for you to learn then! Are you ready to go out to seek your birthstone? Doesn't look like it to me!' he chuckled, gathering up his vine trap and carefully laying the noose back out beneath the branch, covering it carefully with leaves.

'I can fire a bow, best in the Beck,' I said, puffing out my chest. 'I will be ready when the time comes,' I added. That's what my Pa had always told me; 'You'll be ready when the time comes'.

The little man stopped what he was doing, stood up and turned to me with a very grave expression on his wizened, dirty face. 'Dickings Thumbleton. Pleased to meet you,' he said sticking out his muddy hand. 'Know this son and know it well; the time comes sooner than you think.'

From that moment, myself and the little man in the mud house became firm friends. I made sure I continued to practice my bow and sword like the others in the village, but I would head off to see Thumbleton every chance I got. I would make my way to the glade and tap on his little muddy door. If his boat was gone I would know he had gone out mushrooming so I would sit on the boardwalk or tickle for fish in the stream waiting for him to come back. He would always greet me the same way; 'Ah Dryden Hadwyn of Millings Beck, sixteen and a harvest!' he'd cackle. 'Come to learn some tricks from an old man?'

We would head out further into the Blackwoods and Thumbleton spent hours teaching me what he knew. How to disguise myself in the forest, covered in leaves, twigs and mud. How to climb the finkles and swing silently through the trees. How to disappear under the waters of the rivers and lakes. He taught me which mushrooms were safe to eat, which would poison me and how to set up traps like the one he caught me in when we first met.

At the end of a long day in the woods, we would sit next to the fire in his cottage warming our feet, drinking tea, and Thumbleton would tell me wild and wonderful tales of adventuring. His old eyes would become misty, his crooked fingers absent mindedly stroking the smooth shells of the snails snoozing on his hat as he spoke."

My Pa's face looked strangely youthful again in the fading glow of the fire as he recalled days from long ago. I didn't speak, waiting for him to continue.

"I left the Beck the day I turned seventeen but after several months of searching I had found nothing. I heard of a witch over in Gloamglade who claimed she knew where to find Forzit, my birthstone. She charged me a pretty penny and I wasn't sure if I could trust her but I was running out of time. I was lucky. It was just as she'd said and I found my stone in the forests of the mountain foothills to the north. Believe me, it wasn't easy but I don't know what would have happened without the tricks I learned in the woods. One thing that no one truly understood was this: Thumbleton taught me everything I needed to know. And he saved my life."

The firepit had died down, leaving the room gloomy except for the candle flickering on the kitchen table. Pa sat back and sipped his mintleaf tea, deep in thought. Eventually he sighed and stood up, walking to the window and folding his arms across his chest as he looked out at the rain pattering on the glass. I rested my chin on my hands, gazing silently into the embers of the firepit. My mind wandered as I thought of Elvyn and of Pa and how differently their stories had turned out. I wondered what my story would be. Duckie and I had been planning to become Seekers since we were very young and in our childish, optimistic daydreams, we always headed off together heralded by the whole village like royalty going to war. We would be lifted on shoulders, presented with bejeweled weapons – Duckie a sword and me a spangled bow - and the women would thread flowers in my hair. We would mount fine horses and gallop out of the Beck in a cloud of dust, heading off to seek our birthstones and inevitable glory.

All children are taught fighting skills from an early age and the different towns and cities favor different weapons; bows and swords in the Beck, curved daggers in the desert lands and tridents and nets in the settlements along the coast. Fletchers Furrow, a village in the forests north of Millings Beck, is home to the most skilled bowmen in Immentia. The people fletch the best quality arrows from the plentiful wood using bright blue Queenfisher feathers which guide the arrows through the air with great speed and accuracy. The Seekers of Fletchers Furrow learn only the bow, thinking any other method a poor substitute for the deadly stealth of an archer.

Most of the people of Immentia would welcome travelling Seekers and offer assistance where they could, giving them food and drink and a place to stay overnight. However, there were some folk who would trade information on the whereabouts of birthstones. They would take farthings from the desperate Seekers and send them off into the wilds to a find a stone that often wasn't there.

Some of the larger cities had huge libraries filled with books; maps and guides, tomes on how best to kill a Doomstrider or how to treat a sting from a Bloodwarbler. The marketplaces would be teeming with people and rumors; "Did you hear that someone saw a Treemouse with a Glisston between its paws outside Haggs Catton?" or "My cousins' brother-in-law found Xalyph in the Avernian Hills - in a birds nest he said it was!"

Many of these stories turned out to be folk-tales or wild exaggerations. Even if there was truth to them, the stones could turn to dust before they were found. Often, stories and hear-say were the only clues we had so as Seekers we have to keep our ears open but be careful who we trust.

Travelling was dangerous with bandits and vagrants loitering on the roads and rivers, hardened men with nowhere to call home, scraping a living thieving and fighting. The wild expanses outside the towns and cities were deadly places and Seekers would encounter dangerous beasts that they would have to outwit or fight to the death.

As I sat there, hypnotized by the glowing embers of the dying fire, I realized that my own time was coming. Soon I would have to leave the safety of Millings Beck and set off on my own quest. The journey that would determine my fate, my future and whether I would be one of the lucky ones who would eventually make it home.

CHAPTER 3

The next morning the sun rose brightly over Millings Beck and at first light, the roosters began their crowing and the pigs could be heard snuffling and snorting in the yards around the village. I awoke in my bed in our loft with Leif still asleep and breathing softly in the bunk above me. Pa slept downstairs in our front room and I always felt safe knowing he was there. This morning though, something had changed. I didn't feel safe anymore. The storm had continued through the night, rain beating down and dripping through the thatch until eventually the thunder had rumbled further and further away into the distant hills.

I sighed and pushed back the blankets, sun streaming in through the small window in the roof. Dust faeries danced and swooped in the beam of light, chasing each other, their tiny brown wings humming softly. "Shoo!" I whispered, waving my hand through the buzzing faeries and opening the roof hatch. They scattered through the air shrieking and a couple shot out through the open window into the morning air. The others followed giggling, their laughter like the sound of wind chimes. Leif stirred and rolled over in his bunk but didn't wake.

I pulled my sleepshift off and washed myself at the basin standing the corner. A fragment of mirror was nailed to a wooden beam and I wiped the dust from it with the back of my hand. My reflection looked back at me; a muddle of auburn curls, cut chin length by my Pa the last time it got too knotted to brush. My eyes were brown coloured, my skin tanned from the sun with a dotting of freckles across my nose and cheeks. I didn't like the way I looked. I didn't dislike the way I looked. I couldn't care less. My grubby blue dress was crumpled on the floor where I had left it the night before and I picked it up, shaking it out before wriggling it on over my head and lacing the bodice loosely. Some of the older girls in the village would lace their dresses so tightly they could barely breathe because they thought the boys liked it better. They would sway around the square or lounge on the stone circle pretending not to notice the admiring glances of the village urchins. I liked my bodice to be loose and I could shoot my bow better if I could breathe easily. Anyway, there were no boys in the village I wanted to catch the eye of.

Of course, Duckie was a boy but I didn't see him as anything other than my friend, almost as a brother. Since we were pups we would practice bow and sword together, play pinecones or venture to the edge of the Blackwoods, daring each other to go further. Mr Burle would watch carefully from his tower. "Hey you two! Don't you be going any further into those woods – I've got my eye you!" We both pretended that Mr Burle was the reason we didn't enter the cool and foreboding darkness of the trees. In the evenings, Duckie and I would sit next to the fire in the taproom of The Twilight Stop inn while the villager's swilled mugs of ale and discussed the weather or the upcoming harvest. As conversation hummed around us, Duckie and I would tell each other tall stories about the goblins and boggarts that we had heard lived in the Blackwoods. We would imagine them waiting for us to enter the woods and get lost before dragging us off to their caves and certain doom.

I smiled to myself as I pulled on my clogs. I could hear Pa downstairs, the cookpot clattering and the sound of him whistling and singing softly as he went about his morning tasks. I climbed down the ladder from our loft into the kitchen below. "Morning love," Pa said, looking up from where he knelt, lighting the firepit and blowing softly on the wood shavings to encourage the flame to take hold.

"Hmmm," I mumbled, not at my most talkative at first light. "Our room was full of dust faeries again this morning," I complained as I pulled out a sack of oats from the dresser and a jug of milk from the cool, covered stone pit near the door where we kept our perishables.

"Oh Fen, they won't bite you!" Pa chided as he stood up, adding some logs to the fire.

"I know," I said, pouring oats into the cookpot and adding the milk. "I just don't like them. Their buzzing and singing annoys me."

Pa laughed. "Well we can't have that, can we? They must be creeping in through that gap in the thatch. I'll fix it today while you're out at practice."

We bustled about the kitchen in silence for a few minutes; me putting the pot over the fire and stirring the porridge, Pa getting out tin bowls and wooden spoons and laying the table. Leif finally emerged, scurrying down the ladder, his eyes drowsy with sleep and his hair a mess of curls.

"Pa, can I play at the beck today?" chirruped Leif. "Diran Crouch has a paper boat and we're going to sail it!" he said excitedly, scrambling up onto a stool and taking his spoon in hand ready for his porridge.

"You can go play after you've done your chores Leif," said Pa. "Feed the chickens, fetch some water and then you need to help me fix the thatch." Pa patted Leif's little head, licking his fingers to flatten down the unruly curls. I ladled porridge into the bowls and we all sat down at the table, pulling up our stools. We ate our breakfasts chattering about our plans for the day; how many targets I hoped to hit at practice, how Diran Crouch's paper boat would get on – I said sink; Leif said sail.

I left the pots for Leif, kissing my hand and tapping it lightly on his head and then Pa's cheek as I headed out of the cottage. Every morning was weapons practice for all the youngsters in the village. We would gather in the meadow behind the Flitwich's cottage, outside the village boundary where targets and practice dummies were set up. We would learn how to swing and parry a sword or knife, how to shoot a bow and how to dodge and roll to evade an incoming strike. Most of us did not yet have our own weapons so we would practice with rusty dull blades and creaking bows from Mr Flitwich's shed. When we approached our seventeenth annum, our families would usually find better weapons to present to the Seekers before we had to leave. Better weapons meant more chance of us coming home but we still needed to know how to use them.

I walked quickly out of our yard and down the alley. The Edsel's cottage was still dark and quiet, curtains still drawn. There would be no practice for the Edsel children today.

I thought again of Elvyn and it darkened my heart despite the bright sunshine of the morning. They would grieve today. Mr Edsel would go with Burle to the old graveyard at the edge of the village. They would dig into the soft ground and the children and people of Millings Beck would bring flowers, lining the grave with a soft blanket of glorious colours and soft petals. Tonight, by the light of the moon, they would lower Elvyn gently down and his family would lay more flowers before covering him in earth and placing a stone above his head. In a way, they were lucky. For many families, there were no final words of comfort, no cold hands to hold one last time and no flowery resting place.

I frowned and shook my head trying to push the thoughts from my mind as I emerged into the main village street where a few people were up and about. Women stood in doorways glancing at the Edsels cottage as they spoke quietly to one another, expressions grim and serious. Mother Flitwich made her way down the street with a large covered cookpot in her hands her eyes downcast. When she reached the Edsels cottage she stopped and placed the pot gently at their door. She kissed her hand and touched the door sadly, wiping a tear from her cheek.

I walked on, up towards the square where I found Duckie exactly where I had left him the evening before; sitting on the stone circle, legs bent up and his chin resting on his knees. He said nothing as he watched me approach and I sat down next to him, pushing my hair back from my face. "You've heard then." I said flatly and Duckie turned his head.

"Of course," he replied gravely. "The whole village has heard. Dagda Folkborn went straight home after he brought Elvyn back – was in a terrible state apparently. He'd carried Elvyn home but was pretty bruised and battered himself. Exhausted they said."

I sighed but said nothing. After a long silence, Duckie spoke quietly. "I'd do that for you, you know."

"You'd do what?" I asked, turning to look at him.

"Carry you home," he said gruffly looking across the square at the watermill, its wheel turning slowly in the beck, sunlight glittering off the water tumbling between its paddles. I was touched by his words and reached out, patting his hand awkwardly. "You turn seventeen three weeks before me," I said lightly. "It's more likely to be the other way around!" I forced a laugh.

He turned to face me. "Not if I find my stone first," he said darkly.

I looked away again, watching a cat stretching before it jumped up onto a barrel outside the door of The Twilight Stop. It settled there, eyes narrowed, surveying the square. "Well," I said, jumping from my seat and stretching my arms above my head. "We'd better get to practice then. You need to get better at your bow if you're going to be carrying me home!"

Duckie laughed at that, getting up from the circle. "Oh yeah?" he challenged me. "I might not be as good as you with a bow and arrow but I'm faster on my feet… last one to the meadow is a fliggart!" he shouted, suddenly taking to his heels and running off, up through the village towards the little gate out to the fields.

I gathered my skirts and took off after him, my clogs clattering along the lane as we wound our way through the men heading to the mill with barrows and women walking down to the beck with piles of washing on their backs. We weaved down the alley and behind the Flitwich cottage, the gate to the meadow standing open as Mr Flitwich stood there, hands on hips waiting for us. "You're late!" he bellowed as we ran past him through the gate and into the meadow. The others were already there lined up, tightening the strings on their bows and aiming arrows as they squinted towards the targets across the field.

Duckie and I skidded to a halt and took our places at the end of the line, panting and playfully digging each other in the ribs. "Right!" shouted Mr Flitwich, hands behind his back as he paced the line, all eyes turned to him. "In a few weeks, four of you will be leaving Millings Beck. It's time for all of you to start taking practice seriously. In light of today's news, I hardly think I need to remind you." He glared directly at Duckie and me and we looked guiltily at the floor. There were ten of us lined up in the meadow, ages ranging from around twelve to nearly seventeen and four of us would be leaving the Beck in the coming weeks. As well as Duckie and myself there was Drifa Goodhill and Harlequin Ebbington. Harlequin was a burly, thick set lad with a tussock of black hair and heavy eyebrows that seemed to be permanently set in a deep furrow. Drifa was dark skinned with long jet-black hair, watchful green eyes and a spiky temper. Her mother was an herb gatherer and would mix her tinctures in the kitchen of their cottage, plumes of foul smelling smoke drifting out of the door into the street. Drifa's father would usually be found in The Twilight Stop swigging ale until his head nodded onto his chest. He would often have to be woken by a swift kick from the innkeeper Mr Crouch at closing time and would stumble off home down the dimly lit lane, weaving and singing bawdily.

We all stood there in the sun, some of the younger ones fidgeting as Mr Flitwich continued pacing the line before turning to face us. "As you know, Harlequin will be the first to go on the 6th of Bloomsbreeze. That's only three weeks away." He looked at Harlequin, who swallowed hard but maintained his steely expression, chin held high and hands clasped behind his back. Flitwich then turned his attention to Drifa. "And Miss Goodhill, you come of age at the end of Bloomsbreeze – the 28th day isn't it?" He squinted at Drifa. She nodded briefly but said nothing, long pale fingers plucking nervously at her skirts.

"Then there's you Duckie," Mr Flitwich continued. "You'll be leaving mid-Emersfire and Fen, you'll head out on the first of Driftleaf." He turned his eyes on me. "Late in the annum to be leaving the Beck," he said. "Make sure you get your Pa to find you warm clothes and sturdy shoes – those clogs won't last out there on the roads." He peered at my filthy shoes, a small hole in the toe of each.

"Yes, Mr Flitwich," I replied looking down, a little shame-faced and wiggling my toes. Mr Flitwich came to a stop again further down the line and turned to face us. "I suggest between now and then you speak to your elders, catch up with any visitors coming through the village and chat to the merchant caravans to see if they've heard of any birthstones on their travels. Any information you can rake up to plan your search, all the better."

"Yes, Mr Flitwich," we four intoned, our expressions somber, the younger ones' eyes wide and fearful. Flitwich unclasped his hands from behind his back, folding his arms over his barrel chest and casting his eyes once again up and down the line. He was quiet for a moment, looking carefully into each one of our faces.

"I will do everything I can to make sure you're all the best you can be," he said, his tone softening. "I just hope it will be enough to keep you safe and get you back to the Beck where you belong."

CHAPTER 4

The next few weeks were filled with days of practice out at the meadow, each of us honing our skills on our favored weapon. For me it was the bow and for Duckie the sword. Girls tended to be better with a bow than a sword as it took physical strength to swing and drive the heavy metal weapons while the bow depended more on stealth and accuracy. We all needed to be proficient in both types of arms but in those final weeks it was important that we were good at both but excelled at one.

After practice, my Pa and I spent many afternoons in the Blackwoods as he showed me the tricks of the forest that Thumbleton had once taught him. Dickings Thumbleton no longer lived in his little mud house by the pond in the woods. Pa took me there one day but the dwelling was derelict and crumbling, the little windows and door overgrown with grasses and ferns. There was no fire burning in the grate of his front room, no boat moored outside and the boardwalk had long since sunk beneath the black water of the pond. "Where'd he go Pa?" I'd asked as we stood in the glade, mud streaking our faces.

"I don't know Fen." Pa replied, his eyes sad. "After I found my stone and returned to the village, I came here looking for him every day but there was no sign. Maybe he moved on. Maybe he died out there, looking for his mushrooms. You know Fen," my Pa said, wrapping a strong arm around my shoulders, "Even if we find our stone in time, we don't live forever and Thumbleton was very old. I just hope some of what he taught me will help you one day too."

Life in Millings Beck continued somewhat as normal. The villagers harvested the wheat, bringing it back from the fields on groaning carts, their horses sweating and puffing in the late afternoon sun. The inn was still abuzz with voices and laughter in the evenings but there was a sense of building tension as the days passed. Late one afternoon, a merchant caravan approached the Beck on the southern road. Burle saw them coming, their heavily laden carts swaying slowly up the winding lane, outlined black in the twilight. He hallooed the rest of the men in the village and closed the gates, drawing down the heavy bar on the inside before returning to his watchtower. The caravan stopped and the merchants set up camp a little way outside the village, unfurling their tents and posts and tethering their horses. As was customary, one of the visitors approached the watchtower and, when Burle was satisfied that they meant us no harm, the village gates were opened leaving the merchants free to enter Millings Beck and set up their stalls in the square.

We rarely received travelling caravans in the Beck so Leif and I watched them from our cottage window, peering out inquisitively as they passed in their long heavy robes carrying sacks of fruit, barrels of honeyed mead and spits of roasted meat. Pa came home to find us there, our noses pressed up against the glass, pointing and exclaiming at this and that as the merchants made their way through the village. We begged to be allowed out to go up to the square but Pa packed us off to bed, our eyes bright and mouths watering.

As the days lazily drifted from one to the next, the villagers held Seekers meets in the inn, bringing with them the few books and maps we had in the Beck. The maps were incomplete and, by the villagers own admittance, probably inaccurate. All of the papers were old and torn, covered in scribbles and handwritten notes; locations and roads marked and then corrected over the years as each Seeker returned to the Beck and imparted the knowledge of where they had travelled and what they had seen.

As the maps showed, Millings Beck was a small speck of a village in the central region of Immentia, at least a day's journey from any other settlements. There were many towns, villages and hamlets that littered the landscape of this vast and beautiful land as well as coastal ports and huge cities. Immentia was surrounded by endless seas to the south, east and west that no one had explored in recent memory. There was no record or report of what lay beyond the seas in any of the maps or books written hundreds of annums before so the people of Immentia sailed around the coasts from port to port but few had dared to cross the seas to discover what lay beyond.

In the northern reaches of Immentia were the Mountains of Fellscar, a huge range of snowy peaks and deep crevasses that spanned the width of the world from sea to sea. Just as the seas were endless, the mountains were impassable. In the same way that none had travelled across the waters, no one knew what lay beyond the Fellscars. Any brave explorers who had set out across the endless seas had either turned around when they ran short of food and water or did not return to tell the tale. Any foolhardy adventurers who attempted to cross the Mountains of Fellscar would be forced back when their companions began to drop dead from the cold or when they could make no further progress through the unforgiving crags and deadly chasms.

In order to prepare the young seekers of the village for their quest, Burle would gather us together and sit in the Twilight Stop reading from the books, pointing out routes on the maps and the positions of the cities and settlements. He would describe the creatures we should expect to encounter in which types of terrain on our arduous journey. He would show us drawings of all the birthstones, explaining the colours and shapes and reminding us of the danger should we get too close to a stone that was not for us. The power of another stone can kill so we all memorized the descriptions and illustrations of each; the deep red, diamond shaped Rubine; the perfectly spherical glass-like Forzit; the bright green teardrop of Veridian.

Harlequin's seventeenth annum was approaching quickly and he had become quiet and distant. Day after day he remained practicing in the meadow long after the others had gone home, a dark silhouette in the dwindling light, swiping and stabbing his sword until his arm could no longer lift the heavy blade. The night before Harlequin was due to leave, all of the villagers gathered in The Twilight Stop, each of them approaching him to share some final words of encouragement, advice or simply to wish him luck. They offered up a few farthings if they could spare them along with small parcels of food to help him on his way. The Seekers would usually head off with a small pack on their backs so could not carry much, but people wanted to do whatever they could to help. Harlequin accepted their kind words and gifts, his face stoic and eyes hard.

The next day, Harlequin left before the sun came up as the village slept. Burle said his mother had stood in the watchtower silently watching him walk away down the road, his figure getting smaller and smaller until eventually, she could see him no more. She stood there for hours gazing out at the distant hills until her husband came to fetch her, holding her and stroking her hair, whispering quiet and comforting words as she wept.

Time passed and on the afternoon before Drifa's seventeenth annum her family held a feast for her in the square and the whole village came out to celebrate. It was un-said but everyone knew that Drifa may not get the chance to do so again. The trestle tables were brought out of the inn and into the afternoon sunshine of the square along with casks of ale as a travelling picador played his fiddle and the children danced around his feet. All the folk in the village brought food; apple pies, and legs of chicken as everyone sat down together, lifting mugs of cold ale, toasting Drifa and wishing her a happy annum and safe return.

The next day Drifa readied herself and a bleary eyed Mr Goodhill sharpened her weapons and checked her pack. She sat for a while out in the meadow – not practicing, just sitting there on the dewy grass in the hazy early morning light plaiting her hair. She was eventually waved off by a throng of villagers, warm embraces and final words from her family as she went out of the gates and then looped up and around the village boundary, heading north towards Fletchers Furrow and the mountains beyond. The children followed her a little way, cheering and larking about, pretending that they were going too until their parents called them back to the safety of the village. Eventually the people dispersed, returning to their household chores or trudging to the inn to while away the rest of the afternoon, speculating on the day's events and the fate of the Seekers of Millings Beck, Harlequin and Drifa. And what would become of them.

CHAPTER 5

"No, Duck you're doing it all wrong!" I chastised Duckie as he aimed his bow carefully at the furthest target in the meadow. "Your elbow and forearm need to be in line with the arrow – otherwise you'll never hit it!" I said, moving behind him, straightening his arm and squinting my eye down his line of sight.

"Fen, I'm not as good as you are with a bow!" Duckie snapped. "I wish you'd stop telling me what to do!" Duckie lowered the weapon and stamped his foot childishly as he turned to me, his brows furrowed. "I haven't time to get any better. I am leaving tomorrow so what's the point?" He asked glaring at me, his expression a mixture of anger, fear and frustration.

I stood back, hands on hips, puffing out my cheeks as I blew a strand of hair from my face. My tone softened. "I know. Let's forget about practice. There's not much more to be learnt by tomorrow and you're more than good enough with your sword anyway. You probably won't even end up having to use a bow. You'd be better off having a sit down with Burle and Flitwich to go over your route again."

Duckie turned his glare away from me, aiming his arrow back at the target as he straightened his arm and let the arrow fly. We both turned to watch it as it whizzed through the air, shot a foot wide of its mark and disappeared into the depths of the Blackwoods. "Now look what you made me do," Duckie said angrily, dropping the bow to the ground and letting his arms fall limply at his sides. He sat down heavily in the grass, legs crossed and head down, his fingers pulling at the green fronds at his feet. I sat down next to him, looking off across the meadow. The afternoon was cloudy, a little chilly, and we could hear the familiar sounds of the village as it went about its day; the churn of the water mill, the chickens clucking and squawking, and the occasional high-pitched laugh of a child and the low hum of voices in the square.

"So," I turned to Duckie, breaking the uncomfortable silence. "Where will you go first?" Duckie looked up and out across the fields, his fingers still pulling up blades of grass, his expression pensive. "I think I will go to Andorta," he said thoughtfully, our cross words forgotten. "Burle says it's only a couple of day's journey and the roads should be easy enough. I just need to make it through the pass beyond Haggs Catton and then they say you can see the city from the other side of the mountains. It's still a ways from there on foot but at least when I get there I can rest up for a while, ask about."

I stretched out on the grass, leaning back on my elbows. "Make sure you keep an eye out on your way. There could be Zaphite anywhere." I squinted up at him. "You could find it before you even get to Andorta. Don't forget what you're out there looking for."

Duckie lay back in the grass alongside me. "As if I could forget," he said wearily. "I can barely think about getting from Millings Beck to Haggs Catton in one piece let alone looking for my stone on the way."

I pulled up a daisy and absently pulled at its petals. "Just remember," I said mimicking Mr Burle, my voice stern and gruff. "They turn up in the most unlikely places, sometimes when you least expect it." Duckie gave a small rueful smile and shook his head at my weak attempt to amuse him.

"What about you?" he asked me. "If you like, I'll wait for you in Andorta and I can ask around about Rubine stones at the same time. I can bunk up somewhere, do some odd jobs for a few coins and trek out from there and back every couple of days looking for stones. If nothing turns up, I can wait for you and we can decide what to do next. We'd always planned to go together after all." Duckie looked at me expectantly as I swatted at a fliggart that had landed on my arm, its spindly legs and darting antennae tickling my skin.

"Alright," I agreed. "You go on ahead and see what you can find out and I'll come as soon as I can." I slapped again at the fliggart on my arm and flicked its squashed remains onto the ground. Duckie seemed to relax at that, lying back in the grass, hands behind his head as he stared up at the cloudy sky.

I leaned over on my side, my chin resting on my palm as I looked at him. I took a deep breath. "You do know though, that if one of us finds our stone before the other then they will have to come straight home? It's too dangerous and I don't want to get both of us killed if one of us has already found what they're looking for."

Duckie squinted down at me, confused. "What do you mean? We always said we'd come home together?" he questioned me.

"I know Duckie," I said softly. "But it's not safe out there. I think as soon as one of us finds our stone, we should head straight back to Millings

Beck. If I don't find my birthstone, I'd rather die out there and I don't want you to see it." I sat up and looked straight at him. "There'll be no carrying me home Duckie."

Duckie sat bolt upright. "There's no way I'd leave you," he said stubbornly. "We need to stay together. That's what we always said!"

I looked away again, refusing to meet his eyes, my face cold. "We were just pups then. I'm sorry Duckie but I need you to agree to this or I won't come and meet you at all."

Duckie's face was shocked, his expression imploring. "But Fen…" he started.

"No Duckie, I mean it. You leave me or I leave you. Either way, if we find a stone we come home." My voice was terse, my tone serious and I could tell by his face that Duckie knew that I meant what I said. He nodded and swallowed hard. I turned my gaze back out across the meadow, towards the Blackwoods. I knew he'd rather wait for me in Andorta so we could travel together for a time than not be together at all. If he didn't agree to my terms, I could go in the opposite direction and be on my way to the city of Avern on the other side of Immentia before he even realized I wasn't coming.

"Alright," Duckie agreed quietly. He kissed his palm and offered it out to me. I did the same and we shook on it; a binding promise but I knew that at least one of us was lying. I knew in my heart that if Duckie found his stone first, I'd want him to come back to the Beck. I wanted him home safe with his family, free to carry on his life, look out for Leif and my Pa and eventually fall in love with a nice girl and live out his annums happy and content. I also knew that if I found my stone first, I wouldn't leave his side until we'd searched every inch of Immentia.

The next day I was awake before the sun came up, laying in my bunk watching the shadows slip away as the dawn crept slowly into our loft. I hadn't slept, thinking about seeing Duckie off and the long, dreary days that would follow waiting for my time to come when I could set out to join him. We met together in the soft morning light at the stone circle and played a final game of pinecones. Duckie lost, 6 to 4, and I dared him to leave the village, battle for his life and find his birthstone. He didn't laugh. He was quiet and remote, his mind a long way from Millings Beck, preparing himself for the journey ahead of him. He went over the maps one last time with Burle and received the usual well wishes from the villagers who pressed coins and food into his hands, Drifa's mother offering up a gauze parcel of healer's herbs.

The sun was rising in the sky by the time we all gathered at the village gates chattering amongst ourselves, Duckie's mother fussing over his clothes and checking his boots were laced right. "Now Duckie," she said, pushing apples and nuts into his already bulging backpack. "Remember to take the southern road until nightfall and then find somewhere to rest – don't travel at night. There's Mother Bruma's place about a day's walk from here, remember we showed you on the map? I've not been there myself but she's always happy to help young Seekers. She'll take you in for the night."

Duckie looked embarrassed as his mother licked her fingers and wiped a smear of dust from his cheek. "Mother I know, you told me a hundred times and I've been over the route a thousand times more."

His mother smiled sadly and clasped a hand to his cheek. "I know my love. Send word to me when you get to Andorta. I've sewn an extra farthing into your coat lining so send us a letter if you can."

Duckie laughed. "I might need that farthing for more important things than letters!" He drew his mother into a warm embrace, his face nestled in her hair. "Try not to worry mother, if you don't hear from me then it just means I am busy trying to come back to you all the sooner."

I watched him there, holding his mother at the village gates, at least a head taller than her and he suddenly looked very different to me. No longer my childhood friend with his cheeky smile and teasing words but a grown man, ready to go out into the world and face whatever awaited him. Water sprung to my eyes and clouded my vision as Duckie approached me, his face apprehensive but determined.

"So, Fen," he said as I blinked the tears away. He didn't touch me. He knew me well and I had always been prickly, preferring to keep my distance even from those I loved. We'd be more likely to dig each other in the ribs or pinch each other's ears than show any sign of affection. I stood back, arms stiffly folded across my chest. "So," I echoed him, smiling and biting my lip to stop it from trembling. We looked at each other for a few moments and a lone teardrop escaped and dripped down my nose. I quickly swiped it away with my dirty fist, embarrassed.

"Oh Fen," Duckie said, suddenly grabbing me in a bear hug. "Don't be sad. I'll see you in a few weeks' time! I'll be well settled in Andorta by the time you get there. You know they have a tavern there for every day of the week, not to mention the belly dancers and fighting bears! I will hardly even miss you!"

I gave out a half laugh, half sob as I pushed him off me. "Oh, I can imagine Duck, I'm quite sure you won't even remember who I am!" I stepped back and took both his hands tightly in mine. "You take care of yourself," I murmured softly, squeezing hard.

He nodded resolutely. "See you soon Fen," he replied, searching my eyes for a moment. Our hands dropped and Duckie said his final farewells to his family before turning and trudging off out of the gates and down the lane. As I watched him go, I had to fight the urge to chase after him, grab him by the arm and drag him back to the safety of the Beck. He was nearly out of sight before he turned and gave one final wave and we all stood there, hands raised, watching him as he disappeared from sight.

His mother finally let the tears overcome her as she buried her face in his father's shoulder. Pa walked up behind me and draped his arm across my shoulders. "You alright pixie?"

"I just want to go now Pa," I replied, frowning in frustration. "I don't know how I am going to stand another few weeks here on my own, just waiting."

Pa smiled down at me fondly. "I know Fen," he said gently, stroking my hair. "But if you were to find a stone too early it could be too dangerous, you might not be strong enough to accept it." I sighed and looked at the ground, scuffing the holey toes of my clogs into the dust. "And anyway," Pa continued, "The time will pass quickly now - there's a lot still to do before you go." He also looked down at my feet. "And we'll start with getting you some new shoes!" He clapped me on the back, his eyes smiling down at me. "Come on. Get yourself to practice and later we'll go into the woods, maybe catch some fish or a couple of rabbits." I gave a half-hearted smile as we turned and walked back up the village street, Pa's arm still snug and warm around my shoulders.

Pa was right and the next few weeks went more swiftly than I expected. My life was a flurry of activity, from daily practice to our frequent trips to the woods where Pa taught me everything that Thumbleton had shown him all those years ago. The days grew shorter and the sun rose lower in the sky each day as the villagers brought in the last of the crops. The leaves began to turn from vivid green to orange and gold and the people busied themselves fixing their thatches, storing food and repairing the village boundary ready to settle in for the cold weeks ahead. I made sure to spend a lot of time with Leif, trying to alleviate his fears and I found that as I comforted him, my own confidence grew and although I was still afraid, an excitement began to build within me.

I didn't really think beyond meeting Duckie in Andorta and a week or so after he left, a peddler arrived with a letter for the Erlands. It was from Duckie, telling them he'd arrived safely in the city and was bunked up at a tavern called The Sprat and Skirmish. He'd had an eventful trip, fleeing from a pack of bandits on the road to Haggs Catton and fighting off a mountain cat in the pass. But he'd arrived safe and sound, his letter making light of his scrapes so as not to worry his mother. Seeing his scrawled handwriting filled me with relief and my fear subsided further. If Duckie could make it there safely then so could I.

The night before my seventeenth annum, Pa, Leif and I had a special supper in our little kitchen. Pa roasted a chicken over the firepit and we shared a berry pie covered in thick cream. A tearful Leif sat on my lap before bedtime and I told him again not to worry and I would be back soon. We sent him off to bed but I could still hear him crying quietly in his bunk until he fell asleep. Pa and I sat at the kitchen table as we had the night Elvyn came home, a night that now felt very long ago. "I have something for you," Pa said getting up and going to the dresser. He pulled out two packages wrapped in cloth and presented them on the table in front of me.

I scooted closer excited at my gifts, fingers fluttering and eager to unwrap them. I looked up at Pa expectantly. "Go on then," he said laughing. "They're for you. Happy annum my little pixie." I unfolded the cloth around the first package and nestled inside were a pair of brand new leather boots, supple and soft, with a small golden dragon fixed at the outside of each ankle. My eyes lit up as I picked up one of the boots, turning it this way and that, wondering at the workmanship. I had only ever had clogs on my feet and had never seen anything so fine.

"Where'd you get them Pa?" I asked as I kicked off a clog and pulled on one of the boots, lacing it tightly and turning my foot so the dragon glinted in the firelight.

"You remember the merchant caravan that came through a few weeks back?" Pa said. "They had a stall of all kinds of finery; shirts and hats and pretty dresses, but I thought these would be more use." I pulled on the other boot and paraded up and down the kitchen, my skirts hitched up, looking down and admiring my new attire.

Pa watched me, smiling indulgently. "You'll be better with your skirts cut down and some breeches on. It'll be easier to move about."

"Hmm," I replied absently, still absorbed in admiring my gleaming new boots.

"Aren't you going to open the other one?" Pa asked me, pushing the other parcel across the table towards me. This package was thin and long and as I carefully un-wrapped the cloth, I saw a leather sheath and a flash of bright colour from within.

"Arrows!" I exclaimed, as I pulled out the contents of the parcel. "Queenfisher arrows!" I breathed, gazing at them; the feather fletching's at one end shining an almost un-naturally vibrant blue, a sharp and shiny arrow head at the tip of each.

"The finest arrows in Immentia," Pa said proudly. "Mr Caulderon was making a trip to Fletchers Furrow a few weeks ago so I asked him to bring these back." Pa sat back in his seat arms folded, his legs stretched and crossed at the ankles. "You'll need to use them wisely," Pa said observing me. "You only have six so make sure your aim is good and you can retrieve them. Don't go firing them off willy-nilly or they'll all be lost and then you'll be stuck."

I laughed, still admiring the fine arrows. "I will do Pa, I'll take a few iron arrows as well and I'll only use these when I absolutely have to." Pa stood and went into the other room.

"And you'll need these," he said, returning holding a short dagger in a leather scabbard and a fine looking bow. "I've cleaned them up," Pa said holding them out to me. "Sharpened the knife and replaced the string on the bow. They were your mothers so I hope they serve you as well as they did her." His voice cracked a little as he spoke, his eyes misty as he handed the weapons to me. "She'd be so proud of you Fen," he added softly. I looked up at him and swallowed hard as he placed his hand on my head. "We've done everything we can to prepare you and I have no doubt that you'll come home to us soon enough. You're ready."

CHAPTER 6

The day of my seventeenth annum finally dawned. I had slept fitfully the night before, tossing and turning, dreaming of savage creatures and dark forests, faces of people I had never met looming in and out of my consciousness. I laid there for a few moments thinking about the journey ahead of me before I threw back the covers, got out of bed and washed at the basin in corner. Leif woke too and sat on his bunk watching me with wide apprehensive eyes as I dressed. Pa had stayed up half the night cutting and re-stitching my dress so the skirts fell just below my hips. He had taken in a pair of his old leather breeches so they fit snugly to my legs and I pulled those on beneath my skirts, lacing my new boots onto my feet. Leif marveled at the boots, his little fingers touching the glinting dragons and stroking the soft leather.

We all ate breakfast together, quiet and subdued. I struggled to swallow my bowl of porridge, my throat felt tight and my stomach was churning with fear and excitement. Afterwards, when the pots were washed and put away, there was nothing more to be done and it was time for me to go. In my mind, I felt like I had already left. The familiar things around me in the cottage looked strange to me, as if they were already misty, far away memories. I looked at my bed in the loft and it appeared to me like the sleeping place of some innocent child, a child I didn't know. I gathered my things and pulled on my old wool coat, tucking the few coins I had into a coin purse and stuffing it into the inside pocket.

Pa and Leif walked me to the village gates, faces watching from the windows as a few other families emerged from their cottages and walked quietly along the lane behind us. Burle came down from the watchtower and Flitwich joined us as my Pa fastened the dagger around my waist. He handed me my pack which held a few apples, wedges of cheese, hunks of bread and some dried meat along with a flask filled with the cool fresh water of the beck.

Flitwich joined us and admired my new Queenfisher arrows, checking each tip to make sure it was sharp. "These will serve you well Fen," he said, sliding the arrows back into the sheath on my back.

"I'll take care of them Mr Flitwich," I answered, hoisting the leather straps of my pack higher onto my shoulders."

"You make sure you do," he said smiling warmly.

I turned to Leif who was holding on to Pa's legs, his little face frightened and lip trembling. I crouched down so our eyes were level. "Now Leif, you've got to be a big boy now and look after Pa." He looked at me solemnly as I spoke.

"What will we do if you don't come back?" he asked, his voice barely a whisper.

"I will come back Leif. I promise you I will do everything in my power to make sure I come home." I stood and Leif dropped his head, clasping his little arms around my legs. Pa gently pulled him away and Mother Erland took him by the hand as he buried his face in her skirts.

Pa turned to look at me and put his hands on my shoulders. "Remember what I said Fen," he said staring directly into my eyes. "You're ready. Don't be afraid. You need to be brave but not foolish. Be careful who you trust. You need to stay alert, keep your eyes and ears open and your wits about you. If you allow fear to take over you might walk right past exactly what you're looking for." He pulled me to him, squashing my face against the rough leather of his waistcoat. I felt tears well in my eyes, but swallowed them back, wanting to be brave, at least until I was out of sight.

"I will Pa," I replied, pulling away from him. "I promise you I will." He kissed his hand and rested it on top of my auburn head. "Go then," he said. "The sooner you leave, the sooner you will come back." I nodded and hitched the straps of my pack up again. I looked at my Pa and then at Leif for a long moment before turning from them and walking out of the gates. The villagers called out words of encouragement and farewells as I put one foot in front of the other and walked off down the road. The morning air was chilly and I fixed my gaze on the distant horizon as I walked. I didn't look back.

I kept walking for most of the day through rolling green hills and coppices of trees, the sun moving slowly across the sky. I planned to stay the first night at Mother Bruma's just as Duckie had done and his Pa had carefully explained to me how to get there. He'd said to stay on the southern road until I reach a crossroads. I should reach the crossroads by late afternoon and take the left turn but leave the road shortly afterwards and follow a track into the forest. The track would take me away from the road but still in the general direction of Haggs Catton and I should reach

Mother Bruma's house in the woods by nightfall.

After a few hours of walking, I stopped to eat lunch at the side of the road next to a stream. I took my bow off my back and sat in the grass, taking an apple and a chunk of bread from my pack. I didn't eat much as I didn't know how long the food might have to last me. As I munched on my apple and watched the minnows darting about in the waters of the stream, I thought I saw something glistening beneath the surface. When I took off my boots and waded in to check, there was nothing there. No stone. "I should be so lucky," I thought ruefully. I only rested a short while but the longer I sat there, the temptation to turn and run back to Millings Beck became overwhelming so I quickly finished the bread and continued walking.

I arrived at the crossroads in the late afternoon just as Mr Erland had said. The roads were still nothing more than narrow lanes, verged with grass and filled with potholes made by the carts and caravans. I stood beneath the creaking wooden sign at the crossroads looking up at the peeling lettering. The sign pointed south to Feybridge and as I held a hand above my eyes to scout the horizon, I could see the Old Man of the Fey looming high into the sky in the distance. The Old Man was a large mountainous crag that loomed over the town of Feybridge like a sleeping stone giant, grey and oppressive. The river Fey hugged the Old Man's ankles, bustling with boats, sailors and merchants trading and transporting goods to the larger towns and cities across Immentia.

I turned to the right, signposted to the town of Boann. The swamps and marshes lay in that direction, the rolling hills flattening out as the road wound away from me. In the far distance, a grey curling mist settled over the landscape and the outline of the road faded into the fog and disappeared. To my left, the road led towards Haggs Catton, the hills undulating into the distance covered in dense forest. Haggs Catton lay on the far side of the forest and beyond that, the trees gave way to a range of mountains and the pass that would take me to the dry, arid plains on the other side and the city of Andorta.

I took one last glance about me and followed the signpost to Haggs Catton, trudging on down the road. The trees began to close in around me, the road sheltered from the sky by the branches hanging high above my head. I walked for about an hour through the forest before I came to an overgrown track winding off to the left into the trees. I peered down it uneasily. The daylight was fading and the track into the woods looked lonely and ominous but I pushed my fear aside and turned off the road, making my way down the track. The path was narrow and flanked with tall grasses dotted with bright yellow flowers and purple clover. The scent of the forest filled my nose; pine needles and the sweet smell of the foxgloves growing up from the forest floor, cheery towers of pink standing tall amidst the thick trunks of the trees.

As I walked my mind wandered. I thought of Pa and hoped Leif was alright. I wondered what they were doing right now and whether they were missing me yet. I walked on, eyes downcast and as I turned a bend in the path, a strange noise infiltrated my thoughts; a humming in the air coming from the trees on my left, gradually getting louder. I froze, ears straining to identify the sound as it came closer. I crouched down in the grass, my eyes darting about me, my hand reaching for the dagger on my belt. The hum became an insistent buzz and through the trees just ahead of me, a dark cloud spilled out of the gloom of the forest and into the air above the pathway.

As I looked closely, I realized that the cloud was made up of a mass of hovering dark coloured bodies, their iridescent wings thrumming in the evening light. "Bloodwarblers," I murmured, my eyes fixed on the menacing cloud as I crouched in the grass. Bloodwarblers were flying insects but each one was the size of a sparrow, coloured a dark red with glassy orange eyes and long pincers on their small heads. The creatures were known to attack and overpower their prey by nipping with their pincers and injecting a small amount of venom before sucking out the unfortunate victim's blood. A bite from one was relatively harmless but a whole swarm could easily kill a grown man.

My mind raced, remembering everything that Pa and Mr Burle had told me. Still I crouched there, frozen in fear as the swarm hovered above the path as if sniffing out the scent of blood before making their move. I knew I had to run. If I stayed here, they would smell me and attack before I had chance to escape, covering every exposed inch of my skin and piercing my soft flesh with their pincers before sucking me dry. I stood up slowly, and inched back a couple of steps. As I rose, the swarm seemed to turn as one, the buzzing escalating into a high pitched frantic warble as they homed in on me. "Run," I told myself, "Run!"

I turned and darted off the path and into the forest, my pack banging against my back as I leapt over tree roots and ducked beneath branches, the pine needles soft beneath my pounding feet. I could hear the swarm following me, gaining ground as the Bloodwarblers flew swiftly through the air. I lost all sense of direction as I weaved through the forest, ducking and jumping as I avoided ditches and fallen logs.

I was panting heavily as I burst from the trees into a large clearing. Just ahead was a tranquil lake surrounded by reeds, damselflies hovering lazily over the still surface of the water. I dropped my pack from my shoulders as I ran and shrugged the bow strap over my head before dropping that too. I looked back to see the mass of Bloodwarblers only a short distance behind me, their orange beady eyes fixated, their pincers snapping together in anticipation. One of the infernal flying monsters reached me before the others and landed heavily on my forearm, its red body shining and wings thrumming as it extended its pincers. I yelped and swiped at it as the pincers dug into my hand and I violently shook it off, blood dripping from the punctures in my flesh. Just as the rest of the swarm was almost upon me, I took a deep breath and hurled myself into the lake, plunging under the surface and kicking my legs as I dived down to the bottom.

The water was clean and clear and I swam downwards, kicking my legs behind me. Heart pounding, I pushed myself through the water towards the far side of the lake where a reed bed grew from the lake bottom. A thought flashed through my panicked brain when I saw the reed bed and I remembered something my Pa had told me. Perhaps one of the forest tricks he'd learned from Dickings Thumbleton was just about to save me too.

As I swam, the dark cloud of Bloodwarblers tracked me across the surface of the lake and I could still hear the sound of their enraged buzzing. I reached the reeds and pulled one out of the mud, my chest burning for breath as I snapped off the end of the reed leaving a long hollow tube. I kicked back towards the surface but kept my head about a foot beneath the water as I brought the end of the reed to my lips and took in a breath. I almost choked as my mouth filled with particles of soil and the last of my breath was expelled into the water, bubbles rising violently to the surface. I tried again and this time got a clear breath through the hollow reed as the warblers swarmed directly above my head. I remained submerged as they swooped and circled above me, clearly infuriated that their meal had escaped.

I floated there just beneath the surface, my skirts billowing slowly around my waist and eventually the Bloodwarblers began to drift away until I could no longer see the seething mass of red bodies rippling through the water above me. I stayed there under the lake water long after the last warbler had disappeared, my pounding heart gradually slowing and my breath coming easier as I sucked air through the reed clenched between my lips. Eventually, my fear subsided and I rose to the surface, slowly raising my eyes and nose above the waterline, scanning the lake and listening carefully. Birds were chirping and the call of an owl sounded off in the distance but the infernal buzzing had gone.

I raised myself out of the lake and struggled onto the bank, my clothes and hair dripping. I laid there for a while, exhausted, eventually laughing out loud in relief at my lucky escape before wringing out my wet clothes and walking back to the other side of the lake to retrieve my pack and bow. The contents of my pack had spilled out and a rabbit was snuffling inquisitively at a wrap of cheese. It looked up as I approached, its nose twitching before it hopped off across the clearing and into the forest.

I took a few deep breaths as I put my things back into my pack and hoisted it onto my shoulders. I inspected my injured hand and sucked at the incisions from the Bloodwarblers bite. The bite was inflamed and swollen but there was not enough venom to do any further harm; Mr Burle had told us that you can suck the venom from a single bite and the swelling should go down in a day or so. The sun was going down and the clearing was quiet as I swung my bow over my head and looked around me. I knew I had run from the forest and into the clearing but from which direction, I had no idea. In my panic to escape the Bloodwarblers I had paid no attention to which way I was running and now, with no sun in the sky to guide me, I had no clue how to get back to the track that would take me to Mother Bruma's. As I scanned the clearing, I decided that as I had dropped my pack in this spot, I must have run in from the trees nearby. I took my chances and headed off into the darkness of the pines.

I walked as the dusk became twilight and the light faded to darkness. The evening grew chilly and I shivered in my damp clothes as I walked. Eventually, as the night closed in, I had to admit that I was completely lost. I had now been walking longer than I had run from the warblers so if I was going in the right direction I would have come across the path by now. As I made my way between the trees, ducking beneath branches and hopping over tree roots, I began to feel increasingly un-easy. Along with the darkening sky, the forest had become strangely quiet. There were no bird calls and no rustling of small animals scuttling across the forest floor. Just an unnatural, eerie silence. I tried not think of what creatures may be lurking in the darkening forest and pushed thoughts of giant Whitefang spiders and razor clawed Titubus lizards from my mind. I began to glance behind me from time to time, trying to shake off the uncomfortable feeling. A feeling I didn't want to acknowledge. The feeling of being watched.

As I made my way through the trees I began to hear strange sounds in the silent night air. The snap of a twig to my right. A grunted exhale of breath in the bushes to my left. The sound of heavy steps, the footfalls landing at the same time as my own but when I stopped to listen, they stopped. I kept walking and from the corner of my eyes, I glimpsed vague movements here and there; a huge shadowy figure loping behind a tree as I turned. What looked like thick dark fingers wrapped around a branch in the dim light, disappearing from view before I had chance to focus. The occasional glint of large orange eyes peeking and blinking in the blackness.

I strode on, walking quickly now, and eventually the strange sights and sounds seemed to fade away behind me. I relaxed a little as I reached a small clearing in the trees and as I tried and failed to get my bearings, I gave in and reluctantly decided I would have to camp for the night. I could be wandering in circles so if I waited till the morning, at least the sun would give me an idea of which direction I should head. I gathered some twigs and branches and lit a small fire in the middle of the clearing, lying on my tummy and blowing on the dry twigs as the flames took hold. I settled down next to the warm fire and attempted to dry my damp clothes, wondering if Mother Bruma had missed me. I hoped she wouldn't send word to Pa and worry him. I pictured him sitting in our warm kitchen, sipping his mintleaf tea and at that moment, I thought I would give everything to be there with him now.

As I ate some dried meat and a handful of nuts, the strange sounds began again. I froze mid chew and looked fearfully about me as the noises continued. The sounds were close now, just beyond the light of my fire and I strained my eyes as my pulse quickened. Something was moving around my camp, out in the darkness of the surrounding woods. I could hear the slow deliberate footsteps again as the thing, whatever it was, circled me as I sat huddled in the firelight. Far out in the forest, I heard a sound I had never heard before; a long, low baying moan which eventually heightened in pitch almost to a scream. It was an eerie, chilling sound and I drew closer to my fire, taking out my dagger and clenching it between my fingers. I crouched on my heels, my eyes wide and fearful as I spun, following the movement of the thudding footfalls circling around me. I squinted my eyes, peering into the blackness, wishing that whatever it was would make itself known. Or just come and eat me and get it over with. The sound of heavy footsteps went on, accompanied by the occasional grunted breath, the large orange eyes peeping from behind the trees in the thickets.

This went on for hour after hour as I huddled there, afraid and shivering as I watched for those glinting eyes, dagger still gripped between my fingers. Eventually the night fell silent again and, frightened and tired, my eyelids began to droop. My head nodded onto my chest and the dagger fell from my grasp as I slumped into an exhausted sleep. The stark white moon moved across the night sky and the firelight faded as the glowing eyes continued to watch from the darkness of the forest.

CHAPTER 7

I woke with a start, still sitting beside the dying embers of my fire, my dagger on the ground at my side. I grabbed the dagger and jumped to my feet, casting my eyes about me in panic. The dawn light was creeping slowly across the sky and unlike the previous night, the forest was now alive with sounds and movement. Birds were twittering amongst the branches and through the trees a deer and fawn stood, heads up and eyes alert as my sudden movement disturbed them. They froze for a second before bounding off and disappearing into the forest, their white tails bouncing through the pines.

I pushed my hair out of my eyes and looked around my camp, shivering in the cold morning air as I remembered the events of the night before. As I gathered up my things preparing to leave, something caught my eye and I looked more closely at the ground. In the soft earth around my campfire, amongst the twigs and pine needles, were the outline of footprints. Five toed footprints. Very like a man's but with one clear difference; they were huge. I placed my own booted foot next to one and it was half as wide again and twice as long. I stared at them in horror. I thought of the circling footsteps, the orange eyes in the dark. If these were the tracks of what had stalked me the previous night then they had come right into my camp. They had emerged from the black depths of the trees and stood over me as I slept.

I shuddered at the thought and as I quickly gathered my weapons and pack, I noticed something else. Next to my pack was a large leaf, carefully folded and deliberately placed. I inspected it and kicked at it cautiously with my toe. The leaf unfurled and nestled within was a handful of blackberries, shiny and plump. I looked down at them in confusion, my mind racing as I struggled to find an explanation for the strange events of the night before, the footprints and the odd gift left beside me as I slept. I quickly kicked dust onto the still glowing embers of my fire and thrust the berries into my pack before hurrying off into the trees.

The sun had come up and I assessed its position in the sky before turning left as I continued my path through the never-ending forest. If I had judged it right then I should come across the pathway again which led to Mother Bruma's home. Although I only left Millings Beck yesterday, it felt like forever ago and I longed to see a friendly face and have some proper food and somewhere safe to rest. As I ambled along, my eyes busily scanned my surroundings and I stopped occasionally to poke with sticks at the long trumpets of the foxglove flowers, hoping I would see the glimpse of a stone within. I found nothing and again wondered ruefully which Seekers were lucky enough to find their stone nestled in sweet smelling petals a mere days walk from home. I had to take care though as I could come across a different birthstone and it would be dangerous to get too close, fatal to touch it. Burle had told us we would know if we were too close to another birthstone; our breath would falter, our eyes would swim and we would be in no doubt that we were in trouble. He had trained us to recognize the warning signs and made sure that we young seekers were finely attuned to our bodies and senses. Our lives might depend on it.

Eventually I emerged from the trees and found myself back on the overgrown path where I had fled from the Bloodwarblers the previous afternoon. I looked up and down the track, ears nervously pricked as I listened for the tell-tale drone of the swarm but I heard nothing. Just the comforting bird-song of the forest and the sound of branches creaking softly in the breeze. Relieved, I turned right and continued down the track that I hoped would take me to Mother Bruma's house.

I walked for an uneventful hour or so and guessed it was mid-morning by the time I rounded a turn in the path and emerged into a glade, bright with wild flowers and butterflies. I should have found the cottage by now and I was worried that I had re-joined the path too far down and had spent all morning walking away from Mother Bruma's. Maybe I had misjudged my directions and I was on a different path completely? Tired and frustrated, I dropped my bow and pack in the grass so I could rest for a while in this peaceful forest glade. I pulled out my flask and drank from it, the familiar sweet water of the beck flooding my tongue and bringing with it a pang of homesickness. I laid back in the flowers and rested my head on my pack. As I gazed up into the trees above me, the pale sunlight filtering between the branches of the pines, I noticed something. Something very odd. I sat upright, my head still turned up to the trees and my brow furrowed in a confused frown. Above me was some kind of structure supported on sturdy wooden beams that crisscrossed between the branches, rusty nails protruding here and there where the joists met. My eyes widened in surprise as I realized I was looking at a little house perched high up in the trees, painted in greens and browns, the colours disguising its outline amidst the branches and foliage. It was cylindrical in shape and built snugly around the thick trunk of the tree, a round door and circular windows at the front. It looked very much like the bird houses we had in our yards in Millings Beck to encourage the finches and swallows to nest and feed on the pesky summer bugs.

I got to my feet, face still upturned as I stared at the strange dwelling high above my head. The house was surrounded by a narrow balcony and as I stood there staring, the circular door opened and a dark-haired figure emerged, a woman with a spray of vivid blooms held in one hand. The woman didn't appear to notice me as she stood on the balcony and extended the bunch of flowers out into the air above the clearing. As I watched she began to sing; a sweet lilting tone, a melody and words I didn't recognize. As she sang, the many butterflies that had been flitting aimlessly about the glade began to rise up from the clover, dancing and circling, gradually looping higher into the air towards the house. Others flew in from the dark shadows of the forest and before long there seemed to be hundreds of them fluttering up into the branches and settling on the flowers held in the woman's outstretched hands. There were so many butterflies I couldn't even see her face anymore, just the blur of many brightly coloured wings; reds and orange, flashes of purple and purest white. As she continued to sing, I saw that she held a small net in her other hand and as the butterflies settled on the buds and petals she carefully caught one in the net and tipped it gently into a jar at her feet.

She did this over and over again, capturing the butterflies one by one as I stood there in the glade, open mouthed and speechless at the spectacle. Eventually the colourful cloud dispersed a little and the woman glanced downwards, finally catching sight of me. She jumped in surprise and let out a little sound, her sudden movement causing the butterflies to flit away into the glade before gradually settling back down onto the woodland flowers.

"Oh, you scared the life out of me!" the woman exclaimed, as she leaned her elbows on the balcony and looked down towards me. "What're you doing down there?" Before I could answer, a look of realization passed across the woman's face and she tapped her forehead with the heel of her hand. "Of course!" she said. "Silly of me. Don't tell me; you must be Fen," she said, her pretty face smiling and a lock of dark hair falling across her forehead. I was still standing there with my mouth hanging open so I collected myself quickly and called back up to her

"Yes. Yes, I am. I'm sorry, I got lost in the woods." She tutted and turned away before emerging again and tossing a rope ladder over the balcony. The ladder unfurled as it fell, its bottom rung swinging down to the base of the tree trunk. "Come on up then love," she called down to me. "I've been expecting you."

I picked up my pack and clumsily clambered up the ladder into the trees where the woman extended a hand and helped me up onto the narrow balcony. I stood there a little awkwardly, looking at the friendly faced stranger. I had to admit that Mother Bruma wasn't what I expected at all. I had thought that only funny little old people lived alone out in the woods, like Dickings Thumbleton, but this lady was only probably forty annums old with a pretty face, her clothes simple but clean. "I'm Mallady Bruma," she said, smiling as she rested a slender hand on my shoulder and looked into my face, concern in her eyes. "Come on inside, and we'll get you something to eat and you can tell me all about it," she said, patting my arm. Her warm expression and soothing tone relaxed me and I dropped my pack on the balcony before ducking my head and following her through the little circular door of the birdhouse.

Inside, the building was constructed from narrow planks of wood across the floor and around the walls. There was just one circular room with another ladder fixed to the wall at the back, leading up to another floor above. The room was immaculately clean and tidy and was built around the boughs of the branches on which it sat. The bend of a thick branch protruded through the floor on one side of the room and a slice had been cut from its top, the flat surface sanded down and oiled to make a narrow table. On the other side of the room was a small stove with a crooked chimney pipe leading outside, a stool and rocking chair turned cozily towards it. The woman gestured for me to take a seat and I sat down stiffly on the stool, my dagger sheath digging into my thigh and my bow still on my back.

"Let me take those things," she said as I pulled the bow over my head and removed my belt. She propped the weapons against the wall and went to a small cupboard in the corner of the room. "Duckie Erland told me to expect you," she said as she pulled a loaf of bread and some cheese from the cupboard. "Lovely lad, just lovely. I thought you'd be here last night but you got lost, you say? What happened petal? It's not safe anywhere these days, I of all people know that, that's why I live up here in the trees after all…" As Mallady carried on chattering, cutting the bread and cheese, I looked around the room curiously. Rows of shelves curved around the walls, each shelf crammed with glass jars and within each one was a few short-stemmed cut flowers. Nestled upon the flowers were butterflies, some fluttering against the glass and some sitting quietly, their wings slowly opening and closing as they sipped nectar from the blooms.

"Fen?" Mallady's voice interrupted my thoughts. "What happened?" she said again. I turned my attention back to her, realizing how rude I was being.

"Well," I began, "I don't think I was far from here yesterday afternoon but a swarm of Bloodwarblers chased me off the path and I got lost." She came over and settled into the rocking chair, handing me a pretty pot bowl overflowing with buttered bread and slices of creamy cheese. I took the bowl eagerly, my mouth watering.

"Those blasted warblers," she said with a frown. "I have something that'll keep them away – remind me to give it to you before you go because I might forget. You just need a powdering of Violet Silkwing behind your ears and they won't come near you." She bit into a hunk of bread and gestured to me to do the same. I fell upon the food, ravenous after the meagre rations I had allowed myself over the past few days.

"I got away but I was bitten by one," I told her through mouthfuls of food as I held out my still swollen hand to show her. Mallady had a good look and made the appropriate sympathetic noises as we ate. She swallowed and daintily wiped her lips with the back of her thumb.

"I have something for that too," she said. "The swelling'll go down on its own but I can dab a bit of Daintylace on it and it'll stop the stinging." We continued to munch in comfortable silence for a few minutes, the captive butterflies thrumming softly against the glass of their jars. As I finished my meal, I pointed to the jars on the shelves. "What are they for?" I asked Mallady. She rocked in her chair and turned to look.

"Oh, that's what I do Fen," she said matter of factly. "Butterflies have all kinds of amazing properties to heal and protect. That's why I live out here. You don't get as many of them in the towns. I collect the butterflies and when they shed the powder from their wings, I use it to make ointments and medicines." She turned towards me again as she continued. "I don't kill them you understand," she said, her face suddenly serious.

"There's no need - they leave their powder on the bottom of the jars and I set them free again after a day or so." She smiled kindly at me. "So," she said, settling back in her chair and rocking gently, her legs crossed at the ankles. "Tell me what happened after the Bloodwarblers."

I spent the rest of the afternoon with Mallady as I told her more about my night in the forest. She said my mysterious stalker in the night was probably a Shadewalker. She told me that she has only seen the occasional glimpse of a Shadewalker as they are strange and timid creatures that prefer to blend into the forest and remain unseen. She described them as huge, hairy animals that walked upright through the woods on their large five toed feet with orange glowing eyes. "They mean you no harm Fen," she said as we sat with our feet up around her warm stove. "They're just inquisitive but generally like to keep to themselves. The folk from the cities tell tall tales, make them out to be blood-thirsty man killing beasts but they're really very gentle." She looked at me and chuckled. "They pass through this very glade some nights," she said. "I don't often see them mind, but I hear them. No mistaking the call of a Shadewalker.... And anyway," she went on, "By the sounds of it, they had opportunity enough to make a meal of you if they wished but instead, they kept guard over you through the night and even left you some breakfast!" I laughed along, and in the warm cozy birdhouse, my terror of the night before began to fade away.

Mallady asked me to stay till the next day and I happily agreed, still feeling exhausted after my adventures. We spent the afternoon gathering firewood and water and I helped her carry various jars out onto the balcony where we released some of the butterflies back into the glade before heading back into the birdhouse. I watched her shaking the powder from the jars into her mortar as she added various herbs and petals, grinding the mixture and tipping it into small tightly sealed phials. She explained that she would travel to the surrounding villages to sell the phials when she could or would trade with peddlers as they passed through. She mentioned that Duckie had stayed with her a few weeks previous and asked what my plans were. I explained that I would be heading to Andorta to find him and she looked at me knowingly, her bright eyes twinkling.

"I was sweet on a lad too when I was your age," she said, with a wink. My face flushed crimson. "It's not like that," I replied stiffly. "He's my friend. All I care about is him finding his stone and me finding mine so we can go home." She looked at me curiously but didn't press me on it further and as the night outside grew dark, we ate vegetable stew together by the fire.

    Mallady had a bedroom on the upper floor of the birdhouse but she set me up a spot to sleep in the downstairs room next to the stove. She laid out a pillow and a patchwork eiderdown before kissing her hand and grasping my palm in hers. "Sleep tight, love," she said kindly before making her way up the ladder, the light from the stove flickering on the glass jars lining the walls. I undressed down to my undershirt, taking off my dress and breeches before settling down under the eiderdown, pulling the soft fabric up to my face as I gazed into the fading glow of the stove. I was tired and warm and as I fell asleep, I heard the call of a Shadewalker. The lonely baying moan rising a long way off in the cold night air as it roamed through the silent forest.

CHAPTER 8

The next morning was glum and overcast and I ate a hearty breakfast with Mallady before it was time for me to go. She pushed a few extra bits of food into my pack as I pulled on my boots, reluctant to leave the safety of the treehouse.

"Now you make sure to call in again if you pass this way," she said. "I remember what it's like being a Seeker – you need all the help you can get so don't think twice about it." I felt a rush of gratitude to this kind woman, a stranger to me, who had welcomed me into her home. She had dressed the bite on my hand with a few spots of powder and she dabbed me behind the ears and on the back of my wrists from a small phial of the Violet Silkwing to repel the Bloodwarblers. She pressed a few more phials into my pack, explaining how each should be used and eventually I climbed back down her ladder to the forest floor. She waved me off from the balcony and as I made my way across the clearing, the butterflies fluttered about the glade and circling up towards her until she disappeared from view.

I carried on walking down the path through the trees that would lead me to the village of Haggs Catton. I felt much better after a good nights' sleep and some decent food so I stepped out brightly, making good time as I marched onwards. The morning was thankfully un-eventful and around midday the track joined a road and the trees began to thin out, giving way to small fields and clusters of finkle trees. In the distance, I could just see the tops of houses that I took to be the village of Haggs Catton and beyond were the mountains through which I would have to pass to get to Andorta.

I passed a few folk on the road as I approached Haggs Catton. Some looked at me suspiciously while others called out a friendly greeting as they headed into the nearby fields with tools and farming implements. As I drew closer, I saw that the village itself was about the same size as Millings Beck but had no boundary fence or gate, just a small tollhouse at the side of the road.

As I approached, a large dog bounded out of the open door of the tollhouse and ran forward barking and leaping up at me. On its hind legs, its head was almost level with mine and the weight of it almost bowled me off my feet. "Down," I said firmly, turning my back on the dog as I tried to evade its excited leaps. "Down!"

"He won't hurt you," said a voice as a man emerged from the tollhouse. "Here Fliss!" the man said sternly and the dog turned from me and bounded back to her master before lying obediently, panting at his feet. The man bent down and patted the dogs' head before turning to me. "Hullo there," the man said. "What brings you to Haggs Catton?" he asked. "You on your way up through the pass?"

I walked closer to him, my eyes fixed warily on the dog at his feet. "I am," I answered, my hand going to my pocket. "What do I owe you?"

He looked at me in surprise before realizing I meant the toll. "Oh nothing," he said with a friendly smile. "We haven't charged a toll in annums. Just use the tollhouse to keep an eye on the road and check on who's passing through." He bent down to stroke his dog, his weathered face turned up towards me. "You're welcome here. There's a tavern in the village if you want some food or a bed for the night. A blacksmith too if you need any weapons repairing."

"Thank you," I answered politely. "I don't know if I'll be spending the night though, I was hoping to make it through the mountains before nightfall. D'you know how far it is?" I turned my eyes to the steep rocky scree beyond the village where a stony path wound through the rocks and up between the crags.

The man stood and followed my gaze, considering my question. "The pass itself is short enough but you'll not make it through before the sun goes down. And then it's another fair distance to Andorta on the other side." He turned back to regard me. "Not sure if you should be on the road at night, a young lass on her own." The man rubbed his chin. "S'safe enough on the pass in daylight but at night there's mountain cats and Dusk Trolls about." I considered the man's advice and thought for a moment, remembering Pa's words: 'Be brave, but not foolish.'

I sighed glumly. "You're probably right. I suppose I will be staying the night then."

The man nodded and stuck out his hand. "I'm Merton," he said as we shook. "If you like, I'll walk you up to The Woodpecker Lass and see you get settled." I thanked him and we walked up the path and into the village, Fliss the dog trotting around our feet.

Haggs Catton was a nice enough place but not as pretty as Millings Beck, the looming mountains casting a shadow over the cottages. Merton pointed out the blacksmiths and the herbalists as we walked, and I told him

I'd stayed the previous night at Mallady Bruma's. He knew Mallady and spoke of her warmly, asking how she was. He also remembered Duckie coming through a few weeks ago and said he'd come racing into the hamlet with a pack of bandits hot on his heels before the villagers had warded them off.

"Cowards they are," said Merton disdainfully. "They'll take on a poor young Seeker on his own but they'll not fight a whole village." I smiled as I thought of Duckie's letter about those same bandits, comforted by the fact that he had walked this lane not long ago and every step I took was leading me closer to him.

We reached the far edge of the village where a tavern stood, a sign above the door painted with a red and black woodpecker and uneven lettering spelling out 'The Woodpecker Lass'. Beyond the tavern, the mountain track led steeply up into the rocky hills, lanterns hanging from stakes at either side guiding the way. Merton commanded Fliss to stay and she lay down obediently outside the tavern as he pushed open the door and we entered a dimly lit room. A few folks were sitting on stools with mugs of ale, barely glancing up as we walked to the bar behind which a large jolly looking woman was standing, polishing the dark wood.

"Now then Merton," she said cheerfully. "What are you doing in here in the middle of the day? Who's keeping watch at the tollhouse?" she added with a cheeky wink at me.

Merton chuckled. "I think we'll be alright for a few minutes Rheda," he said, playing along. "And anyway, I've brought you a customer."

The woman smiled at me, wiping her hands on her skirts. "Ah," she said, "Another Seeker? We've had a few through here lately. What're you looking for love? Ebontium? Veridian? Forzit?"

I smiled at her rosy cheeked face. "Rubine," I replied, the word feeling foreign on my tongue like another language or a mystical place I'd heard of but never seen. "I'm looking for Rubine. But I'm going to Andorta first to meet my friend. We'll ask around and then go from there."

Rheda looked at me thoughtfully. "Rubine…" she mused, one finger held pensively to her lips. "I don't think I've heard about any Rubine round here for a while. Of course, I don't get out of Haggs Catton much anymore and I don't want to either!" she said vehemently as she leaned across the bar. "I could tell you stories of my days as a Seeker that'd make your hair curl!"

"Now Rheda," Merton interrupted. "You'll scare the lass witless telling her things like that."

Rheda threw back her head and laughed loudly. "She'd better be ready for far worse than an old woman's tales!" she crowed, her chest wobbling with mirth. "Sorry love," she said, wiping her eyes. "Don't you be listening to me, I'm sure you'll be just fine. Someone in Andorta'll have some news on your Rubine, I'm sure of it, big city like that." I smiled weakly back at her.

"Anyway, I'd better be getting back," said Merton turning to the door. "I'll leave her with you Rheda. Maybe I'll see you again soon missy," he said to me giving a small wave over his shoulder as he went out of the door.

"Don't mind me love," said Rheda, still chuckling as she tucked her cloth into her waist band. "Now. What can I get you? You want something to eat? Need a room overnight? Got a lovely one on the top floor, window looks right out over the mountains."

I nodded to her. "Yes please," I said as I placed my pack and bow on the floor and jumped up to perch on one of the high stools. "I don't have much money though …. How much is it?"

She regarded my earnest face with kind eyes and then leaned in towards me. "I'll tell you what," she said. "If you're any good with that bow, go out and get me a few rabbits or a pheasant this afternoon and we'll call it even. You can have the room tonight and I'll throw in dinner too. How's that sound?" She beamed at me and I nodded again, happy to accept her kind offer. She nodded over her shoulder. "If you go into the fields behind the inn there should be a bit of game knocking about so come back later and we'll see what you've got."

I hopped down from the stool and Rheda took my pack and stowed it safely behind the bar. I took my bow and arrows and left the inn, walking around the back and a little way into the fields until I came to a coppice of finkle trees. I scrambled up one and positioned myself on a branch with a good view of the surrounding meadow. I sat there quietly for the rest of the afternoon, bow and arrow poised in my hands, managing to shoot two rabbits and a couple of pheasants before returning to The Woodpecker Lass just as night was falling. The sky was streaked with orange and purple as the sun disappeared behind the stark black outline of the mountains. I dropped off the game with a young lad at the kitchen door and headed round to the front of the inn. I saw that the lanterns on the mountain track had been lit, the bobbing lights marking the path through the fading light and up into the hills.

A busy hum sounded from the bar room and I opened the door to find the tavern filled with people sitting at the small tables or standing around talking and laughing. A game of cards was going on in one corner, a couple of young lads arm wrestling in the other and a thin, gaunt man hunched at the bar spooning stew into his mouth. Rheda was serving up mugs of ale to the busy throng but saw me as I came in, giving me another wink and gesturing at me to find a seat. I sat down at a table in the corner and she brought me over a bowl of hot rabbit stew.

"There you go love," she said as she put the steaming bowl in front of me. "You've earned it. And I've made up the bed on the top floor so you just go on up when you're ready." I thanked her and dug into the stew as I looked around the room, taking in the people and catching snippets of conversation; a discussion about the weather, a joke about a long-faced troll, a scandalous rumour about the blacksmiths wife.

As I ate, the thin man at the bar finished his stew and turned on his stool, looking at me directly with narrowed eyes in his pale pinched face. He was short and wiry with thinning grey hair that was smoothed greasily back from his forehead. His skin was sallow and his chin un-shaven, eyes black and sunken. I didn't like the look of him and avoided his gaze as I continued to eat my stew. Eventually he got up from his stool and sidled casually over to me. "Hello there," the man said as he approached my table. His voice was gravelly and a little hoarse and his stance was slightly hunched. "The stew here is quite tasty isn't it?" he added conversationally. I didn't answer him and fixed my gaze on my bowl, spooning up another mouthful of food. "So… you're a Seeker I hear?" the man went on after a long pause and I swallowed my stew and looked up at him.

"That's right," I said, my tone guarded. "Just set out from Millings Beck a few days ago."

He gave me a thin smile that revealed crooked brown teeth. "Ah yes, I know it well," he said and sat down uninvited at my table, watching me eat. "I gather you're looking for Rubine?" he asked and I nodded uncomfortably, thinking word got around fast in Haggs Catton. "And what about your friend?" he added. "The one you're meeting in Andorta? What's their stone?"

I finished the stew and pushed the bowl away from me, regarding the man suspiciously. "Why'd you want to know?" I asked shrewdly and he smiled slightly.

"I travel a lot, pass through a lot of places, see a lot of things. Maybe I can help you find what you're looking for." Again, he gave me that thin lipped smile but his hooded eyes were calculating. I sat back with my arms folded and considered his words carefully. He looked the sort that might have that kind of information but I knew there'd be a price.

"You tell me what you've seen, and I'll tell you what we're looking for," I said finally, waiting to see how he'd respond.

"Clever girl," he said, a twisted smirk on his lips. "As it happens, I've just come from the south. Have you been south yet?" He spoke silkily, raising his thin eyebrows at me. I didn't answer. "Dangerous places out there, especially for you young Seekers," he continued. Still I said nothing. He paused for a moment, realizing I wasn't going to give anything else away. "I can tell you where you can find Rubine." He said finally.

"Pah," I said, looking away, feigning disinterest. "That's easy to say when you know what I'm looking for. What else?" I turned back to him, my eyes narrowed. I knew this unsavory character would tell me whatever he thought I wanted to hear and relieve me of a few coins for his troubles. I wished I'd not revealed so readily to Rheda in front of the whole bar that I was looking for Rubine. I'd be more careful next time. But this insidious fellow didn't yet know which stone we needed for Duckie. If it was all lies he'd have to guess correctly one of the nine birthstones; or maybe tell me the truth. It might be what we're looking for and it might not but I wasn't about to give him any clues.

He looked at me again, and glanced over his shoulders before leaning in towards me, his lips close to my ear. "Zaphite?" he murmured softly, his breath creeping across my skin as my breath caught in my throat. Zaphite was Duckie's birthstone. I pulled away from him sharply and he saw my reaction and sat back, a satisfied smile on his thin pale lips. "Now. Is that worth anything to you?" he asked smugly, folding has hands across his narrow chest.

"How much?" I asked, my voice low beneath the hubbub of the inn.

"Well, it's a matter of life and death young Seeker so information like that doesn't come cheap." The man murmured.

I leaned across the table towards him, my teeth gritted. "How much?" I asked again.

He looked me up and down, obviously trying to assess how much I might have on me. "Oh, I think ten farthings is a fair price." My heart sank. I only had ten farthings to my name. I pondered his proposal for a moment. It would cost me every penny I had and it rankled me to hand it over to the likes of him, charging money in exchange for information that might save a life. But on the other hand, he might really know where we could find Zaphite and if Duckie hadn't found anything out in Andorta, it might be the only clue we had. I had a decent amount of food in my pack and I should get to the city in the next day or so. Duckie would be waiting and hopefully he would have some money. I could always do a few odd jobs while we're there and make a bit more coin before we journeyed on. I weighed it up in my mind and eventually reached into the lining of my coat and pulled out my purse of coins.

"Tell me where it is." I said, as I pushed the purse across the table.

The sinister mans' cunning eyes lit up and he pulled a folded piece of paper from his pocket, pushing it across the table to me and reaching for the coin purse. I slammed my hand over the purse before he could grasp hold of it. He looked up at me sharply, his claw like hand reaching across the table as I picked up the piece of paper and shook it open. On it was a single line of scrawled writing:

"Zaphite, Halftans Crevice, the woods north east of Wistmans Hollow."

I read the words, trying to decipher the location. "Where is this? Tell me exactly where this is," I said urgently, my eyes darting between the man's black shadowed eyes and the meaningless words on the paper.

The man shrugged. "Exactly where it says, little Seeker. North east of Wistmans Hollow. The locals are.... interesting but believe me, I've seen it with my own eyes. You'll find what you're looking for." I let the man deftly swipe my coin purse and he quickly checked the contents before pocketing it smoothly, his eyes glancing again around the inn to make sure no one was watching. I ignored him as he got to his feet, my eyes still poring over the scrap of paper in my hand and without another word the thin man turned and slipped quietly out of the inn.

I sat there in the bar of The Woodpecker Lass a little longer as I pondered the note. I had heard of Wistmans Hollow and believed it to be down towards the south coast of Immentia. A long way from here. I refolded the piece of paper and tucked it carefully in my pack, saying goodnight to Rheda before climbing the narrow stairs to the uppermost floor of the inn. The room was just at Rheda had described with a window overlooking the winding path up the mountain. In the corner was a large tin tub and Rheda thoughtfully sent up some hot water. When the kitchen lad had filled the tub, I undressed and lowered myself into the bath, washing my body and my tangled hair with sweet smelling soap. Afterwards, I dried myself and crawled into the soft bed before blowing out the lamp. I lay there in the darkness, listening to the comforting hum of voices from the bar room below. I fell asleep imagining Duckie tucked up in bed in Andorta, at some tavern just like this one.

CHAPTER 9

The next morning, I woke early and sat up in bed, knees drawn up and chin resting on my hands as I thought about the folded note tucked in my pack. I was reluctant to leave the warmth of the bed but eventually I rose, washed my face and got dressed before walking to the window. I leaned against the glass, looking up at the steep mountain track winding through the rocks, the lanterns still glowing dimly in the dawn light. I collected my things before heading downstairs where Rheda was busy sweeping the floor of the empty inn, humming to herself. I wondered if she ever slept.

"Morning," she said, looking up as she swept. "Heading off?"

I nodded. "I'm hoping to get to Andorta today," I said. "My friend will be waiting for me." She stood upright and leaned on her sweeping brush.

"Alright. Well if you like you can take a bit of that roast pheasant. Let me get it for you." She bustled into the kitchen and returned with a small greasy package that she handed to me. I pocketed the food and thanked her. "Good luck to you," she said kindly, returning to her sweeping as I opened the door and walked out of the inn.

The village street was deserted and the sign above the tavern clanked in the breeze as I made my way to the mountain path, stony beneath my boots. The air was cold and fresh, a breeze blowing back my hair and I munched on the roast pheasant as I walked. The track wound from left to right as it climbed steeply up the mountainside, the cottages of Haggs Catton getting smaller and smaller beneath me. Large birds circled the crags above my head, lazily climbing higher into the sky until they were nothing more than black specs against the clouds. I struggled to catch my breath as the path weaved between two high rock faces and the village disappeared from view behind me. The track ahead was grey and rough with very little greenery; just the odd clump of grass that had managed to take root in the stony ground or between the crevices of the rock face.

Although it was early Driftleaf, the city of Andorta lay out on the plains where the weather was warm and dry for most of the annum. As I walked higher into the mountains the air grew warmer and the clouds began to disperse above me offering patches of bright blue sky and the occasional glimpse of the sun.

I felt excited at the prospect of seeing a city for the first time. I had heard that Andorta housed not hundreds, but thousands of people, the streets crammed with unusual structures and grand buildings. There were painters and poets, actors and street performers who would juggle or play music while folk tossed farthings into their hats.

The people who lived there varied from rich merchants, poor slum dwellers and the landowners who managed the surrounding land, farming grapes and olives in the heat of the sun. The wealthiest families headed up armies of men, soldiers loyal to their masters and to the city itself. All of the cities of Immentia controlled an army of sorts and the cities varied in size and wealth. In the past, the leaders of the cities had occasionally sought to overpower their neighbours and led invasions from one city to another, warring families who would attempt to extend their control over the surrounding lands. In the eastern reaches were the cities of Andorta, Epona and Dracae but they had co-existed over recent years in a fragile and suspicious peace, each city held at bay by the armies of the others.

I walked on through the mountain pass and after a couple of peaceful hours the pathway led me from between the high rock walls onto a flat plateau. As I emerged from the pass and into the open, I stopped and held a hand above my eyes, shielding them from the sun as I stared down at the view before me. The mountains dropped steeply down from the plateau to the plains beneath which extended as far as the eye could see in all directions. The plains were flat and dusty, scattered with wiry grass, low bushes and the occasional clump of trees. In the distance, a herd of wild horses grazed, their coats varying in colour from chestnut brown to black and white piebald. A pack of Slinkferrals lurked a short way from the horses, their noses sniffing the wind, pacing up and down as they waited for one of the foals to wander too far from the herd. Slinkferrals, I knew from the drawings I had seen, are similar to dogs but much larger. They have mottled bodies sparsely covered in mangy hair apart from around their necks where the hair formed a thick mane. Their faces are cunning with a long snout, yellow eyes and sharp menacing fangs extending from their top jaw. The Slinkferrals hunt on the plains and in the many large forests of Immentia, lurking in packs and attacking as one to bring down their prey.

The track wound across the plateau and down the mountain before weaving away from the foothills beneath me, the uneven surface scattered with fallen rocks. On the horizon, the city of Andorta rose up from the flat landscape like a mirage. I could make out the high wall surrounding the city and some of the buildings within, towers and domes standing out darkly against the sky. It felt like an age since I had left Millings Beck and when I'd said goodbye to Pa and Leif, the thought of getting to Andorta had seemed like a daunting task. I took in the view and felt a rush of elation that I had made it this far.

Eventually, I dragged my eyes away from the impressive vista and continued walking down the track, looping back and forth across the mountainside. I stepped carefully on the uneven ground, conscious of the steep drop to the side of me but as I skirted around a large boulder, I glanced down the cliff side. I stopped dead in my tracks, sure I had spotted something glinting from a ledge far beneath me. I stopped and stepped towards the edge of the path, leaning precariously over the side of the scree trying to get a closer look. I stared hard and as I shielded my eyes, I could make out an object shining in the sun about half way down the steep mountain side. My heart thumped in my chest. It was a stone. I was sure of it. I could see the stone glinting but couldn't make out its shape or colour. I knew that if it wasn't Rubine I couldn't touch it but I would need to get closer to see for sure.

I knelt down at the edge of the path and tried throwing sticks to dislodge the stone onto the path about fifteen feet below the ledge but my efforts were in vain. It looked like the stone was wedged fast in a crevice. Eventually I gave up and stood back, hands on my hips, my face frowning. I assessed the drop below me which, although steep, was not vertical and appeared to have plenty of rocky outcrops and footholds. If I was careful, I could probably clamber down and take a closer look. I took off my pack and bow and left them on the pathway as I gingerly made my way over the side and began to make my way down the scree. I lost my footing on the loose stones a couple of times but luckily the rocks I gripped under my hands held fast. As I got closer to the ledge beneath me, I craned my head back to see if I could get a glimpse of the stone, hoping desperately to see the dark red glow of Rubine.

As I leant back, I felt my head begin to swim, the rocky surface next to my face began to ripple and a burning heat began to spread through my body. My vision began to blur as if I was staring down a very long dark tunnel, the edges gradually closing in. As the light around me reduced to a pin prick, I could just make out an oval shape nestled in the crevice, a glowing yellow with vibrant orange in the centre. Just before I fell I remember one last thought flitting through my mind. "Too close Fen. Too close. It's not your stone." My vision went black and I felt my fingers losing my grip on the rocks as I tumbled unconscious to the stony path below.

CHAPTER 10

When the darkness began to fade, my eyes flickered open and I blinked blearily. I was laid flat on my back, my head still spinning and the daylight stinging my eyes. I appeared to be lying on something soft, the cloudy sky swaying above me and the clip clop sound of a horse's hooves in my ears. I tried to sit up but my head swam nauseatingly again so I laid back, breathing deeply, feeling like I might be sick. My head and limbs ached and I reached into my hair to feel a nasty lump on the back of my skull. I winced as I touched it and tried to sit up again, this time a little more slowly. I found myself on top of a high pile of straw on the back of a cart with the road winding away behind me, the mountains in the distance and my pack and bow beside me. I turned and squinted over my shoulder to the front of the cart where a man sat, hunched there with reins in his hand and the swaying rump of a grey horse ahead of him. The man heard the movement in the back and turned his head, a stem of straw sticking out from between his teeth as he chewed on it.

"You're awake then," he said gruffly, glancing at me with piercing blue eyes in his wrinkled face. He had a hat pulled low on his head and he twisted in his seat to face me.

"What happened?" I asked a little shakily as he looked at me, still chewing.

"You tell me," he replied, eyebrows raised. "There I am minding my own business bringing this load in from Catton when I find an abandoned backpack and bow. Next thing, I almost run you over! Laid in the middle of the track you were, out like a light!" I turned and looked back again at the mountains fading away behind us, remembering my perilous climb down the scree to the stone.

"I was…. Looking for something," I said vaguely. "I must've fallen." The man continued to stare at me, a knowing look in his eyes.

"Hmmph," he grunted, before turning his head back to the road. "Well, we're going to Andorta. I assume that's where you were headed?" I scrambled forward through the straw and climbed onto the seat beside him.

"I am," I replied, my mind feeling a little clearer now. "Thank you. For picking me up."

He glanced at me again. "Couldn't just leave you there could I? Those

Slinkferrals would've been all over you before long, laid there dead to the world without your weapons." I smiled slightly at him. He seemed to be a bit of a grumpy old curmudgeon but I really was grateful for his kindness.

As I sat there gently rocking with the movement of the cart and carefully rubbing the lump on my head, I thought of the stone I had seen in the crevice on the scree. I recognized the oval yellow shape of Glisston, the stone of the month of Bloomsbreeze. The stone that Harlequin and Drifa were searching for. I would have to get word back to Millings Beck. Maybe one of them would pass back through the village at some point in their search - perhaps not for several months but they could still get to the scree beyond Haggs Catton in time and the stone could easily still be there. I promised myself I would get the message back to the Beck if I could and my unpleasant tumble from the mountainside mightn't be for nothing.

We rocked along in silence for a while and finally the man spoke. "So," he asked as he clicked his horse into a brisk trot, the plains slipping past us and the outline of the city growing larger on the horizon. "What business do you have in Andorta? You a Seeker?" I nodded and he grunted again. "Thought you must be. Youngsters out on the roads getting themselves into scrapes usually are."

"What about you?" I asked. "What brings you to Andorta?" He cracked the reins lightly on the horse's rump to encourage it to keep up its pace.

"Oh, I travel a lot," he replied. "Mainly I buy produce from the villages and towns and bring them to sell in the cities. I get a decent price in the cities. Folk will pay a bit extra when they don't have to go out and get it themselves." I nodded, understanding how this would be the case. I suddenly wondered whether the man would expect payment for his help and thought of my empty pockets.

"Um," I began awkwardly, "I don't have any money. You know, for the ride and for picking me up or whatever…" my voice trailed off, a little embarrassed.

The man harrumphed again. "Didn't expect anything pup," he said. "I was going this way anyway so no skin off my nose. Maybe you can just owe me one if our paths ever cross again." Relieved, I faced forward again as we continued down the road.

As we approached the city, a few cottages sprung up at the side of the road, most with signs outside. 'Mudkipper and Tatties – two for a farthing!' one read. 'Best ale in Immentia here!' another bragged. One placard was painted red with the outline of a white feather at the centre. The lettering beneath it read 'The Crimson Feather'. I looked at it curiously, wondering what it meant as the cart passed a thatched longhouse with a wooden veranda at the front. On the veranda was a woman dressed in strange clothes leaning against the wooden railing. The woman's lips were painted a bright scarlet, her shoulders were bare and I noticed she had a feather tucked in her hair. As we passed, the woman called out to us. "Hey Mister! How about rolling in that hay instead of delivering it?" She leaned over the veranda and winked, blowing a kiss towards us. The man steadfastly ignored her and kept his eyes on the road, grumbling under his breath.

"Who is she?" I asked, turning in my seat to get a better look.

"Damn drabs," the man said gruffly. "You're too young to understand." As I watched, the woman made a rude gesture at our cart as we trundled away. I didn't really understand what he meant but as we approached the gates of the city, I felt a thrill of excitement. I knew that Andorta was going to be very different to Millings Beck.

CHAPTER 11

As we approached Andorta the cart man slowed his horse to a walk and the city walls loomed high in front of us. The gates just ahead were open but there were guards at either side dressed in tough looking leather armor with metal helmets covering their faces. In their hands were long lances, a sharp curved blade at the tip. The man jumped down from the cart and I reached into the back to retrieve my pack and bow before hopping down onto the road. The horse stood puffing through its flared nostrils, scraping the ground with its hooves as the man gently stroked its nose before approaching the entrance to the city.

"Now then lads," the man called out as the guards lowered their lances. "Just doing my rounds. Got a loadful here from Haggs Catton, I believe you're expecting me?" He put his hand in his pocket and produced a piece of paper that he handed over to one of the guards. The man pushed up the metal plate covering his face and looked at the note.

"Alright, you can go on in," he said, handing back the piece of paper. "Who's your friend?" the guard asked as his eyes turned to me, looking me up and down appraisingly. I folded my arms self-consciously across my chest and backed away a couple of steps.

"Oh, she's just a Seeker," the cart man said glancing back. "Just given her a lift from Catton." The guard looked at me again, his eyes resting six inches below my chin.

"In you go then sweetheart," he said standing back to let me pass. "And who knows, if you're lucky maybe I'll be seeking you later!" he gave me a lewd wink and laughed loudly at his own joke, his comrades sniggering along as they stood aside to let me pass.

I thanked the man with the cart and as he returned to his horse, I walked quickly past the guards and through the gates, eyes cast down, unused to the attention. Growing up in the Beck, the only men you knew were your Pa's age or lads you'd grown up with who would receive a cuff round the ear if they looked at you the wrong way. I was already beginning to see that in the outside world I wouldn't just be little Fen Hadwyn and I no longer had my Pa to protect me. As much as I didn't like to admit it, I knew that I had changed in recent annums and although I took no care over my appearance there was no disguising the fact that I now looked like a young woman rather than the little girl I felt I still was.

As I emerged from the tunnel beyond the gates and into the city, my senses were immediately flooded with unusual sights and sounds. The street was busy with throngs of people and at either side were tall buildings butted up closely against each other, their facades an unusual creamy coloured stone. Some of the buildings had wide bay windows at the front and some had shutters which had been thrown wide open, tables set out, heaving with fruits and vegetables. Crowds of people were milling around with baskets picking up the produce, squeezing and sniffing it and haggling with the shopkeepers over prices. As I made my way slowly into the city I noticed more streets heading off left and right, all equally as wide and bustling with activity. Dark alleyways cut between the buildings, gloomy and dank as the jostling rooftops above blocked out the light.

I gazed around in awe, overwhelmed by the sights, sounds and smells. The buildings were all constructed from the same smooth, pale stone and some were decorated with shining porcelain tiles around the windows or doorways, each tile painted with intricate images; fruit trees, wild horses, mermen and yellow ears of corn.

The women who passed me were dressed in light diaphanous fabrics which hung low to the ground but clung to their bodies, held up by twisted straps around their necks leaving their brown shoulders bare. The men were dressed in smock shirts, belts and light-coloured pantaloons cut wide at the thigh, narrow around their calves and tucked into leather boots. I stood for a moment, looking around me and felt very out of place in my Pa's breeches, dirty cut down skirts and heavy coat. At least my boots were new, I thought as I continued walking up the busy street. As I went further from the gates, the shops dwindled away and the crowds thinned out. The houses were still as decorative with hanging baskets above the doorways, festooned with colourful flowers. There were balconies at the higher windows and people were sitting out, fanning themselves in the sun or stringing washing onto the lines that hung above my head between the buildings.

It was mid-afternoon by now and I was eager to find Duckie, longing to see a familiar face. As I walked I spotted a man in threadbare clothes sitting at the side of the street, his legs bent awkwardly in front of him. At his feet was a crumpled cloth cap and as people passed, he held out his hands calling "Spare a coin for a veteran protector of the city!" Most of the people walking by ignored him and crossed to the other side of the street, averting their eyes. As I approached, the man looked up at me and I realised he wasn't as old as he had first appeared. He was maybe thirty annums with sandy hair and a wind-burnt face, creases at the corner of each eye from too much laughter.

"Spare a coin missy?" he asked in a feeble voice, holding out a grubby hand as I looked down at him curiously.

"I'm sorry," I said, "I don't have any money. I gave it all away."

The man dropped his hand and squinted up at me. "Gave it away?" he said loudly, his feeble begging voice momentarily forgotten. He suddenly laughed out loud. "You won't last long in this city without any coin," he said, chuckling to himself.

"What's wrong with your legs?" I asked, pointing at his twisted limbs which were stretched out in front of him, his feet bent at odd angles. He looked at me, surprised.

"Do you know, missy," he said, turning to look at his legs. "No one has ever asked me that. For over ten annums I've sat in the dirt all around this city begging for pennies and not once has anyone ever asked me what's wrong with my legs!" I shrugged, waiting for an answer. He looked back up at me. "I'm going to tell you something," he said shuffling close to me on his fists. I knelt down to hear him better and he gestured with a dirty hand for me to come closer. I leant towards him as he whispered softly in my ear. "There is absolutely and utterly nothing wrong with my legs!" I drew away sharply in surprise as he threw back his head, laughing loudly.

"I don't get it," I said flatly, confused.

"Oh, you will missy, you will!" the man answered me, still chuckling at my bemused expression. "Anyway, what are you doing in our fair city?" he asked me, leaning back against the wall behind him.

I stood up before answering, still looking warily at his legs. "I'm looking for a tavern - The Sprat and Skirmish? Do you know it?"

"Oh, I know it," the man replied. "Lost a card game in their once. Didn't eat for a week." His face took on a bit of a dazed, far-away expression and I looked at him expectantly.

"So... Can you tell me where it is?" I asked patiently.

"Of course I can. But you don't have any money so I won't." He folded his arms stubbornly across his chest and looked away from me up the street. I sighed. Apparently, absolutely everything had a price. I pulled my pack from my shoulders and delved around inside before pulling out a hunk of cheese and the rest of the pheasant roast that Rheda had given me. I held the food out to him and he looked up at me, an expression of pity on his face.

"You really don't have any money," he stated, not taking the proffered goods from my hands. "I thought you were joking." I shook my head and he sighed. "Keep going up here and then take the second street on the left," he said wearily. "Carry on another five minutes and you'll see the tavern." He pushed my hands away. "Keep your sorry little chunk of cheese – by the looks of it you'll need it more than I will." He gestured me away, "Now push off, you're putting off the punters."

As I walked away, the feeble voice returned and when I looked back, the legs appeared even more crippled than before. Just before I turned off the street, I glanced over my shoulder to see the man looking carefully up and down to check no one was coming before jumping to his suddenly untwisted feet. He threw me a mischievous wink and, quite sprightly made off down an alley, cap jingling with coins in his clenched hand.

I turned into the side street and continued walking, the buildings to my left nestling close to the foot of the city walls that loomed high above. Torches lined the battlements and the shadows of the guards wandering back and forth fell long and black onto the street beneath. Just ahead was a tavern with tables out front, people spilling out through the door into the afternoon sun, mugs of ale in their hands and the air noisy with chatter and laughter. The sign above the door depicted a small scamp-like creature brandishing a three-pronged fork, the words 'Sprat and Skirmish' above its head. I hoisted my pack on my back and as I approached the inn, the people stared at me inquisitively. Uncomfortable under the gaze of these strangers I avoided eye contact as I opened the door and entered the cool darkness of the tavern.

The smell of stale beer was thick in the air and my eyes took a moment to adjust to the dim light. Down one side of the room was a long wooden bar shiny with age, tables and stools lined the walls. In the corner of the room stood a raised platform with small unlit lanterns lining the floor around it, the surface of the wooden platform worn and used. There were a few people gathered in the taproom and as I approached the bar a small wiry man popped his head up, a mug in one hand and a soft rag in the other. He had bright beady eyes and a bald head with a fuzz of grey hair above each ear. When he smiled he reminded me of drawings I had seen of gnomes or dwarves, his wide grin crumpling up the whole of his impish face from ear to ear.

"Hello there," the man said, still polishing the mug with the rag. "Something I can help you with?"

I put both palms on the edge of the bar. "I…. I'm not sure," I said hesitantly, very aware of my empty pockets and of saying too much. "I'm looking for someone. He's a Seeker and I think he's been staying here? Dark hair…. His name's Duckie?" The man's eyes lit up in recognition, giving me another gnomish beam.

"Ah yes, Master Duckie," he said. "He surely has been staying here but he's not here at the moment."

My face fell in disappointment. "Oh. Do you know where he went?" The man put the glass on the shelf and folded his arms, leaning on the bar tapping a finger against his puckered lips as he gazed out of the window.

"I believe he said he was off to the bazaar," the man mused before turning back to me. "I won't tell a lie and I can't. Lightening from above strike me down, that's where he said he was going and if I know Master Duckie, that's where he'll be."

I looked curiously at the man, confused by his vague gestures and strange way of speaking, combined with the soft lilt of his unfamiliar accent.

"The bazaar?" I asked quizzically, raising my eyebrows.

"Yes yes, the bazaar, the bazaar, I'll show you." As the man gabbled, he came out from behind the bar and manhandled my pack and bow off my back before I could object. "You don't worry a jot about those," he assured me. "I will look after your things as if they were my own," he added before putting a hand on my arm and pushing me towards the door. I walked dumbly as the man nattered on, opening the inn door and gesticulating again down the street. "Now you go that way miss, follow the road round and you'll find it." He gave me a gentle push out into the throng of people gathered outside the inn. I stared at the man as he turned away and began flitting around the benches, collecting mugs and chattering incessantly to no one in particular.

I stood there in the street, my face blank and arms hanging limply at my sides. I felt tired, deflated and a little annoyed. I had expected Duckie to be waiting for me at the Sprat and Skirmish not out gallivanting but I reluctantly realised that he wouldn't have known what time to expect me or even what day. I'd have to go and track him down; otherwise I might be sleeping on the streets tonight with the stray dogs and beggars. I sighed and turned in the direction the innkeeper had gestured, walking on through this endless city of crowded buildings, high walls and increasingly peculiar people.

CHAPTER 12

The street curved gently around the foot of the city walls, homes and shops packed together tightly on either side. A few people were wandering up and down as the sun dropped low in the afternoon sky but the air was still hot and humid. As I walked deeper into the heart of the city, I heard shouting and cheering and as I grew closer to the hubbub, I felt a buzz of energy in the warm air. Turning the corner, I entered a large square bustling with people, young urchins running excitedly about the feet of the crowds. On one side of the square was a market with row after row of tents and stalls laden with vegetables, meats, rolls of cloth and barrels of shiny nuts and fruits. Opposite the market stood a huge circular structure, an arena, higher than the city walls themselves with a crescent of high tiered benches at the back and a lower section fenced off at ground level at the front.

The arena was teeming with people and noise, traders walking up and down through the crowds with trays of food and drink, calling out prices and serving customers. At the back of the arena people packed the tiers, sitting on wooden benches or standing and calling out, waving their fists as they looked down into the arena below. The lower level was also thick with bodies so I couldn't see what they were all looking at or what was causing so much excitement. Curious, I made my way through the crowd to take a closer look. As I approached an opening in the fence, the entrance to the arena, a tiny man dressed in red and blue checks jumped out in front of me, bells jangling from his sleeves.

"Ah ha," he crowed in a loud, high pitched voice. "Not so fast my lovely, that'll be a penny if you want to go in or a farthing if you want to go up into the stand. Now what'll it be, what'll it be??" He jigged merrily in front of me grinning, his small palm outstretched and a bulging coin purse on his belt.

I stopped in my tracks, still craning my neck to see over the lively throng. "I don't have any money," I said distractedly. "I just want to have a quick look, I won't be long."

The little man carried on shuffling from one foot to the other. "How long you'll be is of no interest to me petal, I just need my coins!" He patted his purse as I looked down at him, frustrated.

"I told you, I don't have any money!" I snapped as I stepped from one side to the other, trying to get around this annoying little man.

"'Fraid you'll have to wait here then lovely, there's no free entry into the arena!" the man said, cackling as he dodged left and right blocking my way. As we continued our strange dance, a loud sound filled the air above the noise of the crowd. I recognized the trill of a horn or bugle, a short staccato melody building to a long high note which brought a sudden quiet to the bustling throng as they all turned as one to look across the square.

The little man abruptly stopped his jig and his face went pale. "The Amir? No, no, no, not the Amir! Not the Amiress… not now!" the little man muttered to himself, absently patting down his clothes and casting his eyes around in panic. "There's no seats!" he turned to me, hands held up as if he thought I had an answer for him. "There's no seats! No one told me! No one! Oh, my goodness, goodness me." I looked at him curiously and then followed the gaze of the crowd across the square as the little man scurried off away from his post.

On the other side of the square, the throngs of people were parting reverently as a bugler emerged, strutting slowly, instrument held to his lips. The bugler was formally dressed in the same red and blue colours of the small man that was now scuttling towards them, his little feet kicking up clouds of dust as he went. Behind the bugler came several guards carrying flags and behind them came a small group of people strolling regally, heads held high as they made their way across the square. At the head of the group was a man, tall and barrel chested with a huge curved sword hanging from his waist. Behind him came a black-haired woman, thin and pale-faced with a severe expression, casting her eyes left and right disdainfully as the crowd parted. Between them was a blonde girl, probably a little younger than myself but slight and timid looking. Her arms were painfully thin, hanging limply from beneath her draping robes, her complexion white and sickly.

The people in the square fell silent and dropped back, many bowing as the procession passed. The tall man nodded his head now and then, waving his hand slowly left and right as they approached the arena. The little man who had barred my way was trotting alongside the bugler, jumping up and whispering in his ear. He still looked frantic so while he was distracted, I saw my chance and nipped quickly through the gate, pushing myself into the crowd. I lost myself in the throng of people, wriggling my way through until I reached the waist-high fence at the edge of the arena. The arena itself was nothing but a wide circle of hard packed earth, the ground littered with the heads of flowers and small stones that the crowd had presumably thrown down in adulation or disgust.

In the centre of the arena lay a young girl, dirty and motionless in the dust. Another girl, large boned and thick set stood over her breathing heavily, sweat dripping from her brow. I watched as a guard emerged from behind the fence and threw a bucket of water over the prone figure on the ground before dragging her off and out of sight. As I watched, a bony elbow nudged me hard in the ribs and a vaguely familiar voice whispered in my ear.

"What's up?" the voice said. "Never seen a proper fight before, my little penniless friend?" I turned in surprise and it took me a moment to realize that I was looking at the face of the crippled beggar I had encountered earlier. He was now almost un-recognizable, standing firmly on his two feet in clean clothes and a pattern of flames artfully painted across one weathered cheek. He nudged me again, chuckling to himself, enjoying my confusion.

"Is she dead?" I whispered, my eyes wide, nodding towards the arena. He threw his head back and laughed.

"No, little one!" he replied. "Not dead. Not this time. But she'll likely have a sore head tomorrow, not to mention a bit of a shiner!" I looked at his laughing face and back towards the arena as the burly girl strode off beneath the stands, head held high.

"What's going on? What is this?" I asked, still confused.

"This, my lovely," the man replied, throwing his arms up in a dramatic gesture. "Is one of the many and bountiful forms of entertainment to be found in the great city of Andorta!" He laughed again as he regarded my bewildered expression and leaned on the fence, tilting his head towards me. "Lucky you turned up today," he said. "This time yesterday, they hung a man by his neck in this very arena and cut out his gizzards." I looked up at him in horror and he laughed again. "But today," he went on, "Today we have more gentle sport." He gestured back to the arena. "They're Seekers, lovey. Always need to make a few extra pennies when you're travelling and this is as good a way as any. It's fast farthings for the likes of you." He grinned down at me, the painted flames creasing on his cheek.

"What d'you mean?" I asked stupidly. "They fight each other? For money?" I was incredulous at the brutality of his suggestion.

"Oh aye," he said, looking back across the crowd where the Amir and Amiress were entering the gates of the arena. "Some of 'em make a decent living of it while they're here. Show off a few fancy moves and make a name for themselves. The toters like nothing more than a famous Seeker, really gets the folk putting some proper coin down!" As he spoke he gestured at a row of chalkboards propped around the edge of the arena, each one scrawled with names and numbers. Next to each board stood a man or woman who I assumed were the toters, handing out coins to the people coming to collect their winnings. I observed the scene, still shocked at the idea that these people would pay money, baying like beasts, to watch young Seekers fight each other senseless for nothing but coin. As if the Seekers didn't have enough to fight for.

I turned back to the painted faced man beside me, looking into his eyes. "Who are you?" I asked, slowly shaking my head. He laughed again.

"I'm no one little Seeker," he said. "You'll see me here, you'll see me there but I am no one in this city. If you want to call me by a name I will give you my favourite. Gwil. You may call me Gwil." He frowned down at me. "But don't call me it to my face, not in front of others. I need my name to be whatever I choose from one moment to the next – you understand?" I nodded silently, not really understanding but agreeing anyway. He smiled and patted me on the head like a pet. "Good girl," he said.

As we both turned to lean over the fence, I scanned the crowd hoping to see Duckie's dark head in the sea of faces. In the highest tiered seats across the arena there was a flurry of movement as the little man in the red and blue outfit rushed up the steps, shooing the people off the benches. Some of them looked indignant and argued with him but as soon as they saw the bugler and the Amir climbing the steps, his wife and daughter behind him, they quickly gathered their belongings and scuttled quickly out of sight. The little man bowed deeply as the Amir and his family took their places and the bugler stood to attention above the crowd, blowing his horn once more. The people in the arena clapped slowly and respectfully and the little man rushed back down to his place at the gates.

"Who are they?" I asked Gwil, pointing up to the regal family now seated on the stand high above us. Gwil grabbed my outstretched hand and swiftly pulled it back. "Don't point!" he hissed, not moving his lips as he spoke. "Believe me little one, you don't want to catch the attention of the Amir and Amiress. Not in this city." I drew my hand back, alarmed at the fear in his voice. "The Amir is the leader of Andorta," Gwil continued in hushed tones. "Or some say his wife is. They control everything." I stared at the man sitting above us, casting his eyes over the crowd beneath, his haughty cold faced wife at his side.

"Everything?" I asked. Gwil let out a snort.

"Well, there's a council of sorts. The council is made up of the richest merchants and farmers who can contribute an army of a hundred bodies or more for the protection of the city but the Amir's army outnumbers the rest put together. They do as the Amir tells them." Gwil made this last statement with a bitter tone in his voice, and he spat on the ground before he continued. "His wife has his ear. She is a cruel woman, the Amiress Decima, you can see it in her face. She decides everything. When we fight, when we rest, who needs to be punished – and how. *How* we are punished is one of her favourite powers. She's very…. creative." He glanced furtively up at the stands and turned back to me, his expression grim. "The best thing for all of us is to keep out of her way." The painted flames on Gwils face were vivid and bright but his skin beneath had paled. He swallowed hard and looked back up at the Amiress Decima. "I can give you a few words of wisdom little one," he said softly. "If her gaze falls on you for any reason, you're in grave trouble. If that happens, run. Run far and run fast. Just run."

CHAPTER 13

In the arena, the crowd had become strangely subdued, the air charged with a strange and ominous energy as the Amir cast his penetrating stare around the people gathered beneath him. The expression in his wife Decima's eyes was even more chilling and I shrank away from the fence a little, Gwil's words echoing in my ears.

The bugler sounded out another long clear note as a guard stepped out into the arena and cleared his throat. "And now," the guard shouted loudly and clearly, "For your pleasure, and in honour of our great Amir," he bowed formally to the figures in the stand, "I present our next combatants!" He swept his arms towards either side of the arena as two figures emerged from beneath the stands. Both were young men dressed in leather breeches, tight around their calves, their chests bare and their hands wrapped in cloth. One was tall and well built, his skin glistening with a layer of sweat in the evening heat. His hair was dark, held back by a twisted cloth wrapped around his forehead, his chin stubbled and brows furrowed as he eyed his opponent across the arena.

"That one's named Galant," Gwil said in my ear over the cacophony of the crowd. "He never loses," added Gwil nodding sagely. I watched Galant closely as he stood there, fists held up to his face, throwing out practice punches and parrying from one foot to the other.

I turned my eyes to observe the other Seeker across the arena and my breath caught in my throat. Galant's opponent was also tall and dark but held himself with none of the confidence of the young man opposite him. He clenched his fists awkwardly in front of his body, cracking his white knuckles with a look of apprehension on his face. "Duckie!" I shouted before I could help myself. Duckie turned his head slightly and saw me. He glared directly into my eyes and shook his head imperceptibly. My hand went to my mouth and my body tensed as the guard who stood between the two boys raised his hands high in the air and turned his head to face the Amir. The Amir nodded slightly and the guard lowered his hands abruptly, calling out "Set to!" as he stepped back.

The two Seekers faced each other, fists raised, Galant still dancing from one foot the other. Duckie approached his opponent reluctantly, circling him as the crowd jeered, money changing hands with the toters as they assessed each Seeker and the odds lengthened and shortened. Duckie darted in towards Galant and clumsily swung a fist at his face. Galant dodged the blow easily and ducked, jabbing Duckie hard in the ribs causing him to stumble forward and double over with a grunt. Galant came at him again and aimed a swift kick at Duckie's face, catching him hard on the jaw. Duckie's head snapped back painfully and I winced, drawing in a sharp breath and biting my lip hard as I watched.

Duckie recovered himself quickly and turned, aiming a kick at Galant's stomach. Galant dodged back again and Duckie spun with the force if his mis-aimed kick but recovered himself and backed up, his hands protecting his face. As they circled each other, staring eye to eye, Galant suddenly dropped and swung his leg round to try to catch Duckie on the back of the ankles. Duckie saw it coming and jumped above Galant's swinging leg before stepping swiftly forward and aiming a strong punch at his opponent's face. The blow hit home and caught Galant on his mouth, blood immediately dripping from his split lip as he rolled away and leapt to his feet. He wiped his lip with the cloth around his hand and smiled wryly at Duckie, raising a hand in acknowledgement as the crowd jeered. I noticed with irritation that Galant gave off an air of arrogant charm even with blood running from his mouth.

My heart was pounding as I watched and I found myself shouting and cheering with the rest of the crowd, caught up in the excitement. Duckie seemed to have found a little confidence and he came at Galant again, striking out with his other hand towards Galant's ribs. Galant leapt to one side and shot behind Duckie, grabbing his arm and twisting it up behind him. Duckie threw back his head and cried out in pain as Galant kicked him in the back of the knees. As Duckie fell into the dust, Galant threw him onto his back and aimed a flurry of punches into Duckie's face. Gobbets of blood flew into the air as Galant's blows rained down.

I shouted out to Duckie in desperation and tried to scrabble up and over the fence but Gwil grabbed my arms to stop me. "Steady, little one," he laughed as he held me back.

"Let me go!" I cried urgently, trying to struggle from his grip. "That's my friend!"

Gwil held me firmly and whispered in my ear "Stop it now! She's looking – remember what I told you!" I looked up to see the Amiress still sitting stiffly in the stands, her eyes turned on me as she noticed the commotion down at the edge of the arena. Her expression was stony, eyes narrowed and I abruptly stopped struggling under the Amiress's cold and intimidating gaze.

In the arena, Duckie laid on his back, his chest heaving as Galant stood and raised his bloody hands above his head while the crowd cheered. As the people jostled back to the toters, Galant turned and held his hand out to Duckie who sat up, his head hanging as he spat blood into the dust. Duckie swiped Galant's hand away and rolled to his knees, reaching up to wipe his face. Galant smiled roguishly and shrugged at the crowd, raising his hands again and relishing the applause before turning and walking nonchalantly from the arena. He un-wrapped the bindings from his hands as his broad dusty back disappeared into the darkness beneath the stands.

I glanced back up into the tier of high seats to see that the Amir and his family were now on their feet, clapping slowly. The Amir turned and whispered something to his wife who nodded slightly in response. Their daughter stood and clapped obediently but her face was like a mask. She had a smile fixed firmly on her pale face but the forced twist of her mouth made it look more like a grimace. Duckie rose tiredly to his feet and walked from the arena, his head down as the crowd catcalled and tossed stones at his retreating back. I called his name again but he didn't turn to look at me.

"Looks like your friends' had his backside handed to him tonight," said Gwil wryly, resting one foot up on the fence and turning to look at me. I nodded dully in response. Gwil raised his arms above his head and stretched. "Well chicken, as for me it's time to start the night shift. Maybe we'll meet again but remember what I said – no names!" He gave me that mischievous wink again and slipped off into the crowd, disappearing quickly from view.

The Amir and his family were making their way down from the stands, the little man in red and blue virtually sweeping the ground in front of them with his tufty head as he led them out. The crowd around the arena was beginning to disperse and the toters were folding up their chalk boards, coin purses heavy on their belts. Scullery maids and kitchen lads were coming out to light the lanterns outside the taverns around the square in the darkening evening light. The market was still bustling with activity, traders shouting out to the crowds, trying to shift the last of their produce as the arena emptied.

I jostled through the crowds of people spilling out into the square and walked around the perimeter fence of the arena until I found a door that led under the stands. The door was ajar and the air wafting from inside was cool and dank. I glanced over my shoulder before slipping through the door and making my way down a narrow passage, various small rooms leading off on either side. I looked through each of the doors as I went, finding some empty, some with cages full of straw, doors swinging open and nothing within. I was shocked to find that some of the rooms also contained cages which were not empty – a stinking swamp cat snoozing in one cage, a trio of snarling Slinkferrals in another.

I kept close to the shadows as I made my way along the passage, checking each doorway until I arrived at a room dimly illuminated by a single lantern, a few wooden benches set against the wall. On one of the benches sat Duckie, head in his hands, spitting gobs of blood onto the hard-packed ground. I peered around the corner, my stomach fluttering a little as I watched him. "Duckie?" I ventured, my voice nervous and soft. Duckie raised his head slowly. "Fen," he said croakily. "Welcome to Andorta." He managed a small smile as he looked up at me, his nose bloody and his lip swollen, one eye partially closed and starting to bruise.

I walked over to him and rested a tentative hand on his shoulder. He looked up at me gave out a short bark of laughter.

"I wish you hadn't seen that," he said ruefully, gesturing to the arena. "I've fought a few times – won more than once. Couldn't you have turned up on one of those days?" he joked weakly. He pressed a cloth to his bleeding lip. "That Galant's an old hand though; crowd favourite so I didn't expect to win." His voice was a little bitter as he dabbed his mouth.

"Why are you doing it Duckie?" I asked holding out a hand and gently grasping his forearm. He winced and pulled away from me. "It's good money Fen. I get three farthings for every fight – even if I lose. More if I win. I have to pay for my room at the inn and we'll need more coin when we move on from here. I can make as much in one night in the arena as I could in a month out in the olive groves or in the market."

He stood up and pulled on his shirt, pushing back locks of grimy hair from his face. He sighed heavily. "Let's get out of here," he said gathering up his things. "We'll go back to the Sprat and eat, maybe have some ale and talk. It seems like an age since I saw you last, we have a lot to catch up on." I nodded and he swung his arm casually around my shoulders as we walked back down the dank passage, out of the arena and back into the busy street.

As we walked past the square we paused for a moment. Gwil was standing on an upturned drum with a lit torch in his hand, the flickering light illuminating the painted flames on his face. A small crowd had gathered around him as he stood there, dramatically brandishing his torch and beckoning his observers forward. When he had the full attention of the throng, Gwil gave a grand bow. He made a big show of bending his lithe body backwards and slowly bringing the torch to his face. I watched in amazement as he sucked the burning flames into his mouth for a long moment before suddenly standing straight and blowing out a huge plume of purple fire above the crowd, sparks showering from his lips.

The crowd gasped in amazement, many jumping back from the flames which were dangerously close to their heads. As the fire dispersed, Gwil took another deep bow, picked up his hat and proffered it around the crowd. He caught my eye and shot me another wink as he collected his pennies. I smiled but said nothing, remembering his words from earlier. Besides his numerous names, he was certainly a man of varied talents. I wondered how many faces he had to wear to survive in this city.

After Gwil's performance Duckie and I returned to the Sprat and Skirmish as the moon rose in the dark, star scattered sky. The innkeeper agreed to let us share Duckie's room so we went up and I helped Duckie clean up his face at the washbowl. When the smears of dried blood were gone, I could see that his nose was still swollen and there was a dark black bruise under one eye but the damage wasn't as bad as it had looked. We returned to the taproom of the inn and Duckie paid for a platter of meat with roasted vegetables which we devoured hungrily with greasy fingers. We talked as we ate, sharing stories of our separate journeys to the city. Duckie told me how he'd run from the bandits on his way to Haggs Catton and that he'd stopped for a Mudkipper on his way to Andorta; "Tasted like frog" he said, grimacing at the memory.

When he was finished, I took a deep breath before beginning my story. I explained how I had got lost in the woods near Mallady Bruma's place and showed him the now almost invisible puncture wounds from the Bloodwarblers. Duckie's eyes were wide as I described my night in the forest and the mysterious visit from the Shadewalkers. I told him of my experience out on the mountain path, my fall from the scree and the Glisston I had seen. We agreed that we would get a message back to Millings Beck as soon as we could and maybe Harlequin or Drifa could get there in time.

We finished our food and Duckie took our plates and left them on the bar. As he sat back down, I huddled closer to him and he leant towards me in response, the candlelight flickering in his expectant eyes. I lowered my voice as I began to tell Duckie about my strange encounter with the thin man at The Woodpecker Lass in Haggs Catton, explaining about the contents of the note carefully stowed in my pack upstairs. Duckie tilted his head towards me as he listened intently and when I was finished, he scooted his stool closer to the table, his face bright with excitement.

"Fen," he whispered, "I can't believe it! Only a couple of days out of the Beck and you've come up with more than I've managed in weeks!"

I looked at him a little dubiously. "Haven't you found anything out since you've been here?" I asked, disappointed. "No one knows anything?"

Duckie shrugged. "I heard a few things – spent quite a few days out of the city." He sat back in his stool, hands behind his head. "I was out at Azantia Bay on the coast a week or so back. I met a peddler here who said he'd heard a rumour that there was Zaphite in one of the old smugglers caves. I travelled for two days and nights without stopping. I got there safe enough but it seemed I wasn't the only one the peddler had spoken to." Duckie smiled ruefully. "Someone beat me to it. There was another Seeker celebrating in the tavern at Azantia when I arrived." Duckie leaned forward, chin resting on his palms and sighed glumly. "Just the way it goes I suppose."

Suddenly, the bleak look passed from his face and he looked at me hopefully. "What about this Halftans Crevice though?" he said. "This strange fellow didn't even know what we were looking for did he? There's no harm in going there to have a look. Might be something in it." I nodded in agreement. "We need to see if we can turn up anything on Rubine while we're here though," Duckie continued thoughtfully. "We might not pass through another city for a while after we set out." He turned and looked at me seriously. "You paid everything you had for that note in your pack so if there's anything about Rubine in Andorta, I'll find it. And if I can, I'll pay for it. Whatever it takes." He reached over the table and gripped my hand hard, smiling slightly when I pulled away.

We talked some more about how we'd go about making our way to Wistmans Hollow, whether we'd need maps, where in Andorta we might find some word of Rubine stones and what might lay in wait for us. We sat whispering in hushed voices as the inn gradually emptied leaving just a few stragglers propping up the bar, their speech slurring. When even they had headed home for the night, Duckie and I climbed up the narrow stairs as the innkeeper was stacking the stools on the tables. I huddled up on Duckie's bed and he took the floor, laying our coats down on the hard wooden boards before blowing out the lamp. As I fell asleep, the bright moon cast shadows of the patrolling guards walking relentlessly through the night high on the city ramparts.

CHAPTER 14

The morning sun woke me early the next day and I got up quietly, pulling on my clothes as Duckie lay sleeping on the floor. The swelling around his nose had reduced but the bruise beneath his closed eye had turned to a rainbow of blacks, blues and greens. I crept out of the room and went down the stairs where the innkeeper was unlocking the front door.

"Morning miss," the man said giving me that gnomish smile again. "Nice to see you today. It is today already isn't it?" he asked, his eyebrows wiggling. "Of course it is, of course it is. Yesterday was then and now it's today." He bustled back behind the bar and brought me a jug of milk and some bread. I explained I had no money but he didn't seem to hear me so I accepted the food and thanked him, hoping Duckie wouldn't mind picking up the bill.

I asked the innkeeper if he had a piece of paper and a pencil and he brought me them happily, pushing the items towards me across the bar. "Writing home are you?" he asked nosily, peering at me as I bent my head over the paper.

"Something like that," I murmured.

"Need it delivering do you?" he continued. "The cart man that delivers my ale travels through a lot of places – mebbe's he can drop it off for you? He comes here, then to Saltflat Plains, Snails End, then Haggs Catton after that so you just let me know if there's something you need passing on." He smiled at me as he rubbed down the already gleaming bar. "Nice for folk to know their young'uns are alright." I looked up at him.

"If you could do that, I'd be grateful," I said appreciatively and he nodded cheerfully.

"You just seal it up and I'll make sure it gets at least as far as Catton." He wandered off as I sat, hand poised above the paper, deep in thought.

I needed to make sure that the information I sent home would not fall into unscrupulous hands. I needed to get a message to Mallady Bruma to send back to Millings Beck that my Pa would understand but someone else would discard as the innocent words of a Seeker sending a note home. Eventually, I put pencil to paper and carefully inscribed the words:

"Dearest Mallady,

I thought you would want to know that I have made it safely to Andorta. The journey here was delightful – the scenery and the animals! The foliage and flowers! I have never seen the like before in all my annums. Just on the mountain path down to the plains on this side of Andorta I found the most wonderful bloom – bright yellow with an orange centre, the most beautiful flower I have ever seen. It was growing from a crevice half way down the scree and when I saw it, I thought of Harlequin and Drifa. Those yellow and gold petals – I know Drifa would have loved it as much as life itself! You know how she's besotted with flowers. And Harlequin would climb a mountain and down the other side to bring such a lovely gift to his mother. Of course, it will die soon; water is scarce out here so nothing lasts for long. I write this note from Andorta and I hope my family are well. Please do what you can to get this letter to my Pa and tell him I am safe and hopeful. Get this news there as quickly as you can and make sure they pass my best wishes to Harlequin and Drifa. Please be sure to do that.

Your friend, Fen."

I re-read my words, head cocked on one side, and was satisfied that Mallady and Pa would understand my meaning. I folded the paper carefully and wrote Mallady's name followed by the words "care of Merton, The Tollhouse, Haggs Catton" on the outside. The innkeeper allowed me to use his wax seal to close the opening and I noticed that the seal was patterned with the outline of the same dancing sprat displayed on his sign outside. I handed the note to him and he tucked it out of sight behind the bar.

"My man will be coming in the next few days," he said. "So I'll make sure he gets this. He'll pass it on, owes me a favour so he'll get it there, no mistake, good man he is…" the innkeeper trailed off into his now familiar prattle as I nodded along, hoping Mallady would get the letter to Pa. Hoping I had done enough.

The sun was shining through the windows of the inn and the noise of the street filtered through the doorway as I began to eat my breakfast. Duckie emerged from upstairs a few minutes later, gingerly touching his sore eye with his fingertips as he ambled over to me.

"It looks worse today," I said through a mouthful of bread, looking up at his black eye.

"Yes, well," Duckie said, sitting next to me and tearing off a chunk of bread before stuffing it in his mouth. "It'll go down," he mumbled, spitting a few crumbs as he spoke. "Anyway," he added, peering at his reflection in the rows of pewter mugs lined up behind the bar, "I quite like it – makes me look like a proper traveler!" I snorted and shook my head. Duckie swallowed and reached for the jug of milk, taking a long gulp and wiping his mouth with the back of his hand.

"I'll show you around today if you like," he said to me cheerfully as he stuffed more bread into his mouth.

I nodded. "I need to find a way of earning some money though Duckie," I said. "I don't have a penny and I don't want you paying for everything."

Duckie shook his head and reached into his pockets, forcing a small pile of coins into my hand. "Fen," he said as I tried to push the coins away, "You spent all your money getting a tip off for my stone so I owe you – just take it!" I reluctantly accepted the coins knowing he wouldn't take no for an answer.

"I still need to earn some myself," I muttered sulkily. Duckie finished his breakfast and paid the innkeeper whose name, I found out, was Mr Bantertrap but he insisted we call him 'Banters'. "All my friends do," he said, "All of them except the ones I don't like and I can't tell you what they call me! No I can't!" he laughed uproariously as Duckie and I left the inn and went out into the street.

I felt amazingly free and weightless with no coat on and without all my belongings strapped to my back. I almost felt like skipping as we walked down the street in the warm morning air in the direction of the bazaar. Duckie pointed out buildings and shops to me as we went; an herbalist's where they sold illegal juniper grog through the back door. A milliners with a window display of wonderful and elaborate hats, a tall and haughty looking lady inside trying them on as the milliner simpered around her. We passed the arena, now standing empty and Duckie explained that as well as the Seekers fights, it was also used for other types of 'entertainment'. They would set wild animals against each other to fight, sometimes a travelling circus would pass through and put on a display of acrobatics and jongleurs.

He told me that the arena was also used for less jovial and much darker practices such as torture and executions and I remembered what Gwil had told me the evening before. Duckie explained that the councilors of the city would preside as judge and jury and the Amir would decide the fate of those found guilty of any misdemeanor. If a death sentence was passed, the Amir (or as most thought, his wife) would decide the method of execution. Sometimes, if they were lucky, the convict would be put to death by the sword – quick and bloody. Often, the execution would be more imaginative and the unfortunate soul would be trapped inside the arena and set upon by wildcats or Slinkferrals as the crowd watched, betting on how long the battle would last. Occasionally, they would be tied to a high post in the centre of the arena and left there for days in the blistering sun to suffer a slow and humiliating death for all to see. I shuddered a little as Duckie spoke, a chill shivering down my spine. I thought again of the stoic face of Amir with his steely glare and the malevolent glint in the eyes of his wife Decima.

The bazaar was already busy with traders unloading fruit from carts and wagons, women setting up stalls overflowing with colourful scarves and robes in rich silks and satins. I felt hot and uncomfortable in my bodice and leather breeches; even my beloved leather boots were making my feet feel sweaty and sore. I eyed the ladies of Andorta enviously as they floated past us in their thin loose robes with bare shoulders and sandaled feet. As we walked through the stalls, I reached out to touch the wispy fabrics, lifted the exotic fruit to my face and sniffed the sweet unfamiliar scents. Some stalls had a firepit at the back and the traders were selling roasted meat and chunks of vegetables served on wooden skewers. I had never seen anything like the bazaar and my eyes were wide as I took it all in, listening to Duckie as he explained everything to me as we walked.

As we passed one stall, a wizened brown faced woman approached me with a dark green silk robe over one arm.

"Hello there petal," the crone said as she blocked my way, holding the robe out to me as she cast her eyes over my heavy clothing. "You look ever so warm in that get up," she said with slightly over-done sincerity, looking me up and down. "Wouldn't you like one of my robes?" she asked, holding the swathe of cloth up to my face and tilting her head. "This colour was just made for you lovey," she turned to Duckie. "Look at this, young man; don't you think this green is just perfect on her?" I swatted her hands away, embarrassed, as Duckie regarded me with mischievous eyes.

"Oh certainly it is," he said laughing. "She would look radiant in it!"

"Shut up," I hissed at him, glaring from under my brows as the woman flitted around me.

"Seriously Fen," Duckie said his face now earnest as he reached again into his pockets. "I'll get it for you. It's too hot here to wear breeches, you'll be much more comfortable in this," he said persuasively. "And people will stop staring at you..." he added, almost to himself. I reached out tentatively and touched the robe, the green silk light and cool under my touch. Duckie could see I was weakening and he held out a coin to the woman who hurried back to her stall and returned with the robe in a paper bag, pushing it into my hands with a beaming smile.

"Thank you," I said gruffly and Duckie shrugged in response as we walked on through the bazaar.

On the other side of the square, Duckie took me down a wide street, grand houses standing on either side. Guards were stationed in pairs outside most of the doors, all wearing the red and dark blue colours that I had seen on the Amir's guards the night before at the arena. Duckie explained that these were the homes of the councilors of Andorta and the guards and armies in their employ all wore the red and blue colours of the city. We walked to the end of the street until we could go no further, reaching a marble wall of pillars blocking our way and a set of imposing gates, guards standing stiffly on either side. Beyond the gates stood a palace, a huge and beautiful house built from the same smooth creamy stone seen all around the city, its roof tiled instead of thatched with a large gleaming dome in the centre. The outside was surrounded by tall shining pillars, steps leading down to a neatly tended rose garden with a fountain at the centre, the gushing plumes of water sparkling in the sunshine. Along the upper floor was a long balcony with a row of tall windows running along its length, many of them open with pure white curtains billowing in the breeze.

"The Amir's palace." Duckie said quietly as we stood staring. "He rarely comes out apart from to go to the council or the arena. Did you see him last night?" Duckie turned to me questioningly and I nodded.

"And his wife and daughter," I said. "What's her name again?"

Duckie turned back to the house. "His wife is Decima and their daughter is named Ariad." I thought of the sickly-looking girl I had seen at the arena. "They had three other sons," continued Duckie, his voice now a whisper as the guards eyed us suspiciously.

"What happened to them?" I asked, my voice equally quiet.

"Seekers," said Duckie. "Unusual for three from the same family to fail but that's what happened. One year after another, they each went out but never came back."

"Terrible," I murmured still staring at the rows of windows.

"I suppose it is," said Duckie. "The story goes that the Amir tried everything to help his sons – even sent sorcerers and shaman out to find the stones and try to bring them back. They were all killed of course, or disappeared with their fee." Duckie snorted, adding "Stupid really; you can't collect other people's stones. You can only get your own, everyone knows that." I nodded, finding the hopeless story sad and depressing, thinking again of the pale girl Ariad with a pang of pity.

"Anyway," said Duckie pushing away from the railings. "Let's go. There's a lot more to show you."

CHAPTER 15

We spent the rest of the day walking around the city, looking in bookshops and poring over the maps and guidebooks. We stopped at a couple of taverns and Duckie bought cold mugs of ale that we drank out in the sun, watching the people pass by. We talked about our plans and the folded note in my backpack, deciding to stay a while in Andorta so we could earn some money and hopefully find out if anyone knew of any Rubine stones. The afternoon sun was disappearing behind the walls of the city as we returned to the Sprat and Skirmish.

When we got back I left Duckie in the taproom chatting to Banters and I went up to our room to rest. I dozed for a while and when I awoke, I took the small paper bag I had brought from the bazaar and went to the bathroom down the hallway. The room contained a small wooden bench and a ceramic circular tub in the centre of the room. Above the tub a pipe extended from the ceiling with a small lever attached. I looked at it curiously. I had heard that in the cities, water poured freely from pipes but I had never seen it for myself. In Millings Beck, water had to be gathered in buckets and on bath day, it would take ten or more trips down to the Beck to fill our old wooden tub where we would wash in the tepid water, huddled in front of the firepit. I gingerly flicked the lever and jumped back in surprise when water gushed suddenly from the pipe.

Duckie had told me that large water tanks stood on the rooftops in the heat of the sun and when I put my hand under the flow, the water felt warm. I stood there for a few moments, looking in wonder at the clear flowing stream running between my fingers. I pulled off my grubby clothes and stood under the pipe, the water running into my tangled mess of auburn curls and down in rivulets across my dusty, sweaty body. I stood there for a long time, eyes closed, just enjoying the pure pleasure of it before soaping myself down and standing once again under the water until the suds were rinsed from my hair.

Eventually, I stepped out of the tub and sat on the bench, my hair dripping as I tried to drag my fingers through the knots. When I was dry, I un-wrapped the paper package and pulled out the green robe, holding it out in front of me. There were several straps around the neck and the drapes and folds of the fabric felt pleasantly light as I pulled the robe over my head. The smooth cool silk slid effortlessly over my body and I fiddled with the lattice of straps around the top. I wasn't sure if I was doing it right but I ended up with a couple of delicate straps across each shoulder and one looped up around the back of my neck. The front was not cut too low on my chest but the back was open, draping down to the base of my spine. I felt a little exposed with my shoulders and back un-covered but I felt cool and liked the way the fabric moved freely around my legs.

I padded back to our room barefoot and realised with dismay that I would have to put on my boots under the robe. I pulled the boots on and stood, looking down at my feet. People would probably still give me strange looks but I didn't really care. I ran my fingers through my damp hair again before heading down to the taproom of the inn where already I could hear the buzz of people gathering for the evening. Duckie was still sitting on a stool at the bar and when he heard the door open he turned and glanced over, turning away a fraction before his head snapped back. He gawked at me as I shuffled into the room awkwardly, my hands clasped in front of me. Duckie sat back on his stool, looking me up and down.

"Well," he said, resting his palms on his knees. "The lady in the bazaar was right – that colour definitely suits you. I barely recognized you!"

I stood next to him and tutted. "It's just because I'm clean," I said grumpily. "Have you seen that pipe thing in the bathroom?" I asked, eager to change the subject.

"I know," answered Duckie, "I've been talking to Banters about how it works. I'm going to see if I can build one when we get back to Millings Beck."

I laughed, leaning on the bar. "I can just imagine their faces if you did! There'd be a line down the street to use it!" Duckie laughed along at the thought of the villagers of Millings Beck queuing up outside Duckie's cottage, towels under their arms, waiting to try out his new invention. I enjoyed the moment as we took a brief glimpse into the future, as if it was assured and we would both get home safely to live out our days telling stories and playing with water pipes.

We sat at the same table as the previous night and ate the meal brought to us by Banters; chicken legs, the crispy skin sticky with honey and speckled with shavings of lemon rind. As we ate, a man entered the tavern and approached the bar to speak with Banters, gesturing outside as Banters listened carefully, nodding. They shook hands and the man went back out of the door, only to quickly return followed by a couple of other younger men and a beautiful girl with long black hair. They were carrying various musical instruments; a fiddle and a drum, a mouth organ and the girl held a wooden ring about the size of a dinner plate, thin discs of metal attached to it which tinkled and jangled as she moved. They went to the raised platform at the side of the taproom and Banters bustled around lighting the small lanterns that surrounded it as the musicians set up their instruments.

The girl went through the door at the back of the inn and emerged a few minutes later with her black hair tied high on her head, tendrils falling around her face. She had dabbed charcoal around her eyes and her lips were painted and glistening. She was wearing a silk robe of bright scarlet but she had wrapped the lower drapes of it around her waist leaving her brown thighs bare, her leather sandals laced up her calves. She went back outside to the front of the inn and as I craned my neck to look out of the window, I could see her calling out to passers-by, prancing and twirling in the late afternoon sun, trying to entice them into the inn.

The people in the bar had turned to regard the group on the stage expectantly and as the musicians began to play, the taproom began to fill with people, swigging their ale and swaying to the music. I sat there bright eyed, listening intently. The people began tapping their feet and before long, they began to dance, swinging each other round and linking arms, singing along and clapping their hands. One woman came over to our table and dragged Duckie to his feet. He reluctantly allowed her to pull him into the throng and I laughed in delight as he was spun from one dancer to the next, clumsily tripping over his feet.

I was standing now, clapping along and suddenly a firm hand gripped my arm and spun me into the crowd. The inn was a blur of merry faces as I danced, the warm hand reaching down to grasp mine, twisting me suddenly. I spun around and dizzily found my flushed face pressed against the chest of a tall man, the length of our bodies touching. His warm hand was still tightly holding mine, the other resting low on my naked back holding me steady. I looked up into his face dizzily and realised that this was no stranger. I had seen this man before but it took me a moment to place him. It was Duckie's opponent from the arena.

Galant looked down at me, his eyes gleaming as he held me tightly to him, his face close to mine. I stared into his eyes for a moment, transfixed. "Hello beautiful," he whispered softly in my ear, and I could almost hear the smile on his lips. "Has anyone ever told you that you should always wear green?" I wanted to pull away but it was as if our bodies were connected by some electrical force and my skin was buzzing, hot under his touch. The dancers continued to twirl around us and the music faded into the background as we stood there motionless. After a moment, someone nudged me hard in the back with a stray elbow and the spell was broken. I pushed Galant away from me and stood back, my fists in tight balls at my side.

"You!" I said accusingly. Galant raised an eyebrow and laughed.

"You know me then?" he said, without any note of surprise.

"I don't know you," I replied vehemently. "And I don't want to!" I turned on my booted heel and pushed my way through the crowd, returning to our table and sitting down, arms folded and my brows knotted in an angry frown. Duckie was now dancing with the pretty girl who had come in with the musicians, his face alight as she pulled him close, clasping both his hands as the music slowed and the dancers began to pair off, moving together.

I glowered in my seat avoiding Galant's gaze as he stood across the room, nonchalantly leaning against the bar, mug of ale in one hand and his dark hair hanging over his eyes. The band was now playing a soft, slow melody and the energy in the inn faded as the people settled back into their seats, swaying gently to the music. The singer pulled up a stool and put down his bow, holding his fiddle on his lap instead as he plucked softly at the strings. His voice was low but the notes were clear and pure as he sang. I ignored Galant and Duckie as I pulled my silk robe tightly around my body and leaned my chin on my hands, watching the musicians as their faces flickered in the lamplight. I listened intently as the man sang, mesmerized by his voice, the soft notes of the fiddle and gentle tap of the drum.

"I spent my whole life seeking, knowing full well what I sought,
Those stones of red, blue-green and grey, none that can be bought,
I travelled far, I travelled wide and found my way to you,
When I looked into your eyes I sought no other hue.
We fought, we loved, you taught me to be kind,
And everywhere we journeyed you never left my mind.
The Vale of Sighs, the forests deep, the desert sands so dry,

When the darkness came for you, all I could ask was why."

Unexpected tears welled in my eyes and I rubbed them away with my fists, blaming it on the ale. From the corner of my eye I saw Galant walking towards me, still wearing that teasing smile. He took a seat on the bench next to me and I steadfastly ignored him as he sat there quietly for a few minutes, seemingly quite comfortable with the awkward silence. Duckie was still standing at the bar as the dark-haired girl in red flirted with him, glancing at him from beneath her lashes and twisting tendrils of glossy hair around her fingers.

Eventually, I turned to Galant, irritated by his presence. "What do you want?" I asked harshly, my brows furrowed in an angry scowl.

He laughed at my expression and took another swig of his ale. "I just want to talk to a pretty girl," he said, leaning closer to me. "What's wrong with that?"

I looked at him suspiciously. "Shouldn't you be knocking the sense out of someone in the arena?" I asked, a bitter note in my voice and he laughed again, resting a warm hand on my thigh. I pulled abruptly away.

"That's just a job," he said, "I don't particularly enjoy fighting but I'm good at it, I need the money and the people seem to like it so why not?"

I glared at him again. "Why not?" I asked hotly, incredulous. "That's why not!" I said, gesturing at Duckie still flirting across the room. "Have you seen his eye? He's beaten black and blue thanks to you." Galant looked over at Duckie in surprise and I saw a look of recognition pass over his features.

"Ah," he said, nodding. "That's your friend? I remember him from yesterday. Wouldn't take my hand if I recall." He shrugged and looked back at me. "You can't hold it against me. And he certainly seems like he's doing alright now." We both looked back at Duckie who was leaning against the bar, the dark-haired girl snuggling against him, their faces close.

I scowled crossly and tossed my head, looking back to the musicians on the stage.

"Don't judge me too harshly," said Galant, tentatively touching my arm with his fingertips. "I just want to make some money so I can go home." I turned back to him, ready to make another quick sarcastic comment but I saw that his face was now serious, a sad expression passing across his eyes and I softened a little.

"Where are you from?" I asked stiffly.

"Bleakchill Cove," he replied. "It's all the way across on the west coast."

I nodded. "We're from Millings Beck in the valleys. We're Seekers." Galant glanced at me with an intrigued expression before he sighed and nodded understandingly.

"That's what brought me to Andorta," he said. "I'm one of the lucky ones – found my stone north west of here but now I need to get back to Bleakchill." He laughed wryly. "You'd think finding your stone would be the hard part but getting home is going to be just as bad I think."

We both sat there in silence for a few moments and the band began playing another up-tempo tune, the people now dancing a little more drunkenly than before. I watched across the room as the dark-haired girl whispered in Duckie's ear and he nodded before making his way over to me.

"Fen," he began, his eyes bright and cheeks flushed. "I just wanted to tell you…" he stopped abruptly mid-sentence when he noticed who was sitting beside me. "What's going on?" he asked accusingly. "What's he doing here?"

"Nothing," I snapped, embarrassed and feeling suddenly quite disloyal. "We're just talking." Duckie glowered as Galant stood up.

"You put up a decent fight yesterday friend," he said amiably. "No hard feelings?"

Galant offered his hand again and Duckie's fingers flickered unconsciously to his bruised eye. He threw Galant a hostile look and ignored him, leaving Galant's proffered hand hanging in mid-air. Duckie turned his back on Galant and leaned over the table towards me.

"I'm just going out for a bit," he said, gesturing at the dark-haired girl. "Dandy has a friend staying at the Fledgling Angel on the other side of town and the band is going there to play after this. I thought I'd go along for a while." I looked over at the girl named Dandy who was now chatting with another man at the bar, her skirts resting even higher than before on her brown thighs.

"You do what you want Duckie," I replied easily, taking another sip of ale. "I'm going to bed anyway."

"Good," said Duckie quietly. "I'm not sure I like the company you're keeping." Before I could respond he shot another filthy look at Galant and returned to the bar, looping has arm back around Dandy's waist.

As the evening drew to a close, the musicians gathered their instruments and Banters emerged from behind the bar, patting them on the back before happily handing over a pouch of coins. They made their way out of the inn and Duckie followed with Dandy as she giggled and fluttered her eyelashes, hips swaying. As the door slammed behind them I sighed and sat back on the bench, leaning against the wall behind me. Galant was still sitting quietly beside me, the awkward episode with Duckie hanging over us like a fog in the air. "I like your boots," he said suddenly, leaning down and lifting the bottom of my robe so the dragons glinted in the lamplight.

"Thank you," I said flatly. "My Pa got them for me." I felt a pang of loneliness as I thought of Pa and Leif.

Galant looked at me, his expression interested. "Tell me about your Pa," he said. "Tell me about Millings Beck. Tell me how you got here." I looked into his eyes again and saw genuine interest reflected back at me. "Go on," he said, seeing my dubious expression. "I really want to know."

"Alright," I said, sighing. "But first, get me another ale." Galant laughed at that and beckoned to Banters to fill up our mugs.

We sat there late into the night and I told Galant more than I meant to. Again, I will blame it on the ale. I told him about my mother's death, about Leif and Pa and life in the Beck. I told him about my journey to Andorta searching for Rubine and the kind people and strange creatures I had encountered. It felt good to organize all the events in my mind and Galant's handsome and interested face stayed fixed on mine, adding the odd understanding comment or murmurs of sympathy. In between, he told me a little about himself and about his family back in Bleakchill Cove. He spoke fondly of his older sister and her new baby who was only a few days old when he left. He told me how he'd found his stone and as he spoke, his face seemed to change from being just blandly handsome to something else; I saw a depth behind his eyes that I hadn't noticed before. I realised I had misjudged him and he was no different to Duckie and me; just another Seeker trying to get home to his family.

As the inn emptied, my eyes began to droop with tiredness and Galant eventually got to his feet. "Time for me to go Fen," he said. I nodded and stood also, awkwardly swinging my arms at my sides. He rested his hands on my bare shoulders and when he touched me, the rest of my body faded into numbness. All the nerves and sensation charged towards the skin under his palms, tingling with electricity. We stood for a moment staring at each other and I wondered vaguely if he would kiss me. Finally, I freed myself from his intense gaze and physically stood back from his touch.

"Goodnight then," I said quietly before turning and walking away from him.

He laughed at my abruptness. "Goodnight. We'll meet again, little Fen," he added before he turned and walked out of the inn, glancing back over his shoulder as he went out of the door. I headed up to bed feeling drunk from the ale and the dancing. My body felt loose and relaxed and my brain fuzzy. I had an unfamiliar warm feeling in the pit of my stomach and my skin was tingling where Galant had touched me. Still swathed in my green robes, I collapsed into bed and fell asleep, a small unseen smile on my lips.

CHAPTER 16

The door of the inn slammed shut and Galant made his way out into the street. He glanced up at one of the dimly lit windows on the upper stairway before turning and walking away towards the city gates, crossing the main road and heading to his lodgings in the Feather Quarter. As he passed, two shiny black eyes observed him from the darkness. A small furry body was hunched in the shadow of the buildings, ears alert and whiskers twitching. When the street was quiet and empty, the rat emerged into the light of the street lamps and squatted on its silvery haunches. The creature paused for a moment and sniffed the air before scurrying off down the street, hugging the shadows and moving fluidly up and down the doorsteps.

It followed the dirty gutters of the city streets, pausing occasionally as a lone figure passed by or the sound of voices echoed from an open window. The rat kept moving and eventually reached the palace, scrambling up over the low wall and between the railings of the fence. It darted across the rose garden and up the steps, avoiding the guards leaning dozily against the walls. It stopped again as its pink nose tickled the warm air, smelling the enticing scent of food from the large room beyond the tall gleaming pillars, the row of doors and shutters wide open to the warm evening air. Its beady eyes darted left and right before it dropped to its paws and crept slowly behind a swathe of white fabric and through an open door.

The room was well lit with the glow of many thick candles mounted on ornate metal stands, wax dripping as the flames flickered slightly in the gentle breeze. In the centre of the room was a long table laden with the remains of a rich meal; meats and cheeses and platters of fruit. The rat skulked in a shadowy corner, its nose twitching frantically at the enticing scents. At the far end of the room stood a woman, her expression angry as she leaned over the table looking between the faces of two men seated opposite each other.

"Oberon," she said to the grey bearded man to her right, her voice quiet but venomous. "You tell me that your men have found the ruins of Stellium." She slammed her hands on the table. "Have you found the relics or have you not? It's a simple question!" The grey bearded man visibly flinched as she spoke and his hands fluttered uncomfortably across the table in front of him.

"Decima," he said, his voice soothing but trembling slightly. "It looks promising. The relics are in the hands of the best men in my employ but you must give me more time. I am expecting them any day now."

The woman named Decima threw up her hands and strode away from the table.

"You have had more than enough time Oberon," she said angrily, not turning to look at the simpering old man. "We have thrown fortunes of coin away so you can send your men across the seas, beneath the earth and to the highest mountains to see if the legend speaks the truth. What now? What else do you need now?"

The old man named Oberon raised his hands in frustration. "My lady," he said, his voice wheedling, "I received a message from my men and they have the relics in their possession. They are on their way to Andorta as we speak. Once I have inspected the relics, I will have your answers."

Decima turned to look at the old man. "So you keep saying," she said, her eyes narrowing. "Ariad will soon be seventeen annums, the clock will start ticking once again and you have so far brought us nothing." She turned back to the table and focused her steely glare on the other man.

"And you," she said, a note of disdain in her voice, "The great Amir of Andorta. Already you have lost three sons. Are you prepared to lose your daughter too? Can you live with the shame of it?" she slammed her fist down again hard on the table. "Because I cannot!"

The Amir shook his head and stared at the old man from under his brows.

"Decima's right," he murmured. "You must understand how this looks Oberon." The old man nodded, his face worried. "We are the greatest family that Andorta has ever known. We command the biggest army to ever defend its walls and we could rival any other city in Immentia."

Decima's eyes gleamed angrily in the candlelight. "Yes," she hissed at the Amir. "And we could be ruling Immentia right now if you'd not raised three sons so useless that they could not even pass the first small challenge that was thrown at them." She stood back, her features twisted and evil as the shadows flickered across her face. "They couldn't even find their birthstones. All three of them. All failed to find one, little, stone. I am ashamed to call them my sons." The Amir looked down at his hands as Decima leaned in closer to him, her voice cruel. "There are farm boys and drabs, lepers and shanty dwellers that went out with nothing but a rusty knife and succeeded where your boys failed." The Amir didn't look up. "Are we to be humiliated once again?" Decima asked bitterly. "Ariad will fail us too. She barely has the gumption to look a street urchin in the eye – how d'you think she's going to find her stone without our help?" Decima's eyes flashed at her husband who stared straight ahead, his eyes steely.

She sat down in the chair at her husband's side and grasped his hand, her voice softened, tone persuasive. "You are a great man, a great leader," she whispered. "We are destined to rule. Imagine what we could do with those relics? If we controlled all the lands from Dracae to Epona? With those relics, we can build an army with more power than this world has ever known. We could take over all of Immentia and even venture north beyond the Mountains of Fellscar." Decima's eyes were bright with ambition. "With the relics in our possession and Ariad in the bed of a prince of Immentia no one will oppose us. It will be how we always dreamed."

The Amir listened to his wife's entrancing words and eventually he stood and walked around the table, standing over the bearded man. "My lord," the old man stuttered, "Let me assure you, I believe we have found the source of the legend – a task that has been tried and failed for over three thousand annums! It has been an age since anyone has seen the relics. They have become nothing but forgotten folklore known only to those who can translate the sacred tomes of history." He lowered his hands and sat up a little in his seat. "I believe that we have what you seek – and if we do," he paused, eyes glinting as he spoke the words they wanted to hear. "If we do, it will change the world."

The Amir regarded him grimly. "I have faith in you Oberon. You have not failed me yet." He paced up and down slowly as he spoke, his fingers resting on his chin. "If you say you have found the relics then I will give you a little more time. When you succeed I will provide you with wealth that you never imagined possible." He stopped pacing and turned to the bearded man who was looking up at him with frightened eyes. "But my patience will only last so long. The reputation of my ancestors and the future of my bloodline depends on it." The old man's head wobbled and his lips moved but no sound came out. The Amir reached down and gripped the old man's throat. "You get me those relics and you get them soon," his voice was a whisper but the words were clear. Decima looked on with a look of satisfaction in her narrowed eyes. "Fail me and I will punish you. I will punish you and I will punish your family. Fail me and a blazing torrent of hell will be unleashed upon you and those you love of the like you could never imagine." The Amir tightened his grip and the old man's eyes bulged. "Bring. Me. Those. Relics."

The rat's nose twitched again as it rose to its haunches, sniffing the scent of fear in the air. Its silvery grey hair stood on end and its nerves bristled as the need for food tangled with the urge to flee. Eventually, the rat lowered itself to the ground and scurried back out of the open door, through the garden and down the street. It headed for the bazaar where it would find scraps to eat. They may not be as rich as the offerings of the Amir's table but would not be tainted by evil words and the heavy stench of fear that still lingered in its nostrils.

CHAPTER 17

In the days that followed, Duckie and I filled our time wandering around the city and talking with the merchants in the bazaar and the off-duty guards as they swigged ale in the taverns. We still had no news on Rubine and I was painfully aware of the note in my pack and the Zaphite stone at Halftans Crevice, its energy no doubt fading by the day.

Nobody we spoke to knew anything of Rubine stones, or Zaphite for that matter. I began to feel like I would wander this city for the rest of the annum until eventually I would collapse in a dirty alleyway and fade away, my stone never to be found. I dreamt of it sometimes. I dreamt I was running the streets and snickleways of the city, red glints of light leading me onwards but always in the distance and always out of reach. I would wake suddenly, breathless and afraid.

One afternoon after a particularly fruitless day of searching for information, Duckie and I were making our way across the city back to the Sprat and Skirmish. We turned down a dingy alley, our heads down as we walked in silence feeling frustrated and disheartened. The cool darkness was quite pleasant after the heat of the day but the smell of rotting waste and dank water filled my nose so I held my sleeve to my face as we walked.

I was thoughtful and distracted so it took me a moment to notice the noise that echoed between the damp walls, a quiet but repetitive whistle that seemed to come from above our heads.

I stopped and grabbed the back of Duckie's coat, pulling him to a halt as I held a finger to my lips and looked about me. The whistle sounded again and from somewhere ahead of us and was immediately answered from behind us. I spun around and backed towards Duckie feeling un-seen eyes watching us from the shadows.

As I peered into the darkness, a feeling of panic rising, a figure swooped down from above and landed deftly on the cobbles of the alley, a dark cloak obscuring the face. I stepped back in shock and stumbled against Duckie who had also jumped back in surprise.

The figure rose and a dirty, hard featured face looked up at me, eyes cold and hungry. The boy was only young, probably a few annums younger than myself and thin, as if he were half starved. I glanced over my shoulder to see a girl who had emerged from the shadows to block Duckie's way. She was also dirty faced and equally thin with a look of the boy as if they might be siblings, even twins.

I felt for my dagger but the lad already had his blade pointed right at me as he forced Duckie and me to back up against the wall of the alleyway.

"No need for that," the boy said as he saw me reach for my blade. My hand fell back to my side and he nodded. "We're 'ere to 'elp is all," he said casting a glance at his sister. "Can you believe this Belle?" he said. "Trying to 'elp out these nice Seekers and missy 'ere's after cutting my throat!"

"Seems a bit ungrateful to me Wade," replied the girl, a smirk on her thin face showing brown gappy teeth as she leaned close to Duckie with a leering grin. "Don't you want our 'elp?" she said sweetly and Duckie turned his face away from her with a grimace.

"What d'you want?" I said, glancing up and down the alley, hoping to see someone approaching through the darkness to help. The alleyway was empty.

"It's more what *you* want that's the point," Wade said slyly and his sister giggled before her laugh turned into a splutter and then a racking cough. She turned and spat a gobbet of blood onto the ground. I knew that sound. It was the sound of the Sphyx and despite our situation, I looked at the girl with pity as she wiped her mouth with the back of her hand.

"So," Wade went on, raising his eyebrows at me and then Duckie in turn. "Down to business." The boy stepped back and began to pace up and down, tossing his dagger in the air and catching it again nonchalantly. "My understanding is that *you*," he stopped, caught his dagger in mid-air and pointed the tip towards me. "*You* are looking for something. Something red and shiny I believe? If you get my drift," he sniggered.

Rubine, I thought. He knows where we can find Rubine.

"I might be," I said carefully. "What do you know?"

The boy laughed again. "More importantly, what'll you give me for what I know?" he said, rubbing his thumb and finger together. I shot a look at Duckie and he shrugged back.

"I have a few coins," he said, fumbling in his pockets. I also had a few in mine but I weighed up the situation as I eyed this pair of urchins suspiciously. We could hand over the coins we had in our pockets to these two and they could just flee down the alley and disappear into the crowds of the city. But on the other hand, we had absolutely nothing else to go on to find my birthstone. We weren't carrying all the money we had as Banters had said this wasn't wise, with pick pockets and thieves wandering the city. The rest of our coin was hidden beneath the floorboards in our room at the inn so I reasoned that we would only lose the coins we had. I made a snap decision and delved into my pockets, taking the coins Duckie handed over and pooling them in my palm.

The boy's face lit up and I heard an audible grumble from the girl's stomach when they saw the coins in my outstretched hand.

"Tell me what you know." I said, snatching my hand back when the boy reached for the coins.

"Coin first," he said coldly, not taking his keen eyes from my hand. I sighed, knowing I had little option. I handed over the coins and Wade handed them to his sister who quickly tipped them into a hidden purse beneath her clothes.

"Tell me!" I repeated desperately. Wade began walking away and I reached out to grab his cloak and pull him back but he skipped from my grasp.

"Snaptree Grove," he called over his shoulder. "North of the city. That's where you'll find your Rubine. But go now. Might'nt be there much longer!" The two of them slipped away up the alleyway before clambering nimbly up the walls to the rooftops and disappearing from view.

Duckie and I looked at each other uncertainly. He shrugged again.

"It's all we've got," he said quietly.

The two of us hurried back to the Sprat and Skirmish, the boy's words ringing in my ears. "Go now, mightn't be there much longer." The urgency weighed upon me as if it were a physical pressure in my chest.

"Please let this be it," I thought. "Please let this be my stone." Back at the inn I picked up my bow and arrows and Duckie tucked his sword into his belt. Banters gave us vague directions to Snaptree Grove, muttering words of warning as we left the inn. We hurried out of the city gates as the sun was dipping below the horizon, a smear of molten gold glowing over the hazy desert.

Banters had explained that Snaptree Grove was a few hours on foot outside the city. "It's no place for you though," he'd said worriedly. "Folk bigger and bolder than you have gone there and never been seen again! Witches some say, or Harpies. Something evil in them trees that you two don't want to be messing with." His words had frightened me but not surprised me. I had never expected any of this to be easy.

Duckie and I set out briskly in the twilight and kept the city to our backs as we walked in silence. At one point we were forced to circle a pack of Slinkferrals, crawling silently through the brush on our hands and knees, keeping downwind from the beasts. We startled a herd of wild ponies, sending them galloping off into the night, neighing and whinnying in a cloud of red dust.

The moon rose full and bright in the night sky and no wind stirred across our cheeks as we walked, the outline of the city fading behind us as we steadily covered the ground.

After a few hours Duckie spoke. "Look," he said simply, pointing ahead of us. In the distance was the silhouette of an outcrop of woodland, the treetops dark against the deep blue of the night sky. There were hundreds of tiny lights flickering around the trees; glowbugs or fire faeries that scattered as we approached. The trees were stooped and dense with many fine, delicate branches that seemed to hug the broad trunks or wrap around one another in an intricate web of bark and leaves.

"This must be it," said Duckie as we stood at the tree line. I nodded.

"S'pose so." I said in agreement, squinting my eyes to peer into the darkness of the trees. "Come on then."

As we made our way tentatively into the grove a strange sound echoed through the still evening air; a rapid, slightly wet 'snap snap' sound that seemed to come from one side of us, then the other.

We followed a narrow path deeper into the trees, the fine branches stretching and crisscrossing above our heads. 'Snap snap' went the strange sound again and I touched Duckie's shoulder gently.

"What is that?" I whispered, tilting my head on one side to listen. Duckie shrugged and opened his mouth to say something. Before he could speak I saw a dark flash whipping through the gloom behind him and I quickly grabbed his collar and dragged him to his knees.

"Get down!" I cried out and Duckie and I dropped to the floor as a branch flew across the top of our heads with that sharp snapping sound. "What the…" I began but didn't finish as Duckie looked behind me and yelled "Jump! Fen, jump!"

Without turning to look I jumped up as another branch shot in a swift slash beneath our feet. As it flew beneath my boots I caught sight of a bud-like appendage on the end of the branch, a slash of crimson along its centre.

"They're teeth!" I said suddenly. "The branches have teeth!" More branches were now looping towards us from the surrounding trees, bending back like snakes in readiness to strike. The red mouths set in the buds at the end of each branch were lined with tiny but sharp looking teeth, grinning white in the gloom. The silky sound of the branches flying through the air was all around us as Duckie and I began to run through the undergrowth. The toothy mouths snapped at our legs and faces and we jumped, ducked and dodged our way through the woods. I felt sharp bites as an occasional snap caught me on the face or snagged at my hair but I ignored them and carried on running. I saw one branch shoot out from the gloom and swipe at Duckie's arm and he cried out in pain, grabbing at the wound as he ran. "Keep going!" Duckie yelled breathlessly, "There's a clearing ahead."

A set of teeth flew at my face, gnashing hungrily and I dodged them quickly, but lost my balance, stumbling to the ground. I could see the gleaming teeth bearing down on me so as I hit the ground, I crouched and rolled forward into a clearing, landing flat on my back. I heard Duckie drop to his knees at my side panting heavily and I sat up quickly, backing further into the safety of the clearing. At the edge of the forest the deadly branches were still seething in the darkness, turning and looping through the air, snapping in frustration that they could no longer get to us.

"So that's why they call it Snaptree Grove," I said wryly as I laid back on the floor of the clearing to catch my breath, closing my eyes.

A moment later, my eyes snapped open.

"Thought you'd come," said a voice from directly over my head and I found myself looking at the tip of a sword. At the end of the sword was a young man, dirty faced and thin with a scar running through one eyebrow.

"You Seekers are all so predictable," the boy said contemptuously as he prodded my nose with the point of his sword. He stood back and I felt arms grab me under my arms and hoist me to my feet. Circling us in the clearing were three motley looking boys, young but hard faced and dirty, with cunning, hungry faces. As I turned to see who had lifted me to my feet I let out a groan of despair. It was the boy, Wade. The boy who had taken our money in the alley and led us here with the promise of finding Rubine only to find ourselves ambushed. Duckie had recognized him too.

"You!" he said accusingly. "You said…" Wade let out a loud laugh and punched Duckie suddenly in the stomach.

"I say a lot of things, Seeker!" he hooted as Duckie doubled over, the breath knocked from his lungs. "Doesn't mean them's true or that fools like you should listen to 'em, does it Arvid?!"

The other boy with the sword, Arvid, laughed along.

"S'right," he said, prodding me again with the tip of his sword. "We make a good bit of coin off stupid Seekers like you who'll follow any old rogue's tale, off into the wilderness looking for your precious stones."

I looked at him in disgust. "And what about you?" I said. "You must be, what, fourteen annums? Fifteen? I think you'll find those stones to be quite precious too before long." The boy shot me a smile but there was no humor in it and his eyes were cold.

"The likes of us mightn't have to worry about such things," he said bitterly. "Most of us're not likely to see our seventeenth annum." He walked towards me and held the sharp blade of his sword against my cheek.

"You seen the shanty town outside the city? You walked those alleys? You ever been in the sewers beneath the ramparts and seen the people living there, rotting in their own filth?" I swallowed hard and looked away. "Thought not. You know nothing." He stood back and leaned on the hilt of his sword.

"So, I'll tell you what's to happen now," he said brightly. "The two of you will hand over those nice weapons to Grot here, you'll give us the key to your rooms and tell us which inn you've been stopping at." He nodded at the boy named Grot who stifled a maniacal giggle with a dirty fist. "And then," the boy went on, "We'll be forced to tie you up 'n leave you 'ere I'm afraid." He feigned a look of sadness. "We'll prop you up near the Snaptrees." Arvid gestured to the slithering snapping branches in the woods. "Don't like to dirty my blade if it can be helped." His voice was brisk and he spun on his heel, gesturing to Grot to step forward and take our weapons.

We were outnumbered and I knew that Arvid spoke the truth. It was clear that he had lived a hard life without empathy, without compassion and he was not about to show any to us. I doubted he even knew what pity was. I wondered if this was the end of everything for Duckie and me. As I despondently reached up to loop the bow from around my back I noticed that the boy named Grot suddenly paled, his eyes widening in surprise. Before I could turn to see what had alarmed him, a dark hooded figure leapt from the shadows of the forest and hurled itself at Arvid. He was knocked across the clearing, his sword clattering to the floor and a loud 'whoomph' escaping from his lips. Wade pulled out his knife and spun towards the hooded figure whom by now had leapt to his feet. The stranger aimed a swift kick at Wade's gut which sent him sprawling across the clearing. Grot stood there dumbly, watching the mayhem in disbelief until Duckie managed to slip behind him and crack him soundly on the head with the hilt of his sword. Grot swooned unconscious to the floor.

Arvid had recovered himself and his sword and was facing the hooded figure now, weapon held out and a snarl on his face. The two circled each other before Arvid made a move and their swords clashed and sparked together as they fought. Wade got to his feet and approached me with his dagger held before him, eyes flashing with malevolence. I stepped back slowly, not daring to reach for my own weapon, hearing the shwip shwip sound of the branches of the Snaptrees behind me. As Wade drew closer, he suddenly stumbled and fell forward, his weight carrying him towards me. I side stepped out of his path to avoid his blade, turning to see him fall headlong into the branches at the edge of the clearing. In a moment, the hungry Snaptrees were upon him, a tangle of branches and teeth nipping and biting at his clothes and flesh. He screamed and covered his face but there were too many branches clamoring over him and I had to look away.

On the other side of the clearing, the fight was over. The hooded man had brought Arvid to his knees and was standing over him wordlessly, sword pointed at his chest. The figure was breathing heavily as he turned to face us.

"Told you we'd meet again Fen," a familiar voice said. The dark figure reached up and pushed back the hood revealing soft brown hair, a flirtatious smile and dark twinkling eyes. Galant.

CHAPTER 18

After the night in Snaptree Grove, Duckie was forced to acknowledge that we wouldn't have escaped without Galant and over the days that passed, he seemed to put his resentment from the arena behind him.

Time went quickly and I began to feel a building sense of urgency as each day slipped into night and we still had no idea where we should start looking for my stone. I knew Duckie felt it too but he refused to leave until we had some clue about where to find Rubine. Galant was planning to return home as soon as he could but was reluctant to travel alone, knowing the dangers that awaited in the wilds of Immentia. Duckie and I had told him that we would soon be heading to Wistmans Hollow and Galant asked if he could accompany us before continuing on alone back to his home in Bleakchill Cove. We knew there was safety in numbers and, as we'd learned in Snaptree Grove, Galant's skill at fighting would make him a useful ally on the dangerous journey.

Having spent another few fruitless days combing the bookshops and stopping travelers as they came through the main gates, I eventually persuaded Duckie that we had to leave the city. We had spent too long in Andorta and the Zaphite stone at Halftans Crevice could be fading by the day. Duckie had argued with me at first but had finally given in, my determination once again winning out. The night before we were set to move on, I left Duckie at the Sprat and Skirmish and walked slowly through the darkening streets to the bazaar. I wanted to be alone to take a last walk through this city that had been home to me for a while.

When I reached the bazaar, I wandered amongst the market stalls and street performers for a while before I came across a small group of people queuing in the street next to a tent that had been erected in one corner of the square. The red tent was draped with thick velvet curtains at the front and a small placard hung above the opening. As I drew closer, I could make out the inscription; "Althena, the Great Augur of Dracae".

I drew closer still and stood next to a portly man who was waiting patiently at the end of the queue. "What is this?" I asked him, nodding at the mysterious tent.

The man looked at me in surprise. "You've never heard of Althena?" he asked me, raising an eyebrow.

I shook my head in response. "Who is she? What's an Augur?" I asked. The man leaned closer to me as he spoke. "Althena is the most famous fortune teller in all of Immentia – you want to know what your future holds? Althena will tell you better'n anyone. You have a question about where fate will lead you? Althena will answer it."

I looked at the man, impressed. "How much is it?" I asked as someone emerged from the tent and the line shuffled along a little. "It's a farthing," the man answered, "But it's worth it." I felt around in the pocket of my breeches and felt the single farthing that I had brought with me, round and cold in my warm hand. There were better things I could spend my money on but I was intrigued by the tent, the mysterious Althena and the musky aroma of incense wafting from between the curtains.

I dawdled there in the queue, fingers clasped tight around the farthing in my pocket and eventually the man in front of me stepped forward and disappeared behind the curtain. He was in the tent for ten minutes or so and when he came out he shot a wink at me, his face happy but secretive.

"Best augur in all Immentia, young'un," he said to me. "Just like I told you!"

He hurried off across the square without looking back and I ventured slowly towards the heavy velvet curtains. I pulled one back and ducked my head as I stepped into the tent. Inside it was dark except for the light from lanterns of red and orange coloured glass giving off an atmospheric glow. In the middle of the tent was a circular table where a woman sat, draped in a midnight blue robe, an orange shawl wrapped around her head and shoulders, obscuring her face.

On the table sat a glass orb with a candle beneath it, a strange blue flame burning steadily. I entered nervously, letting the curtain fall closed behind me, muffling the din of the busy square outside. The woman at the table turned her head slightly before she spoke, her face still shrouded in the shadows of her shawl. "Come, come, sit," she intoned in a soft creaky voice as I approached the table. I sat down stiffly on the stool opposite her and pushed my farthing across the table. A gnarled hand emerged from the folds of her robe and drew the farthing beneath the table and into a coin purse, landing with a chink.

The woman turned her face towards me and I could see that she was very old, her face brown and wrinkled with drooping lids over black eyes, her eyebrows grey and bushy. "I am The Great Althena," she said, gesturing grandly. I looked at her blankly. She peered at me from beneath her hood. "You'll have heard of me?" she said questioningly. I shook my head. "The Great Althena of Dracae?" she went on, sounding a little indignant and momentarily forgetting the somber, creaky voice. "The greatest Augur in all of Immentia?" I shrugged apologetically. "Never mind, never mind," she said, scowling, "Most people have heard of me you know, but no matter," she chuntered, irritated before she recovered herself and continued on in her dramatic tones.

"What brings you here child?" she asked, laying her wizened hands flat on the table. "What is it you want to know?" Before I could answer she stiffened and her head jolted up as she raised a hand abruptly. "Wait," she said sharply, "I can see it in your aura. I can feel it. I know what you're here for." I watched her curiously as she dropped her head again and waved her hands slowly through the air in front of me, moaning softly. She lowered her hands to the glass ball and hunched over it, the blue flame casting an unnatural glow over her face. "No," she said eventually. "The crystal has nothing for you today. It's the cards, it must be the cards." She reached into the folds of her robe once more and brought out a stack of cards that she deftly shuffled from one hand to the other, the cards flitting through the air between her palms in a blur.

Eventually she stopped and held the cards close to her chest before raising her dark eyes to me. "I know what it is you seek," she said quietly. "The cards know what you seek and they have a message for you."

I finally found my tongue and began to speak. "I....I'm looking for..." I began but the old crone raised her hand suddenly again and hushed me. "No," she said. "No need to speak. Let the cards do their work." I fell silent as she began to lay the cards out in front of her on the table. One, two, three, four cards were laid out face down and when she was finished she sat back muttering to herself before taking a deep breath.

The woman raised her black eyes to me again. "Pick a card," she said gesturing at the four laid out in front of me. "Pick a card and it will speak the only truth you need to know." I looked down at the cards, the reverse of each identically decorated in a blue swirling pattern. "Erm... this one?" I answered uncertainly, pointing at one of the cards. The woman reached out and turned the third card over laying it face up on the table. The card was painted with a peculiar face; large eyes which appeared to be closed, a bulbous nose and a large frowning mouth. As I leaned over to look at it more closely, the eyes of the face suddenly snapped open and the mouth began to move, opening in a large yawn. I jumped back from the table in surprise as the card began to speak.

"Ahhhhh," it said in a high-pitched voice, its eyes flickering around the tent before they settled on me. "Another Seeker is it? So many of you, so many, all looking for those stones." The cards mouth opened, wide and black and it let out a maniacal laugh. "I know where yours is, so I do!" it went on. "No good to me but so precious to you Seeker – so precious!" The painted eyebrows danced up and down as the card spoke but I just stared dumbly at it, shocked. I wondered what kind of dark arts were at work in this tent with the Great Althena, Augur of Dracae.

"So then," the old woman said shortly to the card. "Don't make her wait, we haven't got all day; what is it she needs to know?"

The face on the card cackled once more. "Oh this one, she's after Rubine you see. Oh yes, lovely Rubine all red and shiny and I know where it is! I know where it is!"

The woman tutted and glanced up at me. "The cards can be a little temperamental you know," she said to me apologetically. "Pick another one; let's see what else they have to say."

I looked down at the upturned card whose painted face was now pouting a little, its eyes darting left and right at the other cards on either side. "Don't bother asking them," it said petulantly, "I'm the only one who really knows, the *only* one!"

The card cackled again as I looked down at the other cards. "Um… I'll choose this one" I said. The woman reached out her claw like hand once more and turned the second card over. This one had the face of a woman painted on it, long dark lashes surrounded the eyes and the lips were plump and red.

This card was silent a moment before it slowly opened its eyes and spoke lazily. "What now?" it asked, blinking sleepily. "Can't I get a moments peace?" Its blue eyes settled on me and narrowed. "Let's make this quick," it said. "Rubine is it? I happen to know of it…" The eyes roamed the room again and the red mouth puckered as if the card was thinking. "I'm not getting a name…" it mused, "No name but I can see caverns and tunnels…. There's Rubine in those caverns…Only the dead will know. Only the dead."

The first cards eyes were wide and it stared hard to its left as it listened.

"Don't listen to her," it said conspiratorially, turning its gaze back on me. "She's a dimwit! You look for the water, the great wide mouth and the flowing water and you'll find your Rubine." The second card narrowed its blue eyes again, ignoring the twittering of the card to its left. "Wait. There's something else... I see a graveyard... so many graves... Yes graves of the dead and I think..."

The card was abruptly cut off again by the other. "Graves? Pah – there's no Rubine there. I'm telling you, look for the flowing waters, look for the river's mouth!" My eyes darted from one card to the other, hardly making out what each one was saying as they bickered, speaking over one another. "River?" I asked urgently, "What river? Where is it? What about the graves? How will I find these caverns?"

The cards seemed to have forgotten me now and were busily trading insults with each other. The face with the bulbous nose was poking its tongue out at the other card, the gesture returned by a flurry of curses from between red lips.

I looked up at the old woman Althena. "What do they mean?" I asked, frustrated. "Can't they tell me exactly where I should look?"

The woman shrugged at me and sniffed. "I can only let you choose the cards. Not up to me what they say or don't say. You will have to make of it what you will." The sound of the cards had now become a cacophony of noise and the old woman slapped a hand over both their mouths. Their voices continued as a muffled hum from beneath her palms, four angry eyes looking this way and that, eyebrows bobbing.

Althena took a deep breath and quickly turned the cards over, silencing them. "That's all for today," she said quietly and with that, she gestured me out of the tent. I looked down at the cards again but they were quiet. "But..." I began to speak and Althena silenced me with a raised hand, dropping her hooded head and waving me away. Reluctantly I rose from the stool and pushed my way through the curtains and back out onto the street, my head spinning and thoughts racing.

I stood out in the bustle of the bazaar as people milled around me. Caverns and graves? I thought to myself. The river's mouth? I didn't know the meaning of the clues the cards had given me but at least I had something. I began to walk back across the square, dazed and deep in thought, when a warm voice whispered in my ear. "Going my way beautiful?" I jumped and looked over my shoulder to see Galant standing close behind me. I brought a hand to my chest and let out a laugh. "You scared me!" I said, punching Galant lightly on the arm. He feigned pain as he clutched his arm and laughed easily along with me as we turned and continued strolling across the square.

"What are you doing wandering around town tonight?" Galant asked as we walked. "I thought you'd be back at the Sprat getting ready for tomorrow." I shrugged. "I felt like seeing the city one last time before we leave," I answered. He stopped walking and looked at me questioningly, an eyebrow raised and I felt a buzz of excitement bubbling up inside me.

"I have some news," I said excitedly, turning towards Galant to look him in the face. I had wanted to tell Duckie first but I couldn't contain myself. I told Galant everything that had just happened; the tent, Althena and the cryptic messages from the speaking tarot cards; the graves, the caverns and the river. I could see the excitement on Galant's face mirroring my own and I was touched at how genuinely pleased he seemed to be that I finally had some news.

When I was finished, Galant took both my hands tightly and I didn't pull away. "I can't believe it Fen," he said with a beaming smile. "You finally have some clues at last. A little mysterious but I am sure we can fathom out what they mean." Galant thought for a moment. "Did you tell this Althena where we were going?" he asked and I shook my head. "Hmmm. I can barely even hope this could be true...." He paused for a moment. "Remind me where we are heading tomorrow. For Duckie's birthstone."

I looked up at him frowning. "Halftans Crevice," I replied. "That's what the note says."

"And exactly where is this Halftans Crevice?" Galant asked, a peculiar look on his face.

"It's south east of here, near Wistmans Hollow." I still didn't understand what Galant was trying to say but he looked at me expectantly, eyebrows raised, half smiling. "Wistmans Hollow..." I repeated slowly. "The graves... The graves could mean Wistmans Hollow!"

"The stories say it has one of the biggest graveyards in all of Immentia!" Galant added and I felt another surge of excitement flood through me. I could barely resist jumping up and down as we stood there, hands still clasped. "Come on," Galant said, dragging me by the hand as we clattered off down the dark street towards the Sprat and Skirmish, "Time for a celebration!"

CHAPTER 19

Galant and I arrived back at the Sprat and Skirmish brimming with excitement as I babbled my news to Duckie, telling him everything that had happened with the mysterious talking cards. Galant seemed almost as happy as I was that I finally had somewhere to look for my stone and I began to realize that I really had found a true friend in him. Although he was only accompanying us on the journey, he was genuinely thrilled that Duckie and I both had an inkling of hope that we might find what we were looking for and get home in time.

The three of us drank ale that night with Banters and the other locals who frequented the inn. Even Gwil stopped by in his beggars' rags to say goodbye. During my weeks in Andorta we had developed something of a friendship, sharing a few moments of casual chatter when I passed him in the streets or came across him in some tavern or other. Duckie's friend Dandy showed up and spent the evening dancing with him and playing her tambourine as the rest of the inn sang songs and danced drunkenly as we celebrated our last night in the city.

It was during one of Dandy's performances that I slipped out of the backdoor of the tavern to get some air. I felt a little heady from the ale and needed to escape the stuffy warmth of the taproom. I emerged into the yard behind the inn and sat on the stone steps leading up to the ramparts on the wall above, the night air warm on my bare skin. I was wearing the green robe that Duckie had bought for me when I had first arrived and I still relished the cool silk, thinking of the next day when I would have to put back on my stiff breeches and travelling coat. The light from the leaded windows of the inn glowed and the muffled merriment sounded from within, the music and chatter. The stars twinkled above me and I enjoyed a few moments of solitary silence.

I had only been there a few minutes when the back door of the inn opened and a tall figure emerged. "Hello beautiful." I recognized Galant's familiar careless compliment as he sauntered over to me and I smiled as he approached and held out his hand. "How about a walk on the walls?" he asked me invitingly, his dark eyes blacker than ever in the dim light. I stood and brushed off my robes, ignoring his outstretched hand. "Alright," I replied before turning and walking up the steep stone steps. I went up a little way and looked back when I realized he wasn't following me. When I turned, his face was tilted up towards me, his expression gentle and eyes hazy with a look that I hadn't seen before. "Come on then!" I said impatiently, waving at Galant to follow as I turned and continued climbing the uneven steps. Galant let out a husky laugh as he climbed the steps behind me.

When we reached the ramparts of the walls, I peered around to see if there were any guards nearby. "Come on," I whispered as we emerged out onto the wall and I walked across to lean against the battlement, facing out across the plains. Galant leant next to me, the length of his bare forearm touching mine. In the distance were the mountains where I had fallen the day I had made my journey to the city. I scanned my eyes south, where the mountain range stretched into the distant horizon, just a faint murky outline in the darkness. This was the direction we would take the next day as we began the long journey to Wistmans Hollow.

After a long moment Galant spoke. "Are you ready little Fen?" he asked me quietly. "Are you ready to cross those mountains again and see where fate leads you?" His voice was almost hypnotic and it seemed to hold the promise of adventure and the promise of finding everything we were looking for, our birthstones and more. I wondered again why his close presence didn't prickle my skin like the touch of others often did. I looked up at the stars as I considered his question. Eventually, I turned my head to him and replied. "I am ready. I want to find Duckie's stone, I want to find mine and I want us all to make it home safely. And I think we will." Our faces were close and I looked him unflinchingly in the eyes as I spoke.

"I'm glad I'm coming with you," Galant said, meeting my gaze, his voice soft and our faces so close that I could feel his warm breath brushing across my skin. I felt no urge to pull away, no urge to distance myself. "I want the same things as you Fen," he said. I watched his mouth as he spoke and I forgot myself as he slowly moved his face towards mine. My lips were tingling before he even touched me and as our mouths met gently, warmly, my eyelids closed. I didn't think about anything. I just let Galant kiss me.

After a long moment, Galant pulled gently away from me and I slowly opened my eyes. "Come on," he said straightening, breaking the silence. "They'll be wondering where we've got to." Without another word, he took my hand and pulled me away from the ramparts and back down the steps.

We bundled back through the door of the inn and found that the merriment had continued in our absence. Duckie was dancing with Dandy but he noticed us as we entered and dragged Dandy over, struggling through the lively throng. My face felt flushed and I quickly dropped Galant's hand self-consciously. Galant shot me a hurt look and Duckie eyed us both suspiciously. "Where've you two been?" he asked, keeping his tone light but I heard the note of irritation in his voice. I felt myself blush and looked across the room, not wanting to meet Duckie's eyes. "Nowhere," I answered, flustered. "Just outside. Talking." My head was spinning and my lips still felt hot. I could feel Galant's eyes on me but I refused to meet his gaze, unsure of what had just happened between us. Duckie nodded curtly, still eyeing us suspiciously but he allowed Dandy to pull him back over to our table where Galant and I joined them, a slight tension hanging in the air.

It was true that Galant had grown on me since our first meeting that day after Duckie's fight in the arena. He had seemed a brute to me at first but I had since found that he was friendly and kind and seemed to genuinely care about Duckie and me and the quest we still had to take. I had noticed how the girls around the city would giggle in his presence and flick their hair, looking up at him from beneath their lashes but I had observed this with indifference. As we sat in the inn, Dandy giggling and prattling, thankfully filling the silence, I wondered how Galant and I had gone from animosity to friendship and then to whatever we had become moments ago on this moonlit night on the walls high above the city.

For the rest of the evening the four of us sat together and drank ale, discussing the journey ahead of us. We raised a toast with Banters and the others as they wished us well and as the inn finally began to empty, I said goodnight and went up to bed. Galant offered to walk me to our room but I responded with a stiff laugh and said I could manage perfectly well on my own, not quite meeting his eyes. I climbed the stairs and shrugged off my green silk robe, folding it carefully and placing it in my pack. I pulled on my undershirt and perched on the bed gazing out into the night sky.

As I sat there, I realized what I was feeling. Guilt. I felt guilty that I was sharing kisses under the stars like some village slut with the first boy who had ever paid me any attention. Knowing all the while that Pa and Leif were at home in Millings Beck, thinking of me, frightened for me. Knowing that Pa would be standing at the window night after night, mint leaf tea in hand.

Knowing that Leif would be alone in our loft, tossing in his sleep, haunted by nightmares of birthstones and monsters. And the other thing I knew without a doubt was that I couldn't be distracted, couldn't have my head turned from my task. Because Duckie and I still had the fight of our lives ahead of us.

CHAPTER 20

Bang bang bang! The noise startled me awake on the narrow bed in Duckie's room. I sat up and realized the sun had not yet come up as the heavy knocking continued on our door. Duckie jumped up from his bed on the floor and went to the door, opening it a crack. "Come on you two," I heard Galant's voice, his tone hushed but urgent. "Are you ready to go?" I saw Duckie sleepily rub his eyes as he murmured a few quiet words to Galant before closing the door again.

"What was all that about?" I asked Duckie as he turned back into the room and began pulling on his clothes.

"Just Galant, eager to be off I suppose." Duckie answered me with a yawn. "Might as well get up now," he added, scratching his mussed hair. I shrugged and stood up from the bed, stretching.

As Duckie and I collected ourselves and started gathering our things, Galant knocked again and poked his head around the door. "We need to leave now," he said, almost frantic. "We need to make it to the mountains before nightfall, don't want to be out on the plains in the dark."

I turned to him and pushed my tangled hair from my face. "Alright!" I said irritably, forgetting the events of the night before as the prospect of our imminent journey loomed over me. "We're coming!"

Duckie and I got ready hurriedly and the three of us made our way downstairs. The inn was silent and not even Banters was up when we eventually emerged onto the quiet city street. I was dressed in my Pa's breeches once again with my heavy travelling coat, bow on my back and Queenfisher feathers glinting in my sheath. Galant had on a leather cape, waxed to waterproof it from the elements and on his hands he wore gloves made of delicate scales of metal, a shining cuff around each wrist. Duckie chuntered as we walked but as we emerged out of the city gates and onto the plains, the sun peeped out to light the sky, colours tumbling over the horizon in a cauldron of orange and red.

We left the road and trudged south across the dusty plains away from the city towards the mountains, further south than the pass we had used to travel from Haggs Catton. Duckie had carefully and sneakily copied a map from one of the bookshops in Andorta and we had a good idea of the route towards Wistmans Hollow and hopefully Halftans Crevice. Duckie had guessed that it could be many long days before we made it to Wistmans Hollow. A much longer journey than the trip from Millings Beck to Andorta but we had full coin purses, food in our packs and our weapons were in good order.

We walked in silence as the sun rose slowly in the sky, approaching the foothills where we would be able to make our way higher into the mountains. We had to take a large looping path around a pack of Slinkferrals that were lying in the dust, most of them sleeping as a couple stood guard sniffing the wind. They eyed us hungrily as we circled them but didn't seem inclined to attack although we trod warily, our weapons ready, keeping one eye on the beasts. We passed a few herds of wild horses and a couple of isolated vineyards as the desert plains began to creep up into the hills, the dusty red earth giving way to sparse grassy knolls and the odd cluster of trees. The air around us began to cool and I breathed deeply, enjoying the fresh sweetness after weeks in the cloying humidity of the city.

Around midday we stopped to rest and ate a few pieces of bread and meat from our packs as Duckie pulled out his map to check our position.

"See here," Duckie said, pointing as he chewed on a bit of bread. "We'll be crossing the mountains here, then we'll drop down into this forest," he gestured to a wide green area marked out. "We'll need to cross the swamp before we come to this moorland." Galant and I huddled over Duckie as he pointed out the route on his roughly drawn map. "And here, we should meet a road that leads south across the river. There's no villages marked between the swamp and Wistmans Hollow so we'll have to spend a few nights sleeping rough unless we find a farmhouse or a traveler's tavern." He looked up at us both as he spoke. "Course, we don't know where Halftans Crevice is on the map so when we get closer to Wistmans Hollow we'll have to keep a look out and ask after it if we come across anyone." He shrugged. "Same goes for you Fen. These caverns of yours could be anywhere round and about the Hollow so we'll just have to hope someone will've heard of them." I nodded as I munched on an apple, knowing that much of what we still had to achieve would depend on a great deal of luck.

"Let's keep moving," Galant said, casting a glance back towards the city. "The sooner we can get into the mountains the better. We can find some cover for the night; don't want to be out on the plains when it gets dark." He gestured back towards the desert beneath the hillside where we sat and I noticed that the pack of Slinkferrals had followed us and were now lurking about a half mile away, pacing menacingly in the dust. None of us spoke of the lingering danger as we walked on through the foothills, climbing higher up from the warmth of the plains. I turned and looked back a couple of times at the walls of Andorta fading into the distance and felt very aware of how vulnerable we were once again, having left the safety of the city.

Galant and I didn't speak of the night before. Now that we were back on the road again and I was in my old clothes, it felt to me as if the lingering kiss had happened to someone else, a long time ago. A pretty girl with auburn hair and a green silk gown, a girl I didn't know. But as we walked I could feel Galant's eyes on me. He would touch me in small and seemingly casual ways; placing a hand on my back as we climbed a steep bluff, reach out to pull me by the hand over a large boulder. When a fox leapt unexpectedly from a cluster of dense brush, he put his arm out protectively and pushed me back. Despite myself, I liked the way he was with me. I found myself clasping his outstretched hand when it was offered, I felt myself lingering too long when his arm rested across me. I couldn't explain why I didn't pull away from him. I didn't even want to question it.

The sun dropped low in the sky and the city had long disappeared behind us. We climbed higher into the hills and as the light dimmed, we found ourselves walking through copses of pine trees and grassy clearings. Ahead of us the mountains rose into the sky, the steep sides coated with trees and the tops smothered in snow and wisps of cloud. The temperature dropped cold and I pulled my thick leather coat around me, not missing the green silk of my Andorta robes one bit as the chilly evening air nipped at my skin. The pine trees grew denser as we walked, patches of snow gathering in small drifts against fallen logs and the bases of the tree trunks.

We stopped for the night as the light began to fade. Galant and I gathered wood for a fire as Duckie pulled a few hunks of uncooked rabbit from his pack, skewering the chunks of meat on sticks. We lit the fire and sat huddled in its warmth as we roasted the meat and nibbled in silence, the night air still and quiet. No wind creaked through the boughs of the trees and the creatures of the day had long since scurried to the safety of their nests and burrows. In the distance, I heard a long mournful wail floating across the mountains and through the pines. Duckie and Galant heard it too and stopped chewing, tilting their heads, eyes alert.

"Just a Shadewalker," I murmured, gazing up into the trees as I listened. Galant and Duckie accepted this without question, both knowing the tale of my strange but peaceful encounter with the mysterious forest dwellers.

When we had finished eating I volunteered to take the first watch as the others slept. Galant argued with me at first but I insisted and he didn't press me as the two of them huddled down close to the fire, heads resting on their packs as they fell asleep. I sat there staring into the flames, my knees pulled up to my chin, listening to the Shadewalkers calling to each other far away in the darkness. After a few hours, I nudged Duckie awake and he rose without a word to take my place, hunched next to the fading embers. I lay down in the warm patch where Duckie had been, wrapped my coat around me and slept.

CHAPTER 21

The spider crawled from its hole in the corner of the stone tower, the lanterns in the circular room reflecting off its many black orbish eyes. It tentatively extended its two front legs, spindly and delicate, the fine hairs feeling the air. It sensed humans in the room but this was not unusual and it knew it had little to fear from the large upright creatures that shared its home. As long as it was quiet, so quiet, and moved slowly in the shadows. The spider emerged fully from the hole resting all eight legs on the stone floor, hugging its black body tightly against the wall as it slowly made its way around the edge of the room.

"Decima," the Amir said soothingly to his wife as she stood staring out of the window, arms folded. "We will get them back, we know who has them and where they are going. We will get the relics back."

Decima turned abruptly to her husband, her eyes flashing angrily and the tendons of her neck taut. "Get them back?" she spat, "They should have been in our possession by now! We are wasting more and more time!" The Amir shrank away from her a little before placing a hand on each of her arms, trying to calm her. "Those fools couldn't spot a drab in the feather quarter," Decima hissed. "Yet you trust them with this? We had everything we ever wanted within the city walls and those idiots allowed the relics to be stolen from under their noses!"

"I know this," the Amir said sharply. "I had one of Oberon's men killed today in the arena and the others were made to watch. They will know not to cross us again. There is no room for any more mistakes."

The woman turned back to the window. "And how do you suppose we get the relics back? Who has them?"

The Amir began to pace slowly around the circular room and the spider shrunk back further into the shadows as he passed.

"I had the head of my guard question the innkeeper," the Amir said. "There was only one other guest in the tavern that night and we have a name, and a description."

Decima gave a disgusted snort. "A name?" she asked. "A description? How useful," her voice was heavy with sarcasm.

The Amir glanced up at her and scowled. "Not only that, we know exactly where our thief has gone. They left the city only a matter of days ago. We have this on good authority and I don't doubt Oberon's commitment to correcting his mistake."

A cruel smile spread across the woman's face as the Amir spoke. "I imagine a few hours in the dungeons have strengthened his commitment," she said and let out a bitter laugh. "Did they remove his fingernails as I requested?" The Amir nodded. "All of them?" she pressed.

He nodded again. "His men are on the road now as we speak. We doubt the thief even realizes the power of what they have stolen. They *will* be found and the relics will be returned to us."

The woman walked slowly to a cage hanging in the centre of the room, a small black figure hunched within. By now the spider had made its way halfway around the edge of the room but froze, one leg poised above the stony floor as it saw the creature in the cage unfurl itself from its crouched position. It was a Grimhellion. The creature raised its head, exposing a flat face with small razor-sharp teeth protruding between thin black lips. Large nostrils were positioned above its mouth, malevolent red eyes slanting at either side. Its ears were large flaps of leathery black skin, pricking up and twitching as Decima approached. On each shoulder hung wings, bony and webbed with a set of sharp claws at the end of each. Its tail was long with a forked tip and the appendage swung slowly and deliberately from side to side, like the tail of a cat ready to pounce.

The woman crooned softly as she opened the cage door, allowing the creature to shuffle onto her wrist, its clawed feet gripped tightly. "We were so near," she sang softly to the creature. "So near my sweet, but yet again I must take matters into my own hands." The woman drew the Grimhellion from the cage and walked back to the window. The creature flexed its wings and yawned as its small black mouth opened wide, the sharp teeth glinting.

"We have much to do my pretty one," the woman murmured softly as the man watched her silently. "Much to do, and we need your help." The Grimhellion observed her, its red eyes blinking slowly as she spoke. The woman leaned close to the creature and began to whisper. The spider could see her lips moving, hearing no sound but the Grimhellion cocked its head as it listened carefully to the murmured words.

Decima gently stroked her finger along the creatures back before holding her arm up to the open window. "Now fly," she said softly. "Fly and do as I ask." The Grimhellion extended its leathery wings, whipped its tail and flew from her outstretched arm, circling the room before it swooped out through the open window and into the night.

Decima turned back to her husband, a satisfied smile on her white face.

"The hellion won't let us down. If I don't have those relics in my hands by the first of Snows Bite then I swear to you I will go out and get them myself," her voice was venomous. "Ariad will pass her eighteenth annum and after that," she laughed and the harsh sound prickled the spider's senses. "After that, there will be nothing to stop us controlling every city, every village, every last miserable inhabitant of Immentia."

CHAPTER 22

Out in the woods, the cold morning light crept slowly across our little campsite. Shards of frost had settled on the needles of the pine trees and the sun's rays glittered amongst the branches. We rose quietly, our bodies stiff with cold and our breath misty in the chilly dawn air. We ate a meagre breakfast and walked on, leaving the forested hills beneath us as we climbed higher into the snowy peaks that would lead us across the mountains. The path became treacherously narrow as it wound steadily upwards and the going was hard, our feet slipping on the compacted ice as the sleet stung our skin. We climbed higher still and the sleet turned to a whirling blizzard of snow, the freezing winds whipping the breath from our lungs as we pulled our coats up over our faces.

We had been walking steadily for several hours and finally we made it to the top of a craggy peak, the forested valley just visible through the bitter whiteness. We made our way carefully through the snowy outcrop and back onto the narrow icy path on the other side of the peak. A vertical cliff dropped off to one side of the path and I knew that jagged rocks waited far beneath although they could not be seen in the whirling blizzard.

Galant led the way; his arms outstretched as he balanced against the side of the cliff and stepped carefully along the slippery path. The wind was howling around our ears and speech was impossible as our words were snatched from the air and lost in the flurry.

I walked, head down and eyes watering from the cold, watching my leather booted feet as I put one carefully in front of the other. I almost bumped into Duckie as I realized he and Galant had stopped ahead of me. When I looked up I saw Galant shout to Duckie and point into the sky, but I couldn't make out his words. I shielded my eyes from the snow and above us I could make out a black shape flying through the whiteout, a mere shadow against the hazy sky, wings flapping rapidly as it circled. I saw Duckie call something back to Galant and he shrugged and continued to make his way along the path, glancing up frequently as his eyes followed the black outline above. Eventually the precipitous path widened and we began to descend from the peak, still walking in single file as the snowstorm began to die down. The wind dropped enough for us to hear ourselves and Galant called over his shoulder.

"Did you see that?" he shouted. "That thing in the sky?"

"Must've been an eagle," Duckie called back. "Maybe a falcon?"

Galant didn't reply and I held my tongue. The thing we'd seen circling above us was not like any bird I had ever seen.

The path levelled out as we left the highest peaks behind us and we found ourselves crossing wide snow plains, smooth and immaculately perfect, no black furrows of footsteps marring the surface ahead of us. The wind was still blowing in freezing gusts, sending up clouds of powered snow that whirled across the surface of the snow plain. As we descended down through the mountains, pine trees began to spring up once again and the path wound from left to right in tightly angled bends, each one leading us lower into the shelter of the valley.

As darkness began to set in, exhaustion washed over me as I contemplated another night out in the freezing wilds and another meal of rationed meat or dried fruit. I was chilled to my bones, hadn't felt my hands or feet in hours and there were icicles hanging from the locks of hair falling over my face. I thought of Pa sitting by our warm fire in Millings Beck and for a moment, I could have dropped to my knees right there, curled into a ball and waited for the cold to take me. Just as a sob was beginning to well in my throat and I thought I couldn't take another step, I heard Duckie call out. "Oi!" he shouted, clapping a hand on Galant's back and pointing through the trees. "Over there!" He leant close and Galant followed Duckie's pointed finger into the darkening tree line. As I peered into the woods, my eyelashes frosted with icy crystals, I could see what Duckie was pointing at. Dim lights glowed through the trees and to our left, an obscure path led into the woods, its uneven stone surface barely visible beneath the snow.

We turned and made our way down the path and as we drew closer to the lights we came to a thatched building, a row of small windows along its side. A sign hung above the door and relief flooded through me as I realized we had stumbled across a traveler's inn. I concentrated on putting one numb foot in front of the other until we reached the door and I watched Galant struggle against the wind as he yanked it open. He held it as Duckie and I hurried inside and Galant quickly followed letting the heavy wooden door slam closed, a flurry of snow and gust of cold air chasing us into the room.

My ears were ringing from the cold wind and the frost immediately began to drip from my lashes as I looked around the inn. A large firepit burned in the middle of the long room and wooden tables and benches lined the walls, a rough wooden counter at the far end. The inn was empty except for a figure leaning behind the counter at and a lone patron perched on a stool, a mug in one hand. Galant walked towards the bar as two sets of eyes turned to stare at us. My hands were burning from the contrast in temperatures and I cupped them to my mouth, blowing on my freezing fingers as we crossed the room. I could smell the sweet, heavy aroma of cinnamon in the air and observed the pot of dark spiced wine bubbling over the fire.

Galant cleared his throat and laid both hands on the rough wooden expanse of the bar. The innkeeper was tall and thin, his eyes hard and face prickled with a few days of greying stubble. He mirrored Galant's stance as he loomed over him.

"What d'you want?" the man asked gruffly, raising an eyebrow.

Galant cleared his throat again and stood up a little straighter. "We just need somewhere to stay the night, some food if you have it?" His voice was strong and steady but I knew him well enough to know he was uncomfortable under the older man's intense glare.

"Hmph," the innkeeper said, standing back and crossing his arms as he cast his eyes across the three of us. "You got coin?" he asked meanly. "Costs a lot of coin to stay the night here y'know." We glanced at each other nervously. "Some's can't afford it," the man went on, staring down at Galant. "And if you're one of 'em then you can go right back out the door and spend the night in the woods for all I care."

Duckie started forward but Galant held his hand out behind him, gesturing him back. The other man at the bar rose to his feet and stood poised, eyes darting to the innkeeper and back to us.

Galant stepped forward, closer to the bar and drew himself up to his full height. He leaned his face towards to the innkeeper who didn't move and stared unflinchingly back. "Sir," Galant said through gritted teeth, "We have been on the mountains since first light; we are cold to our very bones. We just want a bed for the night and some food. I am in no mood to argue. We will gladly pay you a fair price but if you would prefer to barter with us then we will readily welcome it." As he spoke, Galant's hand moved slowly to the sword on his belt. Duckie echoed his movement and drew back his coat so the innkeeper would see the blade hanging at his waist. The innkeeper's eyes flickered across the two of them and he raised an eyebrow, lip curling. The other man at the bar took a step back and looked uncertainly at the innkeeper and back at us, as if measuring us up.

"No need for that," the man said grudgingly after a long tense silence, bending down and reaching beneath the bar. As he moved, Duckie and Galant stepped away, their hands again swiftly reaching for their swords. The innkeeper drew back and held up a glass, the other hand held up in a placating gesture. "Your money's as good as anyone's," the man continued, his tone suddenly conversational. "I'm sure we can come to an agreement gentlemen." Duckie and Galant relaxed as the innkeeper moved from around the bar to the firepit, ladling the spiced wine into mugs and handing the first one to me. "Who's your little lady friend?" the innkeeper asked, nodding at me as he handed mugs of wine to Galant and Duckie.

I threw the man a dirty look. "I'm no one's 'little lady'," I said disparagingly. "And I speak for myself." The man laughed heartily at that, clearly finding me amusing. I took a seat at one of the low benches and sipped the wine. It burned my lips but I relished the hot sting as the liquid slipped down my throat and the warmth emanated from my stomach. I clasped my cold hands around the mug and looked over its rim as I drank. The other man at the bar had returned to his seat and was staring at me with a gormless expression on his ruddy face. I stared right back and wondered if he was a little simple. Some hired muscle perhaps, here to help the innkeeper overcharge desperate travelers.

Duckie and Galant joined me at the table and after a few minutes the miserable innkeeper brought us bowls of thin tasteless stew and some dry bread, not speaking as he plonked the bowls in front of us. As innkeepers go, he appeared to be in the wrong job; hospitality was clearly not one his strong points. We spent an uncomfortable evening under the watchful and unwelcoming gaze of the two men. Eventually, we retired to a cold dank room where we settled on slatted bunks, huddling beneath stinking animal skins as the vicious snowstorm howled outside, battering against the windows.

Outside in the woods, a sinister black figure hunched on the branch of a pine tree, its red eyes fixed on the glowing light emanating from the leaded windows of the isolated inn. Its leathery wings were drawn up around its small hairy body as it shielded itself from the cutting wind and watched carefully, late into the night until all the lights went out, one by one. When the inn was shrouded in darkness it took to the air, circled the rooftop and flew off back through the woods and into the mountains.

CHAPTER 23

We moved on early the next morning, not bothering to stay for breakfast with our unwelcoming host and made our way further down into the valleys. Duckie referred to his map from time to time but we seemed to be walking for hours without any sign of a road or any other landmarks of any significance. We came across no villages or dwellings, we passed no other travelers and all we could see on either side was miles of forest.

Galant and I threw worried looks at each other every time Duckie took out his map but we said nothing. We spent another uncomfortable night on the forest floor but at least the temperature was a little warmer now we were sheltered deep in the valleys.

When we awoke in the morning, I found that I had huddled close to Galant in the night and he had one arm slung protectively across me. I didn't have chance to pull away before he lazily opened his eyes and gazed at me with an amused expression. I had scowled and muttered something about rolling over in my sleep before swiftly extracting myself from his embrace. We continued our journey and as the hours passed the pine forests began to thin out, making way for the more familiar lowland woods; finkle trees and brambles interspersed with clearings and wild flowers.

Around late afternoon, we were still trudging in silence when Duckie suddenly stopped and held up his hand

'Shhh!" he said, although none of us were speaking. Galant and I stopped too and regarded Duckie curiously. "D'you hear it?" he whispered. I listened carefully and in the quiet air I could just make out a sound; the melodic tinkling of rushing water. Duckie suddenly turned and ran in the direction of the sound, his pack thumping against his back. Galant and I followed quickly behind and as we burst into a clearing Duckie shouted in triumph.

"Yes!" he cried as we found ourselves standing on the bank of a small but fast flowing river. "I knew were going the right way! I knew it!" Duckie pulled out his faithful map and pointed out a river marked on it, winding through a valley on this side of the mountains.

Galant and I laughed in relief. "Never doubted it friend!" Galant said confidently to Duckie, throwing me a wink.

"This river should lead us south," Duckie said excitedly, pointing to his tatty map. "And then here's where it leads into the swamp."

I followed Duckie's finger, my brows furrowed. "Isn't there a way around the swamp?" I asked apprehensively as Duckie shook his head.

"It's too big," replied Duckie, tracing around the huge expanse of swampland marked on his map. "It would add days to our journey if we tried to go around." We looked at each other, both thinking of the stones at Halftans Crevice and the caverns near Wistmans Hollow.

"Duckie's right," said Galant. "We'll be better going right through the middle. Shouldn't take long. I've spent time in the swamps; I know what to look out for." I nodded, realizing they were right and I tried to swallow the cold feeling or foreboding that was gathering in the pit of my stomach.

We moved on and followed the river as it wound its way through the woods, gradually becoming narrower and more slow moving, its bends forming large deep pools of still and stagnant water. The firm grassy riverbank was soft beneath our feet and rushes and reeds began to crop up through the peaty earth as the finkle trees of the woods began to dwindle. A fog began to gather around us, hanging low about the loamy ground and swirling in slow moving wisps around our heads.

"There it is." Duckie said after a while, pointing ahead of us. As I peered around him through the fog I could see the swamp. There were outcroppings of wiry grass and reeds, growing from the swamp water in tufty thickets and the odd lone finkle tree, boughs bare and creeping through the fog like cadaverous fingers. The swamp waters settled amongst the exposed roots of the trees and the surface of the water was thick with turgid green algae, a fetid stench in the air.

The encroaching fog seemed to swallow the daylight and as we approached, Galant pointed into the gloomy depths of the swamp. "Look," he said. "Swamp devils." I could see strange green orbs floating above the water, glowing ghostlike in the dim light. Mr Burle had told us that these were caused by the swamp gas gathering beneath the water before emerging in bubbles of luminous green. As the bubbles burst, the gas reacted with the air and ignited with a pop and a flash of bright green flame. They were harmless enough but the glowing orbs cast an eerie and unnatural light over the water and a shiver ran through me.

We walked on into the swamp, hopping across tree roots and jumping from clump to clump of exposed reeds. The swamp waters were getting deeper around us and the going became more and more difficult as we moved further into the fog. My beautiful dragon boots were soaking wet and the dragons no longer glinted, weeds hanging in soggy tendrils from the dragon's wings.

Just as our path was becoming impossible we came across an old and decaying wooden boardwalk built on struts buried beneath the water. It was slippery and broken in places but it seemed to form a path through the swamp as it wound its way between the reeds and trees. I wondered who had built it in this strange and haunting place. We walked carefully along the boardwalk, slipping from time to time and having to jump across sections that had rotted away and sunk into the murky water. We helped each other along and once again, Galant would hold out his hand to pull me across the broken slats. I noticed that he would keep hold of it a little longer than he needed to.

Eventually I found that we were walking hand in hand and I only realized when Duckie looked back and saw us, a strange expression flitting across his features.

Night fell and swamp faeries began to emerge from their holes in the tree roots, their wings the same luminous green as the swamp devils. They flitted across the stagnant water and hovered around our heads, darting towards us to pull at a lock of hair before fluttering off, their high-pitched giggles echoing in the quiet air. In Millings Beck, I had only ever seen dust faeries but the tinkling chimes of their swamp dwelling cousins reminded me of home.

As we struggled on, the walkway began to disintegrate completely until eventually the dark mossy wood slipped entirely beneath the water, leaving us no clear path ahead. We all stood there looking into the darkness, nervously eyeing the black swamp water beneath us. The green luminous glow of the swamp devils floating around us lit up our faces with a strange green pallor and the branches of the finkle trees seemed to reach out for us through the gloom.

"We're going to have to go in," said Duckie eventually, making his statement sound almost like a question that he wanted one of us to answer. Galant took a long stick and prodded it into the swamp water as far as it would go before withdrawing it and holding it up. "We won't have to swim," he said looking at the dark wet line on the stick. "It's probably chest height, maybe almost shoulder deep for Fen."

The two of them looked at me doubtfully for a moment before Duckie leaned out over the water and pointed through the murk. "Look; just ahead the boardwalk carries on. We'd only be in the water for a bit…" his voice trailed off uncertainly.

"Alright," I said, shrugging with a casual nonchalance I didn't feel. "Let's get on with it." The two of them looked dubiously at me again and it irritated me. Without warning I shrugged my pack from my back, held it above my head and jumped from the walkway into the dingy water of the swamp. I gasped as the cold liquid seeped into my clothes and splashed at my face but I found my footing and looked back up at Duckie and Galant's surprised faces. "Come on then!" I said, trying to stop my teeth from chattering. "What's up? You scared or something?" Duckie and Galant looked at one another and paused for a moment before gingerly lowering themselves into the water.

As we stepped carefully through the turgid waters, the boggy peat of the swamp sucked at our feet and the weeds and algae pulled at our arms and legs. It was slow going and when we reached the trunk of the first tree, maybe ten or fifteen yards from the next section of walkway, I grabbed the tree trunk and stopped to catch my breath, waiting for Duckie and Galant to catch up. I turned back to watch them making their way through the water, packs still dripping on their backs, arms held out above the water line. As I watched, I noticed a flash of movement behind them as something rose slightly from the water and cut across the surface briefly before disappearing again with a plop. It was so brief I thought the swamp devils were playing tricks on my eyes.

As I squinted into the darkness, I heard the same noise off to my left and I spun my head around just in time to see a pale fin and a flipper disappear back into the swamp water. When I looked back to my friends, still struggling through the clinging sludge, a sudden violent disturbance churned the water behind Galant. He faltered and stumbled before swiftly vanishing completely beneath the black water. Duckie was just behind him and looked on in shock as bubbles rose to the surface where Galant had disappeared.

"Galant!" I shouted in panic, releasing my grip on the tree trunk and wading back out into the open water. "Fen look out!" I heard Duckie cry and I spun round in time to see a creature fly at me from the water; a goblin-like face with black eyes, the body a bluish grey with purple veins running beneath translucent skin. The creature propelled itself from the water, flying towards my face, webbed hands outstretched, gnashing its toothless mouth. Instinctively I flung my fist forward and punched it hard on the side of the head which threw it off course. It let out a choking squeal and spun through the air before righting itself and diving back beneath the surface. I caught a glimpse of flipper-like feet before it vanished and, with a lurch of panic, I realized what these unseen attackers were. Glibs. Swamp creatures that attacked in numbers to drag their prey beneath the water and drown them. Once you were dead, they would leave you there to decay in the gaseous swamp waters before returning to suck at your sodden flesh with their toothless gummy mouths.

I spun wildly in panic to see Galant burst from beneath the water, gasping, dagger in hand as he raised it high above his head before plunging it down into the water. Duckie pulled his knife out too and took a deep breath before diving down and disappearing from view.

"Fen!" Galant cried, "Get away!" I turned swiftly and could see the wooden boardwalk emerging back out of the waters a few yards from me. I made a quick decision and began to stride through the swamp towards the boardwalk, pulling my boots from the sucking mud with every step. Galant and Duckie were thrashing in the water behind me and all around us, Glibs were flitting through the murk, their narrow spines forming a fin that curved out of the water as they circled.

I reached the boardwalk and flung my pack onto the slippery wooden slats, hauling myself from the swamp. Before I was clear of the water, I felt a cold webbed hand grasp my ankle. It took all my strength to pull my leg out of the swamp, pulling the repulsive creature with it, thin fingers clutched around my boot. It opened its black mouth and narrowed its eyes, releasing a high-pitched shriek as I quickly pulled my dagger from my belt and drove it hard into the Glib's spindly back. A black pus pumped from the wound as the creature released its grip and twisted in agony on the moldy slats of the boardwalk. I stabbed at it again and again, almost feeling remorse for its pain, until it stopped its thrashing. I kicked it back into the water and it slipped lifelessly beneath the surface of the swamp.

I jumped to my feet and looked back to see Galant and Duckie still struggling with the unseen hands of the Glibs swarming beneath the water.

"Duckie stand still!" I shouted as Galant was dragged under once more.

"Hold your arms above your head, put your legs together and stand still!" Duckie stopped struggling and did as I asked. I quickly pulled an iron arrow from my sheath and held up my bow. I fired the arrow into the water just inches from where Duckie's legs would be. I pulled another arrow and fired to the other side. I did this another four or five times until the thrashing under the water subsided and Duckie was free of the Glibs grip.

Two translucent bodies floated to the surface of the water, arrows protruding from their skin and black pus seeping from the fatal wounds. Duckie began to move towards Galant who had once more emerged from the water gasping and clearly weakening.

"Duckie no!" I shouted, "Get over here now!" Duckie turned to look at me as I aimed my arrow once again to the side of Galant. "Galant hold still!" I cried. Galant couldn't stand straight but his head was just above the water line. I cursed under my breath and aimed again, firing another arrow that shot through the air and down into the black water. I did this again and again, aiming either side of Galant's body as best I could as he thrashed through the water towards us. Duckie finally made it to the boardwalk and pulled himself out, gasping for breath. More of the Glibs were floating dead to the surface as my arrows found their mark and when Galant drew near, Duckie reached out and hauled him up beside us.

Galant gasped and fell down on his back, spitting out gobs of black water and weeds. A pale blue, long fingered hand was still grasped around his ankle and I fired one last arrow into the blackness. The fingers stiffened, unclenched and slowly slipped into the gloam.

CHAPTER 24

We didn't sleep that night. After our encounter with the Glibs we crossed the swamp as quickly as we could and none of us wanted to rest. Although we were filthy and soaking wet, our packs dripping and double their normal weight on our backs, the adrenaline was coursing through us and we used its energy to walk on through the night. The wooden boardwalk thankfully became more consistent and other than a couple of large gaps where we were able to swing across through the trees, we didn't have to enter the water again. We were aware of the occasional flash of blue spines in the swamp and the plop of a flippered foot as the remaining Glibs trailed us but we knew they couldn't venture from the water.

Galant was limping slightly as one of my arrows had grazed his leg but he didn't complain and allowed Duckie to support his weight when he began to weaken. His face was pale and his eyes bloodshot and I realized with a sickening feeling how close he had come to disappearing beneath the water and never coming back up.

We pressed on and eventually the ground firmed up, the swamp water shallowed off and the wooden boardwalk again disappeared from beneath our feet. The three of us finally stepped onto solid earth, emerging bedraggled from the fog into the grey light of dawn. I took one last look back to see the swamp faeries gathering in clusters on the tree branches before flitting back into their holes as the sun came up.

We continued through woods of finkles, wanting to put some distance between us and the rancid air of the swamp and the deadly creatures that lurked beneath its waters. The sky was heavy with black clouds and thunder began to rumble overhead before the sky spilled sluices of rain down upon us. Still we walked on as the rain dripped from the leaves above our heads until eventually, exhausted, we collapsed beneath the boughs of a large tree. Duckie carefully lowered Galant to the ground and without a word, Galant dropped his head onto his chest and slept.

"D'you think he'll be alright?" Duckie asked wearily, looking down at Galant.

I nodded. "You rest. I'll keep watch for a bit and wake you in an hour or so." Duckie didn't need asking twice and leaned back against the tree trunk, his head falling to one side as he fell asleep. I lowered my dripping pack from my back and opened it, digging around within until I found one of the small phials that Mallady Bruma had given me. It seemed like a long time ago that I had sat with her in the birdhouse above that magical glade filled with butterflies. The phial I pulled out was filled with a dark blue powder and I shook it, holding it up to the light. "Midnight Blue," I remembered Mallady saying as she pointed to one of her jars, a majestic butterfly resting within. A huge red eye decorated the tip of each wing, the wings themselves a dark blue colour that was so deep it was almost black. "This'll treat a small injury," she'd said. "It wouldn't make your arm grow back but it'll help a small wound heal, keep it from infection."

I ripped open the cloth of Galant's breeches and poured some water from my flask over the arrow wound on his leg. I tipped a small amount of the Midnight Blue powder onto my finger tip and gently dabbed it over the shallow but fierce looking graze. As I worked I realized that Galant was no longer sleeping and I raised my head to find his dark eyes watching me.

"Just making sure it doesn't get infected," I said efficiently, my cheeks flushing.

"Thank you," murmured Galant weakly.

"For what?" I said with a short laugh. "For shooting you in the leg?"

Galant chuckled but it turned to a cough and he turned his face away and spat black water into the grass. "Not for that," he replied. "That I could live without. Thank you for saving my life."

I didn't answer and concentrated on dabbing the blue powder onto his wound before tearing a strip of cloth from my undershirt and wrapping it tightly around his thigh. When I looked up, Galant was still staring at me. He smiled tiredly and reached out his hand, gently cupping my cheek. We stared at each other for a long moment and he pulled a green swampy frond from my dripping auburn curls.

"When I said you should always wear green, this isn't exactly what I meant," he said wryly, the familiar teasing tone returning to his voice and a twinkle glinting in his tired eyes.

I swatted his hand away and sat back. "Go to sleep," I whispered, resisting the urge to reach out and smooth the hair from his brow. He nodded as his eyelids drooped and eventually they closed, his chest rising and falling steadily as he slept.

The rain continued to pour down and after we'd all had an hour or so's rest, we got up and moved on. Luckily, our food was wrapped in greased paper so was still relatively dry and Duckie was also pleased to find that his map was still readable, if a little damp and smudged. Now we had passed through the swamp he seemed confident of our direction and led us off through the dripping finkle trees predicting that we would reach a road in the next day or so.

We spent another night in the woods, erecting a lean-to over our heads using Galant's cape to shield us from the incessant downpour. To our relief, the next morning dawned dry and a little brighter and, just as Duckie had said, we emerged from the woods onto a muddy lane around midday. The landscape was bleak; heather covered moorland extending to the horizon in all directions as the road wound away into the distance. The only sound was the cawing of crows nesting in the woods behind us, their black winged outlines circling above. The sky was still overcast and although the rain had stopped, the clouds still looked heavy and troubled, threatening to open at any moment and drench us once more. We were all cold, wet and tired and our food had almost run out. Despite what Duckie's map showed, I hoped we would soon reach some kind of settlement where we could rest, gather some food and dry our things out.

"Where now?" asked Galant looking up and down the road.

"South," replied Duckie confidently. "As long as we keep going south we'll be right."

"How'll we find Halftans Crevice?" I asked.

"It'd be too much to expect it to be signposted I suppose," Duckie sighed, leaning back on his heels. "We'll just have to keep going and see what turns up."

"Are you sure you still want to come south with us?" I asked Galant, purposely keeping my tone neutral. "You could go directly west from here to get home." Galant gave me a long look and I saw Duckie glancing between the two of us curiously. I found I was holding my breath with anticipation as I waited for Galant to answer.

"You don't have to come you know," Duckie interjected. "The quickest route back to Bleakchill Cove is to go directly west from here. We'll be alright won't we Fen?" I ignored Duckie and fixed my gaze on Galant, trying not to look hopeful.

"I'll come," said Galant after a moments pause. "If I head south with you, I can cut back north beyond Wistmans Hollow. It'll take a bit longer but I'll be safer travelling with you." He shot a pointed look at Duckie. "We all will."

Relief flooded through me and I wondered why I cared so much. Never in my life had I really cared about anyone except Leif, Pa and of course Duckie. But I knew that I was different now. Back in Millings Beck I had only known the love of my Pa and my brother and my childhood friend. I cared about Galant because he cared about me. He proved it to me every day in small but meaningful ways. I didn't mind him touching me. I liked the way he looked at me sometimes with an intense expression as if he was taking in every detail of my features, the way he seemed surprised sometimes at my words or my movements. It was the same look you would give to a wild cat that you expected to bite and hiss at you, only to find that it purred when you dared to touch it.

I tried to look nonchalant and shrugged. "Better get going then," I said. "How's your leg?" I asked Galant as we set off down the road.

"Doing alright little Fen," he answered, gingerly patting his bandage.

"That powder you put on it seems to have done the trick." He grinned at me mischievously, and rumpled my hair. "Little auburn headed witch you are." I pushed him off but smiled quietly to myself as the three of us walked on. Although my body was cold and dirty, my stomach hungry and eyes tired, I felt a warmth somewhere inside me that lifted me. It felt like the three of us could do anything.

CHAPTER 25

The Grimhellion swooped down from the mountain peak and flew across the pine forest, its red eyes keenly focused on the landscape far beneath. It reached the foothills where they dipped down to the desert scrub that stretched all the way to the hazy outline of Andorta in the distance. As it circled, the creature spotted two figures making their way up through the hills and it glided on the warm wind, leathery wings extended, ears pricked and alert as it descended.

The two men were heavily clothed in hard leather and were sweating and puffing as they climbed. One was tall and well-built with a long greying beard and a large scar running from the corner of one eye to his lip. The other man was shorter with a wiry body and sharp cunning features, his head shaved and his face tattooed on one side around his eye with the outline of two crossed daggers. They walked in silence until they reached the top of a hill where they stopped and looked back, regarding the plains beneath them.

"We should've set off yesterday Thrax," said the tall bearded one. "I told you we should've. That witch'll expect us to be at least the other side of the mountains by now."

The shorter man named Thrax stopped walking and spat on the ground. "We'll catch up with them," he said. "Oberon reckons the witch's familiar is tracking them. It'll tell us which way to go."

The bearded man sighed and shrugged. "S'pose so. Last thing I want is to end up like Tetch. What they did to him in that arena is an end no man should meet. Not even a heartless, cut throat, good f'nothin like him."

Thrax quickly whipped around and grabbed the other man by his beard, pulling his face down close to his own. "It's Tetch that got us into this Shiv," he hissed. "If that fool hadn't drunk his body weight in ale and passed out instead of guarding those relics we'd be free by now with more coin that we'd know what to do with."

Shiv sank to his knees and looked up fearfully at Thrax, the whites of his eyes rimmed red. "I know, I know, I din't mean nothin by it."

Thrax let go of the man's beard and looked up into the sky. "Look," he said, pointing "That's it. Decima's hellion." The black shape circling above dropped on the wind until it was only a few feet above the mercenaries' heads, its red eyes fixed on them. When it was satisfied it had found its marks it let out a high-pitched shriek and turned, angling its bat-like wings and turning towards the mountains. It soared a little distance away then turned and hovered in the air, shrieking again.

"Told you," said Thrax with a satisfied smile. "All we need to do is follow that thing and we'll find them. We'll find them and we'll find the relics. Like spearing fish in a barrel."

The mercenaries followed the hellion for two days up through the hills, into the forest and over the mountains. When they began their descent, they saw the faint outline of three sets of footsteps marring the smooth perfection of the snow plain. The prints were almost filled in but the shallow indents still stood out clearly against the soft white blanket of snow. The mercenaries stood and observed the footprints, watching the hellion as it swooped and circled, leading them onwards and down into the valley.

They too reached the secluded inn at nightfall and they too received a frosty welcome from the innkeeper and his cohort. Unlike his customers of a few nights previous, these two didn't hesitate to respond to the innkeeper's games. Without a word, Thrax had pulled his sword from his belt and slit the man's throat. As he crumpled to a heap on the stone floor, Thrax swung his sword around and almost decapitated the ruddy faced oaf sitting at the bar. The mercenaries ate stew and drank spiced wine as the snowstorm battered at the windows and rivulets of blood ran beneath their feet.

While they slept, the Grimhellion flew tirelessly onwards into the swamp, darted between the glowing green orbs and then off into the finkle trees of the forest beyond. It smelled the aroma of wood smoke in the air and saw the remains of a campfire before flying on until it reached a road. The hellion hovered there in the darkness, swooping up the road one way and then the other, sniffing the wind before retracing its path back to the inn. It perched on a branch once more, wings wrapped snugly around its body to shield it from the freezing air, red eyes partially open and the smell of death drifting beautifully to its nostrils.

CHAPTER 26

"What d'you think?" asked Duckie as we stood at the edge of the road, its crooked uneven stones disappeared beneath the swirling waters of the fjord in the deep, wide river that blocked our way. "I don't fancy getting wet again," said Galant, "Won't do this any good either," he continued patting his injured leg. Darkness was falling once more as we stood at the edge of the river and a swirling mist gathered around us smothering the moorland. "I don't think we'll make it. We can't even see the other side in this fog," Duckie added peering across the water into the mist.

"I don't think that'd be our only problem," Galant added, pointing out across the river where a silvery shadow was moving and shimmering beneath the surface of the water.

"What is it?" I asked, leaning forward as far as I dare to observe the strange glittering shape.

"Gutfish," said Galant with a grimace, reaching into his pack and pulling out a strip of molding dried meat. "Watch," he said as he tossed the meat into the river.

As soon as the meat plopped into the water, the shimmering shadow suddenly whipped around causing the surface to splash and roil violently. Tiny wiry fins protruded here and there, tiny mouths breaking the surface filled with rows of pin-like teeth. The shoal of Gutfish rounded on the scrap of meat and the sound of the tiny teeth gnashing was audible above the disturbance in the water.

"Why're they called Gutfish?" asked Duckie, taking a step back from the water's edge.

"If you fell in, you'd soon know!" said Galant with a wry chuckle. He turned to Duckie. "If you were to end up in that water, you'd probably hear them coming. Maybe even see them. A silver glimmer off in the murk." Galant leaned closer to Duckie. "Then you'd feel them," he put a hand on Duckie's middle. "Here. They'd start to nibble at your stomach, you'd barely feel it at first. Then when the blood gets into the water, more of them will come and more still, all gnawing and biting. They would chew a hole in your stomach right through to your spine in a few seconds."

Duckie took another step back, his face pale. "They wouldn't," he said disbelieving.

"They would," said Galant turning back to look across the river. "I've seen it happen."

We all fell silent for a moment. Up and down the river were more of the shimmering shoals of Gutfish and we realized crossing on foot would be impossible. We'd have to find another way.

As we all pondered this, I squinted downstream and walked away from the road, peering into the dim light where the river meandered around a bend.

"Wait!" I called back to the others, "Come and look at this."

Galant and Duckie hurried after me through the gathering fog and I pointed out a dark shape extending from the riverside out into the oozing water. "It looks like a dock or a jetty or something," I said, striding further downriver towards the wooden structure. I walked to the jetty and it seemed to be solidly built so I tentatively stepped onto it and made my way along its mossy surface over the water, concentrating on treading carefully on the slippery wooden slats, head down. When I glanced up a face was looming out of the fog towards me; white and smooth, sharp teeth bared in my face. I jumped sharply backwards and my hand went quickly to my belt as my feet slipped from underneath me.

I lost my footing on the jetty and found myself in a bundle at Duckie's feet, dagger clenched in my fist and heart pounding.

"Fen!" Duckie cried out. "It's alright, it's alright! It's dead!" I shuffled back in panic, my leather boots scrabbling for purchase on the slimy moss-covered wood. Duckie pulled me to my feet before he stepped forward to look carefully at the skull fixed firmly on a pole sticking out of the water at the end of the jetty. It appeared to be the skull of a sheep although its harmless origins made it no less sinister as its black eye holes stared blankly back at us through the mist. It had certainly been placed there with some purpose, smaller bones and feathers strung amongst the orbits of its skeletal features hanging almost into the waters beneath.

On the gleaming white surface of the skull were letters, scratched into the bone and then filled with coal soot or something else black, outlining the words; 'Gutfish Moor' it read.

Galant approached from behind us, limping slightly. "What the...." He breathed as he stared at the macabre marker, the strings of bones chinking against each other in the soft breeze. "What is this?" he asked softly, turning to Duckie and me. Before we could offer an answer, a sound echoed from somewhere downstream. We could make out the steady swoosh, twist and drip of a paddle as it breached the still surface of the dark water. We all turned and stared into the fog. The air was a strange mix of sundown and twilight, casting a dark dirty brown glow that seemed to reflect off the water as the light twisted itself amongst the dark tendrils of river mist.

Approaching us up the river was a small boat, a dark figure at its bow and the outline of another skull hanging from a mast in the middle of the vessel. The air was eerily still around us as the boat approached, the silence only broken by the steady splash of the oar as the dark figure twisted it through the water, the sound strangely muffled by the increasingly oppressive fog.

As the boat drew closer, a thin and wheezing voice sounded through the mist. "You got gold pretty rats?" The voice said. "Me only takes river rats for gold, no bits of chicken or leaves or flowers. Just gold." We stood in silence on the jetty as the boat slowly approached. "What be it rats?" the voice continued, "You got enough gold to be river rats? Or you be land rats and walk through the mud?" The voice cackled loudly as the figure threw back its head, one bony hand resting on its oar as the boat gently thudded against the jetty.

The three of us looked at each other and then back down at this strange, small figure nestled in the boat beneath our feet.

Duckie shrugged at me wordlessly so I stepped forward. "We've got a little gold," I said loudly, my tone guarded. "Where'll you take us?"

The figure looked up from the boat and I could see the features of a very old woman with a long protruding chin and hooked nose. Her face was infinitely wrinkled, her eyes completely black and her skin pock marked and littered with dark moles, bristly hairs protruding from each. When my Pa described witches to me in his childhood bedtime tales, this is what they looked like. I knew that the reality was that many witches appeared young and beautiful; this was part of their power. But in the faerie tales we'd heard as children, they'd looked exactly like this strange little woman looking up at us fearlessly right now.

"Elsbioli will take you wherever you want my little rats," the woman said. "So long as it's between Gutfish Moor and Fangs Foss!" She cackled again as she held out a wizened hand and looked up as me expectantly, mashing her gummy lips together.

"What's between Gutfish Moor and Fangs Foss?" asked Duckie, glancing at Galant and me with a raised eyebrow. I raised both mine back at him in response. Elsbioli drew her hands into her robes and as she did so, I noticed that her cloak was covered in feathers. Black raven feathers sewn in neat rows and layers so that they hung around her slight frame as they would a living bird. The black feathers shimmered in the dim light, so black they glinted blue in places as she folded her thin arms and regarded us from beneath her avian hood.

"Gutfish Moor is here, little rat," Elsbioli said, gesturing at the skull sticking from the water. Her eyes fixed keenly on Duckie. "Carrions Crossing is a bit further down the river. Rattlebone Wood is a bit further down the river from that. Shrews Croft is even further down the river. Then there's Fangs Foss. Does this little rat need more explanations? Hmmm?"

Duckie looked away from her intense black eyes and the woman cackled once again. "Come rats, come," she said impatiently as she pushed her paddle into the river and began to turn her boat around. "Gold for Elsbioli?" she asked. "Or a long, long walk or the land rats?" she cackled again as the small dry bones hanging from her mast clattered against each other.

"We're looking for Halftans Crevice," I said as the woman muttered and cursed, her sinewy arms twisting the oar in the muddy river bottom, as the boat turned slowly in the water.

"Ah yes," she said. "Elsbioli likes the Halfs. Good customers up and down the river." She finished turning the boat and looked up at me. "Small rats though, you know," she said, her tone gossipy. "Ever so small. Smallest Elsbioli ever sees." She shrugged. "But a Half's gold is as good as a tall's gold. Gold's all the same size in't it?" she cackled with laughter at her own confusing joke. "Elsbioli's going now," she said in a sing-song raspy voice. "Rat's need to pay up and get on board. Elsbioli has a pick up at Shrews Croft. Can't be late, can't be late." Her strange voice drifted off into an incoherent mutter and she began to push the boat off from the jetty.

"Wait!" I called, "We'll come," I reached into my coat and pulled out a coin, holding it out to her between my fingers.

She stopped suddenly and turned, her feathered robes rustling as she moved. "Ah ha," she murmured, snatching the coin from my fingers, her long finger nailed claw disappearing into her feathers. "One rat." She nodded at me and I stepped carefully down into her boat. She peered up at Duckie and Galant as the boat started to drift away from the jetty in the lazy current. "And the other two rats?" she asked archly.

"Come on!" I said urgently. Duckie and Galant looked at each other briefly then quickly produced coins from their pockets and stepped carefully across from the jetty onto the bow of the boat.

"A good day for Elsbioli!" the old woman crooned. "You know what they say," she sniggered. "Spend days waiting for a rat and then they all come at once!"

Elsbioli pushed the boat firmly away from the jetty and out into the middle of the river. We began to move downstream with the current and the incessant plunge and turn of the oar Elsbioli held in her bony hands. The three of us huddled in the bottom of the boat beneath the clattering bones as we drifted off through the mist.

"What is she?" Duckie muttered to me. "Who are these 'Halfs?"

I shrugged as I dropped my pack off my back and pulled my knees up to my chin. "Dunno," I answered, glancing up at the feathered figure at the helm of the boat. "But she seems to know something about Halftans Crevice so I don't really care what she is. I just want to know if she can take us there."

Duckie looked at me dubiously and nudged me hard in the ribs. "You ask her," he muttered, dropping his head.

"No, you ask her, it's your stone!" I replied childishly, nudging him back harder.

Galant sighed loudly and looked at the pair of us reproachfully. "For goodness sake, I'll ask her!" he said and Duckie and I hung our heads, shooting a quick grin across the boat to one another. Galant stood carefully in the rocking boat and shuffled forward. "Elsbioli," he began, his voice filled with charm as Duckie and I rolled our eyes. "These Halfs. Who are they? Do you know where they live?"

Elsbioli turned her feather-hooded face towards him. "Elsbioli doesn't know where no rats live; half's or tall's." Elsbioli sniffed as she drew her oar from the water and rested on it as we drifted onwards. "Elsbioli only knows where the rats get on and off. Half rats get on at Rattlebone Wood. Sometimes they get off at Shrews Croft where there's tall rats but then they get back on without no tall rats and go back to Rattlebone Wood. That's all Elsbioli knows." She sniffed again and turned back to the river, a crooked hand extending furtively backwards through the black feathers of her robes. Galant pressed a coin into her outstretched hand, clearly understanding the polite protocol for receiving information even in these remote parts.

He turned back to us and brushed his hair from his face. "Sounds like we're getting off at Rattlebone Wood then?" he said with a shrug. We all settled as comfortably as we could in the bottom of the boat as it floated off down the river into the strange orange glow of dusk. The heavy fog made it impossible to see more than a few feet around us as it shrouded the riverbanks on either side and rendered the moorland beyond invisible. The same fog also completely obliterated the outline of the dark creature flying high above us, black wings gliding silently, burning red eyes always watching.

CHAPTER 27

The swamp devils floated slowly through the darkness and Thrax swatted one away from his face as the two mercenaries made their way through the boggy, ankle deep water. Shiv had several dead Glibs over each shoulder, their flesh mottled blue and lifeless eyes partially open. The Grimhellion had settled ahead of them on a rock, a swamp faerie trapped squealing beneath one of its claws. It cocked its head from side to side, red eyes bright and curious as if it were enjoying the faeries distress.

"That thing turns my stomach," said Shiv, eyeing the hellion and curling his lip in disgust.

"It might do," replied Thrax. "But it's the only thing that's going to keep our stomachs inside our bodies at this rate. We can't go back without those relics and if we make a run for it, that witch'll send all the denizens of the earth and sky after us."

He pulled one fur boot from the swamp and set it on solid ground as they emerged from the trees and into a clearing. The men turned and looked back into the darkness of the swamp, watching the hellion as it bent its bony black head and pulled the swamp faerie to pieces, limb from limb, its screams swallowed up into the mist.

Shiv heaved the bodies of the Glibs from his shoulder and down onto the grass. "What d'you think happened to these then?" he asked as Thrax nudged the damp flesh of the blue tinged creatures with the toe of his boot. He kicked one over onto its back exposing an arrow hole.

"Looks like someone passed through here who was handy with a bow," he mused.

"D'you think it was them?" asked Shiv doubtfully. "They're only pups after all.... D'you think they could have done this?"

Thrax shrugged. "Never know Shiv. Some of these Seekers are well trained." He turned to Shiv with a wicked smile and an evil glint in his eyes. "But not as well trained as us."

The hellion rose from its gruesome meal and screeched as it circled above the men's heads, green faerie blood coating its small teeth and claws.

"Where next my little fetid friend?" called Thrax, watching as the hellion turned and flew into the trees. He looked back at the dead Glibs. "There's gold to be made there," he said, kicking once again at the pile of lifeless forms. "To witches, herbalists and the like...." He mused thoughtfully. Thrax turned back to his companion, eyes stony, his face impassive. He gestured to the heap of bodies. "Cut out their eyes."

CHAPTER 28

It became clear that we had all underestimated Elsbioli's river route and her five stops. We had expected an old woman of her years to only be capable of covering a short distance but she pressed on through the night, an unerring black feathered figure at the helm of the boat pushing us on through the darkness for hour after relentless hour. We floated slowly past the empty jetty of Carrion Crossing, its white gleaming skull looming through the mist, feathers waving in the breeze and the clatter of the old dry bones echoing through the still night air. Eventually our heads nodded to our chests where we sat, huddled in the bottom of the boat, and the three of us fell asleep.

As I slept I felt the vague sensation of a warm body drawing close to mine, an arm wrapping tightly around my back. I thought I felt the gentle heat of breath against my cold cheek and the soft brush of a kiss in my hair. I didn't wake and it could have been a dream or a memory of my childhood, a time that felt so long ago now. A memory of falling asleep on my Pa's lap late at night after waking from a nightmare as he held me and comforted me before leaving me sleeping peacefully in my bunk.

How long I slept, I couldn't say but I was woken with a start at the sound of Elsbioli's creaky voice.

"All rats off at Rattlebone Wood!" she called out. "All rats off now, come on, come on." I blearily looked around to see that the fog had lifted, leaving tendrils of light mist over the water and the sky was beginning to brighten on the horizon. The boat bumped against another jetty on the opposite side of the river to where we'd boarded, a replica bony symbol standing up from the water inscribed with the same crude lettering; 'Rattlebone Wood'.

"If rat's wants to go to Shrews Croft or Fangs Foss then it'll be more gold for Elsbioli," the old woman continued as she brought the boat to a stop, heaving her oar firmly into the river bottom. Duckie and Galant seemed to be quite awake and I thought perhaps I had slept too long. I wondered if Galant had watched me and I worried whether my mouth had been hanging open or if I had looked pretty and peaceful. I shook the silly thought from my head and gathered up my pack and bow, standing up unsteadily in the boat.

We all climbed onto the decrepit, creaking jetty and Galant turned to Elsbioli as she pushed off with a grunt. "Hey," he called, "Which way to Halftans Crevice?" Elsbioli looked back over her black feathered shoulder.

"In the giant woods the Half's live," she called croakily. "Don't know about their crevices. Follow the path rats!" she added and cackled to herself as she floated off down the river into the early morning mist.

On the riverbank, the air was chilly and a light frost coated the fronds of grass. A path led downriver and another path meandered away from the bank, through a meadow and towards the forest visible in the distance.

"I suppose this'll be the way then?" said Duckie, pulling his pack onto his shoulders and gesturing across the meadow, his breath misting in the cold air.

"It was lucky that we came across her and that boat," said Galant, gesturing at Elsbioli's fading figure as we headed off down the path. "Sounds like we're almost there Duckie," he added, laying an arm comfortably across my shoulders as we walked. I had grown used to his tactile gestures and was happy to walk with him, our strides keeping pace together as we strolled through the meadow.

Duckie grunted in response but I could tell he was excited and the quickening pace of his stride gave away his eagerness. I was almost as excited as he was. I wanted Duckie to find his stone as much as I wanted to find my own but in a dark corner of my mind lurked nagging doubts; what if the man at the inn in Haggs Catton had tricked me? An innocent desperate Seeker only a few days from home? Wouldn't be the first time. What if the stone was already gone and we were wasting our time? What if? What if....

I reconciled my doubts with the fact that we had no other clues as to where we might find our birthstones. None of us had mentioned the fact that we had seen nothing since we left Andorta. No stone glittering from a mountainside, no stone nestled in a clump of flowers, no stone clenched in the paws or talons of some animal or bird. No stones. Not a one. I thought of Elvyn staggering towards home the night before his eighteenth annum and it felt like that same macabre milestone was bearing down on Duckie and me. In those sunny, lazy days in Andorta it had felt like we had all the time in the world but now, on this distant lonely path, it seemed as if this was the last and only chance we had. I knew that if we failed here, desperation would set in. And it wouldn't just be Duckie's desperation; it would be mine.

We reached the edge of the meadow and paused, regarding the forest ahead of us. The trees were unlike any I had ever seen; their trunks a deep red colour and immensely broad – all three of us could have hidden behind one with ease. The branches hung high above our heads, the trunks soaring into the sky, their tops almost disappearing into the low hanging clouds. The branchless lower trunks stood out starkly against the forest floor like rows of soldiers in a huge army standing stiffly to attention.

As we walked into the trees, I found myself leaning in towards Galant, his arm warm and strong around my shoulders. He had taken off his chainmail gloves and I could feel his warm hand where it rested against my neck. His leg seemed to have improved and I was relieved to see that his limp was barely discernible now. As we entered the woods, I looked around in awe. The giant trees dwarfed us and it was as if we had suddenly been shrunk to the size of goblins or pixies by some witch's spell or poisoned mushroom, lost in a strange land of giants. The woodland surroundings appeared peaceful but hummed with the noise of the forest; twittering of birds and the rustle of unseen creatures in the low-lying bushes.

Duckie marched on ahead purposefully and I turned to Galant as we walked, comfortably entwined.

"So," I began, wanting to ask him something about himself, wanting to know him better. "You never told me where you found your stone," I said. "I know you said it was just before we met in Andorta but where exactly did you find it?" I tilted my face towards him, interested to hear his story.

His brows furrowed and there was a long pause before he answered. "It was out in the desert," he said vaguely and I noticed his mouth tighten.

"Where? Did you have to kill a dragon?" I teased, pushing against him gently.

He laughed stiffly and withdrew his arm from my shoulders, moving away from me. "I wish it was so dramatic Fen," he said, gazing off into the forest.

"So…." I pressed gently, "Tell me the story, I want to hear it." I glanced furtively at his profile and saw his jaw clench and his eyes narrow as if he was recalling something that he didn't want to think about, something that pained him.

"It was nothing Fen," he said, his voice light but with a forced note of underlying tension. "I found it under a pile of rocks. A cairn or something I think it was. I found out about it from someone in the city, went to find it and there it was."

I frowned, having expected some tale of hardship and heroism. "So, you didn't have to fight?" I asked, surprised. "You didn't have to kill?"

Galant turned to me abruptly. "Fen!" he said sharply, "I just told you what happened. I'm sorry if it's not exciting enough for you. But that's what happened."

I recoiled at his tone, shocked and hurt. "I'm sorry," I said, my voice small. "I just wanted.... I just wanted to know your story that's all...." I realized I had tugged at something dark that lay beneath Galant's humour, beneath his charm and beneath his light and carefree words. Something had happened to him. Maybe he thought I would be disappointed in him, maybe he thought I would judge him. I didn't know and I wished I had never asked. He grunted in response and strode ahead of me to catch up with Duckie, leaving me dawdling behind upset and confused. I was soon to find that the truth of his story would surprise me in ways I had never dreamed of and least expected.

CHAPTER 29

The three of us barely spoke to each other as we went deeper and deeper into this strange forest. The morning passed uneventfully and we stopped for a while to eat and fill our flasks at a small pool beneath a rocky overhang, a stream tumbling down from the ledge above. We hadn't bathed properly since Andorta and I felt filthy, grime streaking my face and dried mud crusted under my fingernails.

"I'm going to wash in the pool," I said to Galant and Duckie as they settled down in a clearing above the waterfall and began munching on some stale bread. "Rather you than me," Duckie mumbled, with an involuntary shiver. "It's freezing!"

"I know," I replied, holding out my filthy hands and regarding them with a grimace. "But I feel so dirty and we don't know when we might find water again. I can't bear to go another day without washing." Galant looked at me, his eyes crinkling in amusement. Clearly our earlier spat had been forgotten and I felt relieved to see that merriment back in his face.

"You go ahead Fen," he called to me playfully. "We promise not to look." Duckie sniggered at this and rested his head on his pack, pulling out his tattered map. I rolled my eyes at them and walked back through the trees, under the overhang and down to the pool.

Duckie was right, the water was freezing but as I splashed my face I became accustomed to the cold and furtively glanced over my shoulders to make sure the boys were out of sight before removing my coat and dress. I shivered in my undershirt as I washed my hands and arms. I looked behind me again and tilted my head, hearing the low murmur of Duckie and Galant's voices drifting through the air from the top of the waterfall. I carefully leant over the pool as I washed under my arms and across my chest and neck. The freezing water made my skin goosebumps' and I shivered before sitting upright and closing my eyes, resting my palms on the soft ground as I let the weak early morning sunlight warm me.

"I told you I wouldn't look," a soft voice said behind me and I jumped, raising my arms to cover the thin transparent fabric of the shirt clinging to my chest. I turned to see Galant kneeling behind me, one hand covering his eyes, his lips curved in a mischievous smile. I laughed in relief, keeping my back to him as I looked over my shoulder. "Nothing you haven't seen before, I'm sure," I said primly, thinking of all the girls in Andorta that he had charmed, thinking of all the girls no doubt pining for him back at home.

He lowered his hand from his eyes. "Nothing I have seen before can even compare," he said softly, suddenly serious as he put a hand on each of my arms and rested his chin on my shoulder. His voice had lost that playful lilt and he pulled me back to lean against him. "I can't even remember anything before you," he said, his voice clear and honest as he reached around my waist and lifted me easily, pulling me onto his lap before I could object. I lowered my arms and rested them against his chest to steady myself, our faces inches apart. I held my breath as we stared at each other.

"You really have no idea, do you?" Galant whispered as he ran his fingers over my wet hair. I shook my head slowly and this time, it was me. It was me who moved my hand up into his hair and drew his head towards me. It was me who raised my lips to his. It was me who pressed my cold wet body against him as we kissed sweetly, slowly, warmly. I felt none of the confusion or apprehension that I had felt on the city walls of Andorta. I felt like I knew him now, really knew him, and I felt an unfamiliar urge to pull myself closer to another person.

The moment was abruptly broken by a commotion above us in the clearing where Duckie was resting. Galant and I jumped apart and I quickly grabbed my dress, pulling it swiftly over my head as Galant leapt to his feet and cursed, pulling out his sword as he ran back up the bank to the clearing.

I heard voices shouting, Duckie's voice standing out as he called "Wait wait, it's alright, it's alright!" followed by a strangled gargle and a gruff muttering I couldn't make out. When Galant reached the top of the bank I saw him lower his sword and hold his other hand out in a submissive gesture.

"Whoa, whoa," he exclaimed. "Let's just calm down, we mean you no harm." I hurried up the bank behind him and when I reached the clearing, I stopped in my tracks and my heart thudded in my chest.

Duckie was on his knees in the clearing, a small figure behind him with a glinting blade held at his throat. Duckie was surrounded by an equally diminutive band of heavily armored dwarves. There were five of them wielding large swords and maces, their long-bearded faces threatening and aggressive. One of the dwarves was a little taller than the others and was almost as broad as he was high. He wore a heavy metal chest plate and helmet, a pair of small keenly focused eyes glimmering from beneath his bushy eyebrows. When he saw Galant and me, the tall dwarf stepped forward, sword held out and feet braced in a fighting stance.

"Who goes here?" he demanded in a deep voice, his eyes flickering from one of us to the other. "This land belongs to us. Who goes here and what do you want?" Galant slowly lowered his sword to the floor, bending low so his face was level with the feisty dwarven warrior. "We're just Seekers," he said, "Just Seekers looking for stones. We're lost. We don't mean you any harm."

I stood there helplessly, my bow and arrows laying uselessly on the floor next to Duckie.

The dwarf narrowed his eyes at us and relaxed his stance a little. "You bandits?" he asked, as if Galant hadn't spoken. "Bandits always coming in here, ambushing my people, robbing us, stealing our things."

I stepped forward, heart racing, my hands held out palms up. "Do we look like bandits?" I asked gently. "We're Seekers, just looking for stones and trying to get home to our families."

The dwarf took a step back and eyed me warily. "You's don't look like bandits but that dunt mean you're not still after thieving and skullduggery."

I forced a smile, my eyes glancing back to Duckie who was still being held by the hair with the sharp blade resting on his neck. "We don't want to rob you," I continued, trying to keep my voice steady. "We're just looking for our birthstones." I swallowed hard. "If anything, we'll pay you for any information you have. We're not interested in anything but finding those stones." I tried to ignore the obvious fact that we were disarmed. If the dwarves wanted to take all our valuables right then and there, we were not going to be able to stop them.

The dwarf looked Galant and I up and down carefully again and sheathed his sword. He turned to the other dwarves who had opened up our packs and scattered the contents on the forest floor. "Look like Seekers to me Crab," called one. "Nothing here but dried out bits of food, a map and a few coins." He kicked a small foot against one of our packs. "Their blades aren't up to much either," he sniffed.

Crab gestured at Galant's sword lying on the ground. "Kick that over to me lad and then maybe we'll talk." Galant did as he was asked and Crab turned and nodded at the dwarf standing over Duckie. "Stand down Garrowby," he said and the dwarf muttered and let go of Duckie's hair, throwing him to the ground. Duckie stood up slowly and rubbed his hand carefully across his neck checking for blood as he caught his breath, scowling at the little man.

"So, what's brought Seekers here then?" asked Crab, resting the point of his sword in the ground and leaning on the hilt as he looked round at us.

"We're looking for Halftans Crevice," replied Duckie. "That's all. We heard there were Zaphite stones there."

Crab rubbed his beard thoughtfully. "Zaphite stones eh? What's it worth?" he asked shrewdly, casting his gaze over the contents of our packs. I was relieved that the dwarves seemed open to negotiation. Clearly some code of honour prevented them from cutting us down where we stood and stealing everything we owned.

I stepped forward quickly and the dwarves all jumped to attention again, weapons held out in my direction. I held my hands up again and moved more slowly. "If you can tell us where it is, we'll pay," I said as I bent down to my pack. I withdrew a couple of coins and held them out to Crab. "Anything you can tell us…" I trailed off.

The dwarf leaned over and inspected the coins in my palm before throwing back his head and laughing loudly, his beard bobbing as the others joined in, nudging each other in amusement. "We've no interest in coin lass," Crab said to me, his voice a little friendlier. The other dwarves sheathed their weapons, having clearly decided we were no threat to them.

Crab approached me, his hands on his hips. "The Half's have more coin than we know what to do with. What else you got?"

I looked up at Galant who shrugged. He picked up his chainmail gauntlets from where they lay. "What about these?" he asked, offering them out to Crab.

The dwarves laughed even more loudly at this. "Metal gauntlets? Lads, you seen this? He wants to pay us in metal!" The dwarves were almost doubled over in hysterical laughter at this, deep guffaws booming from their barrel chests. "We probably made those gauntlets," Crab chortled, slapping his sturdy thigh and looking at us with amusement. "Don't you know who we are?" he asked. The three of us looked at each other cluelessly. "We make more iron and steel here than anywhere in Immentia!" Crab continued. "Offering us those gauntlets is like taking fish to the Cove! Like taking oranges to Epona! Like taking wheat to the flatlands!" At his every word, the other dwarves fell about laughing, wiping tears from their eyes.

I dropped my proffered hand in despair. "So, what do you want?" I asked, casting my mind through a mental list of the contents of my pack.

"We want special things," Crab said, walking up to me and staring boldly up into my face. "We want things we don't already have." He narrowed his eyes. "You got anything like that missy?"

I thought desperately and suddenly something clicked in my mind. "Wait," I said, "I might have something…" I gestured at my pack on the ground. "May I…?" I asked tentatively. He grunted and nodded in response, his eyes lighting up with interest. I reached down and went through the small pocket at the side of my pack before my fingers clasped the smooth glass of a phial. I pulled out the healing Midnight Blue powder that Mallady Bruma had given me and held it out to Crab, tilting it so the contents glittered cyan and sapphire in the light. Crabs eyes widened and he watched the phial closely, his head moving from side to side as if hypnotized by its contents.

"Midnight Blue?" he asked, his voice hopeful. I nodded.

The dwarves all stared up at the phial I was holding, each one transfixed, mouths hanging slightly open as if mesmerized by the colours of the magical powder. At this moment, Duckie and Galant saw their chance and both leapt quickly for their weapons, grabbing their swords and moving quickly to one side of the clearing behind me. The dwarves had been momentarily distracted but were soon alert and moved into action, quickly circling Crab defensively with their blades drawn.

We stared at the dwarves and they stared at us, each side with weapons drawn, neither side backing down.

I held the phial just out of Crabs reach and raised my eyebrows. "You can have this if you can take us to Halftans Crevice."

Crab stared at me for a moment. "Stand down lads," he said eventually. "You boys too," he said to Galant and Duckie as if he was intervening in some childish tussle. "We'll take you there, Miss….?" he said to me, hoisting up his trousers as he spoke.

"Fen," I replied. "My name is Fen and this is Galant and Duckie." The dwarf nodded at the two of them before turning back to me. "As it happens we are quite familiar with Halftans Crevice. And for that Midnight Blue we'll take you there. And if you tell us where we can get more," he said with a chuckle, "I have a feeling we'll become firm friends."

Stoneseekers

CHAPTER 30

The bumble bee buzzed lazily amongst the myriad of flowers before settling inside a trumpet shaped bloom of bright fuchsia. It crept inside the soft petals and extended its curled tongue to sip at the nectar gathered at the flowers centre. From across the garden came the sound of wood striking wood and the bee emerged from the foxglove and buzzed towards a lush green lawn where two figures stood, practice swords in their hands.

"Ariad!" the larger figure chastised. "Dodge and roll! Remember what I told you. When I swipe across like this," the man swept his wooden sword in front of him, "You need to duck down and roll clear!" The bee drifted in looping circles between the grey-haired man and the small blonde headed girl but they paid it no mind as it disappeared into a bush of vivid blue buds. Ariad stepped back and puffed out her cheeks before wiping a hand across her brow.

"I'm not fast enough Farran!" she answered hotly. "I'm no good at this!"

Farran lowered his wooden sword and rested it against his leg as he regarded the girl. "You're no good because you're not trying," he told her. "You have to believe you're good enough," he added, stepping forward and gently tapping a finger against her temple. "In here," he said. "You need to start believing you *can* be good enough in here."

The girl frowned and pulled away from him, dropping her sword onto the grass before sitting down and pulling her knees up to her chin. "And how am I supposed to believe that?" she asked plaintively, looking up at Farran. "I don't think you believe it. And my mother and father certainly don't," she added bitterly.

Farran sighed and sat down next to her, looking across the garden and surveying the rooftops of the city beyond. "Ariad," he said patiently. "It matters nothing what I think, or what the Amir and your mother think. When you turn seventeen, the only person who needs to believe it is you." He turned to her. "You are the one who will have to go out and find your stone. Only you."

A dark look flashed across Ariads face. "I'm not so sure about that anymore," she said, almost to herself. Farran looked down at her and raised his eyebrows. "What are you saying Ariad?" He asked. "You know how it is. How it has always been."

Ariad looked pensive. "You don't understand," she said hesitantly. "My mother…. She has plans for me…" Ariad paused and bit her lip. "If she gets her way, someone will present my stone on a velvet cushion in my bed chamber and I'll be married off to some prince of Dracae before nightfall." She gestured at the wooden swords. "All this will be for nothing. A waste of time."

Farran looked at her closely. "No one can bring your stone to you. You know that."

Ariad started to speak but stopped herself and seemed to be considering her words carefully. "I've… Heard things," she said, her voice just a whisper "I've heard them talking. I know what they have planned for me. What *she* has planned for me." she said. "She thinks I'll end up like my brothers. That I'll never find my stone on my own and what use would I be to her then? Dead girls can't marry princes." Ariad sighed, her lip trembling slightly. "I sometimes wish I was some pauper out in the shanties who had been living hard and learning to fight all my life. At least that way, I'd have half a chance of being able to find my birthstone and decide for myself what to do with my life after that. And who knows," she added with a sharp laugh. "I might even have parents who care about me. They might be poor but at least they'd care."

Farran turned to her sharply. "Don't ever wish that Ariad," he said vehemently. "You don't know what you're saying. If you'd grown up in the shanties there's every chance you wouldn't even make it to your seventeenth annum. Do you have any idea how many of them die out there? Of the Sphyx or the Slinkferrals or in some potshop brawl? You'd likely have been dead by now or begging in the gutters." Ariad paled at his words and looked down at her hands.

Farran relented a little. "I know the Amir and your mother are…." He paused, searching for the appropriate word. "Ambitious. I know they have desires beyond Andorta." He rested a hand gently on Ariad's shoulder. "But you know that no single bloodline has ruled over the cities of Immentia in a millennia," he added reassuringly. "They'd need more than a good marriage to have a hope of controlling the eastern cities, let alone the west. And as for the lands beyond the northern mountains…." He trailed off as Ariad looked up at him.

"They will need more," she said quietly. "And they'll have more. There's a man in the dungeons. An old man who knows things... He knows how to get my mother what she wants."

Farran looked down at the girl, confused by her words but afraid to question her further. Under the Amir's rule and his wife's keen eyes, knowing too much could be dangerous. Even deadly.

Rumour had it that before Ariad's mother, Decima, had married the Amir of Andorta, she'd been a hired sword, an assassin. Some said she had been paid by the King of Epona in the south to murder the Amir but at the last moment, he had tempted her with an offer she could not refuse. Some even said she was a sorceress who had bewitched the Amir and now controlled his every thought, his every move, to her own ends. When they were married, she had cast aside her shadowy past and taken to wearing the regal robes and priceless jewels of an Amiress but the calculated movement of her body and the hard look in her eyes betrayed what she really still was. A killer. An ambitious one, biding her time, but a killer nonetheless.

As the pair sat in thoughtful silence, tension hanging in the humid air, a shadow fell across them and an approaching figure blotted out the sun. The Amiress Decima stood over them dressed in a white diaphanous robe that covered her body from her shoulders to her ankles, jewels hanging around her neck and her fingers heavy with gold rings.

"Ariad," Decima said, her voice smooth. "I sent you out here to practice your weaponry, and here I find you lazing about in the grass." She shot a hard look at Farran. "Is this what I'm paying you for?" she asked him, her tone light but her gaze steely. If she had overheard anything, it was hard to tell.

Farran jumped to his feet. "Many apologies my lady," he stuttered. "We were just resting. Ariad is coming on well with her sword. We can move onto real weapons soon I think," he added, pulling Ariad to her feet.

"See that you do," Decima snapped as she turned and strolled towards the palace. "The clock is ticking Ariad," she called over her shoulder. "Your father and I have great hopes for you." She made her way elegantly up the marble steps and spoke softly to herself under her breath, half a smile curving her lips. "In fact, I have great expectations for us all."

CHAPTER 31

After our tense stand-off in the forest, the 'Half's' seemed to be satisfied that we were not bandits out to rob them and they led us deeper into the woods, chatting as we went. They asked where we'd come from, where we'd been and when we asked about the Zaphite stones, Crab winked at us.

"You'll see," he said, "You'll see." The dwarves led us towards a rocky outcrop nestled amongst the huge trees and we picked our way through the stones down into the black, cavernous opening of a damp cave. The cave was lit from within by lanterns hanging from the craggy rock walls and as we descended downwards, a mechanical clanking echoed from deep in the gloom. The path underfoot was strewn with rocks and the little dwarves made their way effortlessly along with their large sturdy feet and small legs. The three of us were not so sure-footed and I grabbed Galant's hand to steady myself. Duckie glanced back at me, nodded imperceptibly at Crab and widened his eyes in a silent expression of confusion. I shrugged back at him and waved him on as we followed the little band stepping out ahead of us.

As we made our way through the dark tunnel, I looked about me and realized that what I had first thought were ordinary lanterns hanging from the walls were not what they seemed. The lamps had hexagonal glass sides and a metal loop at the top suspended from hooks hammered into the wall. But inside, instead of a flame burning from a wick, I was amazed to see the outlines of tiny figures. Fire faeries sat within each glass lantern, some sitting alone, others in pairs or small groups of three or four. Their slender bodies glowed, illuminating the darkness with their flaming wings that flickered red, orange and a deep blue where the appendages joined their delicate shoulders.

The dwarf named Garrowby was walking alongside us and I stopped, gesturing at the lanterns.

"How d'you trap those faeries?" I asked, knowing full well how difficult it was to catch a faerie let alone contain one.

Garrowby laughed out loud. "They're not trapped lass," he said to me indulgently. "They're in there of their own free will. We've an arrangement of sorts." He smiled again at my bemused expression and beckoned me closer to the nearest lantern. "Look," he said, pointing to a small circular well at the centre of the lantern. Some kind of hot, molten liquid glowed from the well and as I watched in amazement, I saw the faeries dipping tiny cups into the boiling liquid before bringing the cups to their lips and sipping daintily.

"What is that?" I asked, my voice low and soft for fear of frightening the faeries.

"Molten iron," Garrowby said. "Fire faeries can't get enough of it. We keep the lanterns filled and the faeries come, drink their fill and light our caves while they're at it." He chuckled again at my face before turning away, ushering us quickly onwards to catch up with the others.

Ahead of us, Crab and the other dwarves had stopped and the metallic clanging and grinding echoing through the cave had grown louder. Just ahead of us was a wide shaft which dropped down through the bottom of the cave. Emerging from the dark shaft were several ropes looped up around pulleys and cogs fixed to the roof of the cave above our heads. As I watched, a wooden platform with waist high barriers around three of its edges arose out of the shaft, grinding shakily to a stop a couple of inches below the surface.

"All aboard," Crab called and the dwarves all stepped onto the peculiar elevator. "Come on. Quickly now," he called as Galant, Duckie and I dithered at the edge of the shaft, glancing at each other nervously. I gave Duckie a push forward and he stepped down into the platform. Galant and I followed and the lift swayed gently under my feet before it began to descend slowly down into the darkness. For a few moments, we were plunged into pitch black but then the shaft began to widen and a light emanated from beneath us.

I blinked and shuffled to the edge of the wooden platform to look around. We had descended into a huge cave; long and wide with sheer vertical walls at either side. There was no visible floor to the cave, just a deep, dark chasm that seemed to drop into endless blackness beneath us. On the rock walls of the cave were wooden boards resting on beams hammered into the rock, almost like streets in a normal town but the boardwalks were built one above the other, up and down the walls of the rock. It appeared that the dwarves could access upper and lower levels on the same side of the crevice by stairways that joined them. Several other lifts like the one we were standing on were moving up and down the crevice, dwarves getting on and off at the various levels as the lift passed each boardwalk. Some of the lifts traversed across the crevice as well as up and down, allowing the dwarves to move from one side to the other.

The air was filled with the sound of cranking pulleys and the loud echo of metal tools striking rock. The smoky acrid smell of molten metal crept into my nostrils. Along the cavern walls were the small doors and windows of dwarfish dwellings carved out of the stone beside the boardwalks, each door painted a different colour and cozy lights glowing from behind the window panes.

Crab turned and looked at each of us. "Welcome to Halftans Crevice," he said proudly as the lift descended down past the highest boardwalks before drawing to a stop on an exposed rock plateau. Above the plateau stretched a huge expanse of rough stone where many dwarves were busily mining ore with pickaxes and shovels, piling it into great mounds as other dwarves filled wheelbarrows before trundling off. More dwarves were hanging, suspended high up on the wall by rope harnesses, pickaxes in one hand as they loosened the ore and dropped it onto the plateau beneath.

Our little group stepped off the lift and Duckie moved closer to me, his head tilted back as he gazed around in amazement.

"I can hardly believe it Fen," he said, his voice soft. "I never thought we'd find it."

I nodded, speechless as I took in the strange smells and sounds around us. "Let's hope they really have Zaphite here," I added, still not daring to hope that it might be true. Before Duckie could answer, Crab approached us, hoisting up his trousers again in what had now become quite a comical and endearing gesture.

"So," he said, "I suppose you want to see this stone of yours?"

Duckie nodded. "If that's alright Mister Crab," he said respectfully and Crab chuckled at Duckie's eagerness.

"You humans and your birthstones," he said, amused. "Us dwarves were spared that curse. We have no use for your stones. Thank the gods of iron and steel, our only curse is being a bit shorter than you lot." He laughed loudly, nudging Duckie in the thigh. "But what they withheld in height, they repaid in brawn!" he added, gesturing to the rock wall, busy with dwarves wielding their heavy tools.

Crab eyed the phial of Midnight Blue I still held in my hands. "That's worth more to us than birthstones," he said. "A fair exchange in my book." I clutched the phial tighter and Galant moved slightly in front of me.

"So…" I said. "Can you show us the Zaphite?"

Crab nodded briskly and turned to the other dwarves who had accompanied us back from the forest. "You lot are dismissed," he said and the dwarves turned to leave. "Not you Garrowby," Crab added sharply as the black bearded dwarf began to head off down the boardwalk. Garrowby sighed and turned back reluctantly. "I'll show our new friends what they're after," Crab went on. "Then you can take them to the Pick and Spark for the night." Garrowby grunted and we all followed as Crab trundled off down the boardwalk along the side of the crevice, greeting fellow dwarves as he passed.

Crab led us to another lift and he stood there whistling to himself, hands clasped behind his back and rocking on his heels as the platform arrived from the levels above. He herded the three of us on, followed by Garrowby who hopped fearlessly down onto the platform as it began to descend lower into the black depths. When we reached the lowest boardwalk, we jumped off the lift and Crab led us further along the crevice as the little windows and doors of the dwarves' homes disappeared behind us to leave rough, bare rock on one side, impossible darkness falling away on the other.

Eventually we reached a wooden barrier blocking our path and Crab climbed clumsily over it, beckoning us to follow. Beyond the barrier the boardwalk came to an abrupt and precipitous stop, the black chasm yawning beneath us, the floor littered with climbing ropes, abandoned pickaxe heads and shovel handles.

Crab stood a few feet from the edge of the boardwalk and gestured down into the darkness. "We tried mining down here a while back," he said as the rest of us came to a halt. "The iron ore's plentiful but its dangerous work," he pointed down in the black abyss beneath us. "We don't think the crevice ever ends," he said, his voice almost a whisper as if he was afraid he would be overheard. "We've dropped rocks down it the size of a man and never heard them hit the bottom." We stared at him wordlessly with wide eyes and a shiver ran through me as I looked cautiously over the edge, standing back as the bottomless blackness made my knees wobble.

Crab eventually broke the tense silence. "But this is where we found what you're looking for," he said, a little more cheerfully as he leaned forward and peered down over the edge. Duckie shuffled forward to stand next to him and I followed, swallowing my fear as the three of us stared down into the pitch black. "There," said Crab softly. "D'you see it?" We followed his small pointed finger and for a moment I could see nothing but darkness. I blinked a couple of times. Finally, I could make out an almost imperceptible twinkle glowing up through the dark, the source small but undeniably bright and vivid.

"I can see it," breathed Duckie, "I can see it! Fen look!" I nodded, saying nothing, a feeling of relief flooding through me. Duckie's search would hopefully soon be over.

"How'll we get to it?" Duckie asked Crab as we stared down into the darkness. Crab shrugged and straightened upright. "Some of us have been down there on the usual mining harnesses. We can probably fix one up to carry your weight but like I said, its dangerous work." Duckie and I looked at each other and I saw his face was pale. "Let's not think on it right now," said Crab firmly. "You must be tired. And hungry no doubt. Garrowby here will take you up to the tavern and get you settled." He peered back over the boardwalk and into the crevice, his face shrouded in shadows. "We'll tackle that problem tomorrow."

CHAPTER 33

Halftans Crevice was still bustling with activity as the dwarves returned to their homes for the night. Tools and picks clanked on their shoulders as they fearlessly navigated the walkways and crisscrossed the crevice on the lifts and stairways. Crab bid us goodnight, promising to come and find us the next day. "I'll see if I can get the boys on with that harness," he said. "Should have something ready for you tomorrow." We thanked him and the three of us took a lift to the higher levels with Garrowby, various other dwarves jumping on and on off and greeting us cheerfully.

When we reached the highest boardwalk, Garrowby led us along the walkway and pointed out the houses, explaining how the dwarves had first settled here and began building their wooden streets and carving out their individual homes from the rock face. We passed the open front of a larger cave, incessant clanking and mechanical noises echoing deafeningly from within. Inside was a complex network of cogs, ropes and pulleys all powered by one huge wheel turning slowly on the floor of the cave. Around the wheel were eight dwarves standing on strange contraptions with pedals under their large feet. Their little legs were pumping the pedals round and round, turning the wheel that powered the cogs and ropes above their heads.

"These lads are driving the lifts," explained Garrowby. "We work in shifts so we're either mining, working the cogs or having a rest; usually in the pub!" he added with a wink. "Keep at it boys," Garrowby shouted to the dwarves puffing away on the pedals. A couple raised a hand and called back a greeting or bawdy joke in response as we moved off.

We passed more caves where dwarves were shoveling ore into huge smelters, the glowing lava casting strange lights and shadows on the rock walls. One cave contained a workshop where dwarves wearing heavy leather aprons were forging swords, daggers and tools, a loud hissing sound filling the air as they plunged the red-hot metal into barrels of water. A dwarfish urchin trotted past us carrying a steaming bucket and ladle, her ruddy face turned up at us curiously. When she passed I saw that the bucket was full of molten metal and the dwarf girl stopped at the next lantern, clambering up to replenishing the well for the fire faeries.

Eventually we reached the tavern where shapes and shadows moved in the window, the buzz of many voices echoing from the doorway. "Here we are," said Garrowby, pushing open the door. "The Pick and Spark." The three of us had to duck down to pass through the dwarf-sized opening but thankfully inside, the ceiling was slightly higher. I could stand up straight but Duckie and Galant still had to stoop a little. The inn was busy with dwarves sitting at stone tables and benches or perched on three legged stools. The bar at the back of the room was carved from rock, its surface worn and smooth and at one side, a narrow stone staircase led upwards to another floor above.

Most of the dwarves fell silent when we entered and Garrowby clapped his small hands together loudly. "Right all," he shouted. "We have some visitors. These folks'll be staying with us for a day or so. I trust you'll make them feel welcome." Some of the dwarves beamed at us with friendly smiles, others looked up from under bushy eyebrows, their gazes suspicious and some had clearly been in the tavern too long and stared at us with glazed and slightly cross-eyed expressions. I raised a tentative hand in greeting as I looked awkwardly around the room.

"Stonedrill!" Garrowby called out, walking towards the bar as a harried looking dwarf scuttled over from one of the tables, his hands filled with metal ale mugs. "You'll be putting them up for the night. Your largest rooms if you please!" he added and all the dwarves guffawed loudly at his joke.

"Quite alright, Garrowby," said Stonedrill the innkeeper as he dumped his pile of mugs behind the bar and wiped his hands on his apron. "You'll be wanting some food then?" he asked, looking at the three of us. "We've got some nice cave mutton on tonight," he added, gesturing to a pot bubbling over an open fire behind the bar.

"That would be marvelous," said Galant charmingly as Duckie raised an eyebrow at me.

"Cave mutton?" he whispered dubiously, making a face.

"Shhh!" I chastised quietly. "Don't be rude!" Duckie raised an eyebrow at me as Stonedrill ushered us to a table and the dwarves shuffled their stools around to make some space. We all took a seat and I smiled to myself as I watched Duckie and Galant with their knees drawn up uncomfortably, almost under their chins.

Stonedrill brought us some of his cave mutton and we didn't ask exactly what was in the grey glutinous stew, not wanting to appear ungrateful. It didn't taste bad and was the first hot food we'd had in days so we devoured it quite happily. When we had finished eating and had downed a few of the tiny mugs of ale, Stonedrill escorted us up the stairs at the back of the tavern and into a narrow corridor lined with doors. The rooms were tiny but cozily lit by the fire faerie lamps, the beds carved from stone but layered comfortably with wool blankets and animal skins. Each room had a small glassless window in one wall which gave a slightly stomach churning view out into the crevice and the dark drop beneath. I realized how tired I was having been on the road for several days with nowhere safe to sleep and I was glad to see a bed, however small.

"You can have this room Miss," Stonedrill said to me as I stooped through one of the doorways. "And you gents can have the two rooms on the other side." Galant and Duckie followed the little dwarf down the hall, leaving me alone in the little stone room. I lay back on the bed, staring at the stone ceiling not far above my head, listening to the muffled voices as Stonedrill asked if we needed anything and made a few inquisitive enquiries about our travels.

When he had gone, I removed my coat and boots and crawled under the blankets, letting my eyes close and my breathing slow. My feet and lower legs extended well beyond the end of the dwarf-sized bed so I lay on my side and tucked my knees up to my chest. I heard the fire faerie in my lantern ting the bottom of the well with its little cup and its high-pitched mutter when it found the well empty. It tutted and I heard the door of the lantern open and a faint thrum in the air as the faerie flew over my head and out of the window, leaving the room in darkness.

I was almost asleep when I heard a noise in the doorway and I sat up to see a figure outlined in the glow from the passageway.

"Galant?" I asked sleepily.

"No, it's me," I heard Duckie's familiar voice whisper through the dark. "Can I come in?" he asked.

"Course," I said, yawning and pushing myself upright, leaning my back against the wall and pulling the wool blanket around my shoulders. Duckie stooped through the doorway and sat down on the edge of the bed.

"What's up?" I asked him gently as I watched his pale face.

"Just thought I'd check on you," he said with forced nonchalance. "See if you're feeling alright. If you need anything. Funny place this isn't it? And those lifts and everything…" He was babbling brightly but his voice was shaky and high pitched. I didn't respond and waited for him to tell me why he'd really come to see me. Duckie trailed off into silence and looked at the floor, wringing his fingers together nervously.

"I'm scared Fen," Duckie said finally in a small voice. "I'm scared that the stones we saw might not be Zaphite. I'm scared I'll fall. I'm scared of going down there and not coming back." He wouldn't meet my eyes and he clenched and unclenched his hands anxiously as he spoke.

I sighed and looked at his face, shadowed in the darkness. "Duckie," I said gently. "We've made it this far. Crab thinks its Zaphite and the dwarves have been down there. They've seen it. There's nothing to be afraid of now, you've almost done it." I gripped his arm as I spoke, trying to sound confident so Duckie wouldn't be able to tell that I also felt his fear.

"But what if it's not Zaphite Fen?" Duckie pressed. "What if I get too close and it's not Zaphite? What if it's Glisston? Or Forzit or Veridian? They all sparkle in the dark Fen."

I shuffled closer to him on the bed and looked into his face. "Remember I told you about the stone I saw on my way to Andorta?" I asked him. "As long as you don't touch it you'll be alright. Even if you get too close and faint like I did, we'll just pull you up again." He stared at me, still unconvinced. "You know what you're looking for Duckie," I continued. "Remember what we've been taught. A Zaphite stone is silver with many facets and shaped like a snowflake. You'll know if it's what you're looking for."

He nodded. "Shaped like a snowflake," he echoed me, his voice sounding more resolute.

"Go to bed," I said gently. "The sooner you go to sleep, the sooner we'll be able to get this done. By this time tomorrow it'll be over." I smiled at him. "You'll have your stone. Just think of it; your whole life ahead of you. You'll no longer be a Seeker."

CHAPTER 32

I slept uneasily that night and in the early hours, I heard someone creep into my room. I didn't have to open my eyes as I felt Galant's warm body lay down beside me on the small bed and felt him pull me towards him. I rested comfortably against him as he gently kissed my forehead as if it was the most natural thing in the world before the two of us fell back to sleep. When I awoke, he was still sleeping and I watched him for a while, looking at his face in the darkness, his mouth relaxed and his chest rising and falling steadily against me. He shifted and his eyes blinked open as he caught me watching him. I pulled away a little and rested my chin on my palm.

"What are you doing in here?" I whispered and he smiled sleepily at me.

"I had a bad dream Fen," he said lightly, teasing me. "Couldn't sleep without you," he murmured, pulling me back close to him. I smiled and rested my cheek on his shoulder.

"So, todays the day for Duckie," Galant said quietly as we lay there in the dark. I nodded.

"Then it'll be my turn." I said. "I'll need to get to Wistmans Hollow. Find this river or these caverns or whatever it was those stupid cards said."

Galant laughed at that. "Those cards might be stupid Fen," he said, "But they might also speak the truth. And we've found nothing else so it's not like you have a lot of choices."

I sighed, knowing he was right. Since leaving Andorta, we had thought of little else but getting here and finding Duckie's stone. I hadn't even given the next part of our journey much thought, it had seemed so far away. I had pushed it to the back of my mind, intending to worry about it when the time came but now it seemed like the time was almost upon me.

We dozed together a little longer before Galant got up and returned to his room to dress. I did the same and when I put my head around Duckie's door I found him sitting there in the darkness.

"You ready?" I asked and he looked up at me.

"As ready as I can be," said Duckie darkly as we headed along the corridor and down the narrow stairs. When we entered the lower room of the Pick and Spark, we found Crab and Garrowby gathered around a table with a couple of other dwarves. On the table lay a harness like the ones we had seen the mining dwarves wearing as they hung high up on the rock face. As we approached, the dwarves greeting was friendly enough but their expressions were serious as Crab held up the harness.

"We think this'll do it," he said, holding out the harness to Duckie who eyed it warily. "We've extended it where needs be," Crab continued. "And we've strengthened the attachments and rivets. Garrowby and the lads here have tested it – we reckon it'll hold you."

Duckie took the bundle of leather straps and looked carefully at the welded rivets and knots of rope.

Crab pointed at the thick length of rope that extended from the belt of the harness. "Even if this one gives," he said, "There's another one fixed here on the front."

Duckie nodded and swallowed hard. "Let's go then," he said. "I'm ready."

Crab looked at him grimly. "Let's hope you are lad, let's hope you are."

We all left the tavern and travelled the lifts and stairways back down to the lowest level. The air was thick and oppressive but at this early hour the crevice was quiet with only a few other dwarves milling about. We clambered back over the barrier and huddled there while the dwarves helped Duckie into the harness, a leg through each of the leather loops and the belt fastened firmly around his waist. Garrowby tied the ends of the long ropes tightly to a metal loop fixed to the rock wall, the dwarves checking over the fastenings and knots once more before they were satisfied. Duckie's hands were shaking and he clasped his fingers together tightly, rubbing them nervously as he stood at the edge of the crevice.

"Right then lad," said Crab. "You'll need to lower yourself over the edge and turn around to face the wall. If you rest your feet against the rock you should be able to edge your way down. We'll take up the slack on the rope so all you need to do is shout up when you reach the stone." Crab reached into his pocket and pulled out a chisel, handing it to Duckie. "Chip out the stone and for gads sake don't drop it! Give us a shout and we'll pull you back up." He beamed at Duckie's worried face. "Easy!" he said, clapping Duckie on the back.

Duckie nodded, his face grey. He turned to me. "Fen," he said. "If something happens, tell my ma and pa…. tell them…" his voice trailed off and I kissed my palm before resting my hand on his hair.

"Shhh," I said. "I know what to tell them. But I won't need to." He looked hard at my face and I nodded resolutely. He turned from me and took a deep breath before crouching to sit on the very edge of the boardwalk. Crab, Garrowby, and the other dwarves took up the slack of the rope and held it taught as Duckie lowered himself over the edge. He hung there in mid-air for a moment, suspended over the black terrifying chasm before swinging himself around and bracing his feet against the rock face.

"Alright," he called, his voice wavering. "Lower me down." The dwarves began to slowly release the rope, Crab muttering a rhythm as it passed between each of their small strong hands. I looked over the edge to see Duckie disappearing into the darkness and my throat felt tight as if someone was squeezing the breath from me. I felt a rush of panic as the full realization of the danger hit me. The next few minutes passed agonizingly slowly as the dwarves continued to lower Duckie downwards, his fading voice calling out occasionally to ask them to stop as he regained his footing or to lower him a little faster. I could still see the stone glinting far beneath us but Duckie had vanished into the dense darkness.

Eventually, after several painful, dragging minutes, his voice called up to us. "Stop! Stop, I'm almost there."

"Can you see the stones Duckie?" I yelled down to him. I held my breath and waited, willing him to say it, to say the words that we'd dreamed of since we were children. The words that would save his life.

Finally, he spoke. "It's Zaphite!" I heard him shout, his voice stronger now. "Fen, its Zaphite!" He whooped with joy and I felt relief flooding through my body, my knees weakened beneath me and I let out a nervous burst of laughter. Galant smiled at me and gripped my hand hard as the dwarves looked on, leaning back, bracing themselves on the rope.

"Told you," said Crab with a wink. We could hear the chip, chip sound of the chisel and I stared down into the blackness, squinting my eyes, trying to see Duckie finally clasp his hands around his birthstone.

The chipping noise stopped and there was silence in the crevice except for the echo of the mechanisms sounding from the lifts above. As I stared hard into the chasm, a bright white light suddenly lit up the rock face and I could clearly see the outline of Duckie hunched far beneath us. He had the stone clasped in his hands and as I watched in wonder, the light glowed brighter from beneath his fingers before tendrils of silver began to run up his arms and across his chest. In seconds, his whole body was illuminated in light from within and I saw him throw back his head as the birthstone shot its power through him. I could see every vein, every muscle in his arms, neck and face as the silver energy emanated through him. The light glowed even more brightly for a second, almost blinding, before it suddenly faded as the outline of my friend once more disappeared into the darkness and the silence fell around us once more.

For a few moments, no one made a sound and I squinted down into the chasm but could see nothing, just the rope fading away into the depths and the remnant flashes of white burning across my vision.

"Duckie!" I called out. "Duckie are you alright?" There was no answer. "Duckie!" I shouted desperately. Galant held me back from the edge and I felt panic rising in me as the silence went on.

Eventually a faint voice echoed up from beneath. "Fen, I'm alright! I'm alright! It feels…. I feel… It was wonderful! Pull me up." Crab nodded at the other dwarves and they began pulling the rope back through their fingers, puffing and cheeks red from exertion. The rope creaked as they hoisted Duckie up and just as my friend began to emerge from the black, just as my panic began to subside, as relief began to flood through me, loosening my muscles and easing my breath, a dreadful sound echoed up from the depths. A small but dreadful sound. A metallic pop and the noise of something small and hard skittering down the rock face.

I looked at Galant, my eyes wide. "What was that?" I whispered, feeling the blood drain from my face. "Duckie what was that?" I shouted over the edge.

"It's the harness!" he called back and I could hear the terror in his voice. "The harness is breaking; the rivets are coming loose!" I heard another metallic pop and the rope jerked suddenly, quickly running through the dwarves' hands. I heard Duckie's strangled shout and when I looked over the edge I saw that the belt of the harness had come completely undone and he was just hanging from one loop under his thigh. "Pull me up!" he shouted, "Hurry!" I watched in horror as the dwarves regained their grip on the rope and began to pull it quickly through their hands. Another metallic pop sounded beneath us followed by another and my heart stopped as I watched Duckie tumble free from the leather loops. He held tightly to the rope for a moment with both hands as his body twisted and swung. "Pull me up! It won't…. I can't…" His voice was shrill, his white fingers straining as he lost his grip on the rope, hands plucking uselessly at the air, trying to grab for the broken harness as he fell.

Time seemed to slow down as our worst fear came true before my eyes. I saw Duckie's arms flailing desperately and I heard his anguished shout falling away from us, fading into the blackness. I screamed and grabbed onto the rope in a futile gesture, the rope hanging slack in my hand as Galant held me back from the edge. "Duckie!" I cried, tears immediately streaming down my face. "Duckie no!" I collapsed onto the wooden boardwalk and scrabbled to the edge, looking over the side, my tears blinding me. The dwarves had fallen backwards, the rope loose in their hands and I saw Crab looking down at it in horror. "No, lad" he whispered disbelievingly, "Oh no."

I was crying violently now, searing gasps of horror, and Galant knelt beside me, pulling me close to his chest as I struggled against him. "Duckie," I called again and again, my voice weak and the words lost in my tears.

"Fen don't, please," murmured Galant and I felt him shaking too as I wept. The dwarves were shocked and silent and the only sound was my own heart rending sobs. I couldn't think straight, I couldn't speak, I could hardly breathe. We had come so close. So close. For it to end like this seemed too impossible and tragic for me to bear.

I struggled for breath, the tears coming in torrents and my mind scrabbling to try to grasp hold of what had happened. Through the haze of tears and the echo of my own hysterical sobs, I suddenly felt a firm hand on my shoulder. Crab bent down towards me, a finger held to his bearded lips.

"Hush lass," he said sharply. "Quiet!" I looked up at him through my tears to see him cock his head, listening carefully. I held my breath and clasped a hand over my mouth, a flicker of hope leaping to my chest. As we listened in stunned silence, I heard a small sound from deep in the chasm. A muffled groan of pain that filtered up weakly from the darkness. I leapt to my feet, and leaned over the edge of the rock, squinting my eyes.

"Duckie!" I called, not daring to even hope. "Duckie?"

After another agonizing moment, a frail voice drifted up from far beneath and my heart quickened. "I'm here. Fen, my leg…. My leg…" his voice trailed off with a painful moan.

Crab and the other dwarves leapt into action. "Garrowby," Crab ordered, "Get a lantern, quick!" Garrowby hurried back along the walkway and unhooked a lantern from the wall, the fire faeries within giggling and fluttering in excitement. The dwarves pulled the broken harness up onto the walkway and tied the lantern firmly to it, several feet from the end, before lowering it back over the edge. We all watched as the glowing light descended, illuminating the rock face as it went.

"We're almost out of rope Crab," said Garrowby as the dwarves fed the rope quickly over the side of the boardwalk.

"We're nearly there," answered Crab, "A bit more, that's it…I can see him!" I squinted down into the darkness and just beneath the lantern was the small figure of Duckie, laid prone on a narrow ledge far down in the crevice.

"Duckie!" I called, relief and vertigo making my legs collapse beneath me as I leaned over the edge. "Are you alright? Can you see the rope?"

I saw Duckie reaching for the end of the rope that dangled above him as he called back. "I can see it! But my leg's bad. I think it's broken."

Crab cupped his hands around his mouth. "Tie the rope around your middle lad!" he called down. "Tie it tight, wrap it around yourself and under your arms and tie it again. We'll get you out!"

Duckie took the rope and wrapped it around his chest, moving awkwardly as one of his legs lay stiff and unmoving.

"Alright I'm ready," he called eventually and the dwarves once again began to pull on the rope. I wiped my eyes, knowing my tears wouldn't help Duckie. It seemed to take forever for the dwarves to pull Duckie upwards and I realized how far he must have fallen. As they pulled him closer, I saw that his skin was white and his eyes were wide but as he looked up at me, I saw a light in his eyes that hadn't been there before.

"I got it Fen!" he called up to me, half a sob in his voice. "I got it."

Eventually Galant and Crab were able to lean over and grasp him beneath his arms and pull him to safety. I couldn't hold back my tears any longer and I fell onto Duckie's shoulders crying hard with fear and relief.

"I thought you'd gone," I mumbled, "I thought you'd gone." Duckie awkwardly patted my head and forced a laugh, his voice weak and shaky.

"Me too Fen," he said, "Just my luck to find my birthstone and then plunge to my death moments later!" I half laughed, half cried at his feeble joke as we huddled there clutching onto each other. "I've never seen you cry before Fen," Duckie said suddenly, looking at me curiously.

"Yes, well," I said, sniffing loudly. "I've never watched you almost get yourself killed before!" Duckie laughed at that but winced in pain as he tried to shift his leg.

"I thought yous'd checked that harness," Crab said, rounding angrily on the dwarves.

"We did Crab!" said Garrowby vehemently, "I hoisted up three of us in that harness earlier on and it held fast!" Crab grunted in response. "This lad probably only weighs half that at the most!" he exclaimed. "Three of you must've loosened the rivets you stupid half-brains!"

Duckie held up a placating hand. "Crab don't, please. They did their best and we got what we needed. I found my stone." Duckie grinned at them, that strange silver glow still emanating in his eyes. "I owe you my life."

Crab began to speak again but thought better of it and shot a dark look at the other dwarves. "Well, I suppose you're safe now," he said, glancing down at Duckie. "But that leg doesn't look right."

Duckie looked at his leg and flinched again, gasping in pain as he tried to move it. "I think I broke it when I landed on that ledge," he said as Galant helped him up, supporting him under his arms.

"Let's get you back to the tavern," said Crab, casting his eyes across all our pale and drained faces. "I don't usually agree with drinking in the morning but today," he hoisted up his trousers, eyes twinkling. "Today I think we can make an exception."

CHAPTER 33

We spent several more pleasant days with the dwarves of Halftans Crevice. They bandaged Duckie's leg with a splint and even made him a couple of iron crutches so he could hobble about. I felt exhausted and weak after everything that had happened but Galant was sweet to me, bringing me dainty goblets of wine and small things to eat. He slept in my room as I tossed and turned, dreaming of bottomless chasms and seeing Duckie falling away from me into the black over and over again. I woke gasping for breath and drenched in a cold sweat to find Galant lying next to me, his arms around me and his soft voice whispering soothing words until I fell asleep, huddled against his shoulder.

Duckie had told us how he had chipped the Zaphite stone from the rock face and described how the light and heat of its energy had filled him and pulsed through his veins before the stone turned to dust in his fingers.

"It was amazing Fen," he told me, his voice filled with wonder. "I can't even describe it. But you'll find out soon enough," he added, "We'll find Rubine next I'm sure of it."

I had just nodded and smiled, just wanting to enjoy these few quiet days in safety with our new diminutive friends before we all had to acknowledge the obvious. The obvious being the fact that there was no way Duckie would be able to continue on this journey with me. With his broken leg, he could barely walk so I knew we had no option but to try to get him home as safely as we could. I would have to continue on alone.

In the days after Duckie claimed his stone, I wondered about Galant. We both knew that he didn't need to be here. He could have returned home alone weeks ago yet here he was, hardly leaving my side as we lingered in this strange underground city.

"What will you do next?" I asked one morning as we laid together, legs hunched up in my dwarven bed. "You should go home now, you've come far enough with us." Even as I spoke the words, I wanted to bite them back, the thought of him leaving me thudding hard into the pit of my stomach.

He sighed and turned his face towards mine. "I don't want to leave you Fen," he said eventually. "I think we need each other."

I looked at him carefully. "What about your sister? And her baby?" I asked and I saw a pained look passed across his features.

"They need me too," he said eventually. "But they'll be taken care of. I want to help you find your stone Fen. I don't want to leave you now." I felt a surge of emotion well up within me and I didn't know if what I felt was gratitude, happiness or fear. All I knew was that despite my misgivings, he had told me exactly what I wanted to hear.

On the evening of our fourth day in Halftans Crevice we gathered in the Pick and Spark with Crab and Garrowby. Duckie was in good spirits despite the pain of his leg but I couldn't linger here any longer and Galant and I had agreed we would leave the next morning. Duckie had begrudgingly admitted that he couldn't come any further with me and I was grateful that he hadn't tried to argue the point. It was so agonizingly obvious that despite his good intentions, he would slow me down and put us all in danger. He wasn't happy about me going on alone, or even with Galant, but had eventually agreed it was the best thing for all of us. Now we had one more problem to solve before we moved on.

The three of us shared a few mugs of ale with the dwarves, making light conversation before I broached the pressing subject that was concerning me. Amid the chatter I shot a look at Galant and he nodded slightly, prompting me to speak.

"Crab," I began. "I have something to ask you. We need your help."

Crab turned to me, stroking his beard and regarding my serious expression. "I'd have thought we've helped you enough lass," he said lightly gesturing at Duckie. "He's not in quite as good a shape as when we found him but he's alive in't he? And he will be for a few annums more thanks to us!" he grinned at me and I smiled easily in return.

"That's part of the problem," I continued. "His leg. We need to get Duckie home. Back to Millings Beck."

I waited for Crab to respond and shot a look at Duckie who was pulling nervously on his lip. Crab took a deep breath and sat back on his stool, stroking his beard and looking at Garrowby thoughtfully.

"It's a long journey," he said finally and Garrowby nodded in agreement.

"A few weeks on the road I reckon Crab," he said, shrugging and folding his arms.

Luckily, I was prepared for their reluctance. "It is." I said. "And I know it won't be easy, Duckie being….as he is." Duckie gave the dwarves a rueful smile but I knew it pained him to be a burden to any of us.

I leaned forward in my seat. "You've got the phial of Midnight Blue," I said and Crab nodded, his expression suddenly interested. "If you or your men can get Duckie home," I went on, "We'll tell you where you can get more." I had played my ace and sat back, holding my breath, hoping it would be enough.

Crab sat up straighter and glanced at Garrowby. "What d'you think Garrowby?" Crab asked the other dwarf. It was Garrowby's turn to stroke his beard as they considered my offer.

"Well," he began, and I knew immediately that my proposition was a good one. "The best thing'd be to take Elsbioli's boat down to Fangs Foss. And from there we can probably hop on a barge north." I looked over at Galant hopefully and he gave me a small smile but said nothing. The two dwarves looked at each other for a moment.

"Alright," said Crab to his comrade, nodding slowly. "I see, I see where you're going. If you can get on a barge you can probably go as far north as Throttlesbottom and from there Feybridge or even Boann."

Garrowby nodded. "And then it's probably only a few days to Millings Beck. If we can catch a caravan or a cart we should be able to make it from there even with hop-along over here." He pointed a thumb at Duckie who shrugged and shot me a cheeky wink.

"So you'll do it?" I asked. "When you get to Millings Beck, Duckie will give you directions to where you can get more Midnight Blue, Violet Silkwing – all kinds of things." I silently apologized to Mallady and hoped she wouldn't mind a few strange dwarves arriving at her birdhouse uninvited.

Crab thought for a few moments before resting both hands on the table.

"Alright," he said. "We'll do it. Garrowby?" He asked and the other dwarf nodded, needing no more prompting.

"I'll round up a few of the lads and we'll set off in a day or so." Garrowby looked over at Duckie. "You got some gold lad?" he asked. "We'll not ride on a barge or even a cart for free and I'll be cursed if we're footing that bill."

Before Duckie could answer I interjected. "We've got a few coins," I said. "We'll give most of what we have to Duckie. It should be enough." I looked across at Galant hopefully, realizing I was making promises we would all have to keep.

He cleared his throat. "You can have most of the coin I've got. Should be plenty." Galant emptied his pockets onto the table and pushed the gold coins towards the dwarves. His clear eyes met mine and his gaze didn't waver as the dwarves looked at each other and gathered up the coins.

"That's settled then," said Garrowby firmly, scooping the payment into his pockets. His eyes twinkled. "Looks like our little happenstance meeting will work out for the best. For all of us." I breathed a sigh of relief that we would be able to get Duckie home. It would still be a long and hazardous journey but I knew that the dwarves were tough and shrewd and there was no one I would trust more with the safety of my friend.

Crab and Garrowby bid us goodnight, promising to meet Duckie the next morning. Garrowby threw a few quick and playful jabs into Duckie's ribs and cracked a few bawdy jokes about their upcoming travels before he ambled out of the inn, raising a hand and as they disappeared through the heavy wooden door.

Duckie laughed along until the door closed behind the dwarves and then he turned to me, his face suddenly serious.

"Fen, I'm sorry," he said, frowning. "This isn't how we planned it." He slammed his fist down in frustration on his injured leg and when he winced in pain I grabbed his wrist. "This isn't how it was supposed to happen." His voice cracked as he spoke.

I smiled at him. "Duckie don't say that. There's nothing to be done about it now. And I know you don't want to hear this but we both know I'll be better off without you." I saw Duckie flinch as my words hurt him but he had to admit that it was the truth. I didn't want him to make this any harder. "And anyway," I went on, "Galant will be with me. Even without him, I'd probably be perfectly alright on my own." Now it was Galant's turn to look hurt and I avoided his gaze, watching Duckie's crestfallen expression. "You just need to get home now," I said. "We're not far from Wistmans Hollow so if the cards spoke the truth, I might only be a few days away from finding my own stone."

Duckie cheered up a little at this. "I hope so Fen," he said.

I nodded encouragingly but Galant stayed silent. "You found what you were looking for," I continued, looking into Duckie's face. "You found it. And now it's time for you to go home."

CHAPTER 34

The following day we left Halftans Crevice. Garrowby accompanied us with two other sturdy looking dwarves named Cleasby and Hopp. Duckie was glum and apprehensive about making the long journey home with his injured leg and I understood how vulnerable he felt even with the dwarves travelling with him. I couldn't help but wish that I was going home with them but I pushed the thought aside. We parted ways on the bank of the river where Duckie and I exchanged a few words of farewell. I asked him to tell Pa I was safe and to tell Leif I would be home soon. He promised to tell Pa I wasn't traveling alone and I hoped this would be some comfort to him when he saw Duckie return home without me. I couldn't bear to spend any longer on goodbyes so eventually I returned Duckie's awkward hug and told him to take care of himself before turning and walking away. The last glimpse I had of Duckie was of him hobbling along the jetty as the feathered figure of Elsbioli emerged from the mist.

I turned away and scanned the horizon, turning my thoughts to the journey ahead. Duckie had given us his map and the dwarves had scrawled out the route to Wistmans Hollow, a long walk heading south east that would take us several days. It felt strange to be alone with Galant and being without Duckie brought with it a sense of loss I can't begin to describe. With every step, I felt that I was going further and further from Duckie and further away from home. We left the huge trees of the dwarves forest behind us and found ourselves wending our way across grassy wolds and through steep sided valleys. Sparse outcrops of trees lined the hilltops and sweet meadow flowers dotted the lush grass. The landscape reminded me a little of home and for a few happy moments I could almost imagine that it was all over and I was making my way back to Millings Beck.

The hours passed quickly and as night fell, we kept walking through the darkness, a bright moon lighting our way. Galant wanted to find some shelter for us to spend the night, perhaps a bank of trees or some overhanging rocks where we could be shielded from the wind. As we climbed to the top of a ridge Galant stopped suddenly and pointed down the hillside that dropped away steeply ahead of us.

"Look," Galant said, grabbing my arm. "See that?" He asked, pointing to the south where, illuminated in the moonlight was a small wood, barely more than a coppice of trees nestled in the bottom of the valley. Tendrils of smoke were curling from between the treetops and drifting away into the darkness.

"Maybe it's a house?" I suggested. "Or a campfire." I had an uneasy feeling in the pit of my stomach. I didn't articulate my fear but I knew we were far from any villages and we hadn't passed a homestead since we'd left Halftans Crevice. I suspected that whatever or whoever was living or camping this far in the wilderness was just as likely to want to kill us as to offer us a soft bed for the night.

"Let's go down and see if we can get a bit closer." Galant said, turning to walk down the hill.

"Wait!" I said, remembering something that my Pa had taught me, a lesson passed on from Dickings Thumbleton. Galant turned and looked at me quizzically as I knelt to the ground and dug my fingers into the soft peat. "Come here," I said to Galant and proceeded to smear his face with mud.

"Hey!" he exclaimed, pulling away from me.

"Shh!" I said sharply, "It'll disguise us so we won't be seen, and block our scent." I streaked my own face with mud and swiped a muddy hand under each armpit beneath my clothes, up my neck and over the other areas of exposed skin. Galant regarded me uncertainly.

"Just do it!" I hissed and with a sigh, he eventually did the same and covered himself in the loamy peat.

"Ready?" he asked when I was satisfied that we were sufficiently covered. I nodded and we began to make our way down the hillside.

As we approached the coppice of trees I could see the glow of a fire and hear a strange sound, a babble of high pitched voices. I couldn't make out if the voices were speaking our language and Galant turned to me and bent low in the grass, holding a finger to his lips as he gestured me to follow. The darkness enveloped us as we crept through the long grass to the outermost trees, the strange babbling getting louder but no more coherent. I took a step forward, my eyes fixed ahead, and my foot caught on something in the long grass almost causing me to fall. I stumbled to the side and looked down, trying to make out what had tripped me. What I saw caused me to stifle a cry in my throat and I felt my stomach heave.

At my feet was a bloody mess; a pile of torn flesh and white bones. In the dim light I could see loops of wet intestines and some other dark lumps that I couldn't identify. Galant heard me gasp and turned back, his eyes falling to the gruesome heap at my feet. His eyes widened but he didn't make a sound as he grabbed me by the hand and pulled me away, dragging me behind a large tree.

My hand covered my mouth and I tore my eyes away as Galant pointed to another tree a few feet from us where another bundle of bloody rags lay. It took me a moment to see that the pile of rags wasn't rags at all. It was a body. A man. His head was slumped forward, clothes black with blood and there was a dark gaping wound across his abdomen. I felt sick but Galant hushed me again, gesturing towards the campfire.

In the clearing in the middle of the coppice was a gathering of small figures, their skin a sludgy green colour, their heads hairless, limbs thin and heavily veined. Their heads were disproportionately large compared to their small bodies and huge ears sat on either side of their skulls. The faces that flashed and jostled around the fire were round with small snub noses, narrow reptilian eyes and wide grinning mouths lined with sharp teeth. They wore strange decorations around their necks that looked like dried prunes or shriveled mushrooms and as they leapt and danced around the fire, they shrieked and squabbled in a strange language I didn't understand.

"What are they?" I whispered to Galant, pointlessly really as I already suspected I knew the answer. I also suspected that their strange decorations were nothing as harmless as dried bits of fruit.

"Oddgoblins." Galant breathed.

I nodded and Mr Burles' voice echoed in my head. "Nasty things, goblins. Kill for the pure pleasure of it and keep your bits and pieces as playthings. Trophies if you will."

I shuddered as one of the Oddgoblins spun through the firelight and I saw that what was hanging around their necks were macabre morsels, a bloody human ear and a couple of severed fingers tied to the dirty strings.

I grabbed Galant's arm. "We need to go," I hissed urgently, realizing the danger we were in. "Now!" Galant nodded and turned away as we began to creep back through the trees. My hard was pounding in my chest and I felt sweat beginning to drip between my shoulder blades. I put down my dragon boot gently in the grass and before I could prevent it, a dried stick snapped under my foot. I flinched and the two of us froze. I squeezed my eyes shut for a moment as the gibbering behind us suddenly and abruptly stopped, a tense silence filling the night air. The fire hissed and crackled in the quiet before the Oddgoblins began to shriek excitedly, clamoring and scuttling around their camp, seeking us out and snuffling at the air. The adrenaline pumped through my muscles and I readied myself to run, terror welling up inside me. Before I could move, a loud thwack echoed through the coppice followed by a meaty thud and I heard a squeal of pain as the goblins screamed collectively in confusion and rage.

The first noise was followed by a deep rumbling growl – almost a war cry - and then another thwack, followed by another. Galant grabbed my arm and we dropped into the grass, rolling to our right into a thicket of bushes. We crouched in the darkness as chaos echoed in the clearing. The goblins were leaping and spinning around the campfire, small deadly looking daggers held in their bony green hands. In the centre of the commotion were two men dressed in furs, one with a nasty scar running from his eye to his lip. The two men brandished huge glinting swords and they swiped their weapons through the seething mass of goblins sending green limbs, blood and chunks of flesh flying.

An Oddgoblin threw itself through the air at one of the attackers in an attempt to leap onto his back but the other man cried out a warning and the fur clad figure spun nimbly and speared the goblin on his sword. As we watched in horror, the two men efficiently and violently cut down the goblins one at a time, dodging the swipes of the daggers and plunging their blades with that horrible slashing sound again and again.

Finally, the smaller of the two men pinned down the last goblin and I almost felt pity for it as I watched it struggling under his foot, whining and keening in terror. The man looked down at it, an intense and awful pleasure in his eyes as he brought his sword down one last time and swiped the creatures head from its body. The eyes were still wide and blinking as the head rolled and settled in the fire, the limbs of the goblin twitching beneath the man's foot.

"And that," said the man, panting a little, "Is that." The other man laughed and pulled his sword from another dead goblin with a squelch.

"Nothing I like more than seeing off a few Oddgoblins," he said. "Be even better if we were getting paid for it," he added, looking around the clearing.

The smaller man turned to him. "Oh we'll be paid Shiv," he said. "We'll be paid alright. When we catch up with those pups and get those relics back. Then we'll get our payment and we'll never have to lift a sword again." His eyes gleamed in the firelight.

"We can't be far behind now Thrax," said Shiv. "We've travelled day and night. I can't remember the last time I slept."

"Hmmm," replied Thrax. "I think the hellion lost the scent back there in the woods but it seems to be back on their trail now." He looked up as he spoke and I followed his gaze. In the tree above the camp there was a black shape perched on a branch, a pair of wings extended as the creature basked in the heat of the fire. Two red eyes glowed in the darkness, an orange flicker in their centers reflecting the flames in the sinister spheres. It tilted its small head this way and that, sniffing the wind before alighting and circling the camp, its eyes peering through the trees. It settled again on a branch and let out a frustrated shriek.

"Can't you smell them you nasty little gremlin?" one of the men said, looking up at the creature in the trees. "Don't let us down now. Keep on sniffing my little black friend." My heart lurched again and I thought of the sweat dripping down my body, the mud dissolving in streaks down my face.

Thrax turned back to the other man. "Doesn't look like these Seekers are going to make it easy for us," he said as he sat on a log and began wiping his blade on the grass. "I thought we'd have been back in Andorta by now, having relieved our sticky fingered friends of those relics. But I have a good feeling. I think we're almost upon them now. Maybe tomorrow, maybe the next day but I reckon we've almost got 'em."

The other man settled down cross legged next to the fire. "How'll we know we've found em?" Plenty of Seekers round and about."

Thrax gave a bitter laugh. "That there is Shiv, that there is. But how many red headed girls travelling with two dark haired lads? Not as many of them around is there?" My heart jumped and panicked thoughts reverberated in my head as I made sense of what I was hearing. Andorta? Seekers? A red headed girl? I realized with a sickening lurch that the men were right. The quarry they were hunting was almost within their reach. They were hunting for us.

I opened my mouth to speak but I was paralyzed by fear and confusion. Galant turned to me and pulled me firmly towards him, as if he thought I would leap to my feet and run screaming into the darkness. As we watched, the two men picked up the dead Oddgoblins and dumped them into the fire, the flames hissing and cracking as the green bodies blackened and melted in the heat. They spoke jovially to each other and made jokes as if they weren't surrounded by blood and gore and dismembered limbs. My legs were numb from crouching so long but I didn't dare shift my weight. I don't know how long we waited but eventually the two men settled down and fell asleep, both of them soon snoring loudly. The black creature in the tree wrapped its wings around its small body and shuffled on the branch, dropping down to hang from clawed feet, the forked tail curled snugly around its head.

When the clearing was quiet, Galant turned to me and whispered. "Stay down. Step away – slowly – and head directly backwards. If they wake up, just run. Run east and don't stop. If we get separated, I'll meet you at Wistmans Hollow." I nodded silently and we carefully shuffled from our hiding place and slowly crept away from the coppice of trees. Painfully slowly. The muscles of my legs were taut and painful from being crouched for so long but I bit my lip as we distanced ourselves from the camp. Eventually we were far enough away that the darkness surrounded us once more and the fire in the clearing was nothing but a dim glow in the distance. I rose carefully to my feet, wincing as my muscles stretched and Galant stood up straight too and pointed wordlessly across the valley. I nodded and we both made our way through the grass and up the hillside.

When we reached the brow of the hill, I turned back and looked down at the dwindling glow of the campfire in the coppice beneath us.

"They're looking for us aren't they?" I said, my voice still a whisper. I turned to Galant and his face was pale and strained underneath the mud.

"I don't know Fen," he replied.

"Why would they be looking for us?" I murmured, almost to myself.

"Let's just keep moving," Galant muttered before he turned and walked quickly into the darkness. I stood there staring down into the valley, my mind casting about for an explanation, thinking back to Andorta and wondered why we were being stalked. I had no answers and after a moment, I turned and hurried off into the night after Galant.

I heard nothing but our light footsteps moving through the grass in the stillness of the evening air as we moved quickly away from the valley.

But, had my ears been keener I would have heard a sound; the rustle of leathery wings from amidst the trees far beneath us. And had my sight been sharper I would have seen the flicker of two red, malevolent eyes snapping open.

CHAPTER 35

We walked through the night and although we were tired, our pace was quickened by fear and the knowledge that as we were seeking my stone, someone was seeking us. I questioned Galant incessantly, trying to make sense of the situation but he had no answers, eventually snapping sharply at me. We trudged on in silence. When the dawn began to peek over the horizon, a low purple glow in the distance, we stopped and I insisted we climb a tree to rest rather than laying exposed on the cold ground. I thought back to my Pa and Dickings Thumbleton again as I climbed nimbly up a tall tree and pulled branches together, looping and twisting them to form a secure nest. Galant watched me with a bemused expression and after much pleading on my part, he climbed the tree and we nestled together amongst the leaves and slept.

We rested uneasily for an hour or so and when we rose, the morning light was still slowly creeping across the landscape. We huddled together in our tree nest and ate an apple each and a chunk of strange tasting cheese the dwarves had given us. The cheese was yellow but mottled with green specks of mold that the dwarves had assured us added to the flavor. It had a smoky metallic taste that reminded me of Halftans Crevice and I thought wistfully of those few days we had spent there in safety. Galant and I scanned the landscape carefully before we climbed down from the tree. We didn't speak of it but I knew that we were looking for two fur-clad figures and a black flying creature of a nature I couldn't describe. I hoped that the men would still be sleeping but I knew we had to keep moving.

I consulted Duckie's map and judged the position of the rising sun before we headed off across the grassy hills, hopefully heading towards Wistmans Hollow. The morning was cold and crisp and the long grass under our feet was drenched in dew, the smell of it sweet and fresh in the air. We walked up and down the grassy hillocks and through small woods, following the paths made by deer and other wildlife. We passed streams and a large tranquil lake, its surface as smooth as glass, the pebbles clear beneath the clean cold water as we filled our flasks. We walked all day, our pace brisk but I noticed Galant looking behind us frequently, making me nervous and jumpy. My eyes scanned the sky constantly, looking for the menacing outline of the flying black devil that was tracking our scent.

As the sun went down I began to worry that we would have to spend another night sleeping in the open but as we crested a large hill, we spotted the brown ribbon of a road in the distance, looping through the meadows. As night fell we dropped down from the hills onto the narrow lane, grass growing in its centre as it wound its way towards an avenue of tall trees. Ravens cawed hauntingly from above our heads and flocks of them circled in the darkening sky before settling to roost in the branches. As we walked down the lane I sensed a strange atmosphere gathering in the air, a foreboding energy. The twilight turned to darkness and a cold wind moaned through the boughs of the trees, the limbs bent low over the lane, a pale mist gathering around our legs. An owl called from somewhere in the darkness and its baleful hoot startled a rabbit from its hiding place, the creature flitting across the path in front of us.

"Shouldn't be too much further now," said Galant eventually and we both knew it was a statement of hope rather than something based on solid fact. The mist was getting thicker with every step and as we walked, shapes began to emerge from the fog ahead of us. Solid dark outlines loomed from the ground, crooked and black, the mist drifting in tendrils around them. "Graves," I murmured as we approached.

Wistmans Hollow was said to have the largest burial ground in all of Immentia and, just as Althena's cards had said, we emerged from the avenue of trees to find ourselves surrounded by gravestones. Row after stark row of gravestones. The lane wound on ahead into a small cluster of cottages where light glowed from a few windows, the gravestones fading into the darkness either side of us before being swallowed up by the mist.

You would have thought that such a place would be named for the graves – Gravesend perhaps, or Diggers Hollow, but I knew that the village was named for something else. Something more ominous than the sinister but harmless slabs of rock that surrounded us. This was where the Wistmen live. Ghosts of the dead haunting the Hollow in the black hours of the night, tormenting the living and searching for a release from their endless darkness.

I shivered as we entered the hamlet and glanced behind me as the mist swallowed up the stony lane and the eerie headstones. The hamlet itself consisted of a few cottages and a large, low building with a sign bearing a picture of a headstone hanging above the door. The small collection of buildings was dwarfed by the size of the graveyard and I shivered again, wondering who could bear to live in such a place. Galant and I stood uncertainly in the lane as the wind whipped up around us, chilling our ears, noses and fingertips.

The only lights were emanating from a couple of top floor windows of a few of the cottages and the low building that took up most of the main street. I walked towards the building and approached one of the windows, carefully creeping up and peering over the sill. My breath immediately fogged the glass and as I gathered my sleeve to wipe it, a hand suddenly struck the window, the flat of a palm close to my face. I yelped and stumbled backwards into the lane as the door of the building swung open and a man emerged, a pitchfork raised in his hand.

"Who's there?" a loud deep voice called. The man turned and squinted in the darkness to see me crouched on my heels and Galant grasping me under my arms as he helped me to my feet.

When he saw us, the man lowered the pitchfork as I struggled to stand.

"Oh," he said, sounding surprised. "What in the world are you two doing?" Galant walked forward warily, rubbing his cold hands together.

"We're Seekers," he said apologetically, "Didn't mean to alarm you."

"Seekers eh?" the man said, looking at me suspiciously, no doubt wondering why I was peeking into his window. "And what exactly are you doing here? You know there's wistmen about?" he stood on his toes and looked warily over our heads to the graveyard beyond. "I suppose it's true what they say," he said to himself, "Only mad dogs and Seekers…."

We looked at him expectantly and finally he held the door open. "I suppose you'd better come in," he said, "No good for anyone hanging around out here with the door open." He ushered us inside and we found ourselves in a long, single story room with a low beamed ceiling. A large table took up most of the space in the centre and another man and a woman were seated around it with mugs of steaming tea and the leftovers of roast chicken on their plates.

I looked awkwardly around as two pairs of eyes stared at Galant and I as we entered the room.

"We just need somewhere to spend the night," I said, tucking my cold hands under my arms. "Is there an inn or a tavern here?" The two people seated at the table looked at me curiously before the man who had let us in answered.

"Nay lass," he said, lowering himself into a chair. "Not enough visitors here to warrant an inn," he said. "Not living visitors anyway," he added with a chuckle. "What're you doing in these parts anyways?" he asked, gesturing to us to take a seat. "Seekers you say? Can't say I've heard of any birthstones round here for a while. Our young'uns usually leave the village before their seeking years – nothing round here for them. Not unless they're especially good at digging." He gave another wry smile as we sat down at the table.

"We're looking for caves," I said carefully. "Or caverns. I've been told there might be stones near Wistmans Hollow but they're hidden somewhere. Somewhere underground." I looked at the man hopefully. "Is there anything like that around here?"

The man rubbed his chin thoughtfully and looked across at the other man and the woman sitting opposite me. "Kale? Blanchett?" he said. "You heard of any caves around here?" The man and woman shook their heads, murmuring no, they knew of no caves. My heart sank and I inwardly cursed Althena and her stupid talking cards.

The man sitting opposite me, Blanchett, reached across the table and grasped my cold hand in his warm one, smiling kindly at me.

"Are you hungry lovies?" he asked, his twinkly eyes glancing to each of us. "Let me get you something to eat and Kale and Ralf here can have a think about these caves of yours." Blanchett got to his feet and cleared the plates from the table, disappearing through a door in the back before emerging moments later with a plate of chicken for Galant and me.

"So," Blanchett said brightly, sitting back down and folding his hands together on the table. "Where are you from?" He looked inquisitively at each of us and Galant and I answered at the same time.

"Millings Beck."

"Bleakchill Cove."

Blanchett looked in surprise at each of us and then clapped his hands together in glee. "I see, I see!" he exclaimed. "Two Seekers meet out on the road, fall in love and go adventuring together!" he chuckled and clenched his hands together against his cheek. "That is SO romantic," he sighed.

I shuffled uncomfortably and glanced at Galant to see him regarding me with an amused expression. "That's right, Blanchett," he said wistfully. "We're very much in love. But Fen here doesn't realize it yet."

Blanchett giggled again and reached over to grasp my arm. "That's right chicken," he said to me conspiratorially, giving me a wink. "You play hard to get. Plenty of time for all that once you've found your birthstone."

The woman, Kale, had been watching the exchange in amusement and smiled indulgently at Blanchett. "Maybe you should've played a bit harder to get Blanch," she said. "Then maybe you wouldn't be stuck here with a group of miserable old gravediggers."

Blanchett clutched a hand dramatically to his chest and threw his head back in mock anguish. "That's right Kale my love. Story of my life. Easy to get and even easier to leave!" They all chuckled and Ralf reached into his pocket to pull out a pipe. He bent forward, lighting the end of the pipe with a candle before leaning back and puffing, his lips making a gentle smacking sound that I found strangely comforting.

"You can stop the night here if you want," said Ralf agreeably, sucking on his pipe and blowing circles of smoke from his lips. "This here's just the village meeting house, there's no tavern. Everyone else is home in their cottages for the night and we'll be heading over soon but you're welcome to hunker down here for the night if it suits." Galant and I glanced at each other thinking of the bitter wind, mysterious wandering wistmen and the more solid and human threat that we knew was stalking us.

Missing the exchange, Blanchett spoke. "Well that's settled," he said, efficiently clearing our plates and disappearing again into the back room. When he returned, he had a mischievous look on his face and both hands behind his back. "Now Ralf," he began, "As you know, we don't get any visitors EVER." Ralf nodded, amused and clearly used to Blanchett's flamboyant ways. "So….. I was thinking," went on Blanchett, "I was thinking that we should crack open the juniper grog!" he pulled a dusty bottle from behind his back and held it up with a flourish. "How about it?" he asked excitedly. "Who's up for a couple of snifters with our new friends?"

I couldn't stop myself smiling at Blanchett's enthusiasm and Ralf and Kale eventually gave in as Blanchett placed a small cup in front of each of us and popped the bottle open with a fizz. When he had poured a shot of the deep berry coloured liquid into each cup he sat back. "So," he said, "What about a few ghost stories? Gads knows we've got plenty of those around here!"

"It wouldn't hurt to stay for a while," said Galant with a shrug. I looked at him, hoping that my face conveyed my concern that the men searching for us might only be a few hours behind.

"We'll need to leave before dawn though," I added, hearing the tension in my own voice. "That's alright, that's alright," said Blanchett merrily, "We understand you Seekers have stones to find, life and death and all that," he smiled kindly at us and I relaxed a little. I sat back, sipping the strong juniper grog and it burned my throat as I swallowed, gradually warming my belly and flushing my cheeks.

As we sat there in the glow of the candlelight, the wind howling outside, Ralf and Kale told us of the history of Wistmans Hollow. They explained that there had been a great battle here hundreds of annums ago when an armada of ships from the city of Avern near the northern mountains had landed at the coast and fought the army of Blackhaven for control of southern Immentia . To this day, descendants of that victorious Armada still inhabited the city of Blackhaven that lay over to the west of the Hollow. The battle was long and bloody and the dead were heaped up in huge piles around the small hamlet of Crabapple Hollow. It took months to bury the bodies and, as innumerable gravestones were erected in solemn rows, the villagers gradually left the Hollow leaving behind just gravediggers and ghosts.

Over time, the village became known as Wistmans Hollow and the ancestors of those gravediggers lived here still.

"The graves still need tending," explained Kale, her expression soft. "My father did it before me, his parents before him. The dead need to be taken care of too and they don't cause us any bother." Ralf grunted, "Most of 'em don't." he grumbled, glancing darkly at Kale. He went on to tell us about the wistmen. The shadowy figures of long dead sailors and soldiers who wandered the graveyard at night, sometimes roaming the lane that ran through the hamlet.

"You'll probably hear them tonight," he told us. "But they won't do you any harm. Just looking for the light is all." We all sat in silence and I felt goosebumps prickle up my arms.

"That's enough for one night," Blanchett said, breaking the solemn atmosphere. "Don't want to scare the poor lovies to death." He rose from his seat and knocked back the last of his grog. "Let's leave them to it," he said to Kale and Ralf. "Don't you two be making me walk home alone!" he chided as Kale and Ralf got to their feet and pulled on their coats.

"The Wretchmen'll be coming up out of the barrow on a night like this. A full moon too." Blanchett added. I was only half listening as my eyes began to droop with tiredness but something in Blanchett's words snapped me awake.

"What do you mean 'coming up out of the barrow'?" I asked and Blanchett looked at me in the surprise.

"The barrow," he repeated. "You know what a barrow is don't you?" he asked as I stared dumbly back at him.

"There's more than just graves around Wistmans Hollow," he explained. "Before the war, the dead of Crabapple Hollow were put to rest in the burial mound on the other side of the village. The barrow."

I looked up at him hopefully. "So this barrow….." I began. "Is it underground?"

A look of realization flitted across his features. "Ah, of course! I see what you're getting at," said Blanchett. "I suppose they might go on further underground. Never ventured down there myself. Ralf?" he cocked an eyebrow at Ralf who nodded.

"Aye, I believe there are tunnels beneath the barrows. I never even thought of it when you asked about caves and caverns. No one from the Hollow has been down there in centuries. Its bad luck. Wretchmen." he added darkly.

"Wretchmen?" I asked.

Ralf looked at us with seriously and glanced quickly at Kale who had a concerned expression on her round face. "The Wretchmen are not like the spirits that wander up here, made of mist and air. They're made of skin and bone. And they don't like to have their sleep disturbed."

I was suddenly excited that we may have found what we looking for, despite the threat of these Wretchmen. They're probably just tales made up to frighten small children, I reasoned with myself; Ralf said himself no one had been down there in a long time. "Can you take us there?" I asked.

Ralf looked at me in surprise. "Now?" he asked, "You want to go to the barrow now?" I nodded eagerly.

Ralf looked at Galant. "We haven't much time Ralf," I implored, "Please take us there. Tonight." Ralf blew softly out through his lips and glanced at Kale who nodded.

"Take them Ralf," she said softly, "If they need to go, just take them." Ralf rose from his seat and pulled his coat on, grabbing a lantern and handing one to Galant.

"I'll show you where it is," he said warily. "But after that it's up to you.

I'll not go in with you. I can't do any more than warn you." The room descended into silence as we all faced each other. Outside in the darkness, the haunting moan of the Wistmen floated over the graveyard, mingled into the fog and drifted away in the wind.

CHAPTER 36

By lantern light we made our way over the hillocks behind the hamlet of Wistmans Hollow. There was a strange smell in the air; the salty scent of the sea, Ralf said, carried on the air from the coast to the south. Ralf came to a stop on a grassy knoll and pointed out across a shallow valley.

"There it is," he said loudly, his voice battling against the wind. My eyes followed his outstretched finger to see the pale outline of an ancient and ornate stone doorway set into the hillside opposite us, grass hanging over the entrance.

"I'll not go further than this," he said. "I'd suggest you don't either, if you have any sense." He gave me a pointed look.

"I wish I had a choice, Ralf." I said. "But I need to see if my stone is in there. Whatever the cost, it can't be worse than what awaits me if I go home without finding it." Ralf nodded and I saw understanding his eyes.

"What about you lad?" he asked Galant. "You set on going too?" Galant didn't hesitate. "Of course," he said simply as if there were no choice for him either and I felt a surge of warmth tingle through me at his selflessness.

"Well, you'd better take this," Ralf said, handing his lantern to Galant as he looked into each of our faces. "Be careful. And good luck." I nodded, watching his retreating back as he walked back towards the hamlet, the wind blustering at his coat. Galant and I made our way down the hill and climbed up the other side towards the entrance to the barrow. As we drew closer, Galant held up the lantern and I could see that the stone doorframe was inscribed with ancient symbols and runes, crude engravings of evil looking skeletal faces.

"They look like a warning," I shouted over the whipping wind as we stepped carefully into the darkness.

Sheltered inside the doorway, we found ourselves in a dark tunnel that descended steeply, more of the stark warning symbols engraved on the walls at either side of us. The tunnel was eerily silent other than the gale blowing across the doorway behind us and we walked slowly, carefully looking ahead as we descended further into the earth. Eventually we emerged into a long high ceilinged room. All around us were looming shapes in the murk; large rectangular tombs in rows along the floor and upright coffin-shaped stone slabs lining the walls. In the lantern light, the glint of many jewels shone from their settings in the stone coverings of the tombs; reds and blues, orange and vivid green. There was an unsettling, musty scent in the air like incense, damp cloth and clammy flesh. The room seemed to have no other doorways other than the one we had entered through and Galant set the lantern on the floor.

"Let's look around," he whispered. I nodded and made my way to the first sarcophagus on the wall to my right, running my hand along the wall to guide me in the dim light as Galant did the same to his left, the two of us circling the room. I stepped carefully on the uneven floor beneath my feet as I approached the first upright stone slab and stared in wonder at the intricate inscriptions that decorated its surface. I could make out words of some ancient language that was foreign to me and some writings in our own tongue that I could understand. There were engraved outlines of the profiles of faces; I assumed it was the face of the person entombed inside or perhaps some long forgotten deity. Amidst the carvings were glinting jewels, set fast in the stone. Some had been pried out leaving a ruinous hole but there were more still set in place than had been removed and I wondered how the jewels had survived down here all these years without being plundered and stolen. I moved carefully from one tomb to the next, warily inspecting the stones to make sure I didn't get too close to a Glisston or a Forzit or some other birthstone that would sap my strength and possibly kill me. As I looked closely at the stones, I was disappointed to see no glow of energy at their centers and I realized that most of the jewels were nothing more than pretty coloured glass. I pressed on regardless, hoping that I would find my Rubine disguised amongst these decorative but useless gems.

As I moved slowly around the room, I was absorbed in the writings and inscriptions, reading the phrases that I could comprehend that hadn't been obliterated with age.

"For Lena. May she rest peacefully for eternal ages," said one.

"Precious Beau. He only caused his mother a single day of grief. On the day of his death," another was inscribed.

"Little Nipjh, who loved Crabapple Hollow. May she walk in sunshine." I smiled slightly at the sight of these loving and heartfelt words, unable to believe that the stories of the Wretchmen could arise from this peaceful place. The inscribed tombs were interspersed with others that looked different from the rest. The covering stones were black, painted with some shining lacquer and no words inscribed these dark resting places. Each of them displayed a single symbol; a sword and a serpentine circle. I wondered what it could mean.

I moved to the next sarcophagus and something caught my eye, a deep red jewel fixed into the tombstone and glinting in the lamp light. My heart jumped as I caught sight of it, thinking I saw a glow of energy at its centre.

"Galant!" I called urgently, "Come look, quick!" In my haste I stepped carelessly forward and my boot fell onto a small step at the foot of the tomb. I felt the stone descend beneath my foot and, much too late, I realized my mistake. I saw that the gem that had caught my eye was nothing more than simple red coloured glass, just like all the others. It wasn't Rubine. As the stone step dropped, it set off a loud rumble that echoed around the chamber. I heard a loud thump as the cover on the first black sarcophagus loosened and dropped to the ground. I stumbled back in horror, my hand reaching for my bow as I watched another lacquered stone covering drop from the next tomb, crashing to the floor in a cloud of dust.

Galant leapt backwards just in time to prevent one of the huge stones flattening him, and called out to me.

"Fen what did you do?" he shouted desperately as we moved to the centre of the room, back to back as we turned, watching the stone coverings drop one by one.

"I don't know!" I replied in panic as a dark figure slowly emerged from the first tomb, lowering one foot to the ground and then the other before turning its head to face us. In the dim light of the lantern, I struggled to make sense of what was walking towards us in a stilted and strange gait from the darkness. Its head was barely more than a skull, wisps of hair hanging from the bony scalp and the body was skeletal with the remains of tendons and shriveled muscle clinging to the gleaming bones. Rows of teeth grinned as it turned its milky, desiccated eyes upon us. It reached down and pulled an aged but sharp looking sword from the tattered remains of its leather belt and as it approached us, it opened its jaw and let out a deafening roar.

More of the cadaverous figures emerged from each of the black lacquered tombs; two, then four, then six of the denizens surrounding us and all roaring in rage, dust and moths flying from their bony maws. I realized my bow wouldn't help me here. There was no soft flesh to pierce with my Queenfisher arrows, no essential organs to damage with an accurate strike. I discarded my bow and reached for the dagger in my belt as Galant unsheathed his sword. The Wretchmen were unintimidated by our weapons and relentlessly approached us, evil malevolence echoing around the chamber.

The first Wretch approached me and swung its sword at my head with a hissing wheeze emanating from its empty ribcage. I ducked the blow and jumped to the side, leaping close to the creature and delving my dagger into its abdomen. I realized my error when my blade met nothing but hard bone and thin air and I realized that this was a battle we had not been prepared for. Another Wretch wrapped its bony arm around my neck from behind and before it could raise its sword, I lifted my feet and kicked out at one in front of me. My feet struck its clavicle then it's spine as the dry bone snapped under the blows, leaving the things skull wobbling precariously on its neck. My sudden movement released me from the grip of the Wretch behind me and I landed on my feet, aiming a swift elbow at the throat of the skeletal form. Its head shot back but it felt no pain and came at me again. The looming figure bore down on me and I desperately searched for some kind of vulnerability, some weak spot. I dropped to my heels and spun around between the two Wretchmen and before the nearest one had chance to turn, I stood and raised my arm, bringing it up hard against the back of the creature's neck. My elbow struck the things exposed vertebrae, the small bones breaking with a crack as the monsters skull shot loose from its body, the rest of it crumpling to a heap of at my feet.

"Go for their necks!" I shouted to Galant who was ineffectually swiping his blade at the bones of the Wretchmen that surrounded him. "Dislodge the skulls!" I cried as another one lumbered towards me. We were lucky that the creatures were not quick, they didn't have the speed and agility that living muscle provided and I wondered what dark magic drove them.

One of the Wretchmen descended upon me with an unearthly roar and I lost my footing, falling hard on my back as the thing bent low over me, its skull a hairs breadth from my face. I turned away as it snarled, a rotting stench emanating from its jaws and I caught sight of a pale and rotted tongue undulating between its teeth. There was pure rage in its milky shriveled eyes and just before it stabbed its blade into my face, I brought the hilt of my dagger down hard on the back of its neck. The snarl died suddenly, the blade dropped uselessly to the ground and the skull fell loose of the body, rolling across the floor, its toothy grin still snapping at me as it came to a stop. I jumped up and ran to Galant who was fending off four of the Wretchmen. As he dodged and rolled, evading the strikes of their ancient swords, I leapt onto the back of the one closest to me and wrapped my arms around its skull, twisting sharply as the bony sphere snapped from its spine. The Wretch dropped like a stone beneath me and I tossed the skull to one side in disgust. Galant had seen this and sheathed his heavy sword, changing his tactics. He dodged an incoming blow and leapt around the back of the creature, knocking it to its bony kneecaps before driving the Wretches skull onto the stone floor.

We fought hard to bring down the remaining Wretchmen but eventually we stood breathing heavily, staring at each other in disbelief. We were surrounded by prone skeletal remains and a slow clattering sound echoed around the chamber as the final skull rolled across the floor. For several minutes we stared at each other in shocked silence. I looked around, regarding the piles of bones and skulls scattered around our feet and felt a strange feeling of guilt and regret at the destruction we had wrought in this peaceful place.

"They were just protecting the dead," I murmured, looking around in dismay. Galant was bent over, his hands resting on his knees, puffing with exertion. "We shouldn't have come here," I muttered, picking up my bow.

"Don't say that!" he exclaimed. "We're doing what we have to do. What YOU have to do." I nodded reluctantly, unable to shake the feeling that we had desecrated the place. I looked around the room to see that the tombs with the inscriptions – Lena, Beau, Little Nipjh, all remained intact and I realized that we had entered their eternal sanctuary and destroyed their protectors.

"There's nothing here." I said, feeling suddenly desolate as a dark wave of despair washed over me. "Just glass. Coloured glass. We should never have come," I said again.

I realized that Galant wasn't listening to me and had walked to the back wall of the chamber, his hand held aloft as he tilted his head.

"Fen, come here," he whispered.

"Let's just go Galant," I replied bitterly, turning to leave.

"Fen!!" Galant repeated and something in his voice made me pause and turn. As I approached him, I felt a light cold breeze brush across my face.

"D'you feel that?" he asked softly, waving his fingers through the invisible wave of cool air. I nodded and looked around, moving forward to press my face to the wall to see where the breeze was coming from.

"There," I said, pointing at a small hole in the uneven, cracked surface of the wall at the back of the chamber. I stepped forward and brought my eye slowly and cautiously to the opening. At first I could see nothing, just darkness, but as I blinked, I could just make out a dim light emanating from beyond the wall, a weak beam casting a shaft of light from a ceiling on the other side. "There's another room back here," I said as I stood aside, letting Galant look through the hole.

"There must be a way in," Galant mused, stepping back. "Look around, there might be a lever or something. Or perhaps another doorway." I nodded and cast my eyes around the gloomy chamber, moving from one opened tomb to the next, searching the walls and ceiling for any sign of a mechanism that would open some invisible door to the hidden room beyond.

Finally I found it. Behind one of the broken tombs where the Wretchmen had emerged, I found a small opening. It was narrow and low but had clearly been intentionally set in the wall.

"Here," I called to Galant, "It's here." I peered into the darkness, feeling the same soft breeze brushing across my skin and, without waiting for Galant, I crouched down and crept through the opening to find myself in another tunnel. I braced my hands against the rough walls as I stepped blindly forward, my heart pounding in my ears. The tunnel turned at an angle and I emerged from the tunnel into another chamber. A crypt. The shaft of light shone down from an opening in the ceiling and my eyes adjusted so I could see what lay in front of me. In the centre of the room was a large stone tomb, raised high on pedestals of carved ebony heads. The heads of dragons. But the sight that met my eyes, the sight that made me stop breathing for a moment was an elaborately carved stone monolith, its surface furrowed with detailed etchings of trees, faeries, and waterfalls. At the base of the monolith was a stone, held delicately by metal fingers, its surface reflecting the dim shaft of light from above. I knew what it was as soon as my eyes fell upon it. I saw its red facets glinting with a power that emanated from within, from the deep hot glow at its centre. I knew immediately this was what I had been seeking. I had found my Rubine.

CHAPTER 37

In the darkness of the crypt I stepped forward slowly, almost mesmerised and as I moved, I heard Galant enter the chamber behind me. He too froze and I heard him gasp when he saw the monolith and the glowing stone. I put one foot slowly in front of the other, my eyes fixed on the Rubine. I thought to warn Galant not to come too close, to stay back so the stone couldn't hurt him but before I could speak, before I could even think, Galant suddenly rushed from behind me. Without a word, he leapt on top of the tomb, falling to his knees in front of the monolith. I felt my heart jump as I realized what was happening. He had already found his birthstone and to touch another would be deadly. I panicked and cried out to him to stop him, not understanding what would make him do something so reckless. Was he trying to get my stone for me? My thoughts ran wildly in desperation. But why? Why would he risk his life to fetch what was right in front of me. Everything I had been searching for was right in front of me!

My mind couldn't grasp what was happening and as I fumbled for the words, I watched Galant reach out for the stone. I let out an anguished cry.

"Galant no! Don't!" I knew that if he touched the stone he would be gone and the stone would turn to dust. The thought of losing him struck me like a physical blow and I didn't even think of the ruined stone, only his ruined, lifeless body that would soon be lying in front of me unless I stopped him.

I rushed forward to pull him away but again, froze in my tracks as my disbelieving eyes watched Galant reach out and tenderly take the Rubine stone from its resting place. I grasped his arm and felt a jolt of electricity shoot through me that flung me backwards across the crypt onto the stone floor. I sat up, wincing in pain from the shock and before I was able to scrabble to my feet, I saw something that knocked the breath from my lungs and caused my knees to collapse from under me. I watched in horror as the stone glowed in Galant's hands and for one dreadful moment, I waited helplessly for him to fall, dead before my eyes. Instead, my mouth dropped open in disbelief as the stone glowed brighter still and I watched its deep red power run in tendrils up Galant's arms. The glow intensified to a blinding crimson as his body suddenly stiffened and his head was thrown back as the energy shot through him. I shielded my face from the light and felt a strange heat burning my skin, the stone illuminating the whole chamber in a deep red glow. The blinding light gradually began to fade away and I lowered my hands slowly from my eyes. The glow subsided and I watched in stark, harsh realization as the Rubine stone crumbled to dust between Galant's fingers. His head dropped forward onto his chest and his breathing echoed around the crypt in harsh rasps, the red tendrils still flickering across his skin.

My mind raced in confusion and suddenly the terrible pieces all dropped into place with a thud that landed in the pit of my stomach and made my vision blur. I remembered how Galant had sought me out, how he had insisted on accompanying us on our journey. How he'd flirted and flattered and protected me over these recent weeks. How he'd held me in the night, comforted me in my nightmares and gently kissed my lips. I thought of how he'd made me feel for him, a feeling I was unfamiliar with and didn't recognize, but knew without a doubt was a feeling of love. He had made me fall in love with him.

It suddenly became clear to me. Suddenly and brutally clear. He had tricked me. It had all been an elaborate act. A contrived plan to accompany us and allow me to lead him to my stone. My mind couldn't understand what had just happened. What had happened to me in these recent weeks, why I'd trusted him and how we were now here in this cold dark place where he'd stolen my very future from right in front of my eyes.

I managed to get to my knees as Galant let his hands drop and I watched the dust of the stone float to the ground in wisps of useless ash. I couldn't speak. I just stared at him as if he was a stranger. He might as well have taken his sword in his hand and run me through.

Our eyes met in silence for a few long moments and I felt the realization and recognition pass across my features. Galant saw it too. I had seen him. Really seen him for what he truly was. A coward and a liar. Worse than that, he had used me. He had broken through to a part of myself I hadn't known existed and had used it to his own selfish advantage. As we stared at each other, eye to eye in that dark crypt, we both knew it and nothing could be done to take it back.

He began to speak but I held up a hand, knowing that to hear his voice would feel like a million tiny stabs pricking my skin. "Don't say anything," I said, my voice flat and lifeless. "Please. After all… this. Please don't say anything." Galant bit back his words and looked away from me. "Was any of it real?" I asked finally. "Was anything you ever said to me, anything you ever did for me, anything you ever told me..." I swallowed hard and my throat felt dry and sore. "Was any of it real?"

Galant stepped down from the tomb and I was sickened to see the glow of the Rubine still emanating from his skin.

"Fen..." he began and this time I let him speak. "I need you to understand," he pleaded. "I had no other choice. I had nowhere left to search so when I found out you were looking for Rubine too, I didn't think anything of befriending you. Maybe see if we could find them together." He reached out for me and I pulled away violently, the thought of him touching me making me feel physically sick.

"And I suppose your sister and the baby was just a sob story. A little sweetener to make us feel sorry for you?" I asked bitterly.

He looked away from me before he answered. "No," he said sadly, looking back and meeting my eyes. "She's real. But she's not my sister. She's just a girl." My stomach lurched as I realized what was coming next. "And the baby.... The baby is my son," he finished, his eyes not leaving my face.

The walls and floor of the crypt seemed to swim underneath me and a wave of nausea gripped my stomach. "Just leave me." I said abruptly, my voice cracking as I felt my legs going weak beneath me and I crumpled to the ground once more. He rushed to help me but I recoiled from his touch as if his very presence would poison me. "Just go!" I shouted, my eyes flashing and he stopped short, his hands held out, frozen. A thought flitted through my muddled mind and I realized that a few hours ago I would have welcomed his soft touch, rested myself against him like a purring kitten. But now, as he stood in front of me, the thought of his skin touching mine made me sick.

"Fen..." he said softly, "I really did start to care for you. Please believe that. I hoped we'd find more than one stone. But this is my child... My son..." his voice trailed off.

"Please," I said, my voice like ice, resting my head on my hands. "Please just go." He stood there for a moment and I didn't look up. Finally, I heard his footsteps as he turned to leave. He didn't utter another word as he left the crypt but if he had, I fear I would have leapt to my feet and cut him down where he stood.

I listened to his footsteps as they faded away down the tunnel and through the chamber on the other side of the wall. My flesh felt cold and I huddled there shivering as red hot tears dropped in huge dollops between my knees onto the dank stone floor. As I crouched there, I could physically feel my heart, the part of me that had cared for him, perhaps even loved him, wrapping itself in steel and then surrounding itself in unforgiving stone before shriveling to a barely beating core. I thought then that I would never use it again. Not for anything but staying alive.

CHAPTER 38

I don't remember much about the hours that followed. I know that I sat in the crypt for a long time, my limbs numb, before eventually getting wearily to my feet. I found Galant's chainmail gloves on the floor that he had carelessly discarded in his hurry to betray me and I picked them up and tucked them in my pack before I made my way out of the barrow. I don't remember walking through the scattered bones in the chamber or leaving the dark tunnel, emerging into the grey light of day and returning to Wistmans Hollow. I have a vague memory of passing through the graveyard and of Ralf's voice calling out behind me, his words carried away in the wind and lost in the cawing of the ravens. I ignored him and didn't look back as I walked away, feeling at least as dead as the bodies buried beneath my feet. I couldn't feel the cold wind as it whipped at my face and my mind was blank as I left the hamlet far behind me, walking through the graveyard and into the woods beyond. I didn't know where I was going and it didn't occur to me to care.

I didn't eat and didn't sleep, despite being so exhausted I could barely set one foot in front of the other. The gloomy sky rumbled over my head before it released a deluge of rain that dripped through the trees onto my stooped head.

Eventually I emerged from the woods onto a muddy road; nothing more than two deep furrows, grass growing along the centre and dense woodland creeping in from either side. I picked a direction randomly and walked, pulling my coat collar up around my face as the rain dripped down my neck. My mind was blank but I continued moving forward. I don't think I knew what else to do. Eventually, when I was too tired to take another step I simply dropped where I stood, collapsing onto the grass at the side of the tree lined road, pulling my coat around me, not really caring whether I woke up.

As I closed my eyes, shivering with cold and soaked to my skin, my mind kept playing back in painful loops; Galant holding me close, his eyes as he kissed me, his charming smile and the lock of hair that always fell over his dark eyes. I wondered how I had been so stupid. At the same time, I wondered what I would do without him. I missed his presence. I missed the feel of his warm arms wrapped around me. I missed the rumbling murmur of his voice in my ear and as I remembered each and every detail of what I had lost, a physical pain stabbed at me deep inside. I loved what I had known and hated what I knew now.

My mistake had had left me with more than a shriveled heart that beat like a ticking clock in my chest. It may have cost me my life.

As my eyes closed, my cheek lying against the soft wet grass, something echoed through my confused mind. A soft lilting voice, a song, a lullaby. It was the almost forgotten voice of my mother as I remember it, before it was ravaged to a harsh gasping whisper by the Sphyx. As I drifted into sleep, I saw in my mind a hazy red sun dropping beneath the hills of Millings Beck, a golden field of wheat swaying gently before us and a soft breeze caressing my cheeks. I felt the soft embrace of my mother as she held me close to her, the sound of her voice, sweet and airy in the warm summer evening. I smiled softly as I huddled in the rain and although I was shivering with cold, a flush of warmth touched my cheeks. It was as if she was next to me, nestling my cold body into hers as the song she had lulled me to sleep with as a child echoed through the creaking boughs of the trees.

As I lay there, a raven settled in the tree above my head, its black wings rustling as it shook the rain from its feathers. The bird cawed loudly and its harsh cry rattled vaguely through my consciousness. If I had been roused from sleep and if I had been able to understand the raven's cries, it would have told me how it had flown to the woods from a nearby settlement, a hamlet surrounded by graves. It would have described a Grimhellion that had swooped through the avenue of trees, disturbing the ravens into flight and it would have told of the two fur-clad figures that followed close behind it.

Had I been able to understand the birds stark raspy calls, I would have heard it speak of a kind man emerging from a dwelling and being beaten to the ground by the figures wielding swords, blood running from the man's face as he cowered on the ground. Had we spoken a common language, the raven would have understood the violent exchange and would have been able to tell me that the man was questioned about three Seekers – two boys and an auburn haired girl. It wouldn't have needed to comprehend their spoken words to see the bleeding man point off across the graveyard and towards the woods.

CHAPTER 39

"Is she dead?" a voice broke through the murkiness of sleep and pricked at my ears.

"Nay lad," said another. "Just cold and wet." I felt a hand on my shoulder, shaking me and I moaned softly, unwilling to emerge from the comfort of the unthinking darkness. "Hey," the voice whispered, "Are you alright pet? Wake up now, come on." I struggled to open my eyes and my lashes fluttered against my cheeks. I mumbled something and tried to brush the hand away, wanting to sink back into the peaceful black. Two hands clasped me beneath my arms and began to pull me to my feet, my head lolling and limbs weak. "Come on lovely, let's get you up," the voice continued soothingly. I tried to speak but found my voice was gone and my mouth and throat were as dry as parchment.

"She don't look good Pa," the first voice said as I struggled to my feet, the two hands still supporting me. I forced my lids to open and looked around to see the owner of the hands, a man with a kind face and jet black hair, his skin the colour of weathered red stone. Beside him stood a child of around nine or ten annums, with wide dark eyes and hair the same deep black. Along the lane stood a train of caravans pulled by hardy looking ponies, the wooden sides of the caravans painted and ornately decorated, lanterns hanging from the curved roofs. The rain was still pouring down from the ashen sky and the horse's shaggy legs were fetlock deep in the mud.

I tried to speak again but no sound emerged from my mouth, just a rasping hoarse groan. I had no idea how long I had laid at the side of the lane but my throat was parched and I was weak from pure exhaustion. The man helped me up from the ground and guided me to the back of one of the caravans. Sheltering beneath the overhang of the roof was an old woman with a woolen shawl pulled close around her face. She held out a wizened hand as the man pushed me up into the back of the caravan and she grabbed my coat, pulling me inside. As soon as the man's hands released my arms, my legs collapsed beneath me and the old woman managed to guide me to a narrow bunk covered in blankets and pillows. I fell into the soft covers, eyes pressed closed, my body shuddering violently and my teeth clattering. The man closed the door at the back of the caravan and I heard the young boy's voice chirruping inquisitively, feeling the caravan heave under their weight as they mounted the front of the wagon, clicking the horses onwards.

The caravan began to rock gently as the horses moved off and I felt a mug being held to my lips, cool water being poured gently into my dry mouth. I swallowed hungrily, choking and spluttering as the water tipped into my airway in my haste to drink.

"Steady there, steady," crooned the old woman as I coughed and wiped my mouth with a grubby sleeve. The water revived me a little and I managed to raise myself up on one elbow, blearily rubbing my eyes. I looked around me at the cozy caravan, two bunks lining each wall and a small window in the door where I could see the muddy lane winding away behind us. The old woman was looking at me closely with shrewd blue eyes, her skin the same red brown as the man that had found me. I knew enough to recognize that these people were Deltics, travelling folk of , and I was reminded of that night back in Millings Beck when the merchants had set up stall in the square as Leif and I had watched from the cottage window. It seemed so long ago.

I regarded the woman hazily and she stood without a word and made her way to a row of cupboards at the front of the caravan. She turned and sat back down on the bunk opposite me, her small hands ripping a piece of bread into small chunks that she offered to me one at a time. I took the morsels and chewed them carefully, the ravenous hunger mixing with a feeling of nausea. I ate one bit, then another and when I reached for a third she held it back from me.

"No more for the moment," she said firmly. "You'll get sick. You can have some more later." She smiled down at me. "You need to get warm now, so let's get you out of those wet clothes." I stood wordlessly, the woman helping me take my pack and weapons off my back and I unsteadily removed my sodden leather breeches and dress. When I stood there, barefoot and shivering in my undershirt, she nodded at me. "That too," she said, turning away tactfully and holding out a clean man's shirt for me to pull over my freezing naked body. "Now wrap up in this," she said handing me a warm woolen blanket and I did as she asked before settling back on the bunk, pulling my cold feet up under me.

The rain was still pattering on the wooden roof of the wagon and the feeling of movement was a comforting sway that soothed my mind. It felt like every pace of the horse's hooves was taking me further and further away from Wistmans Hollow, from Galant and the men who may still be stalking me. The woman settled opposite me on the other bunk and lowered her shawl, her silver grey hair falling in a long ponytail to her waist. She gazed at me for a few moments, her blue eyes bright in the dim light of the wagon.

"So," she began. "What is it you're looking for?"

I looked back at her, a dead weight lying heavily on my chest. "I don't know anymore," I said dully, my voice nothing but a whisper.

She nodded understandingly and pressed her thin lips together. "Best get some rest then," she said eventually as she pulled back the blankets of the bunk and I buried my feet underneath as I lay back with my head on the pillow. She carefully tucked the covers around me and as my eyes closed, I heard her singing softly. The voice was unfamiliar but the words and melody were not. As the hypnotic sway of the caravan rocked me, I fell asleep once more to the sound of my mother's lullaby.

CHAPTER 40

The old woman's name was Mercy and her black haired son and grandson who drove the wagon were Jentus and Dridd. We travelled the roads west for several days and they shared their food with me and made sure I was getting my strength back. They looked at me with curiosity but didn't question me about who I was and where I was going. My Pa had told me that the Deltics were a mysterious people and were often badly treated by the folk who lived in the towns and cities. People thought they were thieves and tricksters who would steal their livestock or cast a curse on any who offended them. Their way of life was simple but steeped in mystical traditions which many mistook for dark magic or worship of evil spirits. They were allowed to trade in the villages and towns but were always treated with suspicion and encouraged to move on once business was done. In the few days I spent with the Deltic caravan, I had nothing but gratitude for what they had done for me. They could have ridden right by and left me there in the mud and if they had, I have no doubt I would have died right where I lay.

The other Deltics in the caravan train were friendly enough when we stopped to feed and water the horses or to camp for the night, but they spoke little, regarding me with shrewd dark eyes. I didn't wish to discuss what had brought me here and to talk of home would, I think, have broken me. I was happy to spend hour after hour laid in the bunk of the caravan, my mind blank, watching the roads disappear like a muddy ripple into the distance behind us.

On the third day, the Deltics were packing up the camp ready to move off again and I went into the woods, returning a while later with a few rabbits which I offered shyly to Mercy as a thank you for their kindness. She took them and patted my hand without a word, the gesture needing no explanation. When the caravan set off, I sat up front with Jentus as Mercy and Dridd played cards inside the wagon. The Deltics were people of few words and they did not consider a silence of any type to be awkward. They spoke only when necessary and I found that to be a pleasant foible of these kind people.

As we travelled onwards, the ponies' rumps swaying in front of us, Jentus finally broke the long silence. "We'll be heading north today," he said simply, casting a glance at me from the corner of his eye. "This road'll take us a bit further west but then there's nothing but the salt marshes." I nodded, considering his words. "You heading north?" he asked casually but I didn't answer. I hadn't thought of much these past couple of days. I had eaten, slept and was finally feeling myself again but I realized I would soon need to decide where my journey would take me next.

"I think I will be going south," I said eventually. I had no particular reason to go south but the road north was the direction of home. I knew that I could not return home, not yet. Despite Galant and the mysterious men who could still be following me for reasons I couldn't explain, I still had to find my Rubine. Or at least I had to try.

Jentus shrugged and nodded. "There's a town on the coast to the south. Baileys Sound. It's a few days walk though. Rough country. No roads either." He glanced at me again. "Might be the only town any safe distance from here so if you're heading south, might be a good place to aim for." I nodded wondering with sudden panic if I should jump down from the wagon right that minute and trudge off into the woods. "You'll stay for a spot of lunch though?" Jentus asked. "We'll be stopping off soon." I nodded gratefully and we lapsed back into comfortable silence.

The caravan pulled into a clearing a few hours later and after we had eaten, I gathered my things, knowing I couldn't delay any longer. I pulled my bow and sheath of Queenfisher arrows onto my back as Dridd admired the blue feathers. The little wide eyed boy reminded me of Leif and I ruffled his black hair as I said goodbye to him, Jentus pressing some wraps of food into my pack. Mercy took both my hands in hers as the others climbed back onto the wagons, her hands warm but fragile, the skin dry and papery. Her blue eyes seemed to see right through me as she stared intently into my face. After a moment, she gestured at the dark woods at the side of the road.

"I think you'll need to be going that way," she said. "Keep the sun behind you and you'll reach Baileys Sound in a few days."

I nodded, swallowing an unexpected lump that had risen in my throat. "Thank you," I said gruffly. "For everything. I... I won't ever forget what you did for me." She smiled and nodded, squeezing my hands tighter.

"You'll find it Fen," she said with a certainty that confused me for a moment; I had never told her I was searching for anything. "Don't stop looking. You'll find it." Tears welled to my eyes at her words but I steeled myself and gave her hands a brief squeeze in return before I walked away, crossing the muddy road as I made my way into the woods. I lingered in the shadows for a few minutes, hidden by the trees as I watched the caravan trundle away down the road and out of sight.

Eventually I was completely alone, the smell of wet grass and pine needles in the air as I walked into the trees. The woods were quiet and although there was no path, the forest floor was clear of undergrowth and I walked quickly, careful to keep my footfalls quiet. As the hours passed, my thoughts drifted and I tortured myself with thoughts of Galant, wondering whether he had made it home yet to his sweetheart and their baby. Every time I thought of him, I felt a wash of shame and humiliation wash over me at how easily I had been manipulated. Although we were equal in age, I realized now that when I met him, I was nothing more than a little girl but he had already become a man. He was already a father. I realized now how I must have seemed to him, like some lovesick village idiot, hardly more than a child. I thought about how he had called me beautiful and I felt sick with shame at how readily I had come to believe him, flattering myself that his words were the truth. I wondered about his girl at home and I imagined that her hair would be long and black and shiny, her skin would be pale and flawless, her features delicate and pretty. I wondered how I could have believed that Galant found me beautiful with my knotted red mop of hair and freckled cheeks.

I walked for a long time but eventually something pulled me from my reverie. A sound ahead of me caused me freeze in my tracks, my head tilted as I listened keenly. I could hear a vicious snarling and growling in the trees ahead of me mingled with sharp cries and anguished moans - the desperate sounds of someone in pain and under attack. My body was suddenly alert and I instinctively dropped to a crouch as I moved carefully forwards through the undergrowth, pulling my bow from my back and poising a Queenfisher arrow between my fingers in readiness. I quietly approached a clearing in the woods and, still crouched out of sight, I pulled back the fronds of ferns that were blocking my view. In the clearing, fur was flying and spittle shot through the air in hot strings as a pack of savage Slinkferrals set upon some unfortunate victim with a ravenous fervor. I smelled the scent of hot fearful sweat in the air as the Slinkferrals ferocious snarling shot clouds of moist breath into the cold air. I shuffled forward carefully and drew back my bow, aiming precisely and shooting at the heavily muscled, furred bodies of the attackers. I didn't know who they had fallen upon or whose blood was spitting forth from each deadly swipe of their claws but I fired nonetheless.

I heard the thwack of my arrow as it struck one of the huge beasts in its belly and it yelped and staggered to one side. I shot another arrow into its side and it dropped to floor as its eyes glassed over. Its bloodthirsty companions didn't appear to notice as they continued their rampage on the poor soul crouching beneath them. I pulled another arrow and another, firing relentlessly into the melee until eventually, three Slinkferrals lay dead in a bleeding twitching heap. I felt no remorse as I emerged from the foliage and coldly observed the carnage. I was eerily unmoved by the death and bloodshed I had wrought and I wondered whether anything would ever bother me again. I realized I didn't even much care for the wounded person I had killed for, cowering beneath the pile of bodies.

As I approached, I expected to see the pink flesh of a human arm, perhaps a leather clad leg ripped with deep clawing wounds but as I drew close, I saw nothing but bloody, matted fur. I looked around, wondering if the victim had escaped into the brush. As I stood there, my bow still poised in my hand, another arrow ready to fire, I heard a pitiful whine emerging from the pile of bodies. I jumped back and pulled the arrow taught, thinking one of the Slinkferrals had evaded my deadly strikes but as I watched, a face peeped out from amongst the tangle of limbs. Its large fearful eyes were weeping and as I was about to fire an arrow into its neck, I noticed teeth protruding from its bleeding gums, two sharp incisors broken off in useless, blunted stumps.

Just before I released the arrow I realized that there was no unfortunate human victim here. I had stumbled across a brutal act of nature where the powerful eliminated the weak. The injured, stump toothed Slinkferral pulled itself clear of the dead bodies piled across it and cowered shivering in the clearing, its fur wet with blood, slaver and sweat. As we stood staring at each other, I noticed that the Slinkferrals in these parts had full, thick coats compared with the mangy looking beasts I had seen in the deserts of Andorta. The fur sat sleekly across the creature's finely muscled body, almost black in colour and mottled with golden dapples, a thick mane around its neck and down its back. The beast regarded me with its head lowered and let out a whine of pain before it turned and licked at a nasty gash on its hind leg. Something about its demeanor made me lower my arrow and I watched it curiously as it slumped, exhausted and cast a plaintive look at me before its huge head dropped to the ground and it fell unconscious.

Darkness was falling but I felt no need for sleep so I climbed a nearby tree and spent the night in the clearing, my heavy coat pulled up around my face. I had watched the injured Slinkferral wake, stagger to its feet and lick again at the wound on its leg whining and keening incessantly. I knew it was no danger to me as I hunched high in the tree, with its broken teeth and bloody leg and I found its snuffling and weeping more of an annoyance. I eventually let my head drop onto my chest as I let sleep suck me down into its deep careless depths.

I dreamed of Galant again. I dreamed he had followed me here, into this distant forest to tell me it was all a mistake and, impossibly, he had my stone. In my dream I saw his handsome face and heard the familiar rumble of his voice as he held out a Rubine stone in his hands, waiting for me to simply reach out and take it. I awoke slowly and for a moment, I thought that the dream was reality and the reality was a dream. As my thoughts ordered themselves more clearly, I felt another surge of sickness wash over me as I realized the unbelievable truth of what had happened. What Galant had done. I swallowed down the sick feeling and rubbed my eyes hard as I looked around the clearing.

Beneath me I was surprised to see the injured Slinkferral sitting on its haunches at the bottom the tree. I cursed quietly and regarded the creature warily. It seemed to have none of the hungry menace about it that its attackers had displayed the night before - in fact, it was sitting there wearing a slightly stupid expression like a simple-minded lapdog. Its eyes were alert but friendly and its tongue lolled from one side of its broken toothed mouth as it cocked its head at me. I wondered if it had taken a blow to the skull which had rearranged its brain, knocked its natural predatory instincts from it as well as its teeth. I climbed down slowly from the tree, one eye on the Slinkferral and my dagger clenched between my teeth should I need it quickly. The huge animal made no move towards me. It didn't flatten its ears or curl its lip in a snarl and I didn't see the hackles rise on its back.

I dropped slowly onto the forest floor, half expecting the creature to leap at my throat at any moment. "Steady there," I said calmly, turning towards it and bending slightly, my eyes looking off to one side as my Pa had told me I should with wild creatures. "What d'you want?" I asked as I retreated slowly and the Slinkferral licked its lips and pricked its ears, cocking its head expectantly on one side. "You want something to eat?" I felt around in my empty pockets and found a shriveled piece of dried rabbit meat. I drew it slowly from my coat and tossed it on the ground at the Slinkferral's feet.

The beast fell upon the morsel and I took my chance, turning quickly as I fled into the trees, crashing through the undergrowth as I went. I ran as far as I could and eventually stopped to catch my breath, my chest burning, expecting to hear the thump of heavy paws following me. I listened carefully to the noise of the forest, hearing nothing but the wind blowing through the leaves and the boughs of the trees creaking above my head. Relieved, I strode on with renewed vigor. My visceral encounter with the Slinkferrals had made me realize that I did want to keep looking. I did want to find my stone. Instead of dwelling on how Galant had manipulated me, cheated me and used me, I thought of my Pa and of Leif and felt a small glimmer of strength flicker deep within me. Perhaps I would find another Rubine stone and all was not lost.

Along with my renewed optimism, another thought lurked at the back of my mind. I thought of the men that had been following us, their dreadful winged accomplice scouring the earth from the sky with its eager red eyes. I wondered whether they were still trailing me and the thought quickened my steps as I strode onwards.

CHAPTER 41

"We're going in damned circles!" cursed Thrax, slamming the flat of his palm against a thick tree trunk as the rain dripped through the branches overhead. His companion muttered incoherently and leaned back on his heels, stretching the tendons and muscles of his back as he tensed his thick arms over his head. "That witch and her cursed familiar will be the death of us, I'm telling you." Thrax continued. "We've been lost in these woods for days. Those Seekers will be miles away by now." Shiv regarded the frustrated Thrax with heavy lidded eyes but said nothing.

"I swear when I get my hands on that little leathery monster, I'll…." A sudden sound silenced him.

The voice was soft and husky but laden with menace. "You'll what?"

The words carried through the air from the darkness of the surrounding trees and Shiv stepped back in alarm, losing his footing and landing on his behind in the mud. Thrax unsheathed his sword and braced himself, legs firmly apart, one set in front of the other in a defensive stance as he looked wildly around into the trees. A tall, thin figure dressed all in black emerged from the shadows and Thrax narrowed his eyes, lowering his sword as Shiv struggling to lift his huge body from the mud.

"Decima…" Thrax breathed in disbelief before collecting himself and dropping to his knees, his head bowed. "My lady Amiress," Thrax corrected himself reverently as Decima lowered her hood and looked down on the man, her eyes appearing almost black in her white face.

"I shall ask again. You'll do what?" she said, her voice smooth and ominously quiet.

"I meant nothing," Thrax stuttered, "I was just… it's just…. We have lost the scent, your Hellion abandoned us and we lost the trail." He looked down at the ground and Shiv stood behind him awkwardly with one knee in the dirt, his eyes averted from the hard black gaze of the woman looking down at them. She was dressed in black from head to foot, a long dark cape hanging from her shoulders. She looked very much like the deadly assassin that she was rumored to be, rather than the subservient wife of an Amir. Thrax wondered if they had underestimated her.

A screech echoed through the trees, breaking the silence as the Grimhellion swooped from the shadows and settled itself delicately onto

Decima's shoulder. She turned her head and nuzzled her cheek against its repulsive black body as the creature tilted its head and narrowed its red eyes.

She turned back to the men at her feet. "My hellion abandoned you because you have failed me. You should have found those relics weeks ago and been back in Andorta. Instead, here you are wandering the woods like a pair of pathetic old women." She looked at them in disgust and the Grimhellion ducked its small head beneath one of its wings, scratching at its fur with its small sharp teeth. "My hellion returned to inform me of your ineptitude and, as you can see, I have had to come and finish the job myself." The two men gibbered excuses and apologies as Decima crooned softly at the creature on her shoulder.

"You should know that your master Oberon has paid the price for your failure," she continued. "Because of your incompetence, I was forced to have his bowels removed in the arena in front of the whole city." She smiled indulgently at the memory. "He didn't suffer too much, although it was unfortunate that we also had to cut out his tongue to quiet the screaming."

The men's faces turned pale and Thrax involuntarily put a protective hand across his abdomen. "My lady," he said, his voice trembling slightly. "We were almost upon them, I can assure you. They were at Wistmans Hollow only a few days since and we know they came this way. We cannot be far from them now, there was no need…."

Decima let out a sharp laugh. "No need?" she barked. "There was every need you fool. Left to you, we would be waiting forever for those relics. And I don't need to remind you that we don't have forever. Ariad is approaching her seventeenth annum and the armies of Dracae and Epona continue to gather strength. I swear to you, I will not leave the future of our family in the hands of the likes of you." She spat on the ground as if the words had tasted foul on her tongue. "Oberon assured me you were the best of your kind. Given that you had already recovered the relics from the ruins of Stellium I had no reason to doubt him. But after you allowed them to be stolen from within the very walls of Andorta by children no less, I should have known that I would have to do this myself. Get up," she said harshly to the men and they rose slowly to their feet, their heads still bowed. "You will come with me. We will find those Seekers and we will recover those relics. And when we do, I will decide what should be done with you. If I feel generous, I may honor part of our agreement and you will escape with your lives and a portion of the payment we agreed. Betray me and I will have you hunted down like the dogs you are. And when I find you, when you see what I have planned for you," she smiled and moistened her lips as if enjoying the taste of fear in air. "You will soon find yourselves begging to meet the same fate as your master."

CHAPTER 42

I had not yet reached the town that Jentus had told me of but I walked on, trying to keep the sun behind me although it was mostly obscured by the incessant heavy rain clouds. I had emerged from the woodland, making my way through grassy meadows that sloped steeply uphill. As I walked, I heard the rumbling sound of water plunging from a great height in the distance and when I crested the hill, my shoulders slumped in dismay. Ahead of me was an impossibly high cliff of rock that extended as far as I could see in both directions. There were no paths or breaks in the rock and the sheer cliff towered above my head, the shadow of it dwarfing the surrounding countryside. I walked down the other side of the hill, picking my way amongst the fallen rocks towards the cliff. I headed towards the noise which gradually grew louder until eventually the rumble became almost deafening as I rounded a curve in the rock face.

Ahead was a waterfall cascading from the sheer cliffs, a huge expanse of water falling vertically down and resounding off the rocks into a deep pool at its base. I was still a fair distance away but the spray carried through the air, wetting my face and splashing up in great white clouds from the pool. I walked towards the falls, mesmerized by the sheer height and force of the water as it rumbled down the cliff. My hair and clothes were soaking and I stepped back a little, shielding my eyes from the spray as I stared up the impossible height of the falls. At the very top of the cliff was a strange rock formation, oddly domed and unnatural on the cliff top, the outline standing out starkly against the gloomy sky. I walked back further into the meadow before turning and squinting up at the cliffs again and as I did so, the strange outcrop came clearly into view. It was a huge head carved from the rock and I could clearly see the outline of a nose and the dark holes of eyes. The water of the falls was pouring from the wide open yawning mouth of the face in a powerful gushing stream, stony teeth protruding through the snow white of the churning water as it tipped over the edge and crashed to the pool far beneath. I stared in wonder at the sight, wondering who had toiled high up on the deadly cliff face to carve out the face and mouth from the unforgiving rock.

I moved away from the deep pool, intending to gather my thoughts and plan my next move. As I lowered myself into the grass, I stared up at the insurmountable sheer cliffs. There must be a way through, I mused, absent mindedly licking my fingers and rubbing at the metal dragons on my boots, polishing off the caked mud so the insignias glinted once more. As I sat there deep in thought, something flickered deep in my memory. The high pitched voice of the talking cards interrupted my thoughts and the flicker ignited to a spark of sudden realization. The mouth. The waters mouth. My heart jumped and pounded in my chest as I rose to my feet and looked up at the stone carved head high above me and the wide open mouth, water gushing from its lips. The words of the cards echoed in my head "Look for the waters mouth." I had thought that they had meant an estuary or a spring of some sort but maybe it wasn't the mouth of a river at all. Was this it? Was this what they meant?

Before I could even comprehend what I had found, an animal slithered up from the pool, small and rodent-like with a long, sleek body and small ears pressed close against its wet head. The River Moppet raised itself up on its back feet and rubbed its small paws together, swiping one quickly over each ear before shaking its body from nose to tail, its red fur standing up in damp spikes. As I watched, it scurried through the grass to the base of the cliff and stood again on its haunches as it looked around, sniffing the air before it dropped back to its feet and clambered quickly and gracefully up through the rocks, disappearing behind the grey-blue tumescent waters of the falls.

I felt a surge of adrenaline course through me and I stood for a moment, frozen as I contemplated the sheer cliff and the pounding waters. Before I could decide what to do or even take a step, a dark shadow fell across me and as I reluctantly raised my eyes to the sky, I already knew what I would see. An unearthly screech sounded above the thunder of the falls and I looked up to see the black winged creature with red eyes, circling above me, its forked tail whipping behind it as it glided. A feeling of dread settled over me like a poisonous fog and the Grimhellion hovered a moment, its small mouth slightly open as its red eyes fixed upon me. Its unsettling evil stare kicked me into action and I ran towards the base of the waterfall, looking over my shoulder to see the hellion spin and swoop back across the meadow towards the woods.

I scrambled up the rocks where I had seen the moppet disappear and the spray from the water blinded me, causing me to wipe the mist from my eyes as I slipped and clambered towards the thundering falls. I pressed my back against the rock face as I found my footing on a narrow ledge and made my way carefully behind the waterfall. One wrong move would send me tumbling into the churning pool beneath me where I would be sucked under and pinned down by the power of the surge tumbling from above. My face was barely a foot from the falls and the thundering water was deafening as I edged carefully onwards. Eventually, the ledge widened and dropped back away from the roaring falls where the rock had been worn away into a cave by the relentless, pounding force of the water.

Through the clouds of spray ahead of me was a set of worn stone steps cut from the rock, climbing upwards along the side of the cave before disappearing into the dark mouth of a tunnel. The steps were soaking wet and slippery with moss but I moved quickly, thinking of the men that would no doubt be close behind me once their sinister companion had alerted them to my whereabouts. I had no choice now but to move onwards and I rested my hands against the slimy wall as I made my way carefully up the steps towards the cavernous doorway.

I hesitated before entering the darkness but as I stepped forward, my eyes adjusted to the blackness and I could make out a dim light ahead of me. I made my way carefully through the tunnel, the deafening thundering of the falls fading behind me, the steady drip, drip, drip of water falling from the rock wall above my head. The dim light gradually became brighter and after a few moments, I emerged from the darkness as the tunnel opened up. I blinked rapidly and looked about me to find that I was perched precariously on a narrow path, steps leading up to my left, carved into the side of a huge cavern. The ceiling of the cave was impossibly high above my head, the pointed tips of stalactites hanging down, shining and marbled as water dripped in rivulets to the cavern floor far beneath. Shafts of light drifted down from narrow cracks scattered across the ceiling where weak beams of dreary daylight broke through. Below the path where I stood was a vast underground lake, the surface black and rippling with concentric waves as the water dripped from the stalactites above.

The path rose steeply upwards along the cavern wall, parts of it carved from the rock itself, parts built from planks and joists, twisting and turning back on itself as it climbed. On the opposite side of the lake were more paths leading upwards and above the water ran precarious rope bridges spanning the breadth of the cavern. The bridges were constructed from slats of rotting planks, littered with gaping holes where the struts had long since fallen loose and tumbled into the black waters beneath. The paths and bridges wound and crisscrossed above me, climbing steadily upwards. On the opposite side of the cavern the highest bridge and path led to a plateau, a solid overhang of rock that loomed out over the depths of the lake.

As I stood there, taking in this vast place in wonder, a sound echoed behind me through the gloom of the tunnel from which I had emerged; men's voices and the screech of the infernal hellion. With a sudden surge of panic, I set off up the path.

The stairway was steep and the steps slippery with moss and as I hurried upwards, another sound caused me to stop in my tracks. This time, the noise was ahead of me. A loud growl echoed through the cave and as the sound reached my ears, a shower of small stones fell from above, landing in my hair and eyes. I reached for my bow, carefully and silently pulling an arrow from my sheath. The sounds of voices were still approaching through the tunnel beneath me as I crept slowly forwards, putting one leather boot quietly ahead of the other.

Before I could move further up the steps, a strong hand suddenly reached down to grab the back of my coat from the path above me. I spun my head wildly to see a huge arm, strongly muscled and lined with thick silvery veins, the fingers gripping my collar. The skin was a stone grey colour but coated in a fine layer of slime, mottled with black specks of algae and oozing pores. The arm pulled me upwards and for a moment, I was suspended over the precipice by my neck, my legs flailing over the abyss, the black pool far beneath me.

I kept tight hold of my bow but the Queenfisher arrow fell from my fingers, clattering and bouncing off the rock walls before it splashed into the water of the lake. My breath was expelled quickly from my lungs and I let out a whoomph of exertion as the huge arm lifted me effortlessly up onto the pathway above. I was flung onto the stone steps and my body seized up as I lay there winded, struggling to take a breath. I drew squeaking, shallow gasps of air into my shocked lungs and my eyes opened wide in terror as I looked up at the creature looming over me. My mind randomly flashed back to that night on the floor of our cottage when Leif had drawn a picture of me fighting a giant and I almost smiled at the memory as the grey skinned monster chomped its thick lips together, emitting animal grunts and snorts, its huge mouth scattering globs of slaver.

The Troggolem's body was crudely wrapped in animal skins, its eyes lopsidedly placed on its huge gormless face and its ears flapped strangely on the side of its bald conical head. I rolled quickly to one side as it brought its enormous fist down clumsily towards my face and my hand clenched at my belt as I reached for my dagger. The creature roared in rage and its eyes widened stupidly as it realized too late that I had evaded its blow. As it raised its fist again, a flash of red flitted through the air behind its head and I heard a now familiar shriek as the Grimhellion swooped from above, its talons extended as it dug them deep into the Troggolem's shoulder. The creature's fist flailed in the air and it threw back its head, emitting a deafening roar of pain as the hellions claws dug into its meaty flesh. The rush of fetid breath from its mouth flattened the hair back from my face and I turned my head away at the stench, rolling again into a crouch against the rock wall. The Troggolem stamped its huge flat feet from side to side as it swiped its fists through the air trying to grab at the black winged Grimhellion that circled and swooped above its head. I scrabbled out of the way as one of the huge feet crashed to the ground where I crouched and I felt the solid rock beneath me tremble at the great weight.

As the golem bellowed in rage, the hellion shrieked and continued to attack it from the air, its talons and teeth ripping and cutting at the grey flesh, a strange black liquid oozing from the wounds. I scrambled to my feet and ran onwards up the stone pathway and towards a rope bridge that led across the expanse of the cavern. I hesitated as I regarded the flimsy looking wooden struts and the fraying rope, looking down for a moment to see two fur clad figures emerging from the tunnel beneath me. I recognized the men who had haunted my thoughts since we encountered the goblin camp and I felt another rush of fear. Knowing I had no choice but to keep going, I took a step onto the precarious bridge, the Grimhellion and the Troggolem still battling on the path below.

The rope bridge groaned with strain as it took my weight and I closed my eyes for a few moments as I took the first tentative steps. The wooden planks beneath me were slippery and damp and I had to stare carefully at my feet to judge which struts looked like they would hold me. I had made it almost halfway across the bridge when I heard an almighty roar behind me. I looked back to see the hellion swoop once more at the Troggolem's face and as it raised its huge hands to protect its eyes, it lost its footing on the narrow stairway. It stumbled clumsily and seemed to hang for a moment over the precipice, its heavy arms flailing uselessly through the air as it tried to rebalance its immense weight. As I watched, it toppled forwards and fell through the air, turning and spinning with a grace the creature had not possessed with two feet on the ground. A terrified roar echoed through the cavern and the Troggolem's huge body smashed against the rocks as it fell, its huge limbs breaking and twisting until it eventually tumbled into the black waters of the lake.

The Grimhellion hovered in mid-air for a moment before throwing back its head and emitting a long shriek of triumph. The two men were making their way up the stone steps, followed by a third figure clad all in black. This one I didn't recognize but there was something eerily familiar about how this third figure moved, the gait and posture. I couldn't make out a face or features but for some reason, the figure in black frightened my more than any other.

I continued onwards across the bridge and was almost at the other side when the last wooden strut crumbled beneath my boot. I let out a cry as my foot shot through the planks into thin air and I fell forward, catching my weight on my hands as my leg dangled in the air beneath me. I pulled myself up and dragged myself forward on to the stone stairway that would take me higher up into the cavern. I looked back at the figures following me and thought for a moment, wondering whether I should cut the bridge down with my dagger. I hesitated. The bridge might be my only way out of this cavern. To cut it down would leave me trapped.

I left the bridge intact and moved onwards up the steep steps. My heart was pounding and I was breathless with fear and exertion but I had no choice but to carry on higher into the cavern. I looked back to see that my pursuers had reached the rope bridge and one of the men was halfway across, treading gingerly across the creaking planks. I took my bow from my back and aimed an arrow at the figure on the bridge but it sailed through the air and fell a long way short, plummeting to the lake beneath before it reached him. I cursed under my breath and hurried onwards, hoping the top of the steps and the plateau would offer a means of escape from the cavern where I could disappear into the wilderness.

I reached the top of the steps and rushed onto the plateau, my eyes casting about for a doorway or tunnel but instead, what I saw stopped me in my tracks and knocked the breath from my lungs.

Ahead of me were the crumbling remnants of an old ruin. Pillars lined the entrance and the dividing walls had long since dissolved to dust leaving the inside of the ruin exposed. The floor was littered with bones and the decorative carvings and inscriptions of the stonework were overgrown with moss and climbing ivy, cracks running up the length of the statues and figurines that stood against the walls. A pathway led through the broken rocks to a curved wall at the back of the cavern.

I forgot about the imminent threat following close behind me as I walked slowly into the ruin, the unseeing blank eyes of the statues watching me as I went, my own eyes staring intently on what was ahead of me. I saw no details of the elaborate carvings or ancient inscriptions. The flaking gold that adorned the walls went unnoticed as I focused on the curved wall in front of me. I could see a story carved out of the rock, the story of a birth, a woman wracked with pain as a baby emerged from between her thighs. The carving showed the child growing to manhood and holding something aloft above his head, clenched between stone fingers as he poised to throw it into the horizon. The façade showed the man surrounded by devils and monsters, figures of men cutting him down until the last image showed him dying, a woman weeping at his side.

Above them was the delicate detail of a cloudy night sky, a moon hanging there with a benevolent expression carved upon its smooth face. Surrounding the moon were stars. Stars of silver, stars of gold, stars of deep blue and glowing vibrant green. Nestled amongst the throng of glowing colours was another star, a large deep red star with a crimson centre that seemed to pulsate in the gloom, almost beckoning me forward with its alluring promise.

I stepped forward slowly, hypnotized by the beauty and wonder of what lay in front of me. I knew what I was seeing but my sense of caution had abandoned me and I only stepped back when I felt my skin flush hot and my vision began to swim, the pillars of the ruins swaying to either side of me. My legs dropped beneath me and I recognized the sensation. I was too close to the stones, those lovely coloured stars in the stone night sky. I was so close to the Rubine stone but I could never claim it when it was surrounded by its beautiful but deadly siblings of Ebontium, Glisston and Veridian. I realized that the stones were protecting each other, no human being would be able to take one without falling victim to the power of the others.

I fought against the swimming sensation and stumbled back but as my vision began to darken, I heard heavy steps approaching from the stairway behind me. As I dropped to the ground and fell into unconsciousness, I realized there was nowhere left to run.

CHAPTER 43

"Don't. Move." My eyes flickered weakly and I wasn't sure what had woken me. Whether it was the menacing voice that whispered close to my ear, the putrid breath that crept into my nostrils or the sharp point of a blade pressing into my side. My eyes snapped open and I knew immediately whose voice was in my ear and whose sword threatened to slip through me like I was nothing more than a sliver of sun warmed butter. I froze and my eyes spun wildly around the dim cavern ruins, settling on the shoulder of a broken statue where, with a sinking feeling of dread, I saw the dark outline and red eyes of the Grimhellion. A wash of relief mingled with my fear as I realized the hunt was over and I was almost glad that I would now discover why.

I didn't speak as the man whose voice had whispered in my ear prodded me with his sword and grunted at me to get to my feet. I glanced to my left and saw the taller of the two men we had seen at the goblin camp, the one called Shiv, going through my pack. The men had dragged me back out of the ruins away from the wall littered with birthstones but I could still see their pulsating power twinkling prettily through the gloom.

"You've led us a merry dance little one," a clear voice echoed from behind me and I made a move to spin around but the man at my back held me firmly poked the tip of his sword painfully into my side. I heard the sound of soft, purposeful footfalls and a figure came into my view, the figure all in black, a shroud covering the face. Intelligent dark eyes stared at me from beneath the shroud and a white hand reached up to pull the covering down. I recognized the face, as I knew I would, and for a moment I clutched at vague memories, trying to place it before I realized who was standing before me.

Decima.

The Amiress of Andorta.

She gave me a small cold smile as the Grimhellion swooped from its perch and landed on her outstretched arm. It shook its leathery wings, emitting a dry rustling sound before it settled back, its neck disappearing into its body and its red eyes narrowing like a satisfied cat. Decima smiled lovingly down at the repugnant creature before she spoke again.

"And now here we are," she murmured, her voice rich with black amusement. "The Seeker, the relics and the birthstones." She turned her eyes to the mercenary who was pulling my possessions from my pack and discarding them on the dusty floor. My mind was spinning in confusion. Relics? I thought of the few things I had in my pack; my green dress from Andorta, a small phial of the Bloodwarbler repellent that I had kept back from the dwarves, some food, my water flask. I had no relics. The thought that I didn't have what they were looking for terrified me but I felt certain I would be killed either way.

The man named Thrax poked me again in the back and wrapped his arm around my neck, pulling my head back so I felt his hot stinking breath on my neck.

"D'you have 'em little girl?" he growled in my ear. "Or is it one of your friends what stole 'em?" I tried to pull away from his grip, grimacing in disgust as he held me close to his body.

"I don't know what you're talking about," I said through gritted teeth. "I'm just a Seeker. I didn't steal anything."

Decima let out a bitter laugh. "Oh you stole something," she said silkily. "I don't particularly care whether it was you or one of your…. companions. But I suspect that something of mine has found its way into your possession." She walked towards me and the leather of her boots creaked slightly as she moved. "And I will have them back. If you don't have my relics, you will tell me where the others went and I will…. resolve the situation with them myself."

I said nothing as Decima's face drew close to mine and I stared into her black eyes. Suddenly Shiv let out a hoarse gasp as he stopped searching through my pack and I saw his eyes widen and his bearded jaw go slack.

"I've got them," he whispered, his voice a mixture of relief and awe. "Amiress…. my lady… I've got them!" His final cry was jubilant and I felt Thrax loosen his grip around my throat as Shiv pulled something from my pack. Something glinting and metallic. Decima spun around and I looked down in surprise to see what Shiv had found amongst my things. Held carefully in his huge hands were Galant's chainmail gauntlets.

"Little liar!" said Thrax, suddenly twisting his arm tighter around my neck as Shiv walked towards Decima, the gauntlets cradled reverently in his palms as if they were the most precious of riches he had ever laid eyes on. He dropped to one knee and held the gauntlets up to the Amiress whose black eyes lit up at the sight. She stepped forward and gently took the gauntlets in her hands, sucking in a deep breath as she held them up to the light and stared at them in wonder.

"Finally," she whispered to herself. "Everything was worth it. Finally we have them."

"I didn't steal those!" I said desperately, confused and frightened. "They belonged to a…. they belonged to a friend."

Decima seemed to snap from her reverie. "Oh?" she exclaimed, looking round at me. "A friend you say? He happen to be tall, dark haired? Name of Galant?" I hesitated and fell silent. I wondered where my loyalty came from and why I didn't hate Galant with a white hot blinding passion for what he had done to me. Not only was he a liar and a traitor but it seemed that he was also a thief. Despite myself, I couldn't force my voice to say his name and put him in danger so I bit my lip and looked away from Decima's penetrating stare.

She suddenly let out a sharp shrill laugh, throwing her head back, white teeth gleaming. "I don't blame you," she said, as if reading my thoughts. "He was certainly handsome. And the best fighter I've seen in the Arena for years." She leaned close to me and licked her pink lips as she rested a cold hand on my cheek. "It's not surprising to me that you followed such a….. charismatic young man." She stood up abruptly. "But unfortunately your good friend Galant is nothing but a dirty thief. An enticing one yes," she smiled. "But still a thief. And what better place for us to find you?" she said and I looked at her in confusion. "What better place to test the power of the gauntlets?" She gestured languidly with one outstretched arm towards the wall of the ruins, dotted with the beautiful but deadly gleam of the birthstones. "I had heard legend tell of the Wall of Vitrius in these parts but I never imagined we would stumble across it." She smiled again. "Most fortuitous. For us, of course. Not so much for you." Shiv smirked at that and let out a snort but Decima silenced him with a look.

She held the gauntlets out to me. "Put them on," she commanded and I felt the stab of Thrax's sword in my side as he pushed me forward. I didn't understand what they wanted from me but I took the gauntlets and pulled them onto my cold hands, the delicate scales of the chainmail caressing my skin. I stood there with my hands held awkwardly in front of me.

"Now go," said Decima, gesturing towards the birthstones glowing ominously in the ruins. "Take some of the stones from the wall. I don't care which."

My heart sank and my stomach lurched. "I can't…" I began, my voice trembling with fear. "There are too many stones… I can only get Rubine… If I get too close to the others... I won't… They'll… It'll kill me!" The words tumbled desperately from my mouth as Thrax pushed me forward with the tip of his blade. I glanced to my right to see Shiv standing holding my bow, a Queenfisher arrow aimed right at me, its deadly tip glinting in the dim light.

"Go!" Decima repeated harshly as she stood back with her arms crossed.

I closed my eyes for a moment as I realized that I had no choice. I could die right here at the sharp end of Thrax's blade or by the searing tip of one of my own arrows. Or I could walk towards the wall of stones and hope to slip into oblivion before they sucked the life from me. As I stepped slowly forward, I thought of everything that had happened to bring me here. I thought of Mallady and the kind man on the cart who had helped me to Andorta. I thought of Duckie and of Gwil with his painted face and circus tricks. I remembered the feathered outline of Elsbioli as she pushed us down the river that night and I thought of the friendly dwarves of Halftans Crevice. Mercy's words of only a day earlier echoed through my mind and I thought of how right she was but how wrong it had all turned out.

As I walked slowly towards the stones I waited for the sickening feeling to wash over me, I waited for my vision to reduce to a pin prick and I waited for my legs to collapse from under me. As I took one step, and then another, I realized that nothing was happening. Instead, the gauntlets on my hands began to buzz and thrum with a strange energy and when I looked down, I could see the air shimmering around my hands. I stared in wonder as I stepped forward and when I looked up, I found myself standing directly beneath the wall, the birthstones glowing and flickering, their light reflecting off the metal sheen of the gauntlets. As if in a dream, I reached out and touched a stone of Veridian that was so close to my face I could see into its depths where the vibrant green glimmered with shards of peacock blue and diamond white. Next to it was another stone. A deep, blood red with a centre so dark it was almost black. My eyes widened in wonder as the glow of the Rubine reflected from the gauntlet as I reached out to touch it. Everything I needed was right there in front of my eyes. I thought of how cruel life was that I could reach out and take it, only to be murdered by the menacing threat that lurked in the shadows behind me. I breathed out slowly as the fingers of the gauntlets closed gently around each of the stones and I plucked them from the rock easily, each one falling into the palm of my hand. I stared in wonder as the light pulsed and I held my breath as I waited for the Veridian stone to turn to dust and evaporate me with it. I looked down at the Rubine stone, hoping to see it explode in a shower of light as it poured its energy into my veins. Again, nothing happened and when I turned back to the three figures beyond the ruins I could see their faces frozen in amazement as a strange energy charged the still, cold air of the cavern.

Decima's voice eventually broke the silence. "So it's true…" she murmured in wonder as I began to walk slowly back towards them, the Veridian and Rubine stones nestled in my palms. Suddenly she halted me. "Stop!" she commanded. "Put them down. Lay the stones on the ground and come back to me." As I lay the Veridian gently on the stone floor I felt another surge of energy ripple through the gauntlets. I walked back towards my captors and I knew my eyes were alight with amazement at what had just happened. "And the other one," Decima said sharply, seeing the red glow of the Rubine still resting in my hand. I paused for a moment, looking at the stone that I had been searching for all this time. The stone that would save me, that would allow me to return home to my Pa, Leif and Duckie. But Shiv was still poised with an arrow pointed at my chest. I had no choice. Reluctantly, I laid the Rubine stone down gently on the ground and as I did so, I felt my future slip from my grasp.

As I walked back through the entrance of the ruins, Decima stepped forward and pulled the gauntlets roughly from my hands, a vague energy still shimmering around them as she held them up to her face. The air of the cavern was almost crackling with electricity as we all stood in stunned silence, regarding the relics in awestruck amazement.

Finally Decima spoke. "You really have no idea what these are do you?" she asked me finally, a curious look passing across her features. "You have no idea what power you have had in your possession?" She laughed aloud at my expressionless face as she walked towards me. "These, my little red headed drab," she said, her thin lips twisting in her white face. "These are going to change the world."

Something about her tone snapped the last nerve inside me and I looked up at her, suddenly angry. "I don't care what they are!" I said hotly. "I don't care! I just want to get my birthstone and go home! Take them and leave me alone!"

Decima laughed again, gleeful that she had provoked me. "I suppose I can tell you now," she said, pacing slowly up and down in front of me as Thrax grabbed my arms from behind. "I can tell you everything. Seeing as we're going to be…. dispatching you anyway, there's no harm in it. And I think you will find my story very interesting little Seeker, cursed as you are."

Decima was enjoying her performance and I looked at the ground in disgust. She reached forward and I flinched as her soft fingers grasped my chin and forced me to face her. She held the gauntlets in front of my eyes.

"These," she said softly, "Are the ancient relics of Stellium. You know what that means?" I reluctantly shook my head. "Stellium is an ancient city," she continued dreamily as her hard eyes misted over. "A city lost forever in the shadows of time. The power of its relics was once knowledge. Over years they became a rumour, then hearsay, then folklore and finally a little believed legend. Then, even the legend was forgotten." She lowered the gauntlets and rested them tenderly against her chest.

She watched my confused and angry face in amusement. "Imagine this, little one," she said silkily. "Imagine a world where Seekers don't have to find their birthstones. They will no longer need to leave their homes and face untold danger in order to survive. They don't have to chase false trails or fight beasts or even leave the safety of their beds to survive. If," she paused and held up a finger. "If they have these." She held up the gauntlets once more. "These will allow anyone to collect any birthstones; Rubine, Zaphite, Forzit, Ebontium. As you have just discovered, any birthstone can be held by these gloves, harmless as pebbles." Her voice was filled with wonder and my eyes widened as I understood the meaning of her words.

She saw the realization cross my features and her black eyes gleamed. "Do you see?" she asked. "Whomever owns these gauntlets can command all the power in the world. They can collect birthstones wherever they may be and provide the gift of life to whomever they choose. They can favour their family, favour the family of those loyal to them." Decima's face was flushed with the fervor of her words and a fine layer of perspiration shone on her pale skin. "Imagine holding the gift of life in your hands. Just imagine…." Her voice trailed off in wonder and the cavern fell silent apart from the constant drip of the water falling to the lake beneath.

As Decima's words sank in I could barely comprehend them. Life in Immentia had always been as it was. It was brutal and it was cruel but it was honest and simple. To move to the second circle of life you had to find your birthstone and no one knew better than I what a trial it was and the deadly journey that we had to take. If what Decima said was true, it would turn the world on its head. The rich would be able to buy their stones, traditional loyalties would be forgotten and the owner of the gauntlets would be able to command armies of the like that Immentia had never known.

The birthstones could be collected and hoarded faster than the Seekers could find them. A vision flitted across my mind of many, many poor Seekers like Elvyn Edsel, returning home and fading away. I imagined the meadows and forests of Immentia littered with the bodies of Seekers whose rightful stones had been collected and taken away by the owner of these gauntlets. The day would come when the poor would not even try to leave their homes, knowing their search would be hopeless. They would be forced to turn to those with power, to give up their freedom, enslavement their only chance to live. As I looked into a future where the natural balance fell into the hands of the evil and the greedy I saw a bleak and hopeless vision for most of the people who inhabited this wild and beautiful land. It was a gift to the privileged few, subjugation for the desperate and a certain death sentence for many.

CHAPTER 44

The silence of the cavern was heavy with tension. Eventually, Decima turned her bright, keen eyes from me and looked to the mercenaries.

"I will be moving on at first light," Decima said briskly as Thrax dragged me towards the wall of the cavern and Shiv began to set up the camp. "So for tonight, I expect you two to make this place habitable."

"What about this one?" Thrax asked and Decima glanced back to me as the mercenary shoved me onto the cold stony ground.

"Tie her up," she said shortly. "We will decide what to do with her before I leave."

"What about the stones Amiress," he said nodding his head at the glimmering wall of gems behind us. Decima glanced across the ruins, the rainbow of colours reflecting in her black eyes.

"They can wait," she said answered. "Ariad needs Xalyph. There are none here. You can come back for the others when we have brought Ariad her birthstone."

"Of course," Thrax said. "I trust our…" he cleared his throat. "I trust our *agreement* is still in place?"

Decima nodded curtly. "Come to Andorta and my husband will pay you your fee." She narrowed her eyes. "But after that, if I lay eyes on you again I will have you killed where you stand. Understood?"

Thrax nodded and let out a throaty chuckle. "Of course, Amiress. You will have no cause to see me or my…. colleague again once our transaction is complete." Decima nodded.

"Good. Now get that fire lit and give me those bedrolls. I don't wish to be bothered." The mercenaries gave one another a look as Decima laid out the bedrolls on the far side of the plateau and settled there, legs crossed, her cloak wrapped around her like the leathery wings of her familiar.

"So," murmured Thrax, roughly pulling my hands behind my back and tying them together. "What happened to your other little friends?" he said, his voice low in my ear. "Left you all alone did they? What about your boyfriend… Galant was it?" I didn't answer and he sniggered. "Sounds like you were in it together to me," he said. "Stitched you right up now though hasn't he love?" he added, a vindictive smirk passing across his ugly features. "Left you to fend for yourself from what I can see. How's that feel? Treated you liked some backstreet drab and then left you to die," he goaded me but I said nothing.

His words couldn't hurt me any more than I had already been hurt so Thrax regarded my sullen face, disappointed by my lack of reaction. He looked like the kind of man who would enjoy a young girls tears and I refused to give him the pleasure. I thought of the hot droplets I had shed on the floor of that crypt and vowed to myself that these men would never see a tear creep from my eyes.

As the two men set up their camp and built a fire, I watched the Amiress, sitting statue-still across the cavern. The gauntlets were laid at her side as she sat there with her legs still crossed and her back straight, eyes closed in her white face. She seemed to be meditating, oblivious to her surroundings with the Grimhellion perched on her shoulder, its red eyes narrowed but still watching.

I stared into the fire and considered what I had learned, the situation I now found myself in. I cursed Galant and I cursed myself. I couldn't have known, but the thought that I had held such powerful magic in my grasp and let it go filled me with horror and I felt sick to my stomach.

I watched silently as Shiv took a dead rabbit from his pack and skinned it, the blood and guts shining wetly in the firelight. They roasted the rabbit, the smell drifting to my nostrils but the men ignored me as they ate. Decima refused the food, not stirring from her trance when Thrax offered it. My throat was parched and dry from thirst and, when he had sucked the rabbit bones clean, Shiv spent a few minutes entertaining himself as he splashed droplets of water across my face. Although I was aching with thirst, I refused to degrade myself by turning towards the meagre droplets and I even stopped myself from hungrily licking the specks that fell on my lips. I hated these two with a deep hot rage that I had never known before and I would have rather died than give them a moment of satisfaction. I wondered why they hadn't just killed me already.

I watched in disgust as they swigged from a flagon of juniper grog and when I saw that the bottle was spattered with blood I thought of Ralf, Kale and Blanchett and I realized with a sickening wrench from whom they had stolen it. Thrax eventually laid down under his furs and settled by the fire.

"Don't stay up too late Shiv," he said with a filthy smirk as Shiv, sitting hunched by the fire, turned his eyes towards me. A sinking, dreadful feeling washed over me and my heart quickened in my chest as I shrank from his gaze.

Thrax quickly fell asleep, mouth hanging open and the occasional grunting snore escaping his nostrils. Decima was still sitting in the shadows, eyes closed, un-moving apart from her chest gently rising and falling as she breathed. Even the Grimhellion's ever watchful eyes had closed and the only sounds echoing around the cavern was the drip of water and the crackle of the dying fire.

Shiv sat playing with his dagger, turning and twisting it in his rough hands as he stared at me, his hard eyes never leaving my face. He took another swig of the juniper grog before lumbering to his feet and stretching lazily.

"Now," he said, his voice quiet, picking rabbit from his teeth and flicking the bits onto the floor. "How's about you and me get to know each other?" Shiv slurred as he made his way towards me, every muscle of my body tensing in terror and revulsion. Shiv knelt before me and cut the rope that bound my wrists. His rheumy eyes fixed on mine and he grabbed my chin, forcing me to look at him, his scarred face so close that I could see the dirt and grime that had settled in the crevices of his skin.

"That's a pretty dress you have there," he whispered to me, nodding towards my beautiful green Andortan robe that was now lying in the dirt on the stone floor. His white furry tongue emerged, lizard-like as he licked his cracked lips. "You wear that for your sweetheart do you?" he whispered, smirking again as his rough fingers stroked the soft skin of my neck. I closed my eyes tightly, turned my head away and drew my legs tightly towards my body.

Shiv's breath smelled of burnt rabbit and grog and as his huge calloused hands reached beneath my coat and clenched clumsily at my body I thought I might vomit. He dragged me roughly to my feet and pulled me tightly against him, dirty hands all over me as my fists thumped weakly against his chest.

"Come on now," he rasped as he pinned me against the stone wall at my back, his body a dead weight on my slight frame. "Bet you let your boys do this don't ya?" he mumbled, "Wearing that green dress?" I let out a helpless scream and he clamped a sweaty and stinking hand over my mouth, stifling the sound. "Shush now," he whispered, "Don't want to wake Thrax do we? Don't think you could handle the two of us!" he sniggered at his disgusting joke and I struggled to breathe as his paw covered my face. I felt a wave of nausea wash over me.

Shiv clutched his other hand to his breeches and undid his belt. When he had loosened his clothes, I felt his fingers go under my dress and fumble at the clasps on my own leather waistband. I suddenly went limp underneath him. I was too tired to fight anymore. I considered just letting him do what he would and, after all, I would be dead in the morning so what did it matter? But, before Shiv could undo the fastenings I felt an unexpected strength well up inside me. I don't know where the rage came from. I think it was a culmination of the degradation he intended to inflict on me, anger at how Galant had betrayed me and the guilt of what power I had released to these monsters.

It welled deep in my stomach and brimmed up, hot and tight through my chest and into my dry throat. I braced myself against the wall behind me and lifted my knee up sharply into Shiv's crotch. As he fell forward, letting out a sharp gasp of pain, I kicked out again at his face. My boot hit him hard in the nose and I felt a sickening but satisfying crunch as the bones broke beneath my foot. He staggered back, one hand clenching his crotch and the other trying to stem the sudden burst of blood from his nose.

I had unbalanced myself and fell helplessly to the stone floor. I knew I had really done it now but I hoped that at least he would hate me enough to kill me quickly. As I lay in the dust, I turned my face slowly to see Shiv bearing down on me, his bloody features snarling as his hand reached for his sword. Behind him, Thrax had woken and was lurching to his feet in confusion at the sudden commotion. I clenched my eyes shut, bracing myself for a death blow from Shiv's sword but, instead, I was shocked to hear a loud noise that echoed through the darkness. An animalistic snarl and a sharp cry, followed by the heavy thud of bodies hitting the ground. I opened my eyes to see Shiv screaming in terror as a huge hairy body pinned him down, the muzzle of a beast lunging at his exposed throat.

I sat up and scuffled back in alarm but as my back hit hard against the rock I realized that this wasn't some random encounter with a cave monster. The snarling, slathering beast that was mauling the prone man was in fact the broken toothed Slinkferral I had previously encountered in the woods. Its eyes were wild and terrifying, the hair of its thick mane standing menacingly on end as its sharp claws savaged the struggling man.

Decima's Grimhellion had taken flight from her shoulder and was whirling around the cavern shrieking in alarm as the Amiress jumped like a cat to her feet. Her lips twisted in nothing more than annoyance as she saw the great beast, spittle flying and great claws swiping at Shiv's neck.

Thrax reached down and pulled out his sword as I struggled to my knees, letting out a warning shout just before Thrax swung at the Slinkferral. It looked up just in time, its lips drawn back over its broken teeth as it wheeled to the side, evading the swing of the blade before leaping at Thrax as the weight of his sword carried him helplessly forward. The Slinkferral's claws swiped a deep row of gashes in Thrax's face as Shiv gasped for breath on the ground, his hands clutching at the wounds on his face and neck. Thrax fell forward, his sword propelling into the stone floor as its hilt hit him full in the face and he toppled to one side, stunned.

I watched the chaos around me for a moment before realizing that this was my chance, maybe my last and only chance. I jumped to my feet and stumbled back through the entrance of the ruins, the wall of birthstones still glittering ahead of me. As the noise of the savage battle resounded around me, I fell to my knees, scrabbling along the stone floor, hands outstretched.

The Veridian stone that I had dropped earlier glowed from the ground next to the wall of stones and I knew I couldn't get much closer. And then, as I gingerly edged my way forward, waiting for my vision to swim, I saw it. The Rubine stone. It was lying passively on the floor of the ruins, its deep red energy glowing like a life blood just inches from my bare fingertips. I paused for a moment and everything that had happened flashed through my mind. I had been this close before but I knew that this time, I wouldn't let it slip from my grasp. I edged towards the stone and slowly reached out my hand, gently lifting the Rubine up between my fingers. As I clasped it hard between my palms I felt a red hot jolt of energy burn through my hands, up my arms and across my chest. As the power surged through my body, I felt all my muscles tense and flood with vitality. Finally, the heat that was welling in my body shot up through my neck and across my face and with one, final, sudden jolt I felt a pure white shock shoot through my nerve endings causing me to gasp and throw my head back as the intense energy thundered through me. When the heat had subsided, I lowered my head, strangely exhausted and exhilarated. I looked down to see my palms filled with a grey ashen powder and I curled my fingers, watching in wonder as the birthstone crumbled to dust.

As I watched the dust float to the ground, I realized that I had done it. I had found my birthstone and as the magic pumped through my veins, my whole future opened up in front of me. I thought of Pa and Leif who, during recent weeks, had faded to black and white memories of people long forgotten, perhaps never to be seen again. Suddenly their faces leapt into vivid colour and I could smell my Pa's mintleaf tea, see the wrinkles around his eyes and feel the soft silk of Leif's hair under my fingers. I could hear the tumbling waters of the beck as it churned through the water mill in the square. I could feel the pinecone in my palm and the gentle touch of Duckie's hand on my arm.

As I knelt in the dust, the sounds of the ongoing battle behind me snapped me back to the present and I leapt to my feet, suddenly filled with an energy I had never experienced before. The cavern echoed with screams of pain and the thud of bodies as the Slinkferral slashed and snarled at the two men who attempted to fend off the massive beast.

The Grimhellion was gone. Decima had vanished. As had the Gauntlets.

I ran across the plateau, avoiding the slashing blades and flying claws and picked up my things, flinging my pack over my shoulder and looping my bow over my head as I made for the steps. I ran down the way I had come, my boots slipping on the mossy stone as I stumbled down the path. When I reached the rope bridge, I found the evidence of Decima's last insult. The bridge had been cut down and lay uselessly against the cliff face beneath my feet, the gaping depths of the cavern stretching beneath me towards the dark surface of the lake.

The dark figure of the Amiress was flying down the steps on the opposite side of the cavern, the hellion gliding alongside. She moved swiftly, gracefully and quickly but I knew I had to stop her. I couldn't let her escape into the world with those relics, I had to stop her for the sake of all the Seekers who would come after me, for all those who needed to rightfully find their birthstones, not buy them or wage war, or give up their freedom for them. I needed to stop her for all the Seekers and for all the people of . I had to get those gauntlets.

I pulled my bow up and put a Queenfisher arrow on the string, quickly stretching the arrow back until the blue feathers brushed my cheek. Decima was so fast, so lithe that I doubted whether I would be able do this. I trained my eye on her and moved the tip of the arrow, leading her with my aim. Just as she reached the doorway at the bottom of the cavern, I held my breath and froze. All the chaos, screams, snarls and shouts faded around me and all I could hear was the thudding of my heart. Time slowed and Decima paused at the base of the steps for one fateful moment. This was her mistake; that one last pause to turn and look back across the cavern to the plateau. For a second, as I released my arrow, her black eyes met mine and I saw the true darkness of her heart; in that moment, I knew that what I was doing was right.

The Queenfisher arrow flew through the air, a slick of blue light shooting straight and swift. As I watched, still not daring to breathe, the arrow found its mark. The dark figure of Decima suddenly lurched back and she fell to one knee. Her white hands came up to her chest and she looked down in disbelief. She raised her pale face upwards and I felt her black eyes burning into me for one last, terrifying moment before she collapsed. Her body rolled gently and she fell from the ledge, tumbling like a rag doll into the black waters of the lake below. The Grimhellion screeched, a strangely haunting keening sound that echoed around the cavern. It circled the lake before swooping through the tunnel towards the waterfall.

The cacophony of the struggle was still resounding above me as I stood leaning out over the precipice, the rope ladder hanging uselessly down the side of the cavern. I had to move quickly. I don't know whether it was the knowledge that it was the only move I could make, whether it was the power of the Rubine still charging through my veins, or whether it was the Slinkferral that fearlessly leapt over the edge of the cliff ahead of me but I knew what I had to do. I took a huge gulp of air and, as two bloody and raging figures emerged above me on the pathway, I grasped the straps of my pack and bow closely to my body and leapt into the abyss.

CHAPTER 45

My body fell like a stone down into the cavern as the black waters of the lake rushed towards me at impossible speed. The breath was ripped from my lungs and I closed my eyes tightly as I hit the water, feet first with the speed of an arrow shot from a bow. I plunged down into the depths and the weight of my clothes and pack dragged me further down into the darkness. Beneath me, a white face was spinning lazily downwards, spiraling into the depths, one white hand extended upwards and a glint of something silver still clenched between the fingers.

Decima.

And the gauntlets.

I let the water drag me down and I reached out, stretching downwards, trying to reach the gauntlets clutched in Decima's dead fingers. The deeper I went, the further out of reach the relics seemed to drift and my lungs began to burn in my chest. But it was no use. I could go no deeper or this would become my watery resting place as well as Decima's.

I struggled against the grip of the lake and flailed my arms through the freezing water, kicking my legs as I tried to push my heavy body back towards the surface. I felt the energy fading from my limbs as I struggled and a stream of bubbles escaped my lips as the last breath expelled from my lungs. I pushed hard against the water that seemed to drag at my body and struggled upwards towards the surface, the outline of the cavern rocks rippling above me. Just when the surface felt only one more kick away, I felt my body losing its battle against the black enveloping depths and the water began to suck me back downwards. For a moment I imagined my body floating blue and pale in these dark waters, my bones eventually rising to the surface to be picked over and sucked on by Troggolems and other unimaginable monsters. My eyes closed in exhausted despair and a few more bubbles leaked from my nose as I began to sink back down into the lake.

As I drifted into the darkness, I felt something grasp the back of my coat and my body was dragged upwards through the murky water, my face breaking the surface as I coughed and sputtered, my lungs gasping for air. I felt myself propelled towards the side of the lake and as my cold blue fingers clasped onto the rocks, a huge body heaved itself from the water beside me and pulled me clear of the lakes grasping depths. The broken toothed Slinkferral stood beside me panting and soaking wet, its thick fur dripping rivulets of water as its golden eyes regarded me inquisitively.

Above me, the two mercenaries were scaling the side of the cavern, clambering down the remains of the rope bridge. I got to my feet, knowing that we were still not out of danger.

I struggled to stand, water pouring from my heavy pack and I scrabbled up the rocks towards the tunnel opening. The Slinkferral leapt up and followed me, its tongue lolling and its eyes glancing warily upwards at the two men. A low growl emitted from its throat as we made it to the tunnel opening and clattered through the darkness and out into the cave behind the waterfall. Outside, the sun was just coming up, a magical orange glow glinting through the tumbling waters of the fall. The light refracted, casting a rainbow of colours across us as we stumbled down the steps, along the ledge and out into the meadow.

When my feet hit the grass, I fell to my knees and relished the feel of the ground beneath me, the heat of the birthstone still glowing in my fingertips. I closed my eyes for a moment and took a deep breath, realising with a rush of elation that my quest was done. I was done. I had found my birthstone and now I could go home.

The Slinkferral whined urgently, its yellow eyes casting fearful glances back at the waterfall and before I could even comprehend the intentions of this strange wild creature, it grasped me again by the collar of my coat as it dragged me to my feet and I fell weakly against the expanse of its huge, furred, muscled body. The animal dropped to its knees and pushed against me with its snout, whining. In response to its nudges and without thinking, I leapt up and straddled the creature's great back, clinging onto its dappled mane as it took flight across the meadow and into the trees. I gripped the warm fur of the creature galloping beneath me tightly as we flew through the forest and I let out a whoop of jubilation. Despite what I had been through and the significance of the gauntlets that I had lost, at that moment, in those brief fleeting moments, I knew I had won everything that mattered the most.

CHAPTER 46

We ran through the night. The dead leaves and twigs of the woodland floor crunched beneath the Slinkferrals feet but eventually the forest fell away behind us and the surrounding landscape changed from woodland to flat, grassy plains, a huge white moon shining down from the night sky. I huddled close to the thick fur of the Slinkferrals mane and considered the peculiar actions of the beast beneath me. I wondered what it would do when it eventually stopped running. Although it seemed to have some strange affiliation to me I wasn't sure if it had followed me to the cavern with the intention of making a meal of me. Did it trace my scent through the woods like it would stalk its prey? Did it think the mercenaries were stealing its dinner and that was the only reason it attacked them? I knew I had escaped the immediate danger only to find myself riding through the countryside on the back of a beast whose only natural instinct was to rip me to shreds.

Eventually, the animal's stride slowed to a loping run, and then a trot and eventually it came to a panting stop. I remained clinging to its back like a limpet, thinking it would struggle to eat me if I stayed back behind its broken toothed, but dangerous jaws. It stood still for a moment, its ears pricked in expectation but instead of turning to savage me, it gently twisted its huge head and nuzzled at the pocket of my coat. It looked up at me with huge imploring eyes and eventually I tentatively hopped down from its back.

As I dropped to the ground, the Slinkferral whined plaintively and lay obediently at my feet, gazing at me with its strange yellow eyes. Even then, the huge creature's eyes were almost level with mine but strangely, I felt no fear. I raised my eyes and we stared at each other curiously for a long moment. Eventually, I reached out slowly and offered my hand, palm down, to the beasts muzzle and it sniffed delicately at my fingers. It snuffled at my skin for a moment before turning that great head and rubbing an ear against my hand. I gently tickled beneath its ear and the Slinkferral leaned its head against me, eyes closing happily as I scratched the warm fur. It was a very odd exchange but in my dazed and exhausted state, I just allowed my instincts to guide me and my instincts told me that, for whatever reason, this animal did not want to attack me as was its nature. I even found a black amusement in the fact that the people I had trusted had betrayed me but here was a creature I had expected to tear me to bits but instead, was nuzzling against me like a new born lamb.

The huge white moon shone brightly in the sky and the grass of the plains around us was as high as my waist. We were on the crest of a low ridge, the grass stirred by the wind and undulating in waves on all sides. Ahead of me, the green landscape dipping away, my ears picking out the sound of water crashing against rocks. I remembered the maps that Mr Burle had showed us and I wondered if I was hearing the sound of the Endless Southern Sea. I sniffed the wind and licked my lips, tasting salt in the air. I knew we had travelled a long way south but it struck me how far from home I was.

I settled down cross legged in the long grass and nibbled on a few sodden wet scraps of meat from my pack. I had some chunks of creamy cheese that Jentus had given me but I offered that up to the Slinkferral who delicately snaffled it from my outstretched hand, careful not to catch me with its jagged fangs. When we had eaten, I lay back in the grass and buried my cold hands in the warm fur of the Slinkferrals neck as it settled its massive body down next to me, laying its snout on its paws as its yellow eyes slowly closed to sleepy slits. I huddled against the animal for warmth and allowed my own eyelids to droop.

Before I fell asleep, I thought dreamily of the Rubine stone and its amazing power that now ran through me. The power that had saved my life. I would be able to go home to Pa, Leif and Duckie and I would be able to continue my life at Millings Beck and live out many long annums there until old age faded the energy from my bones. I would die happily in my bed in our cottage as the sun set over the cornfields and the sound of children in the lane drifted through my window.

CHAPTER 47

I called her Amicus. This strange and unusual creature that should have been a vicious threat to my very existence proved to be the most loyal beast I had ever known. We journeyed for days and Amicus never left my side. We hunted together through snowy pine forests and brought down deer and rabbits that I would roast over an open fire, Amicus dribbling and whining as she waited for me to throw her hunks of the sweet roasted meat. We struggled across open bog land as the swamp faeries flitted around our heads and Glibs grasped for our feet. I struck many down with my dagger and Amicus pulled the ugly creatures from the gloam, squeezing the life from their insipid forms as her broken toothed jaw clenched tightly around their gills.

A gang of bandits ambushed us and, as one came at me with sword drawn, I shot an arrow into his neck as Amicus set upon his companions, effortlessly tearing flesh and snapping bones. I rode away on the Slinkferrals back like some wild barbarian, a cold look in my eyes and blood dripping from my arrows.

We crossed ranges of mountains and a wildcat stalked us for several days, only to be eventually dragged from the bushes by Amicus, its throat ripped out as the Slinkferral looked up at me with its head cocked and eyes bright, pleased with its kill.

One night, we came across a lonely cottage and I commanded Amicus to wait for me beyond the boundary of the settlement in the darkness. A beautiful, golden haired young woman welcomed me into her dwelling and offered me a hearty bowl of stew which I accepted gratefully along with her offer of spending the night next to the warm fire. I was awoken to find the woman straddling me, knees pinning me to the ground and a claw like hand grasped around my throat as her beautiful features transformed into the face of an old crone with white eyes and crooked rotting teeth. Her lips were clenched back in a snarl and stringy hair flew around her scrawny shoulders as she tried to claw out my eyes. Again, Amicus proved her worth as she shouldered open the door of the cottage and pulled the hag away from me, her jaws crushing the witch's windpipe as she screeched and flailed uselessly, the life draining from her wretched form. I flung her body onto the open fire before torching the rest of the cottage and riding Amicus away, the flames snapping and crackling in the night as the fire burned brightly behind us.

We arrived in Boann, to the west of the road that would take me home and we circled the swampy outskirts of the town before I found a cave where Amicus could rest. I shot a few rabbits and left her there, knowing she wouldn't leave without me as I followed the foggy, lantern lit road into the town. I spent the night at the tavern there, a cozy inn called The Boggarts Rest. I sat in the taproom and after a while, a young man approached me, handsome and dark haired with a twinkle in his eye. He asked me where I'd been. I didn't reply. He asked me where I was going. I didn't answer. He admired my auburn hair and told me I was beautiful, his voice soft and husky with seduction. I casually pulled out my dagger and held it to his throat, telling him never to speak to me again or I would cut him and leave him to bleed to death on the floor of the inn.

The next morning, Amicus and I followed the foggy road through the swamps away from Boann. We were met with curious looks from an oncoming wagon of travelers and I knew that Amicus and I must make a strange sight, a bedraggled girl and a crooked toothed Slinkferral. We made our way through the mist to the crossroads where I had stood many weeks before and I regarded the signpost, an immense wave of tiredness and relief washing over me as I read the familiar names. West to Boann, south to Feybridge, east to Haggs Catton and the other weathered, peeling finger that pointed north. North to Millings Beck. We stood there a while at the crossroads as I thought of the girl who had stood here that day, when I had known nothing of the world and nothing of its deathly dangers and harsh cruelty. I also thought of the amazing creatures I had encountered; the Bloodwarblers, the Shadewalkers, the Oddgoblins and the Troggolem. I remembered the kind people who had helped me; Mallady Bruma in her birdhouse, the grumpy cart man who had carried me to Andorta, the feisty but friendly dwarves of Halftans Crevice and the mysterious caravan of Deltics who had saved my life.

Tears welled in my eyes as I murmured to Amicus and encouraged her to walk on, taking the lane north towards Millings Beck. Towards home.

The village gates came into sight at sundown and as we crested the hill on the chalk road I could see Burle closing the gates, ushering the little ones in and no doubt grumbling as he did so. I smiled and felt warmth flooding through me at the sight of the familiar outline of the rolling hills, the Blackwoods in the distance and the outline of the cottage roofs rising above the gates. The burning orange of the sun was dipping behind the buildings, streaking the sky with purple and gold. I could make out the silhouette of Mr Burle as he settled in his tower, no doubt expecting another uneventful evening in Millings Beck. As we approached, the sunset lit up the chalk road in an ambient orange light and before Mr Burle could catch sight of us and fire a deadly arrow at my loyal companion, I hopped down from Amicus's back and commanded her to wait in a coppice of finkle trees at the side of the road.

As I walked towards the village, I had to hold myself back from breaking into a run. Burle saw me long before I was able to call out to him and he jumped from his seat in the watch tower, pulling out his bow in readiness. I held up a hand in a wave and he lowered his weapon, holding his hand above his eyes as he squinted into the dusky light. I heard him call out as he hurried down from his post, the clamoring sound of doors opening up and down the village before the gates opened and a crowd of people spilled out onto the lane.

I broke into a run as I approached the gates and saw Pa at the front of the crowd, scanning his eyes across the horizon. When he saw me, his shoulders slumped and he dropped his hands to his sides, hesitantly taking a few steps forward as if he almost didn't believe it was me. I felt hot tears streaming down my cheeks as I stumbled towards him and as I ran, Leif emerged from the crowd behind my Pa, his little face white and his eyes frightened. When I reached my Pa, the breath was propelled from my lungs as his burly body hit mine and he enveloped me in his strong arms, his breath warm in my hair as he whispered in my ear and held me close.

"Fen, oh my love, oh my little Fen," he murmured in relief. "When Duckie came back, I thought you were lost, I never thought... I didn't think...." Sobs choked his gruff voice as he buried his head in my tangled hair and I laughed as the tears ran down my cheeks. Leif joined us and wrapped his small arms around my legs and I reached down wordlessly to rumple his soft hair.

"I'm here Pa," I said, my voice trembling but joyful. "I'm here. I found it. I found it."

CHAPTER 48

My first night back in Millings Beck was like a dream. After our welcome at the village gates, I had taken Leif up in my arms and held him close, nuzzling my face into his sweet smelling hair. He smelled of hay and mint leaf tea and I cried into his neck as I hugged him. Duckie had come out to see me and he hobbled down the village lane still using the crutches the dwarves had fashioned for him. I was relieved he had made it home but in truth, I had never doubted those dwarves with his safety for a moment. Duckie had clapped me on the back, relief and happiness glowing in his face, glad that I was home safe and had found my Rubine. He asked after Galant and I wasn't sure if he saw the dark look pass across my face or the wince of pain that pulled at the corners of my mouth. I didn't answer his question but promised to tell him all about my travels later and he nodded, confused but not pressing me further. The villagers pulled me this way and that, hugging me and kissing their hands, patting their kisses into my hair. They asked me endless questions about my journey and where I had been, what beasts and strange folk I had seen and where I had found my birthstone.

My Pa fended them off as best he could and put a protective arm around my shoulders as he picked Leif up, settled him on his hip and we made our way back to the cottage. I promised everyone in the village that I was safe and well, I had found my birthstone and I would tell them all the full story tomorrow. I felt another surge of relief as my Pa finally closed our cottage door quietly behind us. He set Leif down on his feet and Leif began chattering excitedly as he scurried across the floor and settled onto a chair.

"Fen I can't believe you're home!" he babbled. "Did you see monsters and giants? Did you see the mountains? I've never seen mountains but I hope I do one day. Did you kill anyone? Did you kill beasts? Did you go to the cities? I want you to tell me everything!" I laughed out loud at his enthusiasm as my Pa looked on, absently stroking his beard as he watched us.

I crouched down beside Leif. "I did all those things, and more!" I said, my voice filled with the promise of tales of adventure. Leif's face was a picture and he was practically gibbering with excitement.

"Tell me!" he said urgently, "Tell me everything!" I laughed again and ruffled his hair, the soft strands feeling strangely foreign but familiar under my fingers.

My Pa stepped forward. "Not tonight Leif," he said gently. "Fen will be tired and she needs to sleep. She will tell you everything tomorrow."

"Will you Fen?" Leif asked hopefully. "Everything? I want to know everything."

"Everything," I promised as I bent and kissed my palm before resting it on his warm cheek. "You go to bed now," I added as Leif allowed Pa to gently push him towards the kitchen and up to bed.

I settled onto a chair in the kitchen and looked around at the warm familiar room as if it was somewhere I had once seen in a dream. I couldn't believe that I was back here. My Pa walked towards me and dropped to his knees as he grabbed my shoulders and held me close to him. His body was quaking and I knew he was weeping silently as he held me and I didn't pull away, letting the emotion pour out of him.

"You're home Fen. I can hardly believe you're home," he said eventually, his voice croaky. He stood and took both my hands in his, looking down into my upturned face. "So many don't...." he went on. "So many don't come back." He pulled my head towards him again and I nestled into his chest, my nose filling with the familiar scent of wood smoke and mint leaf tea.

Before I went to bed that night, I crept out behind the back of our cottage, through the gate and into the meadows. I went to find Amicus waiting patiently for me in the coppice and I guided her back to the village and into our yard. I had warned my Pa about my new friend and, despite my reassurances, he looked on from the doorway of the kitchen, a fearful look on his face. The chickens had screeched and clustered into their coop clucking frantically but when I threw Amicus a few bones from the kitchen, she settled down happily on a heap of straw under the stoop and ignored her feathery roommates.

Back inside the cottage, I pulled off my leather boots and stripped my filthy clothes off in the kitchen, pulling a clean night shirt over my head. I clambered up the steps to the loft and into my old bed, pulling the covers around me. When my Pa came up to say goodnight, he stroked my hair and sat there for a long time after he thought I had fallen asleep. Everything I had been through, everything I had done and everything I remembered seemed to fall away and I felt like a little girl again. Little Fen from Millings Beck. Eventually, my Pa crept off down the steps and I heard him empty the tea pot, blow out the candles and lock the doors. I heard the creak of his bunk in the front room as he settled into bed and the cottage fell silent.

Although I was exhausted, I lay awake for a long time that night, the dust faeries whispering in the dark corners of the loft. The feeling of making it home was indescribable and the relief made my bones ache with a welcome tiredness. But sleep didn't come easily and my mind was troubled as I thought of Decima and the gauntlets. I thought of those glimmering relics resting in the dark waters of the lake in the far away cavern and I wondered what would have changed if I had been able to bring them home. I could have helped Leif find his birthstone when the time came, even gone out to fetch it for him. I could have done the same for the other young Seekers in the village. But how long would I have been able to keep the gauntlets a secret? How long before they fell into the hands of someone who intended to mis-use their power? The gauntlets could change the way we live in Immentia forever; the Seekers quest would no longer be a rite of passage where they would battle the wilderness and creatures of this world to find a birthstone that was destined to be theirs. Instead, they would have to buy it or trade their loyalty, perhaps betray their friends and family, even sell their very souls.

Maybe the gauntlets were best left with Decima in that watery blackness. Cruel and hard as it sometimes was, maybe the way things were was the way they were supposed to be. Maybe we weren't supposed to change it.

I rolled over in my bunk and pulled the covers to my face. None of this mattered tonight, I thought as my eyes closed and I drifted into sleep. Tomorrow was a new day. A day of new life when I could look at the world around me with new eyes. I had a future now. I had a future that some would never have.

Tomorrow I would just breathe. I would breathe and eat and talk to my family and my friends. I would feed Amicus and stroke her thick mane and reassure the villagers that she meant them no harm. I would feed the chickens and fetch cool clear water from the beck so my Pa could brew his mint leaf tea. I would go to the Twilight Stop and tell Burle and Flitwich of my travels as I scribbled on their maps and wrote notes on Bloodwarblers, Shadewalkers and Oddgoblins for the Seekers that would follow in my footsteps. I would meet Duckie at the stone circle in the centre of the square, the sun warming our heads and the tumbling waters of the beck turning the creaking wheel of the mill. As the sun goes down, casting its warm dreamy haze over the familiar roof tops of the hamlet, perhaps Duckie and I will sit awhile and talk of our adventures and our hopes for the future.

And when all that is done, when there is nothing more to be said, maybe we'll play a game of pinecones.

Printed in Great Britain
by Amazon